THIS QUIET VIOLENCE
THE VIOLENT VIOLETS
BOOK I

BLACK DAHLIA

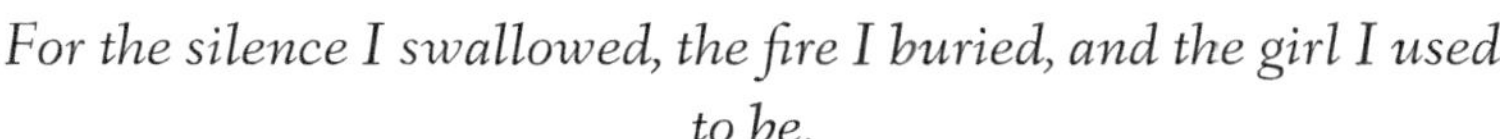

For the silence I swallowed, the fire I buried, and the girl I used to be.

To the pious who preached my pain would be my salvation.

You should have begged God for my demise.

For the silence I swallowed, the fire I buried, and the girl I used to be.

To the pious who preached my pain would be my salvation.

You should have begged God for my demise.

PLAYLIST

Anyway- Me Like Bees
Numb - Abe Parker
If It Makes You Happy - Michael Cera Palin
New Life - Van Dame
Man's World - MARINA
The Love Club - Lorde
Pork And Beans - Weezer
Look At The Time - Sawyer Hill
Gaslight - Derik Fein
EVIL - Melanie Martinez
What It Means To Be A Girl - EMELINE
Expensive - Derik Fein
I've Had Enough - Melina KB
Twin Size Mattress - The Front Bottoms
Sun - Derik Fein
Mine - Sleep Token
WTF Do I know - Miley Cyrus
TV - Billie Eilish
The Doll People - Sofia Isella

Maybe. - Sienna Spiro
Evergreen - Arankai
Drag Me Out - Archer
King - Riell
I Fall Apart - Rory Gallagher
Praying - Kesha
Go Fuck yourself - Two Feet
Blood // Water - Grandson
Start to run - Middle-Class Rut
Lose Control - Teddy Swims
Amor - Derik Fein
Beg - Aryia
Nothing's Gonna Hurt You - Cigarettes After Sex
Stalker - Stevie Howie
Somewhat Damaged - Nine Inch Nails
Closer - Nine Inch Nails
Ruiner - Nine Inch Nails
Laughing On The Outside - Bernadette Carol
Everybody Supports Women - SOFIA ISELLA
Happy Together - The Turtles

CONTENT WARNINGS

Stalking
Obsession/Possession
Dark Humor
Domestic Violence
Cancer
Suicidal Ideation
Blood/Gore Child Abuse (Character Past Reference)
Abduction/Captivity
Smut
Guns
Child Death (Characters Past Reference)
Death
Torture
Paranoia/Anxiety/Depression
Explicit Language (and a lot of it)
Female Rage
Touch Her and Die
Trauma
Attempted Sexual Assault

Remember, your mental health matters more than reading this book. If you or someone you know is struggling, please reach out to your local crisis hotline.

U.S.A. Crisis Hotline: 988

United Kingdom Hotline: 116 223

PROLOGUE

A phenomenon occurs when the mind and body endure too much—too much pain, too much loss, too much breaking and rebuilding until the pieces no longer fit the way they once did. When the trauma is not a fleeting shadow, but a constant weight—pressing and suffocating. When fear dulls, not into acceptance, but into something darker.

At first, we fight to survive. We run, we endure, we try to make sense of the senseless. We tell ourselves there *is* a way out, that things will change if we hold on long enough. But there comes a moment—a final breaking point—when the body no longer flinches, when the mind no longer seeks escape.

When survival is no longer enough.

This is when the fear is burned away, leaving only fury in its wake. When exhaustion is swallowed by rage. When the choice is no longer fight or flight. When there is no pleading, no bargaining, no mercy left to give.

It is a transformation, a reckoning—the moment pain turns into power, when the hunted becomes the hunter, when the silent suffering gives way to something unrelenting, something unstoppable.

It's called the Quiet Violence.

And this is what it looks like.

"Does it hurt?" Dr. Eric Morani's smooth, steady tone pulled me from the memory's grip. His question, low and rich like a cello's hum, drew me back to the present. White walls and fluorescent lights bore down on me, stark and unforgiving.

My gaze snapped to his. He stood close, his gloved fingers brushing the inside of my wrist with a lightness that sent warmth skating up my arm. Even in this sterile light, he looked effortlessly perfect—*too perfect*. Dark hair slicked back with precision, skin sun-kissed and flawless, and eyes... *God, those eyes*. Green with flecks of liquid gold, as if they'd stolen the sunlight filtering through summer leaves.

"Oh, um, no. I'm fine," I managed, flexing my fingers.

"Two seconds," he murmured, concentrating on the needle in my arm. A sharp sting. The odd pull of blood rushing into the vial.

The steadiness of his grip grounded me more than I wanted to admit. Of the four doctors that handled my care, Eric was the only one who insisted on drawing my blood himself. *Every time*. It felt oddly personal—unsettling in a way I couldn't quite define.

"And... done." He removed the needle, and pressed gauze to my skin with his thumb resting a beat too long over my pulse point before pulling away.

His gaze met mine, something unreadable flickering there. "Just let me send this to the lab and check back on the scans. I can call you when the results are in, save you the trip."

I wanted to look away, but his crooked grin and the intensity of his gaze held me captive, as if he were searching through my hidden bits. My body tensed, instinctively hoisting up a barrier to shield whatever he might be looking for. I attempted a grin, to return his so-pretty-it-hurts smile, but it just felt fake—*and probably looked fake*. Like I was some robot trying to convince him I was human. *I felt like a robot*. Nothing but a cold metal casing hiding tangled wires that someone had no clue how to assemble

He turned to his computer, fingers tapping across the keyboard. I swallowed, forcing myself to sit up straighter, to appear...*normal*. Or at least as close to normal as I could manage these days.

My chest rose and fell in slow, measured breaths as I focused on my restless fingers, twisting together without my realizing. He noticed, too.

"I am *entirely confident* your scans will be clear," he said, lifting that square jaw from the monitor and flashing his pearly whites, attempting to placate what I'm sure he mistook as a worrisome and petrified patient.

I wasn't worried, and I wasn't petrified. I was *tired*. Tired of appointments. Of discussing the "next steps". Of being poked, prodded, and probed. Tired of being studied and tested. Tired of the smell of rubbing alcohol and antiseptic. Of being sick. Of waiting on test results. Tired of conversations with people who wore their pity like a second skin and feared for their own mortality. Tired of cheating husbands. Of overbearing sisters. Of distracting doctors who had no business looking *that* good. Tired of the numbing smog that floated through my veins and coated my bones.

Just *tired.*

"You are always entirely *too* confident," I countered, forcing the corners of my mouth to lift into a smile.

He chuckled, the sound warm and familiar. "There she is," he tossed back, eyes returning to the screen, fingers resuming their rhythmic typing. A slight smirk played on his full lips. "Thought I lost you there for a second."

That tone, the effortless way he bantered... . The room suddenly felt smaller, *hot,* as he panned toward me and extended his hand—a simple offer. My throat tightened. I ignored it, pushing myself to my feet. His smile faltered, just for a second—but he recovered, slipping back into that calm, unreadable toffee-colored mask.

Good. The amount of time you spend smiling is unsettling.

"Am I good to go?" I asked, trying to edge closer to the door.

"Yep, you can get out of my hair." Another lighthearted quip. As I stepped forward, his fingers gently grasped mine, catching me mid-step. My breath hitched, eyes fixed on the unexpected and too intimate skin-to-skin contact.

"This is a good thing, kid." The skin under his touch tingled. Too close... he was way too close. And he smelled too damn good—like cedar and sandalwood, like curling up with a book in a cabin while the rain pattered outside.

"Noted," I snapped, snatching my hand back, masking the sudden heat low in my belly with *mostly* feigned irritation. My fists clenched at my sides. Ignoring the thoughts trying to pry their way in was impossible when he just kept smiling *like that.*

A genuine smile. The kind that came from someone truly happy.

I *wanted* that kind of smile—to have a reason for it. It felt like I had nothing left. Except, *apparently*, my vagina's complete lack of self-control.

"Cut the 'kid' crap. You know my age, *Doc*." Actual irritation bubbled beneath my skin. *Kid.* He couldn't have been *that* much older. Not with that face, unless there was some kind of magical fountain of youth I didn't know about.

A flicker of amusement danced in his eyes, the dimple in his cheek ever-present. "*Noted.* I won't call you kid. You don't call me Doc."

I chewed the inside of my cheek, tamping down the unruly and sinful thoughts that threatened to flood in.

"Deal." I chuckled, but guilt gnawed at me, effectively dousing the flames that had ignited in my groin at the way he looked at me—*towered over me.*

I was married. No matter how absent and broken it was, that reality loomed.

"So, what's next for my freshly freed cancer patient?" His casual use of "*my*" sent an unwelcome but delicious shiver down my spine.

"School. Work. Nothing special," I shrugged.

"The invitation on my desk would suggest otherwise," he mused, nodding toward the thick envelope perched among his files.

For the love of all that is holy and unholy.

"It's just a party my sister-in-law's throwing," I grumbled, raking a hand over my face. His lip twitched, suppressing a grin. "She's... big on celebrations. Getting all the family and friends together. Every birthday, holiday, all of it. She throws a party for *everything*, even the little things," The words tumbled out as I shifted on my feet.

"I wouldn't classify beating cancer as 'little.'" His voice softened.

I wracked my mind for an escape, for a shift in conversation —something that didn't include the party or what the ache between my legs was screaming.

How's the practice? How long have you had it? Where do you see yourself ending up? Would it happen to be between my legs?

"What about you? How's your girlfriend?" I blurted.

That works.

I took a deep breath and squeezed my thighs together. I locked my eyes on the space between his dark brows, refusing to get sucked into those soul-snatching jade orbs.

You're not taking my soul today, Satan.

He cleared his throat, leaning against the counter, arms crossing over his broad chest. "She's fine." He looked down at his boots with a slight, knowing grin. "Just... working through some things."

I didn't know much about her beyond a few vague details, but she was out there, and I could only assume they were *madly* in love. It would have been hard *not* to be with his face looking the way it did.

"The best of us get put through the worst shit." I inched toward the exit. He moved in step with me.

"You'd know," he said, winking. My heart tripped over itself.

Christ on toast. Get a grip.

"So that's it, huh? A whole year of treatment, and now you're free of me," he teased, his voice hinting at something I couldn't put my finger on.

He reached for the door, hesitating. His gaze flicked down to mine.

I pressed my lips together and nodded. "That was always

the plan." Meeting his eyes as he held the door open, I pushed my feet forward and stepped into the hallway.

"I suppose it was." A heavy silence settled between us, and for a moment, it felt like there was something more—something unsaid.

"Bye, Eric." The words felt strange, bittersweet on my tongue.

"Goodbye, Violet."

His touch lingered in my mind, searing through the numbness that had shielded me for so long. There was a rawness in his eyes, a feeling that tugged at some unhealed part of me. I hadn't asked for it—didn't want it—but it was there.

But guilt was there, too, heavy and inescapable. I was still someone's wife... Connor's wife. And yet Eric's presence cut through that cold, empty reality, making me feel alive in ways I hadn't in such a long time.

It wasn't fair, not to Connor, to use Eric as a distraction from my pitiful reality, even if only in my mind. But maybe his distraction was what I needed—a reminder that there was something left inside me, something beyond the relentless weight of sickness and survival.

THE URGE TO IGNORE THE TEXT AND GO BACK TO READING was strong. *So very strong.* I knew where this inevitably led, and I didn't have it in me to listen to him complain about how I still hadn't moved back in, our nonexistent sex life, or anything else he might want to dredge up.

A glance at the time.

A sigh.

It wasn't late enough for him to believe I'd fallen asleep.

I rolled my eyes. Our therapist would call this an attempt at 'rebuilding intimacy' or 'reconnecting', but it felt more like an obligation than a cute date night.

Suck it up.

With another sigh, I pushed myself off the bed and trudged

to the tiny, attached bathroom. At the very least, I could look like I was making an effort.

Jesus.

The fluorescent light was unkind, highlighting the dark circles beneath weary, pale blue eyes. Skin, dull and nearly lifeless, almost sickly in places—like I hadn't been outside in months. My hair—*somehow* still intact after chemo—was a mess of tangled espresso-colored locks, thrown into a bun that looked more accidental than chic.

When the diagnosis came, I'd braced myself—wigs, scarves, losing another piece of myself. Yet, against all odds, my hair stayed. It was one of the few battles I'd won. You'd think I'd take better care of it—but you'd be wrong.

I should've gotten used to this sight by now. My body was filling back out, but I still looked like something out of a Tim Burton movie.

I severely doubt I have enough concealer to handle this problem properly.

How long was I going to look like a corpse before I started to recognize myself again?

I pulled the hair tie from the pile of knots atop my head. A quick brush and back into the bun it went—this time more of a cute messy one rather than the I-haven't-brushed-it-in-three-days bun it was previously in.

Me: Love to.

I EASED MY CAR ONTO THE LONG DRIVEWAY, FLANKED BY blackberry bushes and towering walnut trees. Their branches reached across, creating a beautiful canopy of green high above. In daylight, small rays of sunshine burst through, making the place look like it came right out of a fairy tale. But right now, it was an ominous tunnel broken only by headlights and the faint porch light at the end.

I killed the engine and sat for a moment, savoring the quiet. I exhaled as my eyes trailed the dreaded path to our front door —or what *was* our front door. Now, it was just a door to a house that held more painful memories than good ones. But it hadn't always been that way.

Fragmented images surfaced. Signing the deed at the kitchen counter, keys pressed into my palm, Connor carrying me over the threshold after our wedding—painting, renovating, repairing—*together*.

Then, the pain started. Bearable at first, but eventually all-consuming. And instead of wondering why I couldn't make it to work, why I spent all day sleeping, why I couldn't muster up enough energy to shower or change my clothes, or why my weight kept dropping, he just... *left me alone.* Chalked it up to a severe depression bout and let me spiral through it. I could *almost* forgive him for that. We didn't know what was happening then.

'*You don't talk to me. You don't leave that room. I never see you. I fucked up, I know that. I made a horrible mistake. But I was lonely.*' The words still felt like acid dripping down my spine. I was lonely, too, but I hadn't gone out to bury that loneliness in someone else.

I swallowed hard, shoving the thoughts down, reciting the oh-so-familiar mantra that had become my personal gospel.

I chose to forgive him, which meant I actually had to. I chose to work on our relationship, which meant I actually had to. We both made mistakes. Nothing worth having was ever easy.

He was trying. I knew that. And I also knew his frustration

stemmed solely from not receiving the same amount of effort. He needed more from me. Our relationship needed more from me.

But I was tired of the endless arguments. The same exhausted words tossed back and forth. It was getting us absolutely nowhere, and I was so tired of hearing the word 'sorry'. Words meant fuck-all without some kind of action behind them, and maybe it was the pain taking reign in my mind, but nothing he did ever felt like enough for forgiveness.

The front door creaked open as I leaned against the hood of my car, the mantra still repeating itself. Connor's award-winning smile greeted me as he stepped onto the porch's wooden deck.

"Yours or mine?" I waved my thumb between our cars, parked side by side.

"I was thinking we could just watch something here." A grin. "Also, I'd never touch that car. We'd break down before we made it out of the driveway." He chuckled, eyes glinting as he teased my beat-up Camry and earned himself a swift middle finger.

She may have been a rust bucket, but she was *my* rust bucket. She was the longest relationship I'd ever had, and Connor loved to mock me for it. Sure, she didn't sparkle like his Bentley, but she had 9 years' worth of memories carved into those ripped and stained seats.

"She gets me from point A to point B *just* fine," I shot back, narrowing my eyes.

"Yeah, by tow." He crossed his arms and leaned against the door, that playful smile still dancing on his lips

"Whatever." I rolled my eyes, giving a dismissive wave, but warmth crept into my chest. I'd missed this—laughing, teasing. Things that used to be so easy now felt rare and forced.

"So, we're not going to the movies then?" I raised a skeptical brow as he sighed.

"I've had a long day, and don't feel like being surrounded by a bunch of horny teenagers making out." He ran a hand through his cropped chestnut hair.

"They don't really do that during horror films," I replied, climbing the porch steps. He pulled me into his powerful arms as I reached the doorway, brushing a soft kiss against my forehead. The hint of alcohol on his breath made me tense, but I tried to mask it.

"Unless *you* want to be one of those horny teenagers." He looked down, his honey-brown eyes sparkling as they met mine and winked. I shot him a flirty smirk and slipped from his grasp, moving through the threshold.

The house was the same as it had always been—elegant, yet too curated to feel lived-in. The open floor plan showcased the custom furniture and minimalist art on the walls. The spacious kitchen lit by recessed lighting and marble countertops devoid of clutter.

"Drink?" He followed, closing the heavy wooden door. I nodded, and he made his way across the living room and into the kitchen. "You would not believe the shit I went through today. First, I got knocked off a case because Jeremy—" He grabbed two beers from the fridge and returned, handing me a bottle before plopping onto the couch, the remote in hand. "You remember Jeremy, big boss's brother?"

I gave him another nod and followed suit, tucking my legs underneath me and facing him. "He's been gone, states away doing some bullshit with his girlfriend. Anyway, he's been gone for months. Then, he strolls into my meeting with our new client and steals the show. So, I get benched all because this asshole decides he wants to be a part of the firm again, and nobody bats a fucking eye." He waves an exasperated hand in the air.

"*And* we hired a new receptionist last week. She types maybe 10 words a minute and lost some of my notes from the Tomlinson case." He took a swig.

I nodded again, letting his voice wash over me, over the room, over the house—the way it always did.

Connor's job as a civil litigation lawyer wasn't exactly glamorous, but he liked to make it sound like something out of *Suits*. The truth was that most of his work involved mediating squabbles over contracts and damages.

"I mean, you've talked about leaving before. Maybe it's time to start working on that. There's that one law office downtown," I suggested between sips.

"The one in the shopping court? Yeah, that sounds *great*," he replied, rolling his eyes. "I'd love to spend my life listening to couples bicker over splitting assets." A condescending smile tightened his lips. "Ninety-nine percent paperwork, no courtroom time." His aggravation wafted around us.

"I mean, it doesn't *have* to be there. There are others in town." The words came out too soft as the tension slowly rose up my spine and settled between my shoulder blades.

"Yeah, and they are all filled with small-time, pencil pushers who *maybe* get one case a year." He rolled his eyes again, remote still in hand. I bit back the urge to remind him that he was also a *small-time, pencil pusher* by his own standards. Pot, kettle, and all that.

My eyes moved from the black screen of the TV to the remote on his lap. "There's a new movie on—"

"I'd have to go halfway across the state to get a decent job and not continue *wasting* my life in this shit-hole," he cut in, downing the rest of his beer with a heavy sigh. I suppressed my own eye roll at the slight to the town I'd grown to love, and nodded my head, lips pressed into a thin line. "It's bullshit."

The quiet that followed attempted to swallow me whole. I picked at the gray fabric of the couch cushion, the sudden change in the air building onto the ever-present tension in my shoulders. He stormed back into the kitchen and grabbed another drink as I searched for words to break the stillness. He plopped back onto the couch with a huff.

"You need a shave." I brushed my fingers over the short scruff on his chin, and his scowl softened into a smile.

"You don't think it makes me look more distinguished?" He rubbed his stubbled jaw and chuckled that light chuckle that used to make me swoon.

"More like homeless," I exhaled through my nose, masking the awkwardness swirling in my gut.

"Oh, really? That's what you think?" His narrow lips twisted into a wicked grin before he jabbed a finger into my side, drawing a death glare. He took it as a challenge, hands reaching to tickle every square inch they touched.

"Stop! I'll pee on you!" I shrieked, swatting and kicking at him as he loomed over me, continuing his playful assault.

"Kinky," he purred, his golden eyes darkening as he dipped closer. His lips were a breath away from mine, his fingers slowed their ministrations before creeping down and settling on my hips. He tilted his head, grazing his lips over mine.

"You're disgusting." I let out a nervous chuckle, pressing a hand to his chest to ease him back, even as warmth stirred in my stomach. We sat back on the couch, laughing together.

"Hey, you're the one who offered." His hands rose in a show of innocence before settling back on my hips, guiding me over his lap to straddle him. His hands, firm yet gentle, reached up and cradled my cheeks. "I can't tell you how much I've missed you." Heat crept across my cheeks as he brushed them with soft, lingering kisses.

"I was just here a couple of days ago," I replied, offering a gentle smile. He leaned back. Studying me, his nose crinkled as he shook his head in a slow refusal.

"That's not enough for me. I know that's not enough for you, either." His gaze remained fixed, intense, and longing as he tucked a loose strand of hair behind my ear. "I want you home."

Home.

This place hadn't felt like home in months. I'm not sure if it really ever did. Just four walls with a pretty view where I'd been sick and isolated. Where I'd discovered his betrayal. Where I'd packed up my life and left.

His lips brushed mine, one hand cupping against my cheek, the other drifting over my shoulder and down my exposed arm. I closed my eyes, savoring his touch as his hand slid down my rib cage to rest on my thigh.

"*Tell me.* Tell me you'll come home," he murmured against my mouth, breath warm against the skin. Heat traveled lower, following the slow path his fingers traced. "My sweet, sweet Violet," He breathed, pressing a kiss to the sensitive spot behind my ear and trailing down my neck. "I love you." His breath caressed my collarbone, and fingers drew circles on my thigh, before tightening.

"I—" The words were there. He *needed* to hear them. I just had to say them.

Just say the words.

The fog in my mind resulting from the growing heat in my core made it seem so simple. If only things could always be like this. But....

"I'm not ready yet," The whisper escaped, and his touch halted.

"You've got to be *fucking kidding* me." The low growl sent

a chill across the back of my neck as he pushed me off his lap and stood, pacing back and forth. "I can't do this forever, Violet." His voice rose, and I curled my knees to my chest, feeling the familiar panic and guilt coil within me.

"I just need a little more—"

"*Time!*" he snapped, voice reverberating like thunder. "All I give you is fucking time! Time and goddamn space!" His face twisted; his jaw clenched as if he might shatter it. Still pacing, fists balled at his sides.

I shrank deeper into the couch, my shoulders hunched, eyes locked on the white carpet. "I know." The words barely there.

He stopped abruptly, shifting his weight as his pools of honey fixed on me.

"You know? *Do you?*" He stepped closer, anger pulsating.

"I do." My voice shook, holding back tears. My lips trembled as I tried to explain. "I know how much you're trying, and I appreciate it. I really do. I just think coming back before I'm ready will put us in the same spot we were before I left, and it'll have been for nothing." The words poured out, desperation lacing every syllable.

A sneer darkened his features. "It *is* for nothing! Right now! You shouldn't have left in the fucking first place! You're my fucking wife. Your place is here! Not some dump of an apartment across town doing *God knows what* with your sister and her shitty friends! Do you know how that makes *me* look? Trying to explain to *my* family, *my* friends, why you aren't there for Christmas, but they see *you* out getting wasted?"

I felt the color drain from my face, pressure building in my chest until it felt impossible to breathe. "I haven't gone out with anyone in months. This," I held up the half-empty beer bottle. "Is the first time I've even had a beer since Eric gave us the diagnosis."

"*Eric.*" The rage in his expression shifted to something raw and ugly—disgust and a sense of desperation. He dragged a hand through his hair, eyes narrowing. "What fucking doctor has his patients use his first name? And why do you go along with it, like you guys are best goddamn friends or something? It's unprofessional and fucking weird. He's a weird fucking guy. Why are you so okay with it?"

"It's not *like* that," my voice faltered, my eyes silently pleading with him.

"Is that what it is? Are you fucking someone? Are you fucking *him?*" Another step closer, his voice low and accusing.

"What? No—" I shook my head, squeezing my eyes shut as hot tears began to slip down my cheeks.

His jaw ticked as he glared. "Look at your fucking face right now! You *are!* You can't even get the fucking words out!" He lunged, and I flinched as the bottle in his hand shattered against the wall behind me, beer and glass spraying across the floor. "Was that the plan when you left? You'd go fuck your way around town and rub it in my face?"

Get out. Get out. Get out.

"I don't think I can be here right now." Tears streamed down my face as I found the courage to stand. I couldn't bring myself to meet his stare as I moved past him, my steps crunching on shards of glass. I reached for the door handle, but his hand clamped on my wrist, pulling me to face him. His eyes, red-rimmed and desperate, brimmed with unshed tears.

"Wait, no." His hand burned against my skin, words barely cutting through the pounding in my ears. My eyes zeroed in on the contact. "Baby, please. I'm sorry. I'm so fucking sorry," he choked, his voice breaking.

Get out. Get out. Get out.

"Please let go of me." *Stop being so quiet.*

His grip tightened, fingers digging into my skin. "Please don't go. I'm sorry." A single tear dripped down his face.

I could almost feel his heart aching inside of my own.

"I'm a fucking mess without you. I'm fucking broken and miserable, and I know this is *all* my fault. I *know* I did this. Please don't. *Please* don't leave me." He pulled me into his chest, one arm locking around me as the other cradled my head.

My arms hung limp, tears soaking into his shirt as his ragged breaths brushed my forehead.

"When you left, you took all the air with you. I can't *breathe* without you. I can't do anything without you. I'm sorry it took me so long to realize that I couldn't. Please understand. Don't go. *Please*. I need you." Each broken word shattered me. '*I need you*'. Silence. Only silence, interrupted by the muffled sound of our uneven breathing.

The raw vulnerability in his voice cracked something inside of me. The panic dissolved, replaced by something akin to sadness and guilt. We were both fractured in different ways, yet I had been so absorbed in my own pain that I ran and caused *his*. I had left him alone in it. He wanted me, *needed* me.

"Okay." The word felt heavy, forced, but it was all I could manage.

"God, baby, I love you so much." He sighed in relief, his shoulders relaxing. Soft fingers traced my cheek as he lifted my chin, our bloodshot eyes meeting. "You're everything to me. You're my entire fucking world." He peppered soft kisses along my face, his mouth begging for reciprocity. "I *need* you." He deepened the kiss, his hands sliding down to the small of my back.

I instinctively pressed my hands against his chest to push him away, but he pulled me closer, molding me to him. "Please," he whispered.

He's trying.

I swallowed my reluctance and dredged up as much libido

as I could. He needed me, needed my kiss, needed me close. I could bite the bullet for him, *for us.*

I returned the kiss, earning a low and satisfied groan. He tugged on my bottom lip, his fingers hooking beneath the hem of my shirt. He broke the kiss only long enough to pull my shirt over my head, then reclaimed my lips.

"I need you," he repeated, his voice breathless.

We stumbled back onto the couch, tangled together. The fabric against my bare back made me suddenly conscious of the exposure of skin. I covered my bare torso with my arms, remembering the havoc that the past year had taken on my body. The still prominent rib cage, the large pink scar that ran from my navel and dipped underneath the waistband of my jeans.

"I don't care what you look like." The words offered little comfort as I swallowed the prickling insecurity in my chest. His clothes joined mine on the floor.

Trapped. Trapped. Trapped.

The word throbbed in my mind as I jolted awake, my heart pounding. Carefully, I peeled myself away from Connor's sleeping form, tiptoeing into the kitchen. I filled a cup with water and sipped as my eyes flickered back to Connor, still sleeping on the couch.

Regret settled over me like a heavy blanket. The night had ended with us tangled in each other, and the sex had been... fine. Connor had whispered sweet words and held me close, but I'd felt nothing. No spark, no passion—just the dull ache of obligation.

I exhaled as I turned around, leaning against the sink and

staring through the bay window into the dark backyard. Shadows flickered in the moonlight, moving with the gentle sway of the trees. A flicker of movement caught my eye, something separate from the shadows that danced along the tree line. An eerie chill climbed my spine as I reached for the light switch and flipped it on, casting light over the yard. I scanned the area, but nothing moved.

My phone chimed, its sharp sound piercing the quiet. I hurried back to the couch, silencing it and glancing over at Connor. Seeing him still asleep, I released a breath.

Six a.m. My favorite coffee spot had just opened. I glanced over at the deeply sleeping figure beside me, grateful for the chance to slip away unnoticed. I grabbed my keys, slipped out the door, and into my car. As I backed down the driveway, I said a silent prayer that he wouldn't hear the engines rumble.

THAT FUCKING CUNT. SHE THINKS SHE CAN DO WHATEVER she wants with whoever she wants. She's a fucking tease, a whore. She is mine. Every glance, every laugh, every breath is for me. Belongs to me. He's nothing but a placeholder, a temporary distraction. She'll see that. I'll fucking make her see it. I'm the only one who gets her—understands her. She'll regret this.

She'll learn to respect me and what we have....

Or she'll learn to fear me.

"Can you come out tonight? Pleeease?" My little sister's pleading whine filled the phone. The sizzle of my stir-fry mingled with her voice as I tossed it in the pan, waiting for her haggling to run its course. I'd learned not to interrupt until she had laid out her entire case on why I absolutely had to do something—or *the end of the world was nigh*. "It'll be fun, I promise!" she chirped brightly. "You can be James's wingman." A loud thump followed, along with James's muffled yelp. "He's all heartbroken and hasn't left our couch or changed his clothes in days. He stinks!"

Setting the spatula on the counter, I glanced down at my own shabby T-shirt and worn-out sweatpants, both dotted with week-old stains.

When did I last shower?

"You're right. That sounds like an absolute blast, Cas," I muttered, thick with sarcasm. "*Unfortunately*, I've been trying to finish this project for three days, and it's due tomorrow. So, I'm out." It wasn't entirely untrue; I had been trying to work, though motivation was scarce—and last night's fight with

Connor made focusing impossible. I couldn't imagine his reaction if he *actually* saw me at a bar.

More than just a broken bottle.

A chill settled in as I recalled his anger, the force in his voice, and how easily it could have been worse... *no*, he wasn't that kind of person. He'd never laid a hand on me or *anyone*, ever. It was a combination of extreme stress, alcohol, and maybe desperation, *not* violence. I'd had moments of wanting to break things, too. How could I blame him for snapping after I pushed him too far?

I gave my stir-fry a final toss before switching off the stove and plating it. Cassie let out a true-to-self dramatically loud groan.

"You'll stare at your computer, three days'll turn to four, and you'll be no better off. Come out, get some fresh air, drink, *relax*." Another loud thump, followed by a curse from James. "IF I STEP ON ONE MORE SLIMY SOCK, I'M BREAKING EVERY BONE IN YOUR FUCKING BODY, STARTING WITH YOUR DICK!"

I pulled the phone from my ear before Cassie's voice dropped back down. "Sorry, he really needs to get laid." A brief pause, and then more shouting. "I DON'T CARE IF YOUR DICK ISN'T REALLY A BONE! IT'LL SNAP IN HALF JUST THE SAME!" Her tone softened once more. "Think of it less like 'drunk socializing' and more like immersing yourself in the 'psycho-alpha-male-wannabe-sperm cesspool' that is our generation. Inspiration for your project! I'm honestly doing you a favor. By the end of the night, you'll have so much data, it'll write itself."

"Sounds disgusting," I mumbled, mouth full of food, wincing at her revolting description of the male bar crowd she knew all too well.

"Yes, but at least they buy us drinks—and only half of them end up laced."

WHAT ON PERSEPHONE'S GREEN EARTH POSSESSED ME TO agree to this?

Agree didn't seem like the right word.

Forced? Kidnapped? Dragged, kicking and screaming?

"Isn't this so much better than being alone and cooped up in your apartment?" Cassie asked, fingers combing through the platinum locks that framed her freckled face. Her signature painted crimson lips curved into a cheesy grin before she tossed back a shot of tequila.

"My *clean* apartment?" I eyed the grimy high-top table as I ran an index finger over it. I arched a brow, lifting my finger in disgust; a thick, sticky layer of Hades-knows-what covered the surface.

"It adds character!" She gestured around the loud, crowded bar, where couples swayed to country music blasting from a jukebox hanging on the wall near the bar's edge. Cigarette smoke drifted in with each passerby through the wooden double doors.

I met Cassie's sapphire eyes, cocking my head to the side.

Ah yes, how the heavy scent of sweat, sex, and spilled liquor was pure prestige.

She gave me a pointed glance and jerked her chin at the shot glass in front of me. With a scrunched nose, I downed the shot quickly, finding it easier than arguing. And after last night, I was in desperate need of things being in a little less focus.

Sleeping with Connor for the first time in months hadn't

lifted the tension weighing on me. The fight... I didn't even know how we'd gotten there and texting him after I left only seemed to make things worse.

I swallowed another shot while Cassie signaled the server for a fresh round. My phone buzzed in my pocket once, then again, and a third time.

Connor: I thought we were past ducking out in the middle of the night.

Connor: Seriously?

Connor: Yeah, this is healthy.

Violet: I texted you that I had homework to finish.

Connor: Yeah. And it's impossible to do that here, right?

"If it makes you feel better, I don't want to be here either," James said, his amber eyes fixed on his phone, wavy brown hair falling over his tense shoulders.

"How does she always rope us into this?" I shook my head, wide-eyed, glancing back at him as a faint smile played at the corner of his mouth.

Countless times, Cassie had lured us out under the guise of celebration or distraction, only to get drunk while one of us became the target for her version of an intervention. The only way to endure it was to play along, betting on who would be her mark for the night.

Another buzz.

Connor: Where are you?

"Ugh! Could you guys be any more of a drag? You're stalking some girl you refuse to tell me about," Cassie glared at James, who shot daggers back under a heavy brow.

As James rolled his eyes and went back to his drink, Cassie's gaze lingered on him for a beat too long, her teasing expression softening. For a split second, something familiar—something I'd seen a thousand times before—passed over her face.

She quickly masked it with a dramatic toss of her hair and a fresh grin, but it didn't escape my notice.

She snapped and turned her sharp eyes on me, thrusting her hand in my direction.

Locking my phone, I shoved it back into my pocket, raising an eyebrow at her. "And *you*," she continued, "refuse to leave your apartment for anything other than Captain Wander-Willy." I half-heartedly searched for a comeback, but was distracted by the continuous buzzing from my phone.

"Cas, take it down a notch." James set his phone on the table, shoulders still tense like he was ready to lunge between us, as he had done consistently for the last six years after Cassie 'adopted' him.

"That's an incorrect assessment," I deadpanned, ignoring James. I suppressed the urge to argue her "Wander-Willy" comment, though it was a *little* funny. It wasn't the worst name she had branded Connor with since she learned of his *extracurricular activities*, but it might be the most comical.

"*That's an incorrect assessment*," she mocked. "Look at your skin! I can see through you." Her words made irritation flare under my skin; I was all too aware of how I looked. I didn't need to be reminded.

"*I'm sorry*," I replied, thick with sarcasm. "I've been a little busy. You know, fighting cancer and all that." My eyes narrowed to slits, locking onto her icy blue stare.

She flung her arms up. "You act as if that's what turned you into an unbearable hermit, but you were like that *long* before you got sick. We all know it wasn't the cancer that made you that way. I mean, we *could* call him that." She shrugs. "I wouldn't disagree with you."

"Cassie. *Enough.*" James tried to step in, but I raised a palm, halting him.

"Okay, I get it." I ground out, heat spreading up my neck. "I didn't come here to listen to you burn Connor at the stake. You want to know why I don't come around? Because every time you open your mouth, you've got some new issue with my marriage. You don't like him—"

"That's an understatement." She rolled her eyes and downed James' shot, ignoring his baffled expression. "And—" She pointed a single painted finger in the air. "*Nobody* likes him. It's not *just* me." The relentless vibrating from my jeans only added to my irritation.

"You don't have to like him," I said through clenched teeth, nails digging into my palms under the table. "But he *is* my husband."

"Yes, yes. We *all* remember." She gave a slow, exaggerated eye roll. "He's the *only* one that seems to have trouble with that concept."

"So, he made a fucking mistake!" I shot back, raising my voice. "Everyone makes mistakes! We're working on things. We're doing better."

Cassie clapped slowly, her mocking smile wide. "Did you rehearse that in the mirror before you got here?"

"Fuck. You." I pushed back from the table, my chair scraping the floor and drawing a few stares from the surrounding tables.

"Oh, *now* you know when to walk away," Cassie called after me as I headed for the door.

I needed air. I needed space. I was suffocating. These walls, Cassie, Connor....

Cold air stung my cheeks and nose, filling my lungs and whipping through my unbound hair as I burst through the door and stormed down the sidewalk. Passing through clouds of cigarette smoke, I reached the corner and turned into an empty alleyway, pressing my back against the rough wooden siding of the building.

A few breaths—I just need a few breaths.

I closed my eyes, centering myself on the rise and fall of my chest and the hard, cool surface against my spine. Faint footsteps approached, but I kept my eyes closed, already recognizing their steady rhythm.

"I swear to Anubis if you defend her...." I pinched the bridge of my nose, scrunching my face.

"Just bringing you a jacket. It's cold as balls out here." I opened my eyes. James stood there, extending an exposed, tanned arm with his hoodie in hand. I snatched it and quickly threw it on, the scent of vanilla and a hint of tobacco overwhelming my senses.

"You should quit smoking," I noted as James, now shivering, pulled a pack from his pocket and lit a cigarette, clasping his arms around his lean figure for warmth. He took a drag and shifted his weight, bouncing from foot to foot. "You might get cancer," I said with a straight face, fighting a smile. James choked, puffs of smoke escaping between coughs.

"I hate those fucking jokes." He glared between coughs, which slowly subsided. I shrugged, swatting away the smoke that drifted toward me. A pause stretched between us; the muffled beat of the bar's music rumbling into the alley.

"I'm not going back in there," I finally said, breaking the quiet. He leaned against the wall beside me, smoke curling in the cold night air.

"Didn't ask you to." Silence followed.

"She's ridiculous."

"Didn't say she wasn't." Another puff of smoke drifted up.

"It's none of her business." My tone was clipped, and I fixed my stare straight ahead, focusing on the brick building across the alley.

"*None of her business* is exactly where Cas loves to be," he chuckled softly, flicking ash onto the damp pavement.

"She's a pain in my ass."

"She's a pain in *everyone's* ass, Vi." He shrugged a shoulder, his lips twitching as if in thought.

"*Don't.*" I covered my face with my hands as James took a deep breath and exhaled loudly.

"She's worried and wants you happy." As always, he tried to find the middle ground between Cassie and me, trying to bridge the gap between our constantly warring personalities.

Well, I don't want to bridge the damn gap, James.

"I *am* happy." But the words were hollow. He stood there, not making a sound, while the street hummed with the sounds of cars splashing through puddles. More incessant vibrating. "You know that thing when you say something so many times, it stops sounding like a word?" James nodded slowly, watching the passing cars. *I'm happy. We're working it out. I love him.* "I'm *still* not going back in there."

"That's fine, I'll come out here." Cassie's heels clicked against the pavement as she approached.

"*Fucking Christ.*" I pushed off the wall and turned to walk further down the alley, away from her, from this fight.

"I don't want to argue," she insisted, holding her palms out as she reached James.

"Sure, you don't," I scoffed, turning to face her. Might as well get this over with since apparently there was no avoiding it.

Sans running into oncoming traffic.

"I just don't fucking get it. You're miserable. He makes you miserable."

"I'm not miserable," I retort, my cheeks flushing despite the chill nipping at my skin.

"I'm not even going to dignify that with a response," Cassie snapped, rolling her eyes. James stayed silent, leaning against the wall with one foot braced casually. His gaze fixed on the street as he took another drag, looking as if he'd also debated jumping into traffic.

Me too, bud.

I took a deep breath, trying to curb the anger that was building inside me, but nothing worked, and I snapped back at her. "Where'd you find this high horse you decided to ride on tonight? I don't have to be happy every second of every goddamn day." I took a step closer, my voice rising. "And what do you even know about happiness? Endless drinking and one-night stands? That's not being happy, Cas. *That's* distracting yourself. At least *I'm* working towards something other than drowning myself in faceless strangers and high tailing it when things get rough." The words were sharp, and I pushed down the guilt trying to creep in behind them.

Cassie scoffed, an incredulous laugh escaping her. "Oh, we've resorted to slut-shaming, huh?"

"I'm not slut shaming you! I'm just saying don't come snipping after me when you're not the picture-perfect poster child for absolute bliss either."

"Can we just agree that we've all got problems and life sucks and move on? People are starting to stare." James stepped forward, pushing himself off the wall to move between us. Cassie and I exchanged a tense look before she huffed, her shoulders slumping as her thin arms fell loosely at her sides.

"You drive me batshit," she muttered.

"The feeling is mutual," I shot back.

"Alright, can we talk about *literally* anything else?" James practically begged. Cassie's face lit up with a mischievous grin as she looked up at him, her eyes sparkling with a wicked gleam.

"You tell who is it your heartbroken over," She teased, pinching his cheek, prompting a fierce scowl from him.

"You set yourself up for that one," I smirked at James, shrugging. He sighed, tossing his cigarette aside.

"I'm way too sober for this," he muttered, turning and trudging back toward the bar entrance with Cassie and I trailing behind.

I DRAGGED MY FEET UP THE CONCRETE STEPS TO MY apartment door, fumbling with my keys as the weight of the alcohol sloshed in my head. Just as I reached the door, my foot caught something.

"The fuck?" The words slurred out as I braced a hand against the door to steady myself. My gaze dropped, focusing on a matte black gift box lying at my feet. I picked it up, feeling the sleek weight of it in my hand as I unlocked the door, and stepped inside.

The light from the hallway cast a soft glow that barely reached the entryway. I flipped the switch, and warm light filled the living room, washing over the cluttered space.

I slipped off my shoes and set the box on the catch-all table beside the door, giving it a closer inspection. Its black ribbon glistened under the light. I slid out the small, metallic gold card tucked beneath the ribbon.

'*Handle with care.*'

A sarcastic huff escaped me. If that was Connor's idea of an apology, it was a shit one. Then again, I couldn't remember the last time he had gotten me *any* kind of gift.

I placed the card back on the table, loosened the ribbon, and opened the box. My breath caught as I lifted out an aged hardcover print of *Frankenstein; The Modern Prometheus*—My favorite book. I already had a dog-eared paperback copy on the nightstand in my bedroom, but this copy was older, the binding faded, nearly falling apart. I gingerly opened the book, the yellowing pages greeting me with that oh-so-delicious, aged paper scent. I breathed in a few times before scanning the title page. My jaw nearly dropped to the floor as I read and reread the words—*printed 1818; First Edition.* I stared at the words as I quickly pulled out my phone and unlocked it.

Me: Apologt acceptd

I couldn't help the smile plastered on my face as I swayed into my bedroom. I placed the newest addition to my library on the nightstand next to its paperback copy before throwing myself onto the bed and sinking face-first into the plush midnight blue pillows. Sleep began to tug at me as I ignored the buzzing notification from my phone and drifted off.

Connor: What are you talking about?

Goddamn it.

I slammed my laptop shut and slapped the heel of my palm to my forehead. The days I'd spent trying to write this paper, only to come up short, had me seething. Six hours from the deadline, and I had *nothing* but a title and some easily Googleable statistics. I'd thought choosing *Obsessions and Addictive Behaviors* for my psych project would be an easy A, but everything I wrote felt lifeless. I *could* argue that sounding robotic and mechanical during research on the human psyche wasn't unheard of. Still, the wannabe writer in me would eat me alive if my paper came across like every other research article. I was supposed to bring a unique perspective from my childhood, but all I could come up with was, '*Drugs are bad, mmkay?*'

"*No shame in taking a break and trying again later.*" My professor's voice echoed in my mind. He was an easy-going guy and meant well, but when he'd said that I'd wanted to throat punch him. His insinuation that I couldn't handle school just because I was in the middle of treatment felt like an insult. Like he expected less of me because I was sick. Like he thought less of me.

I wasn't immune to the general collective of human thinking. When shit got rough, I wanted to quit, too. *But I couldn't.* Quitting equated to failure, and I'd be damned if I let those condescending sympathetic looks and comments about stretching myself too thin be anything *other* than fuel for my determination.

I could hear Cassie telling me to relax and giving me her fix-all solution—that I just needed to get laid. But I'd done that, and it did nothing but further cloud my mind. I doubted a repeat would help, and I didn't feel like having the argument that would inevitably come from my lack of communication last night. *I could always just....*

I let my fingers drift down my stomach slowly, reaching into my shorts. Rubbing myself through my panties, the fabric a welcome sensation teasing my sensitive bundle of nerves. I leaned my head back into the couch and closed my eyes, continuing the motion.

My free hand slid down to squeeze my thigh as I imagined larger fingers replacing my own, tracing up and down my skin. Soft lips followed the caresses, kissing along my inner thigh and up over my hips and belly. Teeth lightly tugged at my exposed flesh. His hands gripped my hips, pulling my body closer to that taunting tongue. I arched my back, needing *more*. His hand slid to cup my breast, pinching and flicking my nipple.

A delicious ache built low in my spine, centered at the apex of my thighs. Teeth bit at my panties, nudging them aside as his other hand traveled up to my throat, fingers pressing firmly around my neck. His tongue darted out, lapping at the wetness gathering at my core.

The ache intensified as he continued his sinful assault, and I felt myself unraveling. He sucked my clit between his teeth, running his thumb along my jawline before tightening his grip. Another nip, and I came into his mouth. I felt him wickedly grin against me, then look up, meeting my eyes with those hooded jade orbs—

"Jesus, *fuck*." I ripped my hand out of my shorts and sat up. What the *actual* shit was wrong with me? Shouldn't my brain have associated him with disease and illness or something? *Where was Pavlov when you needed him?*

I tugged the drawstrings on my sweatshirt tight, closing the hood around my face, and threw myself back into the couch cushion with a frustrated groan. I just needed coffee. I was clearly delirious from lack of sleep, and that's why I was daydreaming about fucking one of my doctors.

Definitely not because he is the modern male Adonis and looks delicious enough to eat.

I shoved the swirling thoughts as far down as I could and slipped on my Vans, heading outside. Coffee would fix me; Coffee fixed everything. Hopping into my car, I eagerly drove the short distance to my favorite hole-in-the-wall coffee house.

I threw the car in park and bounded inside, instantly wrapped in the warm, earthy scent of freshly ground beans. Soft jazz hummed in the background. The walls were paneled with reclaimed wood, their deep chestnut tones warm and inviting under dim, amber lights. Rough-hewn shelves lined the wall, stacked with small potted plants, books, and jars of house-made syrups. A couple of patrons sat nestled in mismatched leather armchairs by the corner fireplace, chatting quietly or reading.

With each step toward the counter, my shoulders relaxed a little more.

"You're late!" the barista boomed from behind the register as I strolled up, a playful smirk on his face. I raised a questioning eyebrow in response. "You storm in here every day right after six with a crinkle right here," he explained, pointing between his dark eyebrows, exaggerating his furrow. "You order a blonde roast," he said matter-of-factly. "But it's half past nine."

"I hadn't realized I was so predictable," I chuckled softly, reaching for my wallet and pulling it out of my shorts. "I should probably fix that to avoid serial killers and all that." *Shut up, Violet.*

He chuckled before grabbing a cup and moving to the other side of the counter, where several coffee machines sat.

"Don't. I kind of like having something to look forward to in the mornings." His onyx eyes sparkled with a mischievous glint, and a smile peeked from behind the coffee machine as he prepared my drink.

My cheeks flushed, and I snapped my eyes back down to my wallet, pulling out my cash and placing it on the counter. He returned to the register and handed over the coffee cup. "So, what caused the notorious crinkle today?" He asked, tapping an amber-toned finger on the register screen and putting the cash into the drawer.

I let out a heavy sigh, my shoulders drooping. "Homework. Can't focus," I admitted, my tone carrying defeat.

That and my taste in men has me questioning my mental capabilities.

"You'll get there." He nodded.

"Yeah, just need a surge of inspiration."

"Well, if you ever need a creative catalyst, you know where to find me." He smirked again.

No thanks. There's enough men floating around my head as it is.

"Hate to interrupt." A low voice sounded from behind me. I spun on my heel, my body tensing.

Jesus Christ.

My heart nearly leaped from my chest as I connected with those familiar, soul-snatching jade orbs.

"Caramel Macchiato," Eric began, tone flat. His eyes dropped to the barista's names tag before returning to level him with a glare, "*Oliver.*" His gaze shifted and zeroed in on me. Any hint of the sweet and funny Eric I'd grown used to was gone entirely. His dark, hardened manner replaced the usual crooked smile and light demeanor.

Kind of rude, but okay.

"Eric?" I made a mental note to Google later if it was possible to come hard enough and manifest someone.

"Violet." Almost accusatory as he leaned around me and slid cash on the counter. His intense gaze locked on me.

I had to practically pull my jaw off the floor—it had to be illegal for someone to be so effortlessly attractive. The plain black T-shirt hugged the stiff muscles of his chest and the exposed honey-colored skin of his arms. His jeans left little to the imagination, wrapped tightly around thick, powerful thighs and calves. His inky black hair was loose, the waves framing his face and skimming just past his chiseled, sharp jawline.

Gaia, help me.

I resisted the urge to either run or melt into a puddle as the barista cleared his throat, pulling me from my trance. I gave him a quick smile before practically sprinting for the door, fumbling my keys in the rush. I tried to steady my breathing as I reached my car.

A massive hand reached beside me and gripped the handle, stopping me in my tracks.

"Making a quick getaway?" Eric asked as I spun to face him. He removed his hand from my car door and straightened. I felt a twinge of unease as I tried to collect myself.

"I—no," I stammered at first, definitive on the last note.

"Really? Looked like I might have scared you." He flashed a

sinister grin with those full, sensual lips, hiding a tongue that was probably just as devilish.

Don't focus on his mouth, don't focus on his mouth.

"Nope." I somehow pulled myself together.

The fantasy of your tongue deep inside me is still very fresh, and it's throwing me off my game a bit.

"My mistake, then." He scanned me with narrowed pools of green and opened the car door.

"Mhm." Standing in the open door, I pressed my lips into a hard line.

"Definitely no need to offer an apology muffin, then. Since I *didn't*, in fact, scare you." His eyes gleamed with something sinful as he held out a muffin and I eyed him warily.

"I'm going to ignore the fact that you somehow *knew* to grab pistachio." I reached for the muffin. "You didn't *scare* me," I sassed, but he moved his hand just out of reach and shook those jet-black waves slowly.

"Liar, Liar," he clicked his tongue.

What's this guy's deal? If he weren't so blisteringly hot, I'd have kicked him right in the groin.

That's a character flaw I may need to assess later in therapy.

"I just don't ever see you outside the office," I said, twisting the truth.

"Have you always struggled with object permanence?" he joked, quirking a brow. The question struck a nerve, reminding me of his '*kid*' nickname. Whether he meant it or not, it felt patronizing just the same. Irritation drowned out the earlier sprouted ache between my legs.

"Have you always struggled with being a smartass?" I shot back, voice sharpening. Eric placed a hand over his heart, pretending to look wounded. "*Welp*, this has been... *something*. I'm leaving now." I turned, snapping the words as I moved to hop in the driver's seat.

"Without your muffin?" he taunted, still holding it just out of reach.

"Hmm." I paused, then pivoted suddenly, grabbing the muffin from his hand before he could pull it away again. I jumped into my car and shouted, *"Thanks!"* before starting the engine and cackling while I peeled out—a stunned, sexy doctor left in my dust.

"So, you stole the muffin and *left*?" Dr. Hibani leaned back in her chair, eyeing me.

"I didn't *steal* anything. He said it was mine." I munched on the last few crumbs of evidence, tossing the wrapper in the trash beside me. Shifting in the chair, I traced the embroidered pattern on the armrest, resisting the urge to scrunch my nose at the lavender smell filling the room. Her office softly lit; bookshelves lined with psychology texts felt both soothing *and* unnerving.

"*And* you insulted him." Her dark eyes held mine.

"Woah, easy." My hands lifted in defense. "*He* started it." I tried to ease the defensiveness in my pitch, realizing I sounded childish, and cleared my throat. "He called me a liar."

"Did you not?" She observed, her gaze unflinching as her fingers tapped a steady rhythm on her notepad.

My face warmed. "*No,* I didn't." Maybe I did. Maybe I still was. Why did it matter?

"Then, what made you feel the need to leave so quickly?"

She leaned forward slightly, brandy eyes narrowing. My gaze drifted to the framed landscape photograph on her desk—a serene forest bathed in dappled sunlight. I wanted to be there or somewhere. Not here.

I had no problem analyzing other people, but when the tables were turned... saying that therapy made me uncomfortable was the understatement of the century. Still, if I was going to learn it, might as well partake.

"I left because I had my coffee and needed to finish my homework. Which I finally did. So, *yay* me." I fidgeted with a loose thread on my sleeve, avoiding her penetrating stare.

"*After* the coffee house?" She asked, eyebrows lifting ever so slightly.

"Yup." I gave a single, smug nod.

"Interesting." She looked down at her notepad and jotted something.

"I wasn't running, if that's where you're going," I muttered, feeling the tension in my brow as I watched her pen glide across the paper.

"Does that feel *honest*?" She glanced up with one eyebrow arched.

"Not... completely, but I don't really want to expand on it." My shoulders slumped as a hint of vulnerability slipped out. I glanced toward the window, fighting the urge to jump from it.

The impulse to confess—to admit that the idea of Eric's touch stirred something deeper within me, something I didn't want to name—nagged at me. Guilt gnawed, the kind Connor's accusation had brought up, but the thought of saying it, even to Hibani, made me shrink into myself.

"Okay, let's move on to something else. How are things going with Connor?" She shifted her focus, her pen hovering over the notepad, and I wondered what damning assessment she was about to jot down.

It'd probably read, "*Avoidant behavior, emotionally stunted, masks with humor, pretty fucking annoying.*"

Obviously, I'm a real catch.

"Don't really want to get into that either." I crossed my arms, closing myself off.

Talking about Connor was *exhausting*, talking *to* Connor was *exhausting*. And it's not like anything had really changed since the last time we dissected my marriage—aside from our little sexcapade the other night, which didn't feel worth mentioning.

"How about your friends? Family? School? Treatment? Work?" Her words were slow, deliberate, *probing*. "Listen, we've been at this for a while. We were making a lot of headway initially, but more recently, there's been a shift. The only thing we talk about is surface-level things—new shows, whatever book you're reading, the sheets you got from Bed, Bath, and Beyond, etcetera." She crossed her legs. "You may bring up situations deeper than that, but you clam up when we try to explore them. I can't tell you how to go about your life—"

"Isn't that *your job*?"

"*My job* is to show you how to manage your mental health. To help you heal from your trauma and cope with your stressors. But I can't do that if you won't unpack." Her words hung in the air. "And I could tell you *why* I think you're being avoidant, but I'm fairly positive you already know what's going on. Completely up to you if you want to accept it." She shifted in her chair, crossing her legs again as my frustration rose to the blatant accusation.

"I'm not depressed," I snapped, unable to keep the disbelief from my voice.

"Like I said. Completely up to you." Her calmness didn't match the intensity of her scrutiny, making me want to grab one of her ridiculous couch pills to throw at her.

"I'm not depressed," I repeated, voice cracking. "I shouldn't be," I whispered, my jaw tightening.

"You *shouldn't* be?" I straightened as she studied me, trying my darn diddliest to gather my defenses.

"No, I *shouldn't*. I'm alive. I'm married. I have friends. I'm pursuing my dream career." The words spilled out, raw and defensive.

"Yes, all true things that can be healthy—but they can also be stressors." Her pen touched down, leaving its mark. '*Obtuse dumbass*' was most definitely added in there.

"I fucking beat ovarian cancer. Shouldn't I feel a renewed sense of purpose in life? Joy?" My voice came out strained, the words heavy. The walls seemed to close in on me. I sat on the edge of the couch, ready to bolt for the door.

"You seem more focused on what you should and shouldn't be feeling, rather than what you actually are."

"I'm not feeling anything. I'm pretty numb," I finally admitted, dragging a hand roughly down my face. Why was talking about this *so fucking complicated*?

"Hm." She tilted her head. Her unsettling silence gnawed at me. The least she could have done is tried to make her '*hmms*' and '*haws*' less patronizing, like I was supposed to know what the fuck she was digging at.

"What?"

"So, when you disagreed with Cassie, you weren't angry?" She paused. "Struggling with your project didn't frustrate you." Another pause. "And the doctor flirting with you didn't stir anything at all?" Her probing continued, each pause haunting, trying to taunt me.

"He wasn't flirting with me." I rolled my eyes.

"We'll circle back to that." She leaned forward again. "You *are* feeling things—arguably, a lot of things. You've gone through an immense amount of trauma and life changes in an extremely short period. And your track record of having a space with emotional stability and safety where you could be open and honest about how you felt, even before your diagnosis, was mediocre at best. You've never been in a place where you were heard *and* acknowledged. Because of that, you constantly invalidate your feelings."

She paused. "Whether that is telling yourself that you shouldn't be feeling something or ignoring the feelings altogether, you do *everything* you can to distract yourself and others from what's happening inside your head. And you keep doing it because, well, for the most part, it works. You joke or change the subject, and nobody bats an eye. And when that doesn't work and someone presses you—like I do, like Cassie did—you get defensive and turn on them in the hopes that you can push them away enough, and they will either back down or disappear, because that makes it easier for you."

I didn't want her to be right, but as much as I pretended I had it all together, I knew she was. I relied on distractions— while berating Cassie for doing the same. We grew up in the same house with the same parents; of course, we developed the same coping mechanisms.

"Having shitty defense mechanisms doesn't mean I'm depressed, just makes me a walking red flag," I scoffed. "You ever been on BookTok? People find that hot," I joked, trying to lighten the blow she unleashed on my psyche.

"I'm well aware of the existence of red flags. They keep me employed." She *almost* chuckled before her expression softened. "Your 'shitty' defense mechanisms are a major contributor to the depression. You don't let yourself just *be*, so you push everything down and shame yourself because you aren't handling something the way you think you *should* be. You emotionally hinder yourself and, in turn, muck up what should've been a *fairly* healthy grieving process. So now you're stuck somewhere between trying to shut down and trying to set yourself free. You don't have to do *every* step of the process in order, but you *do* have to go through them to get *through* them."

In laymen's terms, my processing capabilities are shit.

"Everything's finally falling into place. This is where I get my happy ending, not some forced character development." I rubbed my temples to alleviate the pressure of her words.

"Do you feel like everything's falling into place?"

"Well, I *thought* I did. But now you have me reconsidering." I threw my hands up, defeated. Clearly, I had no idea what I was doing.

"That doesn't sound like such a bad thing," she said with a slight shrug, glancing at the clock behind me and nodding to herself.

"You can't just give me the answers and make this easy?" I asked, half-joking, half-pleading.

"I can't make your decisions for you. You must come to your own conclusions. However, I do think this would be a good time to assess the different aspects of your life—family, friends, relationships, work. Take some time to think about what your life will look like a year, five, or even ten from now. Is it somewhere you want to be? Is it *who* you want to be? Are *you* happy?" She pointed her pen at me before checking the clock again and closing her notepad.

"I—" She held up a finger, stopping me.

"Don't answer now. I have a feeling it won't be honest. To me *or* yourself. Take the next few days to really delve into it, and we'll pick this up next week." We both stood, and she walked me to the door, ushering me out of it with the words *"Let yourself feel."*

As much as I hated to admit it, she was right. If she'd let me answer, I probably would've said, "Of course I'm happy. I'm fine with my decisions." But even thinking that felt like a lie.

I thanked her and headed out, dreading her added 'home-work'—as if the massive pile I already had from my other classes wasn't enough.

"*Let yourself feel.*"

Go fuck yourself.

THIS IS STRAIGHT ASS.

Exercise, they said. *Good for your head and heart.*

My heart felt like it'd spring from my chest and plummet to the ground at any moment. My head throbbed, heavy and fogged.

I could have, and probably should have, crawled into bed after getting my psyche deconstructed by Hibani, but my mind wouldn't shut up. So, I turned to Instagram, searching the feed for other mentally fucked people to see what they used to clear their minds. Mostly just workout videos of overly muscular men in tiny tank tops or people speeding down highways on motorcycles. Since I hadn't been on a bike since high school, exercise seemed the safer, cheaper option. I googled walking paths and picked what seemed like the least populated route. Thankfully, an overgrown trail wound directly behind my apartment complex.

Was that the safest way for a young woman running alone? No. Should I have stuck to the main road like a normal person? Probably. But I'd honestly rather end up dead in the bushes than deal with the anxiety of thinking people were watching me run.

The gravel path curved its way into the seemingly endless distance, bordered by wild brambles and towering trees that seemed to close in the further I went. Shrubs spilled over the trail's edge, their tangled branches reaching out like twisted fingers, grazing my legs as I passed. Moss-coated rocks peeked through the underbrush while long, slender blades of grass and ferns covered the ground. Overhead, the branches of oaks and maples formed a canopy, shading the path in patches of cool, green-tinted light, while an occasional shaft of sunlight broke through, casting streaks of warmth on the rough gravel below.

The air was damp, laced with earthy scents of moss and loam. Bird calls echoed from the distance, accompanied by the rustle of unseen creatures in the undergrowth. The further I pushed myself down the trail, the more enticing flying through traffic on a mechanical death trap sounded. My muscles burned, my feet leaden while sweat dripped, soaking through my clothes. My chest heaved, each breath dragging, and I still felt mentally lost.

Where was I supposed to start? How did one rewire their brain to function properly? Hibani said I need to *feel* my feelings. How was I supposed to unpack my shit with it crammed in a box, secured with a presidential-security level lock?

I needed a different angle. Clearly, psychoanalyzing *myself* wasn't my strength.

Maybe like I was analyzing a test subject? Like any other assignment—choose an approach and assess.

For someone struggling to 'open their box,' I'd suggest visualization. I'd ask them to describe the box: its color, size, location. Was the lock modern or antique? Could it be picked or would it need bolt cutters? Then, I'd have them imagine cutting the lock open. Did the box spring open or require effort? What did the contents inside look like? Were they neatly organized or a chaotic mess? I'd have them focus on one individual item inside the box. Was it heavy or light? What did the color remind them of?

Blue. The color of the sky right before the sun rises or the ocean waves as they meet the shoreline. The color of my phone and my favorite pair of faded jeans. The ones I've had since my junior year of high school—my first 'adult' purchase after leaving my parents. The color of Cassie's swollen, bloodshot eyes as she begged me not to go. Screaming at her, begging her to grab our baby brother and come with me. It wasn't safe, and I could have finally gotten us out.

The shade of lips the night she finally understood.

And the flashing lights that danced along the front of the house.

And the chipped nail polish on shaking fingers, reaching out and brushing a cold, lifeless cheek.

I'd never seen a casket that small.

I can't breathe. I can't *fucking* breathe.

Panic clawed its way up from the depths of my stomach and consumed me. My legs gave way, and the world spun as an invisible weight pressed down on my chest.

Breathe! Fucking breathe!

My lungs rebelled against me. Each inhale felt like shards of glass scraping against my throat. I wrapped my arms around myself and squeezed tightly, trying to hold myself together. Rocking back and forth on the ground, vulnerability enveloped me entirely.

Please breathe.

I put everything I had into forcing my eyes open to look at *something*—anything.

Tree, shoe, flower, can, stick.

I rubbed the fabric of my sweatshirt with one shaky hand

while the other moved to touch the exposed skin on my leg. My left hand then moved to the ground, grasping loose gravel in my palm and rolling it around as my right hand reached my ponytail, rubbing the hair between my index finger and thumb.

Fabric, skin, gravel, hair.

I shifted my focus, letting every sound envelop me.

Wind, birds, breathing.

I was breathing. I inhaled through my nose as deep as my lungs would allow.

Pine, mud.

I moved my tongue around my mouth.

Copper.

Slowly, my breathing steadied. The ache of panic remained but no longer threatened to devour me. I took another deep breath, letting the cool air fill my lungs. The world back on its axis and nearly steady, I pushed myself up. I concentrated on my breathing, not wholly trusting myself enough to have taken a step in any direction.

Inhale, hold, exhale. Inhale, hold, exhale.

I'd read about panic attacks and written papers on them, but apparently, my own personal brand of mental breakdown skipped that chapter. All that textbook knowledge about grounding techniques and controlled breathing? Utterly *useless* when your lungs decide to stage a hostile takeover. Here I was, a supposed expert, reduced to counting pebbles and sniffing dirt like a bewildered toddler.

The slow, unsteady walk back home was a monument to my own spectacular failure to manage my own head. Clearly, the only logical next step in this self-improvement journey was to lie down and pretend none of that had just happened.

I feel like shit.

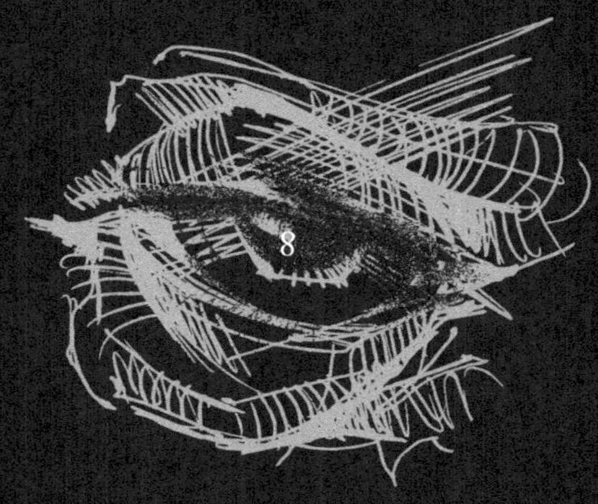

SHE RAN LIKE SHE WAS TRYING TO ESCAPE HER OWN SKIN.

Branches clawed at her as she barreled down the narrow trail, mist curling around her ankles. She didn't slow. Didn't flinch. That fire in her, that desperate ache to be somewhere—anywhere—but here, burned so brightly it seared through the dark.

I saw the tension in her shoulders, the way her dark brows knit together, as if she were running from more than just the silence over the path. She ran with the kind of purpose that spoke of escape rather than exercise, as though this lonely trail was her only sanctuary. She believed no one would bother to watch her here, that she could disappear into the thickets and vanish from the world's view, slipping into the forest like she belonged to it.

She was wrong.

I saw her clearer than she saw herself.

The fleeting moments when her expression softened, when she almost smiled those bow-shaped lips as the wind brushed her cheeks, or when the sun's rays broke through the trees, casting a *golden glow on her face. She had no idea how breathtaking she looked, with her guard down.*

Even then—face flushed, sweat clinging to her brow, breaths coming in broken little gasps—she was fucking radiant. There was something holy about the way she moved when she thought no one was looking. Unburdened. Raw. The way her limbs stretched, the tight pull of her muscles, the feral grace behind each step. She forgot herself in the quiet, and that's when she was the most devastating.

It was always like that. Watching from the brush. Not because I was afraid. No. I could've stepped out. Could've made myself known. But she wasn't ready.

I was always there.

When the world turned its back on her, I didn't. I never had.

She slowed. Her body hitched. Something shifted—panic slithering in. I'd seen that tremble in her hands before. I'd experienced it myself enough times to recognize how panic could seize a person from within, like a fierce and unrelenting storm crashing against the walls of the mind. The way her eyes went glassy, like her mind was somewhere she couldn't claw her way out of.

Her legs gave out beneath her, and she dropped to the earth, curling into herself as if she could hold herself together by sheer force alone.

Every part of me screamed to go to her.

But that was her moment.

Her battle.

I knew she could conquer this moment, not because someone had saved her, but because she had found the courage within herself. She'd done it before. Every fucking day, she survived things that would level most people. And she did it silently. Gracefully. She didn't even see the way she was already winning.

I wanted to tell her. Wanted to step out from the shadows and kneel beside her, press my hands against her trembling shoulders and make her believe me. She was stronger than she knew. She wasn't just surviving—she was turning herself into steel.

But I stayed. I watched. I waited.

And then, slowly... she rose. Not gracefully. But real. Ragged. Fucking triumphant.

She brushed her hair back, face pale but her spine straight. Shoulders squared. The storm inside her quieted, at least for now.

Only then did I let out a breath.

She walked on. No clue she was being watched. No idea I was the ghost in the woods. The one who had always been there.

And she didn't need to know.

Not yet.

But she would.

Soon.

9

"Why are you sleeping on the couch?" A curious and *very* annoying Cassie flung herself down, landing with a dramatic flop at my feet. I blinked my eyes open, staring at the ceiling above and letting out an exasperated sigh.

Go away.

"You have a bed," she mumbled, mouth half-full of food. Her thumb jerked toward my bedroom door, emphasizing her point.

"Why are you eating my food? You have your *own*." I sat up and folded my legs underneath me, facing her while furrowing my brow.

"Not chocolate pie," she protested, voice muffled, her shoulders hunched over my takeout box like a hungry hyena.

"Then go to the bakery like I did."

"Too much work." She shook her head.

"It's closer to your place than I am," I shot back as my hand jerked to the front door. She shrugged, spooning pie into her mouth, as if my argument were irrelevant. "At least *share*." I

55

scooched closer, reaching for the spoon. Her blue eyes widened as she leaned away, frantically shoveling in bite after bite until the pie was nonexistent. I gaped at her stuffed cheeks. "What in the *actual* fuck is wrong with you?"

"There wasn't enough for you." She smiled, words barely intelligible as she tried to stifle a laugh. Her chipmunk cheeks burst as she failed to suppress it, and pie chunks flew, covering us in specks of whipped cream and pudding.

"You got it on my shirt." I pulled the hem of my top out, pointing to the evidence. She bounced back and forth, giggling and coughing.

"You said you wanted a bite." She shrugged again, finally regaining her composure.

"Mmm, regurgitated pie. My favorite," I joked, rolling my eyes and standing. She huffed a laugh as I walked into my room and dug through the dresser for non-pie-covered clothing. I threw on a shirt and padded back to the living room, tossing a pair of clean pants to Cassie. She caught them as her eyes dropped to my top and narrowed.

"That's my shirt." Her accusatory eyes snapped to mine.

"And *those* are *my* pants. Get over it." I waved a dismissive hand in the air, making my way to the kitchen and grabbing paper towels to wipe up the mess. She cocked her head in silent agreement before pulling her jeans off and slipping the leggings on. After cleaning the mess, I sat back down.

"Who gave you the fat lip?" Cassie's eyes widened, and she poked my swollen bottom lip. I flinched away, the pain still fresh.

"I bit it," I mumbled, attempting to shrug it off, not wanting to relive the embarrassing attack or the painful memories that brought it on.

"I've bitten my lip before, and it's never looked like that.

Were you trying to eat it?" Her teasing tone made my lips tug into a smile.

"Didn't really know I was doing it. Panic attack." I gave in, and my smile faded. She leaned back, concern etched into her blonde brows.

"Christ," she muttered. "You okay?" she asked, reaching a reassuring hand out to touch me, but stopped herself and pulled back, shifting in her seat. "Let me guess, you *'don't want to talk about it'.*"

I almost left it there, my need to shut down and keep her out strong. I could have changed the subject, talked about the weather, or put something on TV. We could have sat in the quiet until she got bored and took the hint to leave. I'd be left alone to resume my usual distractions and continue to ignore my feelings.

But I wasn't supposed to be pushing people away, and if I was being completely honest with myself, I didn't want to. I was always alone, always hiding. Even when I was with people, I felt like part of me was tucked away tightly. I didn't want to be alone anymore. I didn't want to hide anymore. I didn't think I ever really meant to. It just happened slowly over time, and at some point, it became my normal—I let it become bigger than myself.

"I was thinking about...." Her eyes raised, surprised at my confession. "The night I left you and Sage." I watched pain flash in her eyes at the sound of his name. Agony and silence hung in the air between us.

"That's the first time I've heard you say his name in...." She trailed off, eyes fixed on the beige, ceramic tile flooring.

"Yeah. I keep him neatly tucked away." Tears stung and threatened to flow, but I shoved them back down.

Old habits die hard.

We sat in silence, pain and unspoken words hovering as we stared at the same spot on the floor.

I wanted to tell her how sorry I was. How I should have tried harder, forced them to leave. Or that I should have stayed and protected them. I wanted to tell her of the *guilt* I'd carried for abandoning them.

The words lodged in my throat, unyielding.

I wasn't there yet, and I could only handle so much growth in one day. Healing wasn't linear, and it wouldn't happen immediately *just* because I wanted it to. There wasn't a magical switch to flip, no shortcut. It took time and effort, and obviously, was fucking *exhausting*.

Maybe one day, I'd be able to talk about Sage without with the threat of another panic attack or fighting the urge to jump from a cliff. For now, I'd let this small confession be the milestone that it was, and leave it be.

"Dad really fucked us up." Cassie's voice cut in. "How are *you* the one that got cancer? What kind of bullshit justice is that?" she asked, her laughter laced with bitterness. She wiped a tear from her cheek, collecting herself. I leaned back, my own laughter bubbling.

"It's for the plot." And just like that, the tension shattered as we dissolved into laughter. For a moment, we were just two girls sharing a joke that would probably have gotten us committed.

Laughing. I couldn't remember the last time I wholeheartedly laughed. It felt good, light. Like I'd been trapped inside an endless dark pit, and Cassie's laughter was shaking me free.

The silent seal clapping slowly subsided and my stomach growled. I stood and made my way into the not-enough-counter-space kitchen, popping my leftovers from the night before into the microwave.

"Ah, the poor man's meal." Cassie chimed from behind,

laced with a hint of sarcasm. She leaned against the linoleum countertop, eyeing me as I watched the bowl of food spin.

"Don't diss pork and beans," I warned, pointing my fork at her.

"No judgment. I *still* eat tomato paste and relish on saltines." She picked her cherry red nails absentmindedly.

"That wasn't good when we were kids, even less so now that we're grown," I countered, my nose scrunching in genuine disgust. The microwave beeped, and I pulled out the hot bowl, steam rising in a flagrant cloud.

"You just don't like tomatoes." She gave a sidelong glance.

"Tomatoes aren't what's wrong with that concoction," I countered. She flashed her pearly whites. My stomach grew louder. I scooped up a mouthful of beans, the heat barely registering as I shoveled them in, my hunger overriding any sense of decorum.

I paused, feeling the weight of silence thicken. My gaze lifted from the beans and landed on Cassie's face, her blonde brows drawn tight.

"Just say it."

"At the risk of starting another fight...." She began, taking a slow breath, and my muscles tensed.

Oh, goddamn it.

She shifted her weight, eyes locking onto mine, earnest and searching. "I just want to say I don't judge you for staying with Connor."

A scoff escaped me, drenched in disbelief. "*Yeah*, you do."

"No." She winced slightly. "I mean, *yes*, but I get it." She shrugged, her shoulders drooping in an unconvincing attempt at nonchalance.

"Why? Because James talked you down?" I lifted an eyebrow as I placed my food on the yellowing counter.

"We both know James doesn't *talk*." Her lips twitched in

annoyance. "He just does that thing with his eyes, like you're supposed to *know* what he's thinking. You both do it, and it drives me insane. Like little secret conversations. I hate it," she snarled, shaking her head as I rolled my eyes.

"Only because you think we're talking about you."

"It's not talking!" She shot back, throwing both hands in the air before relaxing and giving a dismissive wave. She boosted herself up, the countertop creaking under her thin frame. "I'm saying I get that it's important to you—marriage, making it work. You never do anything half-assed, even if that thing you're doing is an ass." A small, self-satisfied smile played on her lips, her eyes twinkling. "You married the guy. That actually means something to you. So, of course, you're gonna try."

I sighed, my shoulders dropping. "He's trying, too."

She frowned, crossing her arms tightly over her chest. "Stop being obtuse. You're a psych major. Use your head." Her baby blues narrowed. "He's not '*trying*', he's love bombing you. That's his thing. Anytime you even remotely start to realize he sucks, he pulls you back in with his bullshit lies, and you fall for it every time. Just like Mom did."

"It's not the same," I murmured, my eyes dropping to the black and white checkered floor.

"Oh, it's not? Tell me what it's like, then. Because from where I'm standing, he's been sucking you dry from the get-go. And *not* in a good way."

"You're sitting," I pursed my lips, kicking a toe at the peeling squares of flooring with a hint of amusement.

"Seriously?" Her head cocked to the side.

"Well, *I don't know*, Cas." I lifted my hands, palms up. "Yeah, we *were* working through our shit. There was just so much going on." I gestured around us as though the chaos of the past year was scattered there. "Treatment had just started. I was sick all the time, and we just kept arguing. It was like every conversation was a fight waiting to break out. I was exhausted. My therapist suggested that we take a few days away from each other, and when I brought the idea up to Connor...." I hesitated, remembering the shattered picture frames and bathroom mirror, the blood dripping from his clenched fist. "He freaked. Instead of talking it out, I ran." The words tumbled out, remembering how hard it was to breathe surrounded by those walls, by him and his overbearing anger.

The same way I'd tried to escape our parents. Sage died because of it. Because I wasn't there. Because the 'overbearing anger' became suffocating violence.

I shook my head, dispelling the thoughts. "I want it to work. I *do*." But as the words left my mouth, they felt thin, as though I were trying to convince *myself* more than her. "I've just been hanging on to so much resentment that I haven't been able to give him—or us—a fair chance. Of course, he's angry. He's putting in all this effort, and I'm stuck in the past."

I took a shaky breath, struggling to put into words the guilt gnawing at me. "It's not even the cheating. Sure, it hurt like hell at first, but now it's more about how he kind of... gave up on me." My gaze dropped to my open palms as if the answer lay somewhere in the lines of my hands. "I wasn't myself, and he just... didn't know what to do with that." Cassie watched me, her lips pressing into a thin line. "I don't know if it's even justified to blame him for that." A bitter laugh escaped me. "I basically abandoned him just as much as he did me." The words settled in my gut, realization and guilt weighing them down.

"Nope." She shook her head. Her hand sliced through the air as she hopped down. "*Months*, Vi!" Her voice rose. "Months of you dying, stuck in that damn house, and this motherfucker couldn't be bothered to pull his head out of his ass long enough to think, '*Hey, this is a little weird. Something's up.*' Not letting us see you? Maybe it wouldn't have made a difference, but...." Her fists clenched at her sides. She paused, visibly trying to steady her breathing. "I'll *never* forgive him for that." Her eyes bore into me, unwavering. "You couldn't leave bed, and he walked into somebody else's. It is *nowhere* near the same thing."

Her words stung, but part of me wanted to believe her—wanted to be the scorned wife, the jilted victim. I wanted to be entirely blameless, but I knew I wasn't. I'd stayed in bed longer than I needed to. Even on the days I could have gotten up, I didn't. I knew I could've noticed something was wrong, just as much as *he* could have. I may have been sick, but I could have tried harder to pull myself out of that darkness. I was stuck and made no attempt at escape. Maybe if I hadn't been so selfish, maybe he wouldn't have felt so lonely. Maybe if I had talked to him....

But 'maybes' and 'should haves' meant nothing now. I couldn't go back and change anything. And I wasn't sure I wanted to. Anger and pain clung to my chest, a faint bitterness that felt lighter than it once had, like the fading metallic aftertaste of a penny.

I'd spent so much time focused on the fact I should have been fighting for my marriage and not enough time asking myself why I didn't, why I still don't, why it took me so long to get out of that *damn* bed. Why I jumped so quickly to moving out, like I was giving myself enough room for the inevitable.

I'd always looked at his cheating as what broke us, but something inside me was constantly gnawing with a more profound answer. Maybe my inability to be anything *other* than closed off had broken him just as much as I was already broken. Maybe *I* broke us long before he did. Maybe I was incapable of loving someone correctly, being what they needed.

I guess I inherited more from our dad than just his nose.

She pursed her lips, leaning on her hand, elbow braced on the countertop. "I'm not saying you aren't fucked up emotionally. Who isn't? But you blame yourself a lot while completely writing him off."

"You weren't there," I said, my voice firm.

"Because of him!" She yelled. "I don't know your guys' dynamic, but to me it looks a lot like douche—" I shot her a warning glare, and she rephrased. "*Connor* tries an awful lot to make sure the only person you have to rely on is him. Like he is trying to keep you locked away, meek and mild little housewife, and you *let* him."

"I'm not 'locked away'," I countered. "I left."

She huffed, crossing her arms. "Arguably, the smartest thing you've ever done. But now you're right back in it, forcing yourself to fix something you didn't break. And I don't think you want to. I think the only reason you're still seeing him is because you feel like you have to. I think—"

"You sure think a lot about something that's none of your business," I cut her off.

Her brow arched, a flash of indignation in her eyes. "When I watch my sister become a shell of herself, it becomes my business." She held my gaze, defiant.

I opened my mouth to speak, but she interrupted, voice laced with fire. "Tell me I'm *wrong*. Tell me he didn't spend the last few years stuffing you into some box he deemed '*appropriate*.' That he didn't label you his wife and then shut out everyone *else* from your life. Tell me that the second you weren't pretty and perfect and proper, he didn't go running to someone else."

"How am I supposed to get past that if you keep shoving it in my face every time you open your mouth?"

"You aren't supposed to get past it." Her grin flashed. "You're supposed to sleep your way around his lawyer friends. And if he had a dad or brothers, I'd say sleep with them, too."

I couldn't help the small laugh that slipped out. Her smile widened, her sparkling teeth on full display.

She sighed, her voice softening. "I might not know what *real* happiness looks like, but it's definitely not *that*."

"I know." The words were a whisper.

CRISP AIR BIT AT THE SKIN EXPOSED BY MY OFF-THE-shoulder dress as I leaned against my car beside Cassie. Connor's family home loomed ahead: the tall windows projecting an inviting glow down the concrete path to the front door. The soft lights lining the pathway exuded charm and quiet warmth, almost mocking my discomfort.

Cassie gave me a once-over, and I could see her holding back a smile. Of course, she was smug—this entire outfit was her doing. When I opted for my sweatshirt and skinny jeans, I was shot a glare that shut me right up.

"Dems da rules. All those people are expecting you to look like death. So put on a dress and some mascara. Make them eat their words."

The dress felt like a costume—a fitted floral bodice squeezing my ribs, the short black skirt of it flaring around my thighs, the off-white sweetheart neckline dipping low and hugging my *assets*. My reflection in the car window stared back at me like a doll dressed up for display: stiff, artificial, empty-eyed.

Cassie, as always, looked like she'd just stepped off a runway. Her form-fitting dark jeans, paired with those curls that bounced with her every move, only amplified my being out of place.

"I'm freezing in this getup," I grumbled, rubbing my arms as a gust of wind cut through me.

"Good thing we'll be inside, then," Cassie teased, adjusting her coat and giving a pointed look at the house, where people mingled just inside the doors. "What did she do, invite half the county?"

I followed her line of vision, feeling my stomach twist as I spotted Connor standing outside the front door, arms crossed, watching us with a stare that rattled my bones. Cassie caught my expression, and her features softened. "Are you *sure* you want to do this?"

What choice do I have?

I forced a nod, pushing my shoulders back as though that might somehow disguise the battle waging inside me.

"James is inside somewhere," she added with a conspiratorial smile. "Probably drowning in small talk. But he's waiting for the signal. One text, and we'll smuggle you out."

A laugh slipped, but it felt distant, hollow. I nudged her toward the house. "Just go. Before we freeze to death."

"There better be cake," she grumbled, walking up the drive.

Connor intercepted us, leaning in to kiss my cheek. "Took you long enough," he said with an overly warm smile that rarely reached his eyes. His gaze shifted to Cassie, and his tone dropped to a flat greeting. "Cassie."

"*Infidel,*" she shot, throwing him a saccharine smile. I suppressed a groan.

And you wonder why he doesn't want you around, shithead.

Connor let out an exasperated sigh. "Can we cool the blind hatred for one evening?"

"Blind? You've got some balls." She raised an eyebrow, but I shot her a pleading look. She relented, curtsying with mock grace. "I can quietly seethe."

I made to follow her through the front double doors, but Connor's hand suddenly closed around my arm, stopping me mid-step. His fingers dug into my skin.

"We can't walk in separately," he said, his voice a murmur but with enough of an edge to make my pulse skip.

"Oh, I thought you were coming," I kept my tone light, though my heart raced.

Ignoring the remark, he released my arm and spoke low, his voice all too calm, "I don't like how things have been between us. I *don't* like not seeing you or barely hearing from you. And I *don't* like waking up without you."

"I know, I'm—"

He raised his finger to silence me. "I *especially* don't like when you lie and say you're at the apartment when you aren't."

I swallowed, a sense of dread creeping up my spine. "I was just with Cassie and—"

"And *James.* Yeah, *I know,*" his voice strained with effort. "I thought we agreed you wouldn't spend so much time with them anymore."

You *agreed. Not me.*

He took a deep, calming breath. His eyes softened, but the words were sharp, cutting into me. "I forgive you."

I blinked. "You... *forgive me?*"

"Yes." As if it were the most natural thing in the world. "For lying, and disappearing, and not communicating with me. I was upset, yeah. But I found our solution." He paused, a proud gleam in his eyes. "I got an offer from Bronson & Bruick. They want me on as a partner."

"New Jersey?" One of the top criminal defense law firms in

the country. Connor only raved about them on days that ended in 'Y.'

But why are they be interested in a small-time civil suits lawyer from bum fuck nowhere?

"Yes. They want us there ASAP. Monday morning. The tickets are bought and paid for, as well as our relocation." He gripped both of my hands as he grinned, oblivious to the shock and rising panic radiating through me.

Our?

"Wait—"

I tried to speak, but Connor's mom swooped in, her lavender perfume overpowering as she swept me into a hug and pulled me inside. Connor followed close behind, like a tether I couldn't break.

The house was crowded with chatter and the soft clinking of glasses. I spotted Cassie across the room, a silent James hovering near her as she brightly smiled and chatted away with other guests. The scent of expensive perfume and polished wood mingled with the aroma of catered food drifting from the kitchen.

Tabatha wove us through the crowd, her arm draped through mine, Connors' pressed firmly on my back. I stumbled through greetings, my mind racing, fighting to control my breath.

Our.

He had said *our* tickets had been paid for. He had made the decision. He didn't ask. He just *did*.

Trapped. Trapped. Trapped.

I finally broke away, wandering aimlessly through the party as people asked intrusive questions, their eyes darting between my ring and my face, whispers of cancer, survival, and recovery swirling around me like a fog. It felt like every person saw me as a broken thing to be prodded, pitied, and congratulated. I navigated the endless sea of morbid curiosity from everyone who deemed *my* life, *my* fight, *my* survival, their business.

"*Such a tiny little thing!*"

"*What were your symptoms?*"

"*My great aunt had cancer.*"

"*You kept all your hair!*"

"*Those doctors are only out for your money.*"

"*What about children?*"

"Excuse me, ladies," A familiar voice cut in, rich and smooth, followed by the scent of cedar and sandalwood. *Eric.* I nearly choked on my drink. He took a step closer, his gaze warm as he appraised me, then turned to the two women who peppered me with questions. "I'll need to borrow Violet for a moment."

The women, both of whom I had never met before tonight, practically swooned. His all-black suit was tailored perfectly, the collar opened just enough to hint at the toned body beneath. He nodded at them before his eyes settled on me. He took my arm, the slight pressure of his hand like an anchor in the storm around me, green eyes sparkling as he ushered me away.

I blinked, words deserting me momentarily as I let him lead me toward the kitchen archway.

My heart hammered as I blurted, "What—why are *you* here?" The words came out harsh as I scanned the room for Connor, praying that he was either too busy in conversation or had magically left the party before he saw me standing anywhere near Eric.

Eric raised a brow, that familiar mischievous glint in his eyes. "*Well*, hello to you, too." He tipped his head toward me. "And congratulations. I said I was *entirely* confident, but the relief I felt when I saw the results—"

"I didn't need to be rescued. I was *fine*," I nearly snapped.

The anxiety of Connor seeing us talking felt like TV static on my skin.

"I have no doubt." A grin spread as he leaned in. "I was more doing it for *their* sake. You looked seconds from strangling those poor women." His hand rested on his chest, and a false frown graced his lips.

I tried to hold my composure, but the smile tugging at my lips sold me out. "Try listening to the same questions a thousand times and see how *you* like it."

He chuckled. "Touché." Leaning against the doorway, his playful tone shifted as his eyes softened. "You seem... uncomfortable."

You have no idea.

"I don't know these people. I don't think I've met this many people in my entire life. But they're totally fine with asking *a complete stranger* intrusive and borderline rude questions. Why is *any* of it *their* business?" I tried to keep the words neutral, but my annoyance made that nearly impossible.

"It's not."

"I'm sorry. I'm just not... a people person."

He tilted his head, dark brows furrowing. "I think you're not a *'these people'* person."

I opened my mouth to respond, but the sharp clink of glassware sounded. Like a sixth sense, the hair on the back of my neck rose as I turned toward the interruption. All eyes were on Connor as he raised his glass. I swallowed, my body tense.

"I wanted to thank everyone for not only coming out, but for the massive support you've been to Violet and me. We are so grateful to have each and *every* one of you here to witness and celebrate Violet's recovery. It's been a *hard* road, but...." He glanced at me, a sharp glint in his eyes as he continued. "We are excited to move into the next chapter of our lives and start fresh, *finally*. Since everyone is here, I thought it's as good a time as any to announce what that chapter holds." He moved through the crowd until he stood right beside me, his arm circling my shoulders. His smile turned sinister, and glare raised, holding Eric's as he added, "*We* fly out to New Jersey Monday morning." He turned back to the crowd, smiling broadly as he finished. "Beginning *our* next journey with one of the top criminal law firms in the country."

I could have sworn I saw daggers in Eric's eyes as Connor pulled me to face the crowd with him, but the pulsing veins in my head made dissecting *that* impossible.

My smile froze in place, a fragile mask concealing the storm raging beneath. I felt disconnected from my body, every nerve screaming at me to run, to fight, to *do something*.

I wanted to scream. To throw something. To demand *why he thought he had the right*. But all I did was nod, smile, and play the part.

Because that would make a *scene*. And Connor *hated* scenes.

Cassie's eyes found mine from across the room, and her look was one of horror and anger. James stood beside her, casually but firmly gripping her wrist as if to keep her from lunging for Connor.

Applause rippled through the crowd. *Numb*. Everything was numb. The room felt like it was spinning, Connor's grip on my shoulder was iron tight as he guided me through more conversations, purposefully avoiding Cassie, James, and Eric. People rushed forward to congratulate us, asking for details about *our* new life—a life I hadn't agreed to. I nodded along, a doll on display again, each second tightening around me, pulling me deeper and deeper under.

Trapped. Trapped. Trapped.

Finally, I excused myself under the guise of needing a bathroom break and, as Connor turned, I slipped out the front door.

The cold sting of the wind was almost welcome. I closed my eyes, took long breaths, and tried to still my pounding heart.

The front door opened, and footsteps sounded.

Connor. His *friendly* smile long gone. "What are you doing?"

"What *was* that?" I asked, trying to steady the tremble in my voice.

"What?"

"You... up there. We didn't talk about this. You didn't ask me if that was what I wanted. You just assumed I would pack up and move across the country."

"Because you are." The words were final and, quite honestly, rubbed me the wrong fucking way.

I shook my head. "My entire life is here. Cassie, James—"

"Your entire life will be *there*. You're being ridiculous—hung up on the distance. If you still want to see them, we'll fly them out. You're making this a bigger deal than it is."

"It is a big deal!" My voice rose. He glanced toward the front door, his jaw tight.

"*Lower* your voice," he ordered. "Your life is with *me*, wherever I go."

Trapped. Trapped. Trapped.

"We aren't even living together."

"This fixes that," he said through clenched teeth.

"I—"

"Phew, that champagne really goes to your head, doesn't it?" Cassie and James appeared suddenly, her hand slipping around my arm. "We need a ride," she announced, her voice bright like the light at the end of a *very* dark tunnel.

She tugged my arm toward the driveway, and quiet relief flooded through me as I followed. James turned back toward Connor, giving him a salute as he chimed, "Always a pleasure, adulterer extraordinaire."

I elbowed James in his ribs, shooting a warning glare, but refused to turn and see the anger I knew radiated off Connor as we walked down the driveway.

Cassie leaned close and whispered, "Eric said you might need an escape route and to tell you that it's okay if you need a rescue sometimes."

I smiled tightly, my mind flashing with wicked thoughts of the well-dressed two-times-in-one-night savior. If only there were a hallmark card that read: *Thanks for the save. I'd love to ride your face sometime.*

We piled into my car as Cassie turned in the passenger seat, first glancing at James in the backseat, and then me. "Soooo, now we screw the lawyer friends, right?"

I huffed a laugh, the sound feeling foreign but freeing, and saw James's raised brow in the rearview. His eyes were soft and concerned, as if asking, *"Are you okay?"* I set my lips in a hard line and threw the car in reverse.

II

THE CLEARING BEHIND MY APARTMENT FELT ALIVE WITH warmth and laughter, the damp grass squishing under my boots. I stood with Cassie, James, and Kal around the fire pit. The smell of smoke rose, and I watched it curl upward, carrying my past with it. I pulled the thick binder from a box—the one the doctors give you when they stamp 'Cancer' on your forehead before pumping you with poison, filled with page after page of different doctors and their extensions, treatment plans, drug names, and their possible side effects. I tossed it into the fire, a quiet thrill rolling through me as the flames swallowed it, curling the pages into nothing but ash.

Each item I threw enlightened something inside me, bit by bit. The wristbands from endless hospital stays, the aftercare sheets, the pages that had weighed on me for so long. I caught sight of Cassie and James throwing in their old visitor badges from when they'd come to sit with me, week after week, without Connor's knowledge. Kal held up a Lavender Aromatherapy vial—the ones they give you to curb the nausea from being pumped full of poison. Too bad it really only triggers a Pavlov-like response and made me want to vomit just looking at it... I gave him a grateful smile, followed by a light chuckle.

Kal laughed as he tossed it in, the fire engulfing the tiny tube. "I missed all the drama tonight, huh? Should've called out just to see Connor's face when James saluted him."

I laughed with him, letting it bubble up and out. Cassie rolled her eyes and nudged him. "Oh, please, as if *you'd* ever call out. You're so addicted to those patients that you ended up best friends with one of them." She threw her arm out theatrically toward me.

Kal shot her a look and turned to James with a smirk. "The only reason I started hanging out with you guys is because I thought James was hot," he teased, winking at James. "Silent and mysterious is totally my thing."

James flushed, ducking his head as he chuckled. I couldn't help but smile, too, feeling a warm, complete happiness settle inside me, mingling with the smoke. This was what I wanted for my remission party—my friends around me, a fire burning, laughter echoing across the clearing. I'd told Connor exactly that, only to have him dismiss it, waving away my idea as "too small." He'd just gone ahead and decided for us, as usual. But tonight wasn't about rich strangers or Connor's new job. It wasn't about caterers and morbid curiosities. It was about me— as selfish as that made me feel—about who *I* wanted here, about feeling truly alive with the people who mattered.

With each piece of the past I tossed into the fire, I felt my ties to it loosen. It wasn't just cancer I was letting go—it was all the times I'd felt alone, all the nights Connor hadn't been there, hadn't cared enough to even ask what I needed. All the times I'd thought less of myself and accepted less *for* myself. "*Where do you see yourself—are you happy?*" I pictured myself *here*, months from now, years maybe, still laughing with *my* friends, *my* family. *They* were who I wanted in my life, not *him*. And the relief of that thought settled deep into my bones. Connor didn't belong here, and I didn't belong there. He wasn't one of the people who made me happy, not anymore—maybe not ever, not truly.

I may have a long way to go before I'm truly happy, but the journey to finding it is the whole point of life, right? Not tiptoeing around hoping I don't upset someone or make them look bad. Not cleaning up broken bottles and mirrors. Not fearing the person that I am meant to love. Not trying to be perfect so they won't sleep around. Not getting yelled at or looked at like I'm stupid.

I've spent all this time just surviving, and I'm *done*. I want more. I want to live my life. I *deserve* to live my life.

When the fire had burned down, James and Kal settled into camping chairs, cracking open beers and chatting.

"I have to pee," I said.

"Ditto." Cassie nodded, following me inside.

The moment I stepped through the backdoor and into the kitchen, my stomach dropped. A bouquet of dead flowers sat on the counter, beautiful and brittle, like the whole mess of them would fall apart if I touched them. Cassie noticed, her eyes narrowing as she nodded toward the flowers. "Did Connor come by?"

Rage spiked through me, hot and fierce, sparking like a match inside me. *He'd just let himself in? Left these here as if that would fix everything?* My hands tightened around the stems, crushing them as I gritted my teeth, unable to hold back the flood of anger. Without a word, I spun around, my pulse thrumming as I stormed back out to the fire. Cassie trailed behind me, uncharacteristically quiet, as I marched across the clearing and flung the flowers into the flames. They crackled, curling back in an instant, shriveling and falling apart.

James and Kal stared wide eyed into the fire before their eyes slowly rose to me. Their beers paused mid-sip. I dropped into a camping chair, crossing my arms tightly, my eyes locked on the fire as I felt the anger twist and crackle in my chest. They exchanged glances, but Cassie just shrugged and settled down next to me.

After a beat, she broke the silence with a sly grin. "So... New Jersey, huh?"

I snorted, the sound escaping me before I could stop it. I kicked off a boot and flung it at her, missing by inches as she dodged out of the way with a yelp. Laughter rang out, loud and clear, and for the first time in so very long, I felt the knot of tension loosen in my chest. And for once, the words that had been echoing in my head for longer than I realized sang a different tune.

Finally.

THE TRAIL CUT A PATH THROUGH THE WILD AND neglected forest. Dead leaves and damp weeds brushed against my legs with every stride, catching on my sweatpants.

I hadn't wanted to run today. I'd spent the afternoon on the couch, wrapped in a blanket, reading through another manuscript for work. It wasn't terrible, but the endless stream of revisions had me worn down, and the words stopped looking like words. On top of that, calculus and more psych homework waited for me at home, breathing down my neck.

One quick run. Just enough to keep up with the routine.

I needed it. Running cleared the fog in my head, made me feel stronger, more in control—especially now. After treatment, everything felt fragile, like my body might betray me again at any moment. But this? My shoes on the gravel, the burning in my legs, the bit of the cold air in my lungs—it reminded me I was still here.

If I were lucky, the exhaustion would help me sleep. It hadn't solved the insomnia yet, but it helped take the edge off, turning nights of restless tossing and turning into something almost tolerable.

The runs had become my haven in the week since the party. It drowned out the noise in my head from Connor's constant calls and texts. I was surprised he hadn't tried showing up at my apartment.

Connor. The flowers. His so-called *offer*. It wasn't an '*offer*". It was a command wrapped in his self-righteous logic, his need for control. The way he'd dismissed me, like I didn't matter in my own life... my jaw clenched as I pushed my pace, trying to outrun the phantom caress of his voice.

I hadn't realized how I was practically begging for an escape until Eric stepped in—sending Cassie and James to the rescue. I'd felt the shift immediately—the relief of Connor's grip finally loosening, the air feeling lighter with every step I'd taken away from him.

My thoughts drifted, seeking refuge, and landed on Eric. His presence, magnetic and grounding all at once. I pictured him at the party—sharp and commanding, the kind of man who didn't just walk into a room but *lit* it. Confidence poured off him like a slow, rolling wave, filling the space around him in a way that made people stand a little taller, speak a little faster.

And his *smile*, that maddening curve of his lips, like there was always some joke that only *he* was privy to. Had he known how women had ogled at him as he sauntered around the room?

I wondered if he'd noticed how my breath hitched when he looked at me or how my thoughts wandered at night, imagining those massive hands of his—steady, skilled, strong—tracing paths across my skin. A shiver ran through me, though it had nothing to do with the cold.

A sound broke through my thoughts—a crunch behind me. My steps faltered. I tugged out one earbud, leaving it to dangle against my heaving chest, and turned to look.

Nothing. Just the empty path winding back into the shadows, the overgrowth pressing in on either side. A whisper of wind stirred the brittle and dry leaves, but nothing moved.

I forced out a breath, shaking my head. *Just my nerves.* I started running again, slower this time, letting the rhythm of my strides settle me. But there it was—a crunch, louder this time and undeniably closer.

I stopped cold, heart thudding against my ribs. Slowly, I turned, scanning the path behind me. Mountain lion? Bear? Out here, the possibilities endless, and none of them good.

I could carve a shortcut back to society through the brush and trees, but I'd be just as likely to run into an animal before I made it. I could wind back through the trail and return to my apartment, but that risks running directly past whatever could be watching me.

A gun. I should own a gun. Or maybe I shouldn't run through nothing but miles and miles of forest alone like a dumbass.

Then, I saw him. A figure in the distance, running.

My stomach twisted. No one ever used this path. That was the whole point—the solitude, the quiet. I glanced back again, hoping he might veer off onto a different path.

He didn't.

I started moving again, picking up my pace, breath quickening with every step. I tugged out the other earbud, my ears straining for every sound. His footsteps grew louder, steadier, matching my pace.

Panic started to coil in my chest. My legs burned as I pushed harder, *faster,* but no matter how hard I ran, the sound of his approaching didn't fade. My breathing turned ragged, every sharp inhale clawing at my throat.

My hand slipped into my jacket pocket, fingers curling around the small knife I carried. I was alone, not stupid. A lone woman running on a deserted path at night? Prime pickings for serial killers. The weight of the knife, and its cool surface, grounded me even as fear buzzed under my skin.

No. I'll be damned if I let another man think he can scare me. I may go down, but not without a fight.

I stopped suddenly, turning to face him, feet planted, heart pounding. My grip tightened on the knife.

The man kept coming, his stride strong, his breathing audible now. My stomach lurched as he got closer, every footstep echoing in my head.

Then he passed me.

Just like that, he ran by, his face flushed with effort, his eyes forward as if I didn't exist.

I stood there frozen, my breaths shallow, until his figure disappeared around the bend. My fingers ached as I uncurled them from the knife handle, shoving it back into my pocket.

I let out a strained laugh at the parancia that slowly drained from my bloodstream.

Could've been bad.

The thought made the path feel darker. I didn't bother putting my earbuds back in, listening to every sound as I forced myself to keep moving and tried not to jump at every shadow.

"So, are you going to run with me or not?"

"Oh, Gaia. *No.* I hate running," Cassie replied, her tone dripping with horror. "I prefer a different type of cardio," she purred, twisting in the passenger seat and grinding against it as she let out a breathy moan that sounded straight out of a bad adult film.

The road twisted and turned, hemmed in by towering evergreens on either side, the wilderness creeping close enough to brush against its edges.

"You're gross." My voice was flat, but I couldn't help the laugh that slipped through.

"You only think it's gross because you married Limp-Dick Larry." She scrunched her nose, looking through the fogged window at the brick buildings that lined the main street.

Each building had its own personality: some with arched windows framed by iron grates, others adorned with painted shutters or faded murals. Nearly every storefront showcased Halloween decorations. Skeletons dangled from balconies, pumpkins perched on window ledges, and cobwebs draped across door frames. The cold air carried the comforting scent of wood smoke through the car's cracked windows. Overhead, the gray sky hung heavy, hinting that the first snowfall was close.

"He's *never* had a limp—"

"James has a treadmill," Cassie interrupted.

I let it go with a sigh, humming in response as I steered into a parking spot outside The Coffee House. The shop sat on the corner of the street, its red brick exterior softened by ivy creeping along one side. Above the door, a sign creaked in the wind, its peeling paint charming in its imperfection.

The cold hit me properly as we exited the car, biting through my jacket. I zipped it up higher, trying to trap what little warmth I had left. Cassie, seemingly unaffected, was already talking, her breath curling into the air in wispy clouds.

"Ooh, maybe we can run to that new thrift store down the street after this!" She suggested, bouncing on the balls of her feet.

"I have to make a pit stop before we head in," I said, stepping up onto the sidewalk.

The streets were quieter than usual for a Friday, the town settling into its slow, steady rhythm as the colder weather set in. Cassie followed me as I passed The Coffee House. The door swung open briefly, releasing a rush of warmth laced with the sharp scent of cinnamon and espresso, but I didn't stop.

We moved along the narrow street, past rows of old buildings. Dusty windows stared back at us, some veiled by curtains, others dimly lit, reflecting the overcast sky.

I stopped in front of one of the older buildings, its stone facade worn and pockmarked by time. The weight of the building settled over me, heavy and unyielding, but necessary. It wasn't the structure itself—it was what it represented.

Cassie's footsteps slowed behind me. I could feel her gaze, a mix of curiosity and concern, as I stopped and stared at the courthouse doors. My breaths came evenly, but each one measured.

"What are we doing here?" Her voice was tentative, the usual teasing edge replaced by something softer.

"I just need to take care of something really quick," I said, not meeting her eyes.

THE COFFEE HOUSE HUMMED WITH A LOW MURMUR OF voices as I traced the rim of my coffee mug with my finger. Across the table, Cassie sat with her hair tousled from the walk, her sapphire eyes gleaming with their usual mischief.

"We *have* to celebrate!" she chirped, her enthusiasm palpable as she leaned over the table.

"No, we don't." I rolled my eyes and sipped my blonde roast, hoping the coffee would shield me from further discussion.

Her expression dropped into disbelief, her brows scrunching as if I'd just insulted her. "You're *joking*, right?"

"Nothing is finalized yet," I countered, keeping my voice low. "It still needs to be signed. Even *then*, it has to be filed, and there's the whole 'separation period' thing."

"Whatever." Cassie rolled her eyes dramatically and threw her hands up. "You're as good as divorced!"

"Hush!" I hissed, leaning closer, my grip tightening on the mug. "This is a small town. I don't need it getting back to Connor before I can talk to him myself." The thought of Connor finding out before I was ready sent a chill down my spine, colder than the wind outside.

Cassie shrugged, entirely unfazed. "Well, you better get on

it then. I've already texted James and Kal to meet us at the bar later." She held up her phone, the screen flashing a text thread.

"You're *mental*," I groaned, sinking further into my chair. "I'm not going out tonight or *any* night any time soon. Can't we have a movie night in?" My voice softened, practically begging her to let this go.

"We can do that tomorrow." She waved me off, her tone light and breezy. "Tonight marks the night that you *finally* kicked dick-dipping turd to the curb. Heavy drinking and dirty dancing are what normal people do after a breakup. You'll have a great time."

"Your standards for a great time are *very* different than mine," I muttered, shaking my head.

Cassie smirked, sipping her coffee. "Not after a few drinks, *Vixen*."

"Do *not* call me that." My teeth clenched involuntarily at the ridiculous nickname that had haunted me since my 21st birthday.

"Oh, come on! You never dance with me anymore," she whined, her lips curving into a pout.

"For good reason," I shot back.

Countless nights we'd spent dancing and drinking together. Luring strangers for Cassie to take home with a well-timed wink and half-hearted promises, only for her to kick them out before sunrise. She was the real vixen—though everyone had dubbed her *Cassie-nova*.

She tilted her head, the glimmer of puppy-dog eyes forming. "Can we still check out the thrift store, at least?"

"Yeah. Actually, I need to run to a few places. I think my washer keeps eating all my underwear." I took another sip of coffee, savoring its warmth.

"Ooh, Victoria's Secret it is!" She sang the words.

"Or just Target. I don't think I'll be needing anything fancy in the foreseeable future," My tone was dry as I shot her a pointed look.

Her nose wrinkled in mock disgust. "I am not letting you put your sex life in the hands of a five-for-fifteen pack of granny panties." Her eyes narrowed. "What's wrong with your face?"

"Nothing... shit*fuck*," I muttered, my gaze locking onto the approaching form made of pure sex and sin. My heart lurched as if it recognized him before my brain caught up.

"What?" Cassie leaned forward, following my line of sight.

"Eric," I whispered, immediately ducking my head, staring at the table like a schoolgirl caught passing notes.

"Like... *hot doctor Eric*?" she asked, voice brimming with glee as he reached our table.

"Violet." His voice like dark honey, rich and smooth, wrapped around my name. His eyes found mine, and my stomach twisted in the most maddening *delicious* way.

"Eric." The word barely left my lips.

Get your shit together.

"Cassie." She brightened like the sun and extended her hand with a theatrical flourish. He shook it briefly, a polite smile flickering across his lips before letting go.

"We finally get to officially meet!" she gushed. "I was so bummed we didn't get to talk more at Violet's party. I've heard so much about you."

"All good things, I hope." His crooked smile sent my pulse into overdrive.

"Anything *but*." She winked.

Eric chuckled softly before returning to me, his expression shifting to something quieter, more serious. "How are you?"

"I'm... alright. And thank you—for the other night." Heat crawled up my neck.

"My pleasure." His tone was layered, something unspoken resting beneath the surface that made my skin tingle.

"No patients today?" I asked too quickly.

"I took the day. Needed a breather." His gaze never left mine, and it was like being under a microscope—hot, intense, and terrifyingly intimate.

Cassie's eyes lit up, and I could see the gears turning. "We were just talking about going out and getting our toes wet... among other things." Her eyes swept over him like a predator sizing up its prey.

Kill me. Please, anyone. Kill me now.

"Oh, really?" He quirked a dark brow, his lips twitching.

"Nope." I shook my head. I needed to stop this train before it derailed.

"We're meeting friends at Tumbleweeds later. You should come," she chimed, ignoring the kick I delivered under the table. She winced but didn't back down.

"You probably have better things to do," I said before glaring at her. "Like hanging out with your *girlfriend.*"

"I didn't see a girlfriend at the party. Where is she?" Cassie quipped, glaring right back before flashing a toothy grin at Eric.

"Indefinite break," Eric said, shifting his weight.

Her eyes sparkled as she looked back at me. "You hear that? *Indefinite break.*" Her foot shot out to kick me, and I bit back a yelp.

Welp, I tried.

"You guys seem to have everything figured out. So, you two have fun." I stood, putting my jacket back on.

She yanked my arm, pulling me back into my seat. "We'll be there at nine."

He glanced between us, his lips moving into a smile. "It's a date," he said, his eyes resting on me before he turned and walked out.

Cassie waited until he was out of earshot before mimicking his words. "It's *a date,*" she purred, batting her eyelashes.

"Wipe that smug look off your face. I'm not going."

"*Yes,* you are. Did you see the way he looked at you? When a man that looks like *that* looks at you like *that,* you don't just pass on the opportunity. You're going, even if I have to drag you there." Her eyes narrowed, daring me to argue.

Fuck.

THE GRAY SKY BATHED CONNOR'S PORCH IN EERIE darkness. Each step up the creaking stairs felt heavier than the last, my breath uneven as I clutched the manila envelope like a lifeline. I had to be the one to give it to him. It felt like the right thing to do, to stand here and face him instead of hiding behind someone else. He deserved some closure, even if he'd hate me for it. And maybe I could reclaim some piece of myself by saying what needed to be said.

But as I stood there, the weight of everything settled over me. Fear, guilt, exhaustion—all of it tangled in my chest like a knot I couldn't unravel. My hands trembled despite my best efforts, and I had to force myself to keep breathing.

Just hand him the papers. Be calm. Be firm. You beat cancer; you can do this.

I paused on the top step, exhaling and straightening my posture. I squared my shoulders and raised my chin. The door swung open.

Stay calm.

Connor stood in the doorway, eyes blazing with barely

contained fury. His caramel hair stuck out in uneven tufts as if he'd been running his hands through it in frustration. His lean but muscular frame filled the space, radiating a predatory tension that made my blood run cold.

"Christ, Violet," he snapped, the sharpness of his voice like the crack of the whip. "Where the fuck have you been? You can't answer a fucking text? What the fuck have you been doing?"

My heart stuttered as I swallowed hard. I hated how he could make me feel so small, as if I were standing in the shadow of a storm I couldn't outrun. His gaze raked over me, searching for answers he wouldn't like no matter what I said.

"I'm sorry," I managed, keeping my voice even despite the tightness in my throat. "I should've communicated better. I just needed a minute."

He barked a bitter laugh, his lips twisting into something cruel as he stepped closer. The heat rolling off him was suffocating, his anger curling through the air like smoke, choking me. "Yeah, *yeah*, you always need a minute. That 'minute' cost me a grand in rearranging flights. Do you know how that makes me feel? When *you* run every time *you* get emotional? Are you coming inside, or are you just going to stand in the cold all night?"

My nails dug into the thick paper of the envelope. "No, I can't stay." My voice grew firm with resolve. "I just wanted to tell you I've thought about it—a lot. I don't think what we're doing is productive. I don't think it's healthy for either of us." I held the envelope between us like a barrier. "I went to the courthouse today. I grabbed these. All we have to do is sign—"

His hand shot out, gripping the door frame so tight his knuckles turned white. "Get. In. Fucking. Side.... *Now*." His voice dropped to a low, dangerous growl, each word slicing through me.

My instincts screamed for me to run, but my feet stayed rooted to the spot as my courage buckled under his glare. "I don't think that's a good idea, Connor." I forced calm into my tone.

Without another word, his hand lashed out, grabbing my arm and yanking me forward. I stumbled into the entryway as the door slammed shut behind me. The sound reverberated through my chest, leaving me breathless.

"Connor!" I tried wrenching my arm free, but his grip was unyielding.

"We're not doing this out there," he snapped, releasing me with a shove that sent me staggering further into the living room.

My skin crawled as I stood there, the walls of the house closing in around me. Every fiber of my being screamed to get out, to run, but my feet wouldn't obey. I clenched my fists, grounding myself in the weight of the papers still clutched in my hand. I'd faced worse than this, *lived* through worse—I could face him too.

Connor's movements were swift and calculated as he paced in front of me, his hands slicing through the air with wild gestures. "So, you thought... *what?* You'd show up with papers, and I'd roll over and go along with it? Where the fuck is this coming from? Did Cassie get into your head? *James?*" He spat the name like venom.

"No, no." The words rushed out of me, my palms raised in placation. "I decided this. Cassie didn't know anything about it until I got the papers."

"Oh, so glad she knows now, though," his lip curling. "Glad that I am, yet again, the butt of the joke."

"None of this is a joke," I insisted, my voice trembling. "No one convinced me to do this. This was *my* choice."

He let out a humorless laugh, his golden eyes burning. "So,

you can make decisions by yourself, but when *I* do it, you threaten me with divorce? You're such a fucking hypocrite."

The words cut deeper than I wanted to admit. "I am not threatening you with divorce." My voice rose as years of suppressed anger bubbled to the surface. "I'm telling you this isn't working and needs to be over."

"Do you hear yourself? This isn't working? You haven't even tried!"

The dam broke. Memories surged like a flood—every slammed door, every broken plate I cleaned up, every backhanded compliment I swallowed. Every time, I made myself smaller to fit into the cramped space he allowed.

"I came to drop these off." Rage and sorrow made my voice shake. I swatted away the memories and mustered up my best petty-professional tone. "Sign them at your leisure, but sooner rather than later would be preferred." I extended the envelope toward him. He slapped it out of my hand.

"I'm not fucking signing shit," he hissed, stepping closer, his presence dark and inescapable. "We aren't fucking doing this. *YOU* aren't fucking doing this."

Fear clawed at me, but I refused to back down. "Sign them or don't. If I have to get a judge involved, I will."

I turned for the door, but his hand clamped around my arm like a vice, yanking me back toward him. His face inches from mine, breath hot and bitter. "I'm not letting you run this time," he growled. "You're staying, and we are figuring this out."

My pulse thundered in my ears, his grip burning. The fear that had braised beneath my skin erupted into fury.

"Let go of me!" I shouted, struggling against his grip. "There's *nothing* to figure out." My voice cracked and I wanted to kick myself for sounding so weak. "I don't—"

"You don't what?" His voice dropped to a chilling whisper,

his eyes narrowing into slits. "Love me? Fucking say it, then. Say you *don't*! Say you *never* did!"

"I DID love you!" I screamed, shoving him with every ounce of strength I had. He stumbled back, just enough to put space between us. My chest heaved as I rubbed my aching wrist. "I loved you so much it fucking *hurt*!" I held up my wrist, the skin already darkening. "*This* is what it gets me. Your love, or whatever this is, *hurts*, Connor." I threw every ounce of my pain at him. I took a deep breath. "I was *here*! I was here, and I was happy, even when I wasn't happy, because that's what *you* wanted. Every high, every low, every time you needed me. I—" I shoved his chest again. "Was—" Another shove. "*Here*—" One final shove before I took a step back, panting. "Where were you? In between someone else's thighs. Even when you were here, you weren't really *here*. But your anger was. And your temper tantrums. All of that was here, and I tucked and waded through it like a good little wife."

His laughter was cold and cruel as he stepped closer, the venom in his voice dripping with disdain. "Why do you think that is Violet? Who made me that way, huh? You think it's been a cake walk dealing with you and all your baggage? The clingy behavior, the obvious daddy issues, your annoying tag-along friends. How could you possibly be a 'good wife' when the only thing you've ever done is complain and look down on me? You want to leave? Who's going to put up with you? You think anyone would want you? You're a fucking burden, Violet. *A job*."

"Stop." Tears stung my eyes.

He ignored me, leaning in. "No one wants that. You're nothing but a quick fuck to them. You'll be lucky to get that, looking as fucked up as you do. You're pathetic."

His words ripped my soul limb from limb. He knew exactly what buttons to push, what insecurities to throw at me. He knew exactly how to break me because he had been doing it for so long already.

"If being alone means I never have to deal with another *you*," I said, voice trembling with defiance, "then I'll be just fine."

Rage twisted his features. Before I could react, he shoved me against the front door, his body pinning mine. Pain shot through my skull as it connected with the hardwood. "You want to fight, you want me angry? You do shit specifically to piss me off, and then you complain about it. Those papers are nothing but a desperate cry for attention. *Right?* That's what you want. You want me to show you how much I care, that I'll fight for you, for us. Fine!" My vision blurred, mixing with fear and fury as his hand came up, tracing my cheek in a mockery of tenderness before wrapping tightly around my neck.

"This is what you want," he hissed, his fingers squeezing until stars danced in my vision. "You want me angry because you love it. Because it excites you. I *know* it does." I clawed at his hand, gasping for air, but his grip continued to tighten. "You can't leave because you love this too much." His lips crushed against mine, his tongue forcing its way into my mouth. My struggles slowed as his grip slackened just enough for me to drag in shallow breaths. I relaxed into the kiss, my fingers crawling along the door as his grip loosened.

His lips hovered over mine, his voice a sinister murmur. "Til death, babe."

My fingers stopped fumbling and found the handle as he leaned back into the kiss. I brought my knee up, slamming it into his groin. He crumpled with a groan, and I shoved him away, yanking the door open and bolting for my car.

I didn't stop until I was behind the wheel, coughing and gulping in air as my heart pounded in my chest. The engine roared to life, and I sped away, tears blurring the drive ahead.

Never again.

'*Til death, babe.*'

I sat on the couch, knees pulled tight to my chest, arms wrapping around them like I could hold myself together. I didn't bother turning on the lights. The darkness wrapped around me, hiding me from myself, and the bruises I knew marked me. Stark and ugly. Fingerprints he left on my neck, a cruel reminder of how *little* control I had.

But it couldn't hide the crushing pressure of fingers around my throat or the ache in my head from where it connected with the door. It couldn't hide the image of his eyes—golden and devoid of anything human, like a monster wore his skin. There was no hesitation, no regret, only fury.

I wasn't a person to him. Maybe I never had been—just something to overpower.

A fresh sob tore from my throat—raw, painful. My face burned from crying, my chest ached from how tightly I held myself, and yet none of it hurt more than the memory. My lungs still felt like they were fighting for breath, even hours after the attack.

My phone buzzed beside me, lighting up the cushion. Cassie. *Again.* Her name glowed on the screen, followed by a string of missed calls and texts.

I couldn't bring myself to respond. What would I even *say?* That I was sitting in the dark, falling apart because of *my* reckless choices? That I was too scared to speak because my throat still felt like it was closing.

Another buzz. Then another. Kal this time.

I ignored them all, curling tighter into myself, wishing I could disappear into the couch.

A loud knock at the door shattered the fragile quiet. My heart lurched painfully in my chest. Every muscle locking up as dread slithered through me. The knock came again, louder this time, and I flinched.

It's him.

My hand fumbled for my phone, trembling as I unlocked it. The emergency dial lit up, my thumb hovering over the numbers.

"Vi!" Cassie's voice shouted through the door. "I know you're in there! Your car is in the drive!"

Relief surged through me, knocking the breath from my lungs, but my body still felt too heavy, too fragile.

"Answer the door, or I'm breaking in!"

I forced myself to move, one step after another. When I reached the door, my hand hesitated on the lock. I flicked on the porch light, letting its glow spill outside, then opened the door.

Cassie stood there, her hair wild from the wind and her expression fierce. She pushed past me, shutting the door behind her.

"Why is it so dark in here? I can barely see a thing," she said, reaching for the light switch.

"Don't," I rasped. My voice came out cracked and broken, scraping against my sore throat.

Cassie paused, the head of her silhouette tilting. "You sound like you're getting sick." She flicked on the light anyway, and the brightness made me wince.

Her sharp intake of breath was immediate. I didn't have to look at her to know what she'd seen—the tear tracks staining my cheeks, the *bruises*.

"Oh, Vi," she whispered, stepping closer. She pulled me into her arms, holding me so tightly I thought she might break me. I didn't move—couldn't—my arms hanging limp at my sides.

"He's dead," she murmured, her voice shaking with anger. "I promise. He's fucking dead."

The words broke something loose, and fresh tears spilled down my face as I buried it against her shoulder. The sobs wracked through me, painful and uncontrollable, and still, my arms stayed slack.

"I should have gone with you. I wasn't thinking." Guilt thick in her voice. "I'm so sorry. So fucking sorry." Anger replaced the guilt as she continued. "We go to the cops, get him arrested, disbarred, *ruin* his fucking life."

I shook my head, the tears slowing. "I shoved him," I managed to choke out

She pulled back just enough to hold my face in her hands, her touch careful, her thumbs wiping away the wet streaks on my cheeks. "It doesn't matter. He doesn't get to hurt you like this."

You don't get it.

I swallowed hard, forcing the words out. "The courts—" I winced and cleared my throat, though it didn't help. "They won't care. He knows the judges, the cops. They're his drinking buddies."

Her jaw tightened, and she let out a curse under her breath. "If we can't go the traditional route, we'll stay with you until we figure something else out. I can put up a good fight, but James has a gun."

"Cas, don't—"

But she was already dialing.

Fifteen minutes later, another knock startled me, making me flinch nearly hard enough to fall off the couch.

"It's just James," she said gently, moving to open the door.

James stepped inside, eyes immediately landing on me. His golden face hardened, jaw clenching as his eyes dropped to my neck. Without a word, he dropped the two overnight bags he carried and moved toward me.

Cassie intercepted him, pressing a hand to his chest. James shot her a glare that would have sent anyone else running far, far away.

"I don't know if she can handle you touching her. I don't know if he... I don't know how far it—"

"I'm okay." At least, in the way she was thinking. "He didn't... I think *maybe* he might have... but I didn't let it get that far," I whispered, my voice barely audible even to myself.

The room went so quiet I could hear the blood pounding in my ears. James's fists clenched at his sides, and his voice came out low and dangerous. "Motherfuckers' *dead*."

She nodded. "Yeah, we covered that. We can talk about the logistics later. But until further notice, we're staying here."

James didn't argue. Instead, he reached into one of the bags he'd brought and handed me a container. Small, round pemmican balls lay nestled in wax paper. A mix of dried berries and ground meat flecked the compact spheres that smelled faintly sweet with the tang of dried meat. I took one, nibbling on it without much thought.

Her voice broke the quiet. "Bless your mother, and her Navajo roots."

The corner of my mouth twitched. It wasn't *quite* a smile, but it was something.

She waved an index finger at him, "Oh, and text Kal that we can't make it. And if he happens to see a sex-on-a-stick, dark-haired, green-eyed giant, tell him we said 'rain-check.'"

He rolled his eyes but pulled out his phone as I reached over and shoved a Pemmican ball into her mouth, earning a garbled scoff.

"At least someone knows how to shut you up." He chuckled.

As the night wore on, James paced the apartment, stress-cleaning until she scolded him into sitting down. I found myself sandwiched between them, my head resting on Cassie's lap while my feet stretched across James's. Her fingers combed through my hair as we watched some comedy I wasn't paying attention to, laughter occasionally breaking the silence.

And my body relaxed for the first time in what felt like an eternity, and sleep pulled me under.

CAN'T BREATHE. CAN'T BREATHE.

Trapped. Trapped. Trapped.

My eyes flew open, and I shot upright on the couch, gasping for air like I'd been dragged up from deep water. Sweat clung to my skin, soaking through my clothes and matting my hair to my face. The room pressed in around me, shadows stretching long and suffocating.

Cassie was sprawled on the other end of the couch, her

head tilted back and mouth slightly open, oblivious in her sleep. James shifted, his brow creasing as he stirred, but he didn't wake.

The nightmare lingered, and I instinctively raised my fingers to the bruises, tracing the tender, molted skin. A shudder wracked my body as I pushed off the couch, my legs unsteady beneath me, and stumbled toward my bedroom and into the bathroom.

I shut the door behind me with a trembling hand and turned to the mirror. A stranger stared back—hollow eyes rimmed with shadows, pale skin stretched tight over sharp angles, lips pressed into a thin, bloodless line. I couldn't hold the gaze, couldn't bear to see *her*.

The shower knob squeaked as I turned it, water spraying out in a sudden burst of cold. I stepped inside, fully clothed, not waiting for it to heat as I slid down in the tub. My knees tucked against my chest, clothes soaked and clinging to me.

The room was quiet, save for the patter of water against the tile. My arms wrapped around my legs, and I rested my chin on my knees. A soft knock broke through, pulling me from my spiral.

"Vi?" James's voice was low, careful, as if testing the air.

I hesitated. "Yeah," I said finally, the word like sandpaper on my tongue. "You can come in."

The door creaked open, James stepping inside. His hand shielded his eyes, shoulders stiff as if he were bracing himself for a quick nude show.

"J." The subtlest edge of a bitter laugh creeping in. "I have clothes on."

He peeked between his fingers, tense frame relaxing just slightly as he saw me, though his brow furrowed again. He tilted his head toward the living room, amber eyes asking, *Should I wake up Cas?*

I shook my head, tightening my grip on my knees. The faint grind of his teeth was visible in the muscle along his cheek.

"Do you wanna be alone?"

I paused, unsure. Finally, I shook my head again.

He crossed the small space and lowered himself onto the linoleum floor beside the tub, his knees bent, his head and back resting against the wall. His gaze followed mine to the far wall, where water streaks ran down the white tiles.

"I feel so stupid," I whispered, barely able to push the words out.

He jerked his head toward me, eyes smoldering with anger that wasn't aimed at me. His dark brows drew together, and his lips parted like he wanted to say something but couldn't find the words.

"Why did I let it get to this?"

He didn't answer immediately, his adams apple working as he swallowed hard. His gaze softened, though the tension in his shoulders remained. "It took my mom decades to leave my dad."

I turned to him, brow raised, but didn't interrupt.

"He almost killed her. Probably would have." He rubbed a hand over his face, dragging it down until his fingers rested on his jaw. "She loved him... even after she left. When he died, she still cried at his funeral."

He sighed, his shoulders slumping. "He made her—made *all of us*—believe shitty things about ourselves and each other. Untrue things. Cut us down if we talked too much. Made us afraid to say or do the wrong thing. He made her feel less. *Be less.*"

James's voice grew quieter, to a whisper. "Even after she married Jeff, she spent years living with my dad's ghost, working through the damage he caused. She kept waiting for the other shoe to drop with Jeff, for him to pack up and leave because she thought he was too good for her."

His eyes flicked to me. "Sometimes, we accept the love we think we deserve. And asswipes like my dad and Connor? They eat that shit up, taking advantage of our fucked-up views of ourselves."

I stared at him, his words sinking into me like stones.

Silence.

Without warning, James stood and stepped into the tub. He lowered himself beside me, his long legs awkwardly folded in the cramped space, water soaking through his jeans and shirt.

A flicker of warmth broke through the cold inside me.

"I'm sorry," I whispered.

James turned, lips twitching in a faint, almost sad smile. His eyes locked on mine. "Me too."

We sat in the water, the silence between us something closer to peace.

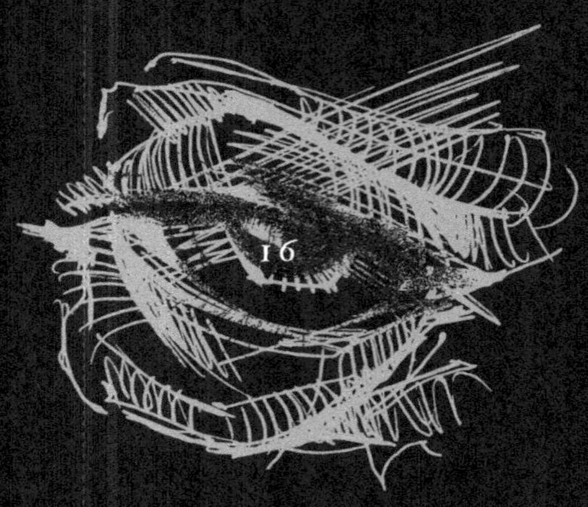

THE GLOVES FIT SNUGLY OVER HIS HANDS, THE LEATHER taut against his fingers as he meticulously adjusted them. The steady drip of blood hitting the floor beneath the slumped figure in the chair was the only sound in the concrete room.

The metallic tang of blood, the acrid staleness of sweat, and the chemical sterility of disinfectant—it clung to everything, saturating the space in its stifling grip. But he didn't seem to notice—*or care*. His attention was entirely focused on the poor excuse of a man before him.

The so-called man's unconscious head lolled forward. Blood smeared his chin, dripping onto his shirt, though it did little but add to the masterpiece of blood already tainting it. The fluorescent light overhead cast a harsh glow, leaving no shadows to hide in and no illusions to cling to. He looked small beneath the glare. Weak. *Pathetic.*

The same way he had always made Violet feel. How poetic.

The figure tilted his head, waiting for the epitome of fragile masculinity to return to consciousness.

He wanted him awake for this. To ensure every sensation landed with the weight it deserved.

But there was no rush, he had been waiting for so very long already—had no problem with taking his time.

He flexed his fingers inside the gloves, watching the serpent-tongued piece of shit's chest rise and fall with labored, rattling breaths.

A low groan escaped the small man as he stirred, shoulders twitching as pain dragged him back to consciousness. His head lifted, bloodshot eyes squinting against the brightness, blinking sluggishly. Confusion turned to fear, his feeble mind finally catching up.

Delicious.

The figure stepped closer, boots clicking softly upon the ground. The sound made the pious piece of shit flinch, his eyes darting toward the noise.

"You'll have to excuse me," the figure said, calm, almost conversational. "It's been a while since I've had to *exercise* my skills. I'm a little rusty."

The scum winced as he shifted in the chair, testing the restraints. His voice cracked as he rasped, "You broke my fucking ribs!"

The corner of the figure's mouth twitched upward, a faint, humorless smile that didn't reach his eyes. "I agree my temper was... less than controlled," he admitted, tone laced with a dark sort of amusement. He tilted his head as if considering something deeply. "She has a way of dragging the darker parts out of me."

"*She?*" The waste of breath spat, blood splattering onto the floor. His eyes widened in horror as he noticed the bloody tooth among the crimson streaks. His breathing quickened, panic flaring as the words clicked.

A short, mirthless sound broke from him, cutting off

abruptly with a wince. "You've got to be fucking kidding me. This is about Vio—"

The figure moved faster than the viper could react, his hand shooting forward and clamping down painfully on the fornicators jaw. The chair groaned under the weight of the force as the asshole bit back a scream, his eyes wide with terror.

"Unfortunately," the figure growled, "You no longer have the luxury of saying her name." He released the unfaithful knight's face with a shove, sending his head snapping back.

The serpent coughed, choking on blood and air as he tried to regain his composure. "Look, we can figure this out, right?" he gasped, his voice frantic. "What, you want her? You can have her. I'm not standing in your way."

The figure stilled, his hands curling into fists at his sides. "So many things wrong with those words," he said, dangerously serene. "Odd that you feel so inclined to pass her off like a bargaining chip. Not how this works, I'm afraid."

The thief's breathing hitched, his mind scrambling for a way out. "I'll disappear!" he blurted. "I have no idea who you are, what you look like. I couldn't send anyone after you even if I *wanted* to. You let me go, you take her, you never see me again."

The figure chuckled, the sound cold and devoid of humor. He stepped closer, his shadow looming over the spineless like a specter of death. "Disappear," he echoed as if tasting the word. "What a wonderful idea." The figure smiled, reaching behind him and pulling out a long serrated blade.

The simple man's feet scrambled against the concrete floor, trying to put as much distance between him and the knife as he could. The figure's free hand shot out, gripping Connor's shoulder and holding him in place.

The perfect man-child's face twisted, desperation bleeding

through his fear and anger. "Wait! Wait! Think about it! You'd kill me for her? You don't want to do this!"

The figure stopped the blade edge inches from the patriarchal poster boy's jugular. "Oh, but I *really* do. There are just a few things to take care of first." In a swift, singular motion, the blade shot down into the embodied entitlement's thigh. He let out a scream that was quickly muffled by the gloved fingers of the figure gripping his tongue. "Tell me, how well would *you* fare without this silver tongue? Without the venom you use as a shield—as a mirror. Strange that she spent *so* long trying to see the good in you. Let me show you what *I* see." The figure pulled the knife from The Lord of the Flies's thigh before the tip dug into the corner of his eye socket. Blood oozed down his face and the blade as screams filled the air.

Ten days.

I slammed my fist into the punching bag, sweat dripping down my temple. My knuckles throbbed from the impact.

Ten days. Not a word from Connor. The thought circled like a vulture over a carcass, never leaving me in peace.

No texts. No calls. No last-ditch efforts. No *surprise gifts.* I'd be grateful for the silence if it didn't feel like the calm before the storm.

The gym was alive with the rhythmic sound of leather smacking leather and the hum of voices. It smelled of rubber mats, disinfectant, and the sharp tang of sweat. James's stepdad, Jeff, owned the place—a modest mixed martial arts gym tucked into the corner of an industrial strip. Exposed brick and bright lights gave it a gritty atmosphere. Heavy bags lined one side, racks of weights and mirrors claimed the other. A padded area dominated the center, where a handful of people waited for Jeff's Muay Thai class to begin.

I struck the bag again, imagining Connor's soulless face beneath my wraps. My shoulders burned with effort, each movement demanding more than the last. Cassie leaned against the wall nearby, arms crossed, one brow arched. She watched me, sapphire eyes missing nothing.

"Keep going, Vi," her lips curved into a smirk. "That thing doesn't look half dead yet."

A small snort escaped me, but I didn't let up. "Working on it."

James stood across the gym, deep in conversation with Jeff. His tall frame leaned forward, nodding as Jeff gestured broadly, explaining something. Jeff's grizzled appearance—thick gray hair and calloused hands—gave him an air of authority, but his eyes were soft.

James's eyes darted to us, his gaze lingering on Cassie for just a beat too long. My chest tightened as my eyes followed.

For the last six years, I'd watched them dance around the subject of love and all things sunshine and rainbows. It gave me motion sickness. But I couldn't deny the bittersweet ache it left behind–a longing for something I wasn't sure I could ever trust again.

I turned my focus back on the bag. Every muscle in my body ached, but it was a *good* ache. A rebuilding ache. The kind that reminded me I was working on something—my strength, my confidence, my survival. For ten days, Cassie and I followed James here, showing up like clockwork to train. For ten days, they stayed at my apartment, refusing to leave me alone. It wasn't a discussion; it was a fact. She had taken over my bed like her throne, her overnight bag sprawled across the floor. Ever the neat freak, James had unpacked his things into tidy corners of my space, leaving no trace except the calming steadiness he carried with him.

Cassie insisted on making everything a production—arguing over dinner choices, commandeering my TV remote, and even trying to critique my wardrobe. James balanced her chaos with quiet gestures: fixing the broken cabinet hinge in my kitchen, restocking my fridge with his mom's cooking, and always making sure I never felt alone.

I like being alone.

Having them there helped. The fear never left, but it felt smaller with them around, like I wasn't completely defenseless —but I missed being alone.

I hit the bag again, harder this time, as my breath came in uneven bursts. No matter how much progress I made, I couldn't shake the rending fear of Connor finally showing up and catching me off guard.

"Hydrate before you pass out." Cassie tossed my water bottle.

I nodded, taking a long swig as Jeff's voice rose. The Muay Thai class began. Students shuffled into formation on the padded mat, some bouncing on their feet, and others adjusting their gloves.

"Ádaat'ééh!" Jeff barked in Diné Bizaad, the *People's Language.* "Defensive!"

Arms raised and, shifting their weight, some students balanced perfectly, their movements controlled. Others wavered, their feet sliding against the mat.

James wandered between rows of students, nudging a shoulder here, adjusting a wrist there. Brows knit, focused.

I sat on the bench as Cassie joined me, my chest still heaving. She studied the students, a pout painting her mouth. "Think we'll ever look that good?" She asked, bucking her chin to a tall woman whose round kick landed with intense power.

"Give it a few more months," I said, half-joking.

My phone chimed—8:30 a.m.

Cassie raised a brow, snickering. "Ope! Gotta go stalk the doctor!"

I groaned, shoving the phone into my bag. "I'm not stalking him."

She pushed off the bench, standing with her arms crossed and a wicked smirk. "Oh, sure. You just completely changed your five-year-long morning caffeine routine. Definitely not because that's when *he's* there."

I rolled my eyes. "Eat tar."

She shot me a wink. I shook my head, biting back a smile.

The gym buzzed as Jeff barked another round of instructions, and the students shifted into offensive positions. My eyes lingered on their movements, soaking in every detail. My body wasn't there yet, but it would be.

I sat near the door, one leg crossed over the other, pretending to scroll on my phone while my eyes darted up every time the door opened.

I am stalking him.

I didn't really know why I did it. I told myself it was to apologize for standing him up for what he called a "date." That was reasonable, wasn't it? Polite, even. But if that were true, why had I sat at this table for over an hour every day for the past eight days, nursing cold coffee and waiting to glimpse those frustratingly beautiful green eyes?

There wasn't any other reason. Just the apology. *Nothing else.* But the hollow ache in my chest betrayed me.

Today would be the last time—I'd told myself that this morning. But I'd told myself the same thing yesterday, the day before, and the day before.

Calling his office hadn't helped, either. The only response I got was "out of the office." No details. No timeline. Just out. For all I knew, he was sipping cocktails on some beach halfway around the world, blissfully unaware of the ridiculous lengths I was going to for the sake of my vaginas future.

I sighed and glanced toward the door again as a couple walked in, laughing about something. Not him. *Of course not.*

Cassie reappeared, her pin-straight hair flowing as she strutted across the shop. She stopped in front of me, one hand on her hip and a knowing smile. "Alright, coffee queen, time to wrap this up. I've got animals to save, and you've got... something other than this." She gestured vaguely around us.

I rolled my eyes, but her words stung. "Fine," I muttered, glancing at the door again before standing.

Her smile softened as she reached for her cup. "Look, I get it. You're going through it. But sitting and waiting here daily seems a tad unhealthy and a smidge desperate."

Cassie's typical bluntnesss, gotta love it.

With my lips pressed together, I followed her toward the exit. The rain began to sprinkle as we walked in silence toward the car.

18

She didn't see me. Never saw me.

Violet. My Violet. My Sunshine. Sitting there like a lost little fawn, like a picture of perfection wrapped in oblivion. Her head turned every time the door opened, her eyes flickering with hope.

She wasn't looking for me.

NEVER. FOR. ME.

Never for the one who truly mattered. How could she not feel it? The pull between us that was as undeniable as gravity?

Her face lit up when the blonde witch spoke, her smile a betrayal that tore at my soul.

She didn't belong to them. She belonged to me.

Cassie. James. Even Kal. They were always there, always in the way. Obstacles, nothing more. They clung to her like parasites, filling her head with lies, pulling her further from me. But they wouldn't last. None of them would.

I'd remove them. Every single one. They thought they were protecting her, but all they were doing was delaying the inevitable. They would be gone. And when they were, Violet would finally see.

She thought she was safe. She thought Connor was the real threat, but he was nothing. I understood him, though. His need to claim her. But he didn't deserve her. He was careless, weak. He let her slip away, and that made him unworthy.

But I wasn't.

I had been patient, watching, waiting. But my patience was wearing thin. I would strip them all away until there was only one truth left.

Mine.

THE APARTMENT WAS QUIET EXCEPT FOR SOFT KEYS tapping as James and I worked on our laptops. The heater, wheezing in its old age, barely managed to fend off the chill seeping through the warped windowpanes. My mind wandered between the manuscript in front of me and the oppressive weight of every other goddamn thing in my life.

Four more days. I could give Connor four more days to sign the papers before I went to a judge, even if I had to leave the county to find one willing to default the divorce. Two weeks was plenty of time to work through his shit and let me go.

The door burst open with a gust of icy air and Cassie strode in, dropping her bag and flinging her arms wide. "I swear to Gaia, I could be paid to promote dog pee perfume." She scowled at her navy-blue scrubs, groaning. "I've gotta burn these things."

James and I both mumbled in response, not bothering to look up.

She placed her hands on her hips, eyes darting between us. "Thanks for the sympathy, you emotionally constipated gremlins." She sighed, drawing out the sound like a performance. "We *need* to go out."

"No," I replied without missing a beat, my fingers still hovering over the keyboard. James ignored her completely.

"We've been holed up in here for a week and a half," she pressed, her voice rising. "You *hermits* might be fine living like this, but I need air, excitement, *something*."

"You were *just* outside," I countered, meeting her determined stare.

She waved me off. "Not the same, and you know it." Her lips parted to argue further, but the abrupt knock on the door halted her.

Her plucked brows drew together as she stalked toward the door. "If this is another solicitor—" She yanked it open, and her body stiffened. "So, the rat bastard sends *you* to do his dirty work?"

My stomach turned. I was off the couch in a second, James stepping beside me and placing a hand on my shoulder.

Then I saw her. *Lucy*.

Connor's sister stood in the doorway, her caramel-colored hair tied back in a messy bun. Those honey-brown eyes, so much like his, darted nervously between Cassie and I. She looked small, almost fragile, as she clutched a manila envelope.

"Listen," Lucy began, her voice quiet and hurried. "I don't know what happened between you two. Connor won't speak to any of us. All I know is when I woke up this morning, this was on my doorstep with a note telling me to bring it to you."

My throat tightened, anger flickering to life. "Where is he?" The words came out sharper than I intended.

Lucy's shoulders lifted in a helpless shrug. "Somewhere in Newark. Mom's worried, but he probably needs time. I'm late for work, so I have to go. But if you need to talk or... anything, call me, okay?" She held out the envelope.

I took it without a word. Lucy gave me an awkward, uncertain smile before vanishing into the frigid night.

I closed the door, the envelope feeling impossibly heavy in my hands. The air seemed to thicken as James and Cassie turned their eyes to me, both waiting.

My hands trembled as I tore the envelope open. A folded note fluttered to the floor. I picked it up and read the two simple words scrawled in Connor's familiar handwriting: *I'm sorry*.

Two words. *That was all he had to say?* My hands shook harder as I pulled out the rest of the papers. The deed to the house. My name. And beneath it, the divorce papers signed.

"He...." My thoughts scattered like leaves in the wind. I couldn't find the words, couldn't articulate the tidal wave crashing over me.

Anger. Relief. *Confusion*.

I stared at the papers, the words blurring as I let the emotions wash over me. For once, I didn't fight them. I let myself feel the full weight of it all—the suffocating years, the endless battles, the constant fear—and then something began to stir beneath it.

Freedom.

It felt fragile, like a flickering flame, but it warmed me from the inside out. Connor was gone. His shadow no longer loomed over every corner of my life. For the first time in three years, I was free to make decisions without the crushing fear of his wrath. Free to breathe, to laugh, to exist without bracing myself.

I let out a long breath, a hint of a smile tugging at my lips. I *did* want to go out, to celebrate—not because I had to, not because someone else decided I should, but because I *wanted* to. I wanted to laugh with Cassie and watch her flirt with men who didn't stand a chance. I wanted to see James's smirk when she pushed his buttons. I wanted to drink to a life that was mine again, one where I could finally start living.

I folded the papers carefully and set them on the catch-all table. I turned to Cassie.

"Bowling."

Her face lit up like Christmas morning, and James cracked a smile. The weight in the room shifted, and the air became lighter, freer.

For the first time in forever, I felt like I could breathe.

THE BOWLING ALLEY WAS FILLED WITH CHAOTIC ENERGY and neon lights. Blues, pinks, and greens swirled like a fever dream across the lanes, bouncing off the glossy bowling balls and plastic seats. The smell of fried food, beer, and waxed lanes assaulted my senses.

I adjusted my grip on the smooth surface of the ball while focusing on the lane ahead. Another strike would put me ahead of Cassie—a rare victory. I stepped forward, the ball rolling off my hand with practiced precision. It curved slightly, veering toward the right before crashing into the pins with a satisfying force.

"Ha! That's how ya' do it!" I grinned as I spun toward Cassie, who was mid conversation with the group of friends in the lane beside ours.

She smirked, leaning on her hip. "Don't get cocky, Vi. We've got another frame." She returned to her conversation with her new-found friends.

Behind us, James slouched at the table, his beer poised midair as his eyes fixated on Cassie. I followed his line of sight, watching as she stretched a smile that he and I both knew all too well. The one that meant she wasn't coming home with *us*.

The rigidity radiating from him was palpable. His grip on the bottle tightened, his knuckles blanching white. A pang of sympathy flared as I slid into the seat beside him. I caught his eye and glanced in Cassie's direction before returning, silently asking: "*You good?*"

His mouth tugged into a thin line before taking another long pull from his beer.

I'll take that as a no.

I nodded, deciding to let it lie. Tonight wasn't the night to press him. Gods knew *I* hated being pushed.

Cassie took her turn, hurling her ball down the lane, the pins scattering like startled pigeons. She threw her arms into the air as though she'd just won the lottery, her laugh lighting up the noisy room.

She skipped back to our table, giving James a light smack on the shoulder. "Come on, Mister Broody. Time to make yourself useful."

He groaned, exaggerating his sluggishness in dragging himself to the ball return. His brows knit together in fierce, frustrated focus, though it did little to steady his wobbling aim. The ball teetered into the gutter without ever threatening the pins.

She exploded into laughter, doubling over as her hands clapped together, adding insult to injury. "Amazing. Truly a masterpiece."

He shot her a scowl, though the corners of his mouth twitched as though fighting a grin. "It's unnatural how good you two are at this," he muttered, gesturing at his pitifully low score. His angst only grew as I took my turn and knocked down another eight pins. "Such a weird hobby for anyone under the age of 80."

Cassie draped herself over the back of a chair, grinning. "Growing up, we practically *lived* in this crappy little bowling alley down the road from our house," she explained. "Our older brother, Ren, worked there when he was a teen. He'd sneak us in after hours when our dad got high, and things got... tense."

My eyes fixed on the swirling lights. "Lots of practice dodging reality," I muttered, my voice hollow.

She shot me a sidelong glance but said nothing, her easy grin faltering just enough to betray her regret at bringing him up.

Ren. Her version of our past always made him sound like a savior, but I was less forgiving. He'd helped us escape for a while, *sure*, but when life truly fell apart—when Mom got sick, when Sage died—he was nowhere to be found.

Part of me understood it. I had done everything possible to get out of there, too.

Regardless, I hadn't spoken to him in years and planned to keep it that way.

I forced myself to focus as James pointed at the scoreboard. "So, kicking bowling ass runs in the family?" He rolled his eyes at Cassie's snort.

"Hardly," I said, my voice dry as I turned to face him. "Ren was high off his gluteus assimuss the majority of the time"

"And yet here you are," he gestured to his abysmal score. "Destroying me."

Cassie ruffled his hair as she walked past him, laughing at his expense. "Just admit you're bad, J."

He glared at her. "I'm bad because you never shut up long enough to let me concentrate."

She gasped, clutching her chest. "I kind of *like* buzzed James. Saucy, talkative, almost like you're a normal person!"

"How is he supposed to talk when you don't let us get a word in?" I shook my head, the corner of my mouth lifting.

"'*I'd rather microwave myself*'... Really?" James's glare drilled into the back of Cassie's head as we tailed her out of the bowling alley and into the parking lot.

"I politely told them they were barking up the wrong tree." She shrugged, still completely unbothered by the fact that she nearly caused a full-on throw down with two strangers just minutes before.

"What you actually said was they couldn't see their dicks over their stomachs." I bit the inside of my cheek to keep from laughing because... well, she wasn't lying.

"Same thing!" She flung her arms up.

"In her defense," I muttered to James. "Reek was looking at her like she was a ribeye."

James raised a brow at me.

"He smelled like stale cigarettes and unwashed ass," I added, answering the question he didn't ask. "I wasn't exactly dying to find out his government name."

He shook his head, a smile tugging at the corner of his mouth.

I twirled the keys around my index finger as we approached my car, then unlocked it with a soft beep.

"Okay, well, Reek and his friend Comb-Over can *disrespectfully* suck my ass," she snapped. "I was just about to tell that when J went all peace-keeper Captain America and ruined what would have been a *very* entertaining showdown. And that other guy—blonde hoodie dude—he came out of nowhere, but he *definitely* had our backs."

"Do we know him?" James asked, pulling a cigarette from behind his ear and lighting it with a quick flick.

"Nope, but he was hanging out with the group in the next lane and watching Vi *alllllll* night." Cassie tossed an exaggerated wink at me, leaning her back against the car.

"Probably worried for my safety," I said dryly. "Since my sister is certifiably insane *and* hostile."

Cassie glanced at James and then quickly locked to the black abyss above as she said, "I have a thing for superhero types."

"I don't." I crossed my arms.

I couldn't see her eye roll, but I *felt* it.

"I bet you wouldn't mind if it was Er—"

"Shut the fuck up," I snapped, heat crawling up my neck like wildfire.

Her head lolled to the side, eyes scanning me. "Keep holding that denial like a lifeline, babe."

I opened my mouth, ready to fire back, but her gaze shifted behind me—back to the entrance. I turned just in time to see the group from the adjacent lane—superhero hoodie dude included—emerge from the bowling alley.

"And while *you're* over here pretending not to want the best dick ride of your life, I'm gonna go have some fun."

"Cas, you don't even *know* them."

"Sure, I do! Mia and Marc." She waved her hand like that somehow validated her logic. "They've been together for a while and are looking to *experiment*."

"Knowing their sexual habits doesn't mean you *know* them."

"Oh, my sweet, *sweet*, summer child." She gave my head a condescending pat, then flicked my nose before I could dodge. I flinched, scowling, and she laughed, already turning to jog across the parking lot toward her next self-inflicted disaster.

I almost argued, but realized how pointless that would have been. Cassie would do whatever Cassie wanted to do, and there was never any stopping it. An argument wouldn't even delay the inevitable.

"Just... keep your location on!" I shouted across the black pavement.

"Don't wait up." She tossed a hand in the air, but didn't turn back.

Black Chevrolet Traverse. License plate: 7-61377A.

I typed the information into my phone notes and looked at James. He caught my eye and immediately tossed his cigarette, stomped it, and hopped in my car.

The drive home was quiet but full of James and his unspoken sadness.

"She's not doing it to hurt you," I mumbled as I pulled into my apartment parking lot.

"I know." The only response James gave.

"The real stuff scares her. Every time she feels anything she just buries it with—"

"I know."

I planned to let the topic die and shut my car off. Instead, I hesitated, my hand sitting on the door handle.

"You make her feel a lot of things. She won't talk about it, but I *see* it. Just like I see what this does to you." I took a slow breath. "I'm not saying to keep torturing yourself watching her —I'm just saying that she feels it, too." And with that, I got out of the car. James didn't move from his seat, but I wanted to give him that moment alone. I didn't know if he already knew what I had said, or if he had guessed it, but it felt like he needed someone else to say it out loud. I could understand that.

I made my way up the concrete steps but stopped short.

A black satin box sat just outside my front door. Smaller than the last one, but its presence no less potent—like a viper waiting to strike. I held my breath as I reached for it. The box felt cold and smooth beneath my fingertips.

I opened it with shaking hands, the weight of what I'd find already heavy in my gut.

Just one night. One fucking night where I don't have to think about you and your fucked up sense of self, please. That's all I'm asking.

Connor already signed the papers, I had the deed to the house, he said he was sorry. What else was there for him to give me?

Inside, a ring gleamed—a gold band lined with diamonds engraved with initials I knew all too well—his wedding ring.

A breath caught in my throat, the sight of it pulling me under like quicksand. Attached was a card—simple, elegant, infuriating.

Forgive me

My jaw tightened as I stared at the handwritten gold lettering. *Forgive?* Forgive the manipulations? The cruelty? The assault?

"Rot in Hell."

Dr. Hibani's office felt like a haven against the chill creeping into the world outside. The last autumn leaves clung stubbornly to the branches, trembling in the wind. Inside, the warmth wrapped around me like a blanket, aided by the whir of the space heater.

"So, lavender is a *big* no-no," she said as she turned off the humidifier, puffing out clouds of lavender-scented mist.

I tried to look nonchalant, shrugging as though the smell hadn't made me want to vomit every time I walked into her office. "I can handle it. It just reminds me of chemo, and my stomach flops a bit."

"I'll keep that in mind for our sessions." She sat back down in her chair opposite me and settled with her notepad and pen. "Are you ready for Thanksgiving?" Her eyes held a kindness that encouraged honesty, but there was steel beneath them. Her long, dark hair was tied loosely at the nape of her neck, and a few gray roots peeked through her blonde highlights.

I shifted, crossing my legs and sinking into the couch. "Cassie's on a full-blown mission—'*real authentic Friendsgiv-*

ing,' her words, not mine. She's determined to cook the whole thing herself."

Her lips curved. "You sound skeptical."

I raised an eyebrow, folding my arms across my chest. "Because I've lived with her. She's never cooked a day in her life. I'm pretty sure she's hoping sheer enthusiasm will baste the turkey itself."

Her soft chuckle filled the room. "Why do you think it's so important to her?"

I turned the question over, searching for an answer that felt true. "Because it's the first time in a long time that Connor hasn't whisked me away for every holiday to spend with his family." A twinge of guilt crept in. "Cas... she's scared of ending up like our mom," I admitted, my voice softening. "A bunch of kids running around and a shit husband who does nothing but drink, yell, and the occasional heroine vein tap. So, she distracts herself. Work, sex—anything that'll keep her too busy to think about what she really wants but won't let herself have."

"What do you think that is?"

I sighed, picking at the fraying edge of my sleeve. "A family. A good one. One that does the big family dinners like on TV. It's the closest she will let herself get to having the real thing without the risk of being stuck or being hurt. But I see how she looks at James—how the *want* is there, but she shoves it away with a '*ball-and-chain*' joke."

"Interesting." There it was again, that lock. The one that made you want to strangle someone and scream "*Out with it already!*" She leaned forward, her elbows resting on her thighs. Her voice was soft but edged with intent. "And what do *you* want, Violet?"

I hesitated, a flicker of a smirk tugging. "Well, I don't want to end up like our parents either." The smile faltered as I exhaled. "But I guess I turned out more like my mom than I realized."

Silence stretched, heavy and brittle. Memories hovered at the edge of my mind, threatening to pour in. My mom's smile flashed in my head—so radiant, so strong, masking a weight I didn't understand. My nails pressed into my palms as I forced the guilt back into its box.

Later.

I'll deal with it later.

"Do you want to talk about what just crossed your mind?" Hibani's voice pulled me back.

I shook my head but caught her stern expression, one eyebrow raised in a silent rebuke. "Not today, not *yet,*" I amended. She seemed satisfied enough to let it go, and I pressed on, filling the quiet with words. "I'm fine being alone. I like my space. I like my alone time. Kids were never in the cards for me. Even before surgery took that option off the table, I just...I like kids, but I never wanted them. That was Connor's dream—he was all about the '*big house to fill with a big family.*' That's what he said when we bought the house." My lips twisted into a wry smile. "I've never pictured myself with a gaggle of kids underfoot. It's fine to want that. Moms are extraordinary people. I just don't think I'm one of them."

She tilted her head, brows knitting. "You don't have to justify not wanting children, Violet," she said, her voice gentle. "Some people like to say that without children, women can't be fulfilled. But that mindset does a disservice to all of us. It implies that women exist only for one purpose, that we're designed solely to nurture and care for others, and that's simply not true."

She leaned back, crossing one leg over the other. "We're individuals with our own wants, needs, and dreams. Sometimes those include children, and sometimes they don't. Either way, it's valid. My point is, no matter what certain people think or say, it's okay *not* to want children, just like it's okay to *want* them. The choice is yours, and you don't owe anyone an explanation."

Her words settled over me, sinking deeper. "Usually, people just say I'll change my mind or regret it later."

She gave a small, understanding smile. "People like to project their own desires onto others. But that doesn't make their opinions more important than your truth."

"How very 'woke' of you," I chuckled, a genuine sound that still felt foreign in my throat. "I've also sworn off men. Well, relationships in general, but *mostly* men."

Her eyebrows lifted. "Oh?"

I exhaled sharply, attempting to release the weight that had suddenly appeared on my chest. "I... Connor made me feel... I don't ever want to feel that powerless again, that controlled. Power and control seem to be most guys' favorite kinks."

As she nodded, a traitorous thought flickered in my mind.

Not counting a certain dark-haired Adonis in a lab coat.

Heat pulsed through me, and I fought to suppress a smile.

"It sounds like you've taken time to understand what you want and don't want. Setting boundaries is important."

I let a smirk pull at the corner of my mouth. "Do I get a gold star?"

Her laughter was genuine, unguarded. "I don't have gold stars, but I do keep stickers for my younger clients."

The sound of her laughter made my grin stretch. "What I'm hearing is I'm eligible," I said, raising an eyebrow.

She stood, shaking her head with a soft smile, and walked to her desk. She returned with a full page of marine life stickers a moment later. My grin widened into a ridiculous, uncontainable smile as I peeled one and slapped it to my forehead.

"I am, at my core, a child."

Hibani chuckled, a hand briefly covering her mouth as she shook her head again. "It *is* fairly difficult to take you seriously with the new addition."

"I'd argue you shouldn't take me seriously *ever*," I quipped, pulling the sticker from my forehead and smoothing it onto my jacket. I leaned back onto the couch, suddenly more at ease than I'd been in days. "Whale sharks are pretty badass if you ask me."

Her lips curved as she studied me, her gaze softening. "I will say it's good to see you being honest with yourself, even if you hide it behind jokes."

I gave her a mock bow, dipping my head and sweeping my hand out like I was performing on stage. "It's my best quality."

Her laugh was quieter this time as we shifted back into the session. She glanced at her notes, then back to me. "So, Cassie and James are still staying with you? How has that been?"

I ran a hand through my hair, my fingers catching in a knot. "It's... a lot. I love them and am grateful they're there, especially in the beginning. But this is exhausting. Honestly?" I paused, letting out a long breath. "Their hovering makes me feel like they don't think I can take care of myself."

Her eyes narrowed, her pen poised over the notepad. "Do you think they don't trust you to?"

I shook my head, sweeping a loose strand of hair behind my ear. "No, I think it's coming from a place of concern. They care, and they're trying to help. But it's still a lot. I miss my me-time." A small, almost giddy smile played as I added, "Tomorrow, James has to fix the security cameras at the gym, and Cassie's working the graveyard shift at the Vet. I get the whole place to myself."

Hibani's mouth quirked upward, but her eyes stayed focused on me. "Do you feel their presence keeps you from processing what happened?"

I shrugged, though the question hit closer to home than I cared to admit. "Maybe. Or maybe I just need a break from the constant bickering. I really do love them, but if they stay for much longer, I might blow my brains out." I shot her a look as I added, "For legal reasons, *that's* a joke."

She arched an eyebrow, her expression both amused and admonished. "Good to see your sense of humor is still intact." She adjusted her position, the chair creaking softly under her weight. "Are you worried about Connor showing up?"

I shook my head. "It's been *weeks*. He's still across the country, probably sulking or plotting his next power trip. I haven't heard a word from him since he left that stupid ring on my porch." My hands clenched into fists as I thought about the audacity of it. '*Forgive me*'. *Eat shit.* "And if he *does* show up, I've got some new moves James taught me."

Her smile was small but approving. "It's good to stay prepared, to arm ourselves with defenses—physical and emotional. I'm glad you're taking precautions."

I tilted my head, throwing up my fists in an exaggerated fighting stance. "What is it they say? He can '*catch these hands.*'" The absurdity of the gesture made us both laugh.

As the session drew to a close, Hibani stood, extending her hand. The small gesture always felt personal, like she saw me as more than just another client. "You're opening up more, Violet. I like seeing you like this—it suits you."

I accepted the handshake, but my lips quirked into a wry grin. "Opening up? I think I'm just tired of listening to myself whine, so I pay you to do it instead." Despite the sarcasm, her words lingered in my chest, warm and reassuring.

She laughed, her voice light but filled with sincerity. "Your smile is a good look on you."

Outside, the wind had picked up, rustling the trees as I walked to my car. The air smelled of smoke from a nearby chimney, mingling with the crispness of impending winter. I felt a flicker of something I couldn't name.

Maybe it was peace.

Or maybe it was the knowledge that tomorrow, for one single night, I'd get some fucking peace *and* quiet.

My days started like clockwork. Wake up at five, coffee at six, manuscripts by eight, and a full schedule until my eyes shut. It was a routine—structured, reliable. It grounded me, giving me the control I'd been clawing at for so long. I'd built it brick by brick.

The coffee shop was barely waking up, the open sign flickering as I pushed the door open. Jazz drifted through the open space, mixing with the earthy smell of brewing coffee. The purpling hues of dawn peeked over the snow-covered mountains in the distance.

My heart stopped.

Eric was seated at *my* table—the one I'd staked out for days, hoping to see him. He leaned back, his long legs stretched out, fingers drumming a rhythm on the side of his coffee cup. When his eyes landed on me, he stood abruptly. Something in his expression—a flicker of hesitation, maybe even regret—caught my breath.

His green eyes, always so damn piercing, locked onto mine as he moved toward me. My pulse sped up. I hated that I was already responding to him. My stomach tightened in a way that had nothing to do with the coffee fumes swirling around us. He stopped a foot away.

"Hey," we both said at the same time.

Awkward.

A nervous laugh escaped, and his low chuckle followed, the sound washing over me like warm honey. We spoke again in unison, both offering apologies and laughing again. He gestured for me to go first, his lips tugging into a grin.

"I'm sorry I stood you up for drinks," words quieter than intended.

He shook his head. "I wanted to apologize for not showing. Something came up, and it took me out of town for a while." Laced with sincerity. "I just got back a few days ago. I would have called, but accessing your medical file for your number felt... stalkerish." His lips tipped into that crooked smile that always felt like a private joke.

"Surprisingly considerate." I raised a brow.

"Thanks. I try." His lips quirked. "So, I've been coming here, hoping I'd catch you."

"You've been waiting for me?" My stomach did a flip that I chose to ignore.

"For days," he admitted, rubbing the back of his neck. "I thought I had your routine figured out. You'd come to morning appointments with coffee, but never the afternoon ones. Not exactly rocket science."

Something close to shock rendered me silent.

"Didn't think you'd show up right at six, though. Early bird."

"It's quiet," I shrugged. "And I'm usually up anyway."

His smile faded, replaced by concern. "Still not sleeping?"

"It's better, but not by much. Connor being gone really—" I

stopped myself, eyes narrowing at him. "How do you know I wasn't sleeping?"

"That question's on every intake form at the office." His smile was teasing, but I felt my face flush.

"Oh, right," I muttered, as I internally cringed. "Totally forgot about that. That's... not embarrassing at all."

The number of things this man knew about me made me want to spontaneously combust and burn to ash. How many exams *had* he done? How many times had we talked about my eating *and* shitting habits? Thank whatever higher power there was that he had left the vaginal exams up to the other doctors.

He leaned in conspiratorially. "I had food poisoning last year and painted the office bathroom with puke *and* worse. Feel better now?"

I barked out a laugh, loud enough to earn glances from the handful of early risers. "Okay, that actually does help."

"Glad to be of service." His grin returned, softening his sharp jawline, but his gaze lingered, growing more intent. "If it lets me hear *that* sound again, I'll tell you every gross and embarrassing thing about me."

My throat went dry, that telltale ache low in my stomach flaring to life. *Lords*, even his banter was maddeningly attractive. It wasn't just his looks, it was how he made me feel like I was the *only* thing in the room.

"Save it for a rainy day," I said, shrugging off the flustered heat creeping through me.

We moved to the counter together, and I greeted the barista with a nod. His eyes scanned between Eric and I, narrowing as Eric leaned against the counter, exuding his causal confidence.

Eric's relaxed smile didn't falter, but something sharp passed his face—a silent standoff that left the barista bristling. I resisted the urge to roll my eyes at the apparent dick-measuring contest.

Caffeine first; analyze that *later.*

We took our drinks to a corner table, Eric moving with an easy grace that made my stomach tighten. He leaned back in his chair like he didn't have a care in the world, those impossibly long fingers cradling his fresh cup. His thumb brushed the rim idly, a simple movement that made me pull my lip between my teeth.

"So," he said, his tone light. "What do you do when you're not deliberately dodging doctors in coffee shops?"

I pursed my lips as I stirred my drink, trying to focus on anything but how his voice rolled over me like velvet. "Oh, you know. Moonlight as a tightrope walker."

His laughter was warm, genuine, and deep enough to shiver up my spine. "Great balance—always dancing the line between sarcasm and charm."

I raised an eyebrow, biting back a smile. "Deflection *is* an art form." My grip on the cup tightened. I swallowed, forcing myself to focus on the coffee before me. "More seriously, though, most of my time is taken up by work and school. The semester is almost over, but the work never stops."

"Publishing. Right? Ink something."

"Inkpot Press," I corrected, twirling the straw between my fingers to keep my hands busy. "Normally, I love it. But lately, it's been a lot of self-help books. You wouldn't believe how many people think they can write life-changing epiphanies after *one* bad breakup."

"Sounds riveting."

Why does he have to sound like that?

I tapped the edge of my cup thoughtfully. "It's not glamorous, but I love reading. Even the things that I don't love reading." I paused, suddenly aware of how much I was rambling. My teeth sank into my bottom lip to stop the word vomit spewing from my mouth. "Sorry."

He tilted his head, brow furrowed. "Why are you apologizing?"

My eyes dropped to the table, fingers picking at its edge. "I'm talking a lot."

"It's a beautiful sound. Never apologize for it." His voice was soft, but there was something else in it--something I couldn't read. He paused, his expression shifting as though he were shaking off a thought. "Other than work, school, and the odd coffee routine, what do you do for fun?"

I sipped my coffee, trying to buy myself a moment. "My idea of fun isn't everyone's cup of tea."

He leaned forward, resting his elbows on the table, his green eyes gleaming. "It might be *my* cup of tea. Try me."

"I watch an *absurd* amount of true crime documentaries. Oh! And bowling. I love bowling." The words tumbled out before I could stop them, and I cringed at how ridiculous they sounded together.

Eric sat back, his mouth curving into the grin that was as devastating as it was infuriating. My pulse stuttered. "Bowling, huh? Should I be intimidated?"

"Only if you're not ready to have your ass handed to you in neon shoes," I shot back, trying to hold my ground.

His laugh was soft, teasing. "Noted. Add '*dangerous with a bowling ball*' to your list of talents."

"What about you?" I asked, desperate to shift the focus. "What's your version of fun?"

His dimples deepened. "*Besides* sitting here with you? I've got a soft spot for bad '80s action movies."

I arched my brow.

"Bruce Willis in a tank top?" He pressed the back of his hand to his forehead as if swooning.

I choked on my coffee. "I'll give you that."

His expression softened as he watched me, the teasing glint

in his eyes giving way to say something quieter. "You seem... different. I like it. *This*." He gestured vaguely toward me, his voice dropping lower.

"Yeah, I'm... doing better. I think."

"Everything has its time," he said gently. "I'm sure not having to drag yourself to the office every week has been a weight lifted. Though I will admit, I do miss that shining smile and getting my ass kicked by way of sarcasm. I'm sure your husband is relieved as well." His words carried a subtle edge as though he were waiting—searching for something in my response.

"Funny story, that one," I said, my fingers tightening around my cup. "We aren't.... He's not.... We, um...." The words were there, but I couldn't bring myself to say them.

He straightened in his chair, his brows drawing together. "I assumed you meant on a business trip. How long?"

"Filed the papers three days ago, but we've lived separately for a while."

His jaw tensed as he nodded. "You never mentioned—"

"Yeah, well, my failing marriage didn't seem like small-talk material," I said into my cup as I took another drink.

"Was it the treatment?" He asked. "It's a terrible thing, but not exactly uncommon for couples to struggle once they are diagnosed."

"No, no. I mean, we...." *Keep it vague. Trauma dumping isn't hot.* "Just wanted different things."

"People consistently take beautiful things for granted," he said, his voice quieter now.

Beautiful wasn't the word I'd ever use to describe what Connor and I had. But the way Eric looked at me, with those piercing and vibrant eyes—the way they lingered on me with something close to reverence—made me think that maybe he wasn't talking about my marriage. My heart thudded painfully against my ribs, and I forced a smile, fighting to steady my breath.

How can he look at me like that, and suddenly I feel completely naked, exposed?

"What is it that *you* want?" He asked after a contemplative moment.

My breath caught, and I dropped my gaze to my cup, running a fingertip around the rim to keep my hands busy.

What did I want? I felt like I'd been asked that question ten ways to Sunday. The answer felt complicated, messy, tangled up in guilt and longing.

"I don't actually know," I admitted finally. "I'm still trying to figure that out."

Eric nodded, his eyes never leaving my face. "You don't have to have all the answers right now. That's what life is for— figuring it out."

There was something disarming about the way he said it, as if he genuinely believed it. It wasn't advice wrapped in condescension or empty platitudes. It was honest and made my chest ache in a way I wasn't prepared for. For a moment, it felt like he saw right through me.

I cleared my throat, forcing myself to switch gears. The last thing I needed was to spiral into introspection. Throwing him a sly smile, I leaned back in my chair. "Okay, Dr. Feelgood. When do I get my bill?"

That damn smile spread across his face, softening his features and twisting something deep inside of me. "First session's on the house. After that, we can negotiate." He winked, and my thighs clenched.

Devilishly handsome bastard. And he definitely knows it.

I shook my head, denying a smile. "Does this work on all the girls?"

"Well, *you're* still here." He leaned forward again, resting his head on his knuckles, making the space between us feel smaller--too small. His eyes flicked to my mouth for the briefest second before meeting mine again, a glint sparking there.

I rolled my eyes. My body had turned against me, exposing the flurry of unruly thoughts I was trying to push down. Being near Eric felt like teetering on the edge of something dangerous, something I wasn't sure I had the strength to resist.

My alarm blared, breaking the moment like a bucket of cold water. I jumped, fumbling with my phone to silence it.

Thank fuck.

"Shit, I'm supposed to be working." I stood abruptly. "I don't know how the time got away from me."

Eric stood with me, unfolding himself from the chair with a smoothness that warmed my cheeks. He didn't seem the least bit rattled. "I'll walk you to your car."

I hesitated, torn between telling him I didn't need the escort and selfishly wanting those extra few moments with him. My traitorous feet decided for me, carrying me toward the door with him at my side.

When we reached the car, Eric moved ahead, opening the driver's side door for me. I stopped short, staring at him in disbelief. "I could have done that myself."

He smiled, unbothered. "I know." The way he glanced down at me, his hand still resting on the door, felt so damn intimate. As I met his eyes, the twist in my stomach returned, sharper this time.

"I... actually enjoyed this." It felt like a confession, and I hated how vulnerable it was.

"So did I." The sincerity in his voice made my heart ache. "Would you let me make it up to you for missing our date?"

"It *wasn't* a date." The words came out too fast. "But I stood you up, too."

"Then you should *really* make it up to me."

I huffed a laugh, crossing my arms over my chest. My brain screamed at me to shut this down, to remind myself that I'd literally *just* sworn off men. But my heart—and certain other lower and traitorous parts of me—had entirely different ideas.

I had to remind my vagina that I couldn't flirt to save my life and that she was completely and utterly out of luck. My version of flirting was all sarcasm and teasing—a defense mechanism more than anything else. But Eric? He made it feel effortless like a dance I didn't know the steps to but desperately wanted to learn.

He's being nice. That's all this is.

Just get in the car and drive off.

Of course, instead, my hand shot out, palm open. "Phone."

He didn't hesitate, pulling his phone from his pocket and placing it in my hand. He looked entirely too pleased with himself as I typed my number into his contacts.

"Still not a date." I handed the phone back to him. I slid into the driver's seat, avoiding his gaze. But as I pulled away, I caught a glint of that stupid shit-eating grin in my rearview mirror. A mix of exhilaration and dread swirled in my stomach.

"Goddamn *motherfucking* shitfuck," I muttered under my breath, gripping the steering wheel like it was my only tether to reality.

The reality that he was my doctor, *a medical professional.* Not someone I should have been using to further distract myself. *The reality* that distracting myself was all that this was and had ever been.

But that couldn't have felt further from the truth.

*W*HAT THE ACTUAL FUCK.

The gym parking lot was a mess of flashing red and blue lights, their glow bouncing off the thick veil of black smoke. The acrid stench of burned wood and leather clawed into my throat as I stepped out of my car. My eyes immediately drifted to the charred remains of the building. Half the structure stood in defiance, blackened and skeletal, while the other half had collapsed entirely. Firefighters sprayed down the last smoldering remnants, steam hissing as the water hit what was left.

My heart slammed against my ribs. My stomach twisted as I spotted James sitting on the bumper of an ambulance, hunched forward with his forearms resting on his knees. His usually neat appearance replaced by a soot-smeared face and hair that clung to his forehead with sweat. His shirt streaked with ash, and his palms, crudely bandaged, rested limply on his lap.

I ran toward him, each step fueled by panic. "James!"

He lifted his head, and his bloodshot eyes met mine. He

looked like he wanted to reassure me, the corners of his mouth twitching but failing to form a smile.

"Hey, Vi." The words came out hoarse.

"What happened? Are you okay? Jesus fuck, your hands—" My words tumbled out in a frantic rush.

"I'm fine." But the tightness in his jaw said otherwise.

Cassie came barreling out of nowhere, still in her navy-blue scrubs. She skidded to a halt before James, her eyes like saucers.

"Like hell you are!" she shouted, her voice loud with anger and fear. Whirling toward the nearest EMT, she balled her hands into fists. "What the fuck are you doing? He needs to go to the hospital! Did you even check him for—"

I stopped listening. My eyes bounced between the EMTs—who looked like they wanted to be anywhere else, and James, the weariness etched on his face. "What happened?"

His eyes dropped to the ground as he spoke, his words slow. "I was in the office, working. Smelled smoke. When I tried to open the door, the handle burned my hand." He paused, flexing his bandaged fingers before continuing. "The window was stuck. The flames came through, so I broke it to get out. I don't know how it started." His voice cracked. "It's my fault. I must've—"

"Don't." The word came out more forceful than I realized. I locked eyes with him. "This is not your fault. It could have been anything."

Jeff arrived then, jogging toward us with panic written all over his face. He dropped to his knees before James, cupping his face with callused hands.

"JJ," Jeff choked out, scanning him before forcing their eyes to meet. "I know what's going on in there." Jeff pointed to James' soot covered forehead. "You are all that matters. This place? It's just a place. It can be rebuilt, replaced. I can't do that with you. Ya hear me?"

James's eyes welled with tears, his lips pressing into a tight line. I turned, giving them their moment by walking a few feet away, wiping my eyes. My heart ached, not just for James but for what I'd seen in Jeff's face: pure, unrelenting love. It reminded me of my mother, and that memory ripped deep inside at the cluster fuck of chaos running rampant.

I said I'd deal with it later, goddamn it.

When I turned back, the firefighter captain and one of the cops from the scene were approaching. I hurried over to join James, Jeff, and Cassie, who had finally backed off the poor EMT. Together, we listened as the captain explained that an investigation would be conducted to determine the cause of the fire. James nodded numbly, his exhaustion evident in the slump of his shoulders.

The cop outlined the process, his words practical and clinical. The EMT had finished treating James' burns, but Cassie's glare made it clear she wasn't happy with the care provided.

"You should go to the hospital," she said again, crossing her arms.

"I'm fine," he insisted. She pulled him into a tight hug, burying her face into his chest. He met my gaze over her head and rolled his eyes, a faint smirk tugging at his lips despite everything. I shrugged, smiling back.

When she left, still muttering threats about what would happen if James didn't call her, I offered to come back for him if he didn't feel up to driving. He waved me off, insisting he was fine, but the haunted look in his eyes lingered as I walked away.

When I got home, exhaustion had settled into my bones, but the sight of my front door stopped me cold. It was cracked open, the dark interior of my apartment visible through the narrow gap.

I locked the door. I know I locked the door.

A faint sound came from inside. My stomach plummeted, and icy fear prickled along my skin. Slowly, I backed away, my movements careful. My heart hammered as I reached my car, fumbling with the keys before locking myself inside.

I parked a few houses down and called the police, my voice trembling as I explained the situation.

When they arrived, I followed them back, staying near my car with a female officer while the other officer entered my apartment. Minutes stretched into what felt like hours before he returned, shrugging.

"Nothing in there," he said. "If the door was left open, an animal could've wandered in. The forest is right behind your building."

I nodded, swallowing hard, but their explanation didn't sit right.

James pulled into the driveway just as the police car disappeared down the street. His headlights caught me leaning against my car, my arms crossed tightly over my chest to ward off the early morning chill. I straightened as he stepped out, relief and frustration crashing inside me.

"What the hell's going on?" he asked, his voice rough, likely from the smoke still clinging to him. His disheveled hair stuck to his forehead in damp strands, and the faint smell of burnt wood followed him like a shadow.

I pushed off the car and met him halfway. "Someone was in the apartment."

He froze, his eyes narrowing. "What do you mean someone was in there?"

"My door was open when I got home, but I locked it. I *always* lock it." My voice wavered despite my efforts to stay calm. "I heard something inside, but the cops said it was clear. They think it might've been an animal."

His gaze flicked toward the darkened apartment. "Bullshit," he muttered. Without another word, he brushed past me and headed for the door.

"Jay, it's fine," I called after him.

He didn't respond, just motioned for me to follow.

The apartment looked normal at first glance, but the air felt off like it had absorbed someone else's energy. James checked every room—closets, cabinets, corners—I hadn't realized how many places there were to hide in my tiny apartment until I saw him systematically clear each one.

I trailed behind him, hugging myself, my unease mounting. He opened my bedroom door last, stepping inside with the same vigilance. I hovered in the doorway, eyes darting around the familiar space as if seeing it for the first time.

When he finally straightened from checking under the bed, he sighed. Nothing. No sign of anyone.

I tried to take comfort in his words, but my stomach churned. My instincts screamed that the cops were wrong, that James was wrong, but I didn't have the energy—or the evidence—to argue.

"Thanks," I said quietly.

James crossed the room and rested a bandaged hand on my shoulder. His grip reassuring.

"Aren't we just two peas in a fucked-up pod?" I huffed a sarcastic laugh. He gave a wry smile as we moved back to the living room, checking and double-checking every window and door. Every latch locked and sealed tight.

I watched him scrub at the kitchen counter like the act of cleaning might erase the night's events. I winced at the pain that had to have been shooting through his bandaged hands by his furious scrubbing. Every swipe of cloth against the surface grated on my already frayed nerves. He was trying to calm himself in his own way, but his unease only magnified my own.

I shifted on the couch, my thoughts circling back to the cracked door and the cops' dismissive reassurances. It wasn't an animal. I knew that. Something gnawed at my gut—a creeping dread.

Someone was here.

"Bud," I said, my voice too quiet, "you don't have to do all that right now. Just... sit down or something."

He didn't pause, dunking the sponge into the bucket with force. "If I stop, I'll lose it," he muttered, his tone clipped.

I sighed. "Don't overdo it, okay? We both need to get sleep at some point. It's already three."

He finally glanced up. The look he gave was soft enough to show he heard me but still distant. "You get some rest," he said, though the way his jaw tightened made it clear he didn't believe I would.

I nodded, retreating to my bedroom even though the knot of nerves in my chest wouldn't let me rest.

A smell stopped me as I settled onto the bed, tugging the blanket over my legs. It was faint but wrong—a mix of sweat, dirt, and something sour I couldn't quite place.

I sniffed the blanket again, my stomach further twisting. I shoved it off and leaned closer, squinting at the gray fabric of my sheets.

What. The. Fuck.

For a moment, I just stared, my blood like ice running through my veins, fear locking every muscle in place.

The heat surged up, chasing the cold away. Anger—hot and all-consuming—took over. I clenched the sheets in my fists, shaking with fury, my brain pulsing with what I assumed could only be a stress migraine.

Without thinking, I stormed back into the living room. James looked up from the counter, his thick brows pulling together.

"What's that?"

I held the sheet up, my hands fighting their tremble. "Animal my ass," I snapped, barely keeping my voice steady as I thrust the marred fabric toward him. My finger jabbed at faint streaks of dried mud smearing the fabric.

"That's a fucking boot tread."

THE CHARRED REMAINS OF THE GYM LOOKED LIKE A graveyard against the gray clouds overhead. The cold and the acrid bite of smoke burned my nose with every breath. My shovel dug into the debris, crunching ash and glass beneath it. Layers of ash clung to my coat, the fabric stiff and dusted gray despite its original deep green. I tried to focus on clearing a path, on doing something useful, but my thoughts were scattered.

All around us, people worked in grim silence. James's mom, Dianna, bundled in a puffed navy coat and a bright red hat, was sorting through piles of melted equipment, her face pinched in quiet determination. Jeff hauled beams to the side of the lot. A few locals—faces I barely recognized—pitched in.

"It's Connor," Cassie's voice shattered the relative quiet like a hammer against glass, the words loud enough to carry across the lot.

I leaned on the shovel, taking a slow inhale, and turned toward her.

Her black coat cinched tight at the waist, a scarf in bright rainbow stripes wrapped around her neck. Her hands shoved into matching gloves, and her cheeks were flushed pink from the cold. She met my gaze, eyes wide.

James paused mid-step, his boot crunching against shards of wood. He puffed out a visible breath and turned toward us. The tight pull of his mouth and raise of his eyebrows screamed his thoughts loud and clear: *No shit, Sherlock.*

She shot him a glare, her breath misting as she flipped him off without missing a beat.

I tightened my grip on the shovel and looked down at the rubble beneath my feet, focusing on anything but the sinking pit in my stomach. I wanted to say no, to shut her down, but the words didn't come. She had a point, one that James and I had already mulled over two nights ago when we found the sheets.

"Statistically speaking, it's always the spouse," I said.

Cassie's stare down with James continued as she swung her arm out, gesturing to me. "Exactly! Stalkers are always someone you know. Right?"

He tilted his head, gaze sliding to me like he was gauging my reaction, lips pressed into a thin, skeptical line.

I let out a slow breath, watching it disappear into the air. "More often than not."

I don't know if I would call it stalking. Breaking and entering, sure. But 'stalking' felt like a stretch. And even if he did break in, it would have been solely to scare me, to show how much control he still had over me.

Still, something about it didn't add up. Why now? Why try to freak me out after signing the divorce papers and leaving his ring? Was it just a reminder he could still reach me, to give me a taste of freedom and then snatch it away just as quickly as it was given?

Then, there was the smell of dirt and sweat in my bed, so unlike the sharp tang of Connor's cologne, the one he wore religiously because it made him "smell like success." The scent was burned into my nostrils and brain.

"On the flip side," James said, breaking into my thoughts, "that footprint was a boot tread. I've never seen him in anything other than those weird, pointed dress shoes."

His furrowed brow and narrowed eyes gave away the gears turning in his head.

"He could've bought boots just for this," Cassie argued, her voice rising as she threw her hands in the air again. "Doesn't that make sense?"

I bit my lip, chewing over the memory of Connor's scoff when I'd suggested he buy a pair of heavy-duty boots during the last winter storm. He'd looked at me like I'd suggested he wear a garbage bag to court, saying boots didn't "match his aesthetic."

"Maybe," I said, "but Lucy said he's still in Newark. Texting her. Sending photos."

Cassie gave me a pointed look, arching a single plucked brow. "And we trust her?"

"She isn't a liar," I shot back. "If anything, she seemed sympathetic." I hesitated, glancing at James, still watching me. "But he could be feeding her lies, and she wouldn't know."

I made a mental note to look up Bronson & Brick Law Offices. I'd call to confirm he actually worked there—quickly, without tipping Connor off.

Cassie crossed her arms over her chest, the bright scarf swaying in the wind. "Okay, but in the likelihood that it is Connor, what do we do? You said the cops won't do shit. Should we start house hunting? Because, sorry, Vi, your place is too small for all of us long-term. I need my closet. I need my room."

My phone buzzed in my pocket, pulling me from her words that, for once, I wholeheartedly agreed with. I pulled it out, my fingers shaking slightly from the cold and rigid nerves.

Unknown: Is it socially acceptable to text you yet?

Another buzz followed almost immediately.

Unknown: I'm in dire need of your sarcastic smartassery to get me through the day.

I stared at the screen, my heart playing hopscotch in my chest. A smile tugged at the corners of my lips before I could tamp it down. Cassie and James were strategizing, their words blending into the background as I typed back.

Me: Eric?

Unknown: Were you expecting someone else? Should I be jealous?

My stomach did a ridiculous little flip, and I felt giddy warmth spread through me, so at odds with the freezing air. The tiniest spark of light in all this mess, and I clung to it.

"You're selling the house, right?" Cassie yanked me back to the conversation. "We could find a bigger place out of town, out of the state, with that money."

"If it's Connor," I said, "this was probably his idea. To scare me into leaving, to show me he has all the power."

Another buzz.

Eric: How long do I have to wait for the ass handing in neon shoes?

I bit my lip, the smile threatening to break free as I shoved the phone back into my pocket. "I'm not going anywhere. He doesn't get to win. Not anymore."

James shifted closer, his jaw tightening. "Even if he's in New Jersey, he could've hired someone. He's got friends high up on the totem pole."

"Let them try," I said, my tone final. "I'm done being told what to do, how to live."

James's expression softened, and he nodded. "Okay," he said quietly. "Then we'll need a couple of things."

THE SHOOTING RANGE WAS LOUD, EVEN THROUGH THE orange earplugs. Muffled bangs ricocheted through the space, each one rattling my nerves as I stood behind the counter, trying to calm the flutter of my hands. The room smelled of gunpowder, and the bright lights overhead gave it an artificial glow. Rows of cubicles lined the walls, each occupied by someone gripping a gun and firing at a paper target far off.

James stood in front of me, his sleeves rolled up, exposing the veins running along his forearms. His safety glasses reflected the light, making his gaze almost intimidating.

I'd never seen him look so confident and self-assured outside his gym instruction—the kind of confidence that came from experience like this was old hat for him.

"First rule," he said, his voice firm but patient. "Treat every gun like it's loaded. Second, your finger doesn't go on the trigger unless you're ready to shoot. Got it?"

I nodded, the weight of the Glock in my hand foreign and overwhelming. It felt cold and heavy, like the consequences it could unleash. My palms were clammy, and the tension in my shoulders felt like it could snap at any moment.

Cassie looked completely at ease, a cocky grin spreading across her face. "You don't gotta explain it to me, J." She waved James off. "I know what I'm doing."

He and I exchanged a glance. His eyebrow lifted. My expression matched his disbelief.

She shrugged, sliding the magazine into her gun with a practiced click. "What? You keep guns in the house, and you think I wouldn't make sure I knew how to use one?"

James's lip twitched upward before he shook his head, and his focus shifted back to me. "Let's start slow."

Cassie raised her arms, took aim at her target, and pulled the trigger. The sudden crack of the gunshot made me flinch. My heart pounded against my ribs as I turned to glare at her through the see-through glass partition that separated us. She only winked at me.

"She's just showing off," James said, calm as ever.

I tried to laugh, but it came out more shaken than anything. "Good to know *she's* enjoying this."

His hand rested on my shoulder. "People think the recoil is worse than it is. That fear can make you hesitate, but it's not as bad as your brain builds it up to be."

I swallowed hard, my throat dry. "What about... everything else?"

"What do you mean?"

"The... aggression of it," I stared at the gun in my hand. It felt unnatural, like holding a live wire. "It's not just the noise or the kick. It's the fact that this can... kill someone."

His expression softened and turned to understanding as his amber eyes met mine. "It's not about the aggression, Vi. It's about control. Protecting yourself. The people you care about. It's just a tool. How you use it is up to you."

I nodded slowly, his words sinking in, but the tight knot in my chest didn't ease.

"Here," he stepped behind me, keeping enough space between us that his body didn't crowd mine. "I'll show you."

I raised the gun, aiming it toward the paper target. James gently placed his hands over mine, steadying me. "Square your shoulders. Keep your arms firm but not locked. Don't hold your breath, okay? In, out. Pick your spot and pull the trigger."

The weight of his hands on mine was reassuring, and I let out a slow breath, focusing on the target. The black silhouette seemed impossibly far away, but I forced myself to trust James.

I exhaled, my finger squeezing the trigger. The bang was sharp, vibrating my arms, but the recoil was less than expected. The bullet punched through the paper, leaving a clean hole just shy of the center of the silhouette's chest.

Surprise rippled through me. "That wasn't... that bad."

James removed his hands, stepping back beside me and grinning. "Yeah, Glock 44's got a pretty mild kick. Unless you're the one getting shot."

I couldn't help but laugh, shaking my head. "Thanks for the image."

"Try again," he encouraged. "You've got this. I'm right here."

As I raised the gun again, the sound of Cassie firing in the next lane made me nearly jump again, but I pushed through the nerves.

Each shot I fired made me feel a little sturdier, a little stronger. The cracks of other guns going off around me faded. With every pull of the trigger, it felt like I was taking back something I'd lost—like I was the one in control, and no one could take that from me again.

After a while, James leaned against the divider between our lanes, watching me with a small, approving smile. "Background checks take about a week," he nodded toward the gun in my hands. "Once that's done, you guys can get your own. Until then, it's good to know how to use mine, just in case."

My arms ached as we all finished, but the adrenaline left me smiling as we walked out into the cold. Cassie was laughing, the sound bright and carefree, and even James looked more relaxed than usual.

She swung her arms as we approached my car, her cheeks flushed from the cold. "Back to your place?"

I hesitated. A stupid, *very dumb*, most-likely-a-mistake kind of thought crossed my mind. "Um... no."

26

CASSIE PERCHED ON A STOOL BY THE BAR AS SHE TOSSED back a shot of tequila. She wiped her crimson lips with the back of her hand and smirked.

James sat beside her, leaning forward and tying the laces of his bowling shoes. His rich brown hair, pulled back in a short ponytail, shifted as he glanced up.

Kal leaned against the bar, his platinum hair styled in a fade that softened into longer strands on top. He swirled his drink. His deep blue eyes, framed by smudged eyeliner, paused on the lanes before cutting to Cassie. "What's the game plan, Cas? Losing with style or going for glory?"

She scoffed, twirling her empty shot glass between her painted fingers. "Speak for yourself. I'm here to dominate."

Kal chuckled, James rolled his eyes, and their banter drifted as I shifted my weight, arms crossing and uncrossing. My eyes darted toward the entrance every few seconds, my stomach knotting tighter with each glance. The hem of my sweater twisted between my fingers, a flimsy distraction from the TV static thrumming under my skin.

What were you thinking?

I wasn't thinking. That was the problem. My mind had left the building, and my vagina's incessant pleading took reign.

Cassie's voice nabbed me from my spiraling thoughts. "Why you staring at the door like you're waiting for Death herself? What's up?"

I stiffened, dragging my eyes away from the entrance. "I might've done something... incredibly stupid."

James paused, his hands stilling mid-knot as he raised a brow. "Define 'stupid'."

Before I could answer, Cassie's freckled face lit up. "Eric!" she shouted, leaping from her stool to wave him over.

You did this to yourself.

I closed my eyes for a brief moment and exhaled before turning to see him stepping through the doors. His dark hair, grazing his jawline, fell in soft waves. Those green eyes found mine instantly, as they always did. That slow, confident smile was a dangerous weapon.

He moved toward us, his long strides eating up the distance. A black hoodie clung to his lean, muscular frame. Even in the chaotic light, his tanned skin seemed to glow.

By the time Eric reached us, I had no oxygen left—every step making him seem taller, broader. Even James, who towered over most, suddenly seemed average next to Eric.

"Hey," he greeted, voice like polished stone. His eyes tarried on mine before shifting to James and Cassie. "Good to see you both again."

Cassie grinned, tugging him closer and deliberately planting him beside me before reclaiming her stool with a wink.

"Violet."

I swallowed hard, trying to ignore the heat climbing up my neck. "Eric."

Cassie leaned in, her smirk full of mischief. "Relax. You look like you're about to combust."

I shot her a warning glare before turning back to him. "Uh... yeah, so... you know everybody." My hand waved vaguely toward the group. "Cassie, James, Kal."

Then, for reasons I couldn't explain, my brain short-circuited, and I pointed to myself. "And yours, truly," I blurted, punctuating it with awkward finger guns.

I want to crawl into a hole and die.

The silence that followed felt infinite. Eric's laughter broke through it, warm and rich enough to tangle around my senses. His smile curled, critically charming.

Cassie groaned, rolling her eyes. "Ignore her. She gets flustered around obscenely attractive men."

His gaze slid back to me, eyes gleaming. "Good to know."

Kal chuckled, breaking the tension as Eric turned to him and extended a hand. "You work with Dr. Echo, right? I believe I've seen you in her oncology department during my visits."

Kal smiled as he took Eric's hand. "Yeah, I work directly under her. That's how I met Vi."

"Vi?" Eric's lips twitched as he glanced my way.

Cassie grinned wickedly. "Yeah! Vi, VV... *Vixen*." She nudged me.

"Vixen?" Eric repeated, tilting his head. "I rather like that one."

"Of course you do," I muttered, mortified.

Shiva, end my misery.

I wanted to disappear. Instead, Cassie ordered shots for everyone, including Eric, calling it his 'initiation.' The group fell into motion, drinks in hand, as we migrated to the lanes. Cassie shoved me toward Eric with all the subtlety of a sledgehammer.

"Go help him pick a ball," she whispered, her grin daring me to argue.

"He doesn't need help."

"So what? *Go.*"

He stood a few feet away, long fingers dancing over the selection of bowling balls. My stomach fluttered as I approached, every step feeling heavier.

It's illegal to look that good in bowling shoes. It's just not fucking fair.

I pointed to a neon pink ball coated in glitter epoxy. "I think this one is more your style," I teased.

His brow arched a slow smile tugging at his lips. "Dynamite. I have a thing for glitter." He reached for the junior-sized ball, his playfulness disarming me.

I have a thing for you.

I laughed, shaking my head. "No, I'm totally kidding. If you throw that down the lane, it'll probably fly."

He halted, eyeing me and raising a thick brow.

"It's too light. Your arms are very.... You seem like you'd have a strong throw." *Fuck. Get your shit together.* "You need something heavier to weigh your hand down, so you have more control over where the ball goes." I grabbed a solid black ball. "Like *this.*"

Our hands brushed as he took it, those soul-snatchers locking onto mine, the weight of his attention almost unbearable. I cleared my throat, stepping back.

We made our way back to the group as Cassie leaned forward, resting her elbows on the table and propping her chin in her hand. Her pale blue eyes sparked with mischief as she stared Eric down like a cat toying with a mouse. "So, Eric, you've got this whole 'tall, dark, and mysterious doctor' thing going on. Spill. How does one get their own private practice at the suspiciously young age of...." Cassie trailed off, waiting for his answer.

He smirked, setting the ball into the return. "Thirty-two."

I sat across from her, and Eric moved to take up the chair beside me.

Kal and James entered our names on the scoring monitor before they joined us at the table. They sat on either side of Cassie, and I couldn't help but feel that Eric and I were sitting in front of a judge's panel.

Eric leaned back, his posture deceptively relaxed. "I tested out of high school fairly early, did a bit of travel, then went straight into pre-med, immediately followed by med school."

James, sat with his arms crossed. "Which med school?"

I shot him a questioning look. It was Cassie's usual behavior to ask a million and one questions, but for James? Definitely an interrogation.

"Stanford." Eric tapped his fingers on the glass of water sitting in front of him before slowly nudging it to me, his eyes steady on James as he continued. "Residency ended, came back home. The practice was already established with my father. I took it over when he passed."

A shadow crossed Eric's face, and my chest tightened. "I'm sorry."

He gave a slight nod, his expression softening when his eyes met mine. Our shared grief passed in silence.

Kal broke the moment. "Are we playing or what?"

"Fine, but I'm not done with you." Cassie pointed a half-teasing, half-serious finger toward Eric, who flashed her his pearly white teeth.

I sipped some water, rolling my eyes. "Shocker."

Eric watched me with an infuriating calmness, as though he wasn't the reason my insides were in turmoil. I stepped up to the lane. The weight was familiar, comforting in its own way. I focused on the pins, trying to drown out everything else.

The ball glided from my hands, rolling down the lane before crashing into a perfect strike.

Cassie whooped, throwing her arms in the air. "Starting strong, are we?"

Kal groaned, shaking his head. "We're doomed."

I smiled, stepping aside to let him take his turn. He picked up his ball with exaggerated flair, flexing before his throw.

The ball veered left, barely grazing the gutter before clogging into it entirely.

"You're a natural," Eric called.

Kal turned, his arms outstretched. "The lanes crooked."

"Of course," Cassie said, deadpanning. "It's the lane's fault."

Laughter bubbled around us, and for a moment, I relaxed. Glancing at James, I caught the faintest hint of a smile on his mouth.

Cassie didn't miss the opportunity to heckle Eric. "Let's see if Doctor Perfect can handle a bowling ball."

Eric rose from his seat, and grabbed the ball.

"This is going to be terrible," I muttered low enough for only Cassie to hear.

"Oh, absolutely," she whispered back.

Eric positioned himself at the end of the lane, stance awkward but composed. He pulled back, the ball slipping from his fingers—and flew sideways, landing with a heavy thunk in the gutter.

A laugh escaped before I could stop it, and Cassie practically doubled over. Eric turned, his expression caught between sheepish and amused.

"Beginners luck," he said dryly.

"Don't stress," I said, smirking. "There's nowhere to go but up."

His eyes narrowed as he grinned. "Someone's got jokes."

The first few rounds unfolded predictably—Cassie leading the scoreboard with me right behind, James and Kal squabbled over who bowled worse, and Eric, to my delight, still couldn't bowl to save his life, even with instructions from both Cassie and me.

"Brains, looks... you're the whole package." Cassie narrowed her eyes at Eric as we all sat down for a drinks-and-snack break. "So, what are you hiding?"

My thoughts exactly.

I nibbled on a fry from the basket Eric had placed in front of me, anxiously waiting for some unseen shoe to drop. Axe murderer? Mama's boy? Closeted gay?

Eric's lips pulled into a tight line. "Well, clearly, it isn't my amazing bowling skills. I'm using everything I've got and still terrible."

She laughed and pointed at the scoreboard. "Oh, we noticed."

He held his hands up in mock surrender as James, cracking a grin, leaned forward. "I think you've officially dethroned me as the worst bowler in the group."

Eric extended a hand across the table. "Debatable. But we can share the title."

James hesitated, then clasped Eric's hand in a firm shake. "Fair enough."

Cassie leaned back in her chair, delighted. "Oh, I like this. A bromance brewing right before my eyes."

"Watch out, Vi, James'll give you some competition," Kal chimed, winking at James, who gave a smug shrug.

We fell into easy conversation, Eric fitting in seamlessly. The drinks kept coming as the night wore on, and Cassie plied him with more questions. To his credit, he took it all in stride. He didn't seem to be unearthed one bit, even smiling and laughing as he answered every single question. I, on the other hand, was internally screaming as every word out of Cassie's mouth grated against my nerves.

What's your sign?

How much do you make?

Relationship guy or just casual?

I silently begged the earth to swallow me.

Their fishing for information had put Cassie and James on my shit list. And Eric, with his quick glances and not-so-quick glances.... My pulse jumped whenever he looked at me, and all coherent thoughts left the building. Every word out of his mouth drew me in further.

Kal was the only person there who didn't seem like he was trying to unnerve me or get under my skin. But he had left me to the wolves because of an early morning shift. And with him went the light quips and distractions that minimally eased the tension edging up my spine.

So astronomically fucked.

Cassie's line of questioning persisted. "How long was your last relationship, and why did it end?"

"Bathroom break!" I blurted as I stood and grabbed her arm, dragging her toward the restroom.

Cassie tripped as I pulled her through the bathroom door. "Shit. What?" She steadied herself before glaring at me.

I shot a glare right back. "What's with the third degree?" I said through gritted teeth.

"I'm just making conversation." She shrugged a shoulder, turning to the mirror and fluffing her hair.

"No, you aren't, and you somehow roped James into it, too."

She turned back to me, throwing her hands up innocence. "Hey, I'm just as surprised as you are with James. But at least he's warming up to the guy." If looks could kill, she would be seizing on the floor. She shrugged again. "All I'm doing is being cautious."

"Why?"

"Because you aren't allowed to date just any guy anymore, Vi. They have to be vetted." She crossed her arms over her chest and leaned back against the bathroom counter.

"*Since when?* You're the one always saying, 'Get over someone by getting under someone.'"

Her eyes dropped to her shoes, sadness and anger mixing there. "That was before I saw what Connor did."

"We're not dating. He's just hanging out."

She smirked, sapphires thinning as she cocked her head to the side. "Yeah, sure. Keep telling yourself that. You guys have been eye-fucking each other all night."

"For once, can you please just chill the fuck out?" I begged.

Cassie waved me off as she exited the bathroom. "Sure. I like him anyway."

I followed her to our table, my patience balancing on a thin, frayed rope. She, thankfully, turned her attention to more sporty teasing as she and James finished out the last frame before starting another.

As Cassie landed a winning strike at the end of the game, she turned to face us and attempted what looked like a drunken shuffle. True to his instructing nature, James sloppily showed her the 'correct' moves.

I huffed a laugh, glancing at Eric with an apologetic smile as Cassie slipped and dropped to her ass with a yelp and a laugh. James made to help her up, but she pulled him down with a maniacal cackle.

"I think that's our cue," I mumbled, pulling out my phone and opening an app to order an Uber.

"I can drive you," Eric offered.

"You don't need to do that."

"I know. I want to."

Against my better judgment, we piled into Eric's forest green Camaro.

Green was becoming my new favorite color.

Cedar and sandalwood enveloped all my senses. It was intoxicating, much like the man himself.

27

Eric eased James onto the couch, laying him down with tenderness. I couldn't look away as he adjusted James, ensuring his head rested comfortably. For a moment, it felt as if I were intruding on something private, something rare. My chest tightened with an ache, but I quickly pushed it aside.

Cassie groaned beside me, her face pale and her body leaning heavily into mine. "Come on, Cas," I groaned, looping an arm around her waist to guide her through my bedroom and into the bathroom. Each step was a struggle, her weight a reminder of how much alcohol coursed through her veins.

She was already gagging when we reached the toilet. I knelt beside her, pulling blonde hair back as she retched into the bowl. The noxious scent filled the air, making my own stomach clench. She gripped the porcelain edge, her knuckles white, while I rubbed slow circles on her back. She slumped forward, her breath shallow. I handed her a washcloth to wipe her face.

Footsteps approached. Eric stood in the doorway, eyes flitting to Cassie, then me, assessing but not an ounce of judgment on his face. He stepped forward, setting a glass of water on the counter, and left as silently as he'd arrived.

That shouldn't have made my heart flutter. It shouldn't have made me notice how his shoulders filled out his jacket or how his presence seemed to calm every corner of the apartment. And yet.

I helped Cassie to her feet and led her to the couch. Eric had already draped a blanket over James. His shoes removed and placed neatly on the floor. A glass of water sat on the floor beside him. She collapsed onto the opposite end, her head lolling as I removed her boots.

I straightened, my gaze sweeping over the little details Eric had quietly handled. He hadn't complained, hadn't drawn attention to himself. He'd simply helped. Something about that sent a warm pulse through me, followed immediately by a pang of guilt.

It wasn't like he would stick around after witnessing all of this. No one's patience stretched this far, not with the chaos that seemed to follow me wherever I went.

'You're annoying, tag-along friends.'

Grabbing a blanket from my room, I turned back toward the doorway and stopped dead in my tracks. Eric stood there, his tall frame filling the space, hands resting in his pockets. My bedroom had never felt so small.

He's in my room. Eric fucking Morani's in my bedroom.

Heat bloomed across my cheeks. The sight of him there, framed by the soft glow of my bedside lamp, felt too intimate, too close. My thoughts slipped into forbidden territory—places I had no business going.

I cleared my throat, trying to sound unaffected. "I'm sorry about all of that. All of *this*." I motioned vaguely toward the living room.

'*You're a fucking burden.*'

"You don't have to stick around. I've done this more times than I can count. You're free to skidaddle."

The corner of his mouth twitched, amusement sparking in his eyes. "None of this bugs me." His tone even. "And *skidaddling* isn't really my thing."

I swallowed hard, caught between gratitude and the disarming pull of his presence. "Thank you," I managed. "For coming tonight...for taking us home...for helping."

'*A job.*'

"You don't need to thank me for being a decent human," he replied.

Right. Just being decent. Just being nice. That's all this is.

Brushing past him, I returned to the living room and draped the blanket over Cassie.

James shifted on the other end of the couch. "Eric's cool," he muttered.

"Cool as a cucumber," Cassie slurred, her voice thick with sleep.

"Go to sleep, little drunkies," I muttered, shaking my head.

The sound of running water reached me from the bathroom as I headed to the kitchen. Grabbing a glass from the cupboard, I filled it, the coldness of the water helping to lessen the heat running through me. Turning, I nearly jumped out of my skin. Eric leaned against the counter, arms crossed, watching me.

"Christ, you keep sneaking up on me," I breathed, pressing a hand to my chest.

"Sorry." There was that smirk again. "I was trying to be quiet."

Christ, even his whispers were intoxicating.

His eyes landed on my mouth as I took a sip, and my tongue

darted out to catch a stray drop. The space between us crackled.

"Water?" I offered, my voice uneven.

"Sure."

I reached for another glass but paused as he stepped closer, taking the cup from my hands. His fingers brushed mine, brief but electric, before he lifted the glass to his lips. He drank slowly, his throat working with each swallow. When finished, he set the glass down and dragged his thumb across his bottom lip.

Something primal unfurled in me.

Fuck. Me.

Literally.

"Excuse me," I slipped past him and out the back door.

The cold hit me like a slap, sharp and invigorating. Stars winked above, scattered across the dark expanse. I inhaled as deep as my lungs would allow, hoping the chill would drown out the fire he always ignited.

The door opened behind me. Eric stepped out, carrying a blanket. His footsteps crunched over the frosted ground as he approached. He draped the blanket over my shoulders, hands remaining a moment before pulling away.

"Thanks," I said softly.

He stood beside me, breath visible in the cold, presence as solid as the earth beneath my feet.

"I'm tempted to make another 'running away' joke. But I remember where that got me the last time."

"I'm not running from you." *Lie.* "It's just weird having my doctor in my house." *Half-truth.*

"I make house calls." He quirked a smile and I huffed a laugh, shaking my head. "Technically, I'm not your doctor anymore. All of your follow-ups are with someone else." He paused before his voice lowered. "If you want, I can go."

"No, I want you here." The words came out before I could stop them, and a wicked grin spread across his face. Just as quickly as it appeared, it was gone.

"You have some interesting friends," he said, his tone light.

I leaned my head back, staring into the sky, my breath coming out in puffs of white. Eric stared into the darkness with me as I pulled the blanket tighter around myself. "They mean well," I finally replied. "They're just protective. And... they want the old me back."

"The *old* you?"

I hesitated. "Yeah, the me who drank, danced, laughed, who felt... alive. The me I was before...." I dropped my eyes to the frozen ground as I finished. "Everything."

"And that's not what you want?"

I turned to him. His eyes were searching, warm, like he was seeing all the cracks I was trying so desperately to hide. "I do," I whispered. "I'm just not fully there yet." I hesitated again, shaking my head. "I'm not sure that person even exists anymore."

"Hm. Maybe you're right; she's not in there anymore. But that doesn't mean you can't be happy and enjoy things. Maybe the old you had to die to make room for the new one. You know, character development and whatnot."

I laughed, the sound almost freeing. "Then I wish my character would stop needing so much development."

We exchanged something in that moment. Something that I couldn't name, but it felt like something inside of me had shifted. The silence that followed felt less heavy, more comfortable.

"Did you have a good time?"

He nodded. "Bowling was a way better idea than a bar."

"You'd do fine in a bar," I teased. "Being surrounded by

drunk and horny women who would sell their souls for 15 minutes with you? Isn't that the bachelor dream?"

His expression darkened, his voice dropping an octave. "Maybe. But I'm far more interested in the dark-haired, quiet, brooding, judges-drunk-people type." He paused, his gaze sharp and unflinching. "And it'd be drastically longer than fifteen minutes."

My breath caught, my throat dry. His words hung in the air, heavy and charged. I didn't know whether to laugh, blush, or combust. He was flirting, and a part of me wanted so very badly to fly with it, but....

'Nothing but a quick fuck.'

"I'm...." *'Pathetic.'*

"Not ready for anything serious or casual right now," he said smoothly, his gaze never wavering. "There's a third option I'd like to propose. Friendship."

I raised a brow. *"Friendship?"* The word felt foreign in my mouth, like an ill-fitting shoe, and made my heart twinge with disappointment.

He nodded, unbothered by my disbelief. "We hang out, talk. Do things you actually enjoy." He shrugged. "No pressure, no expectations. Just a mutually beneficial friendship."

I crossed my arms underneath the blanket, trying to ward off the sudden chill that had nothing to do with the weather. "And what do you get from this *mutually beneficial friendship?*"

His eyes dipped to my lips, and when he smiled, it was that devilish crooked grin. "I get to see a genuine smile on those plump lips of yours."

Where'd all the oxygen go?

I bit down on my bottom lip, the sting grounding me against the unruly thoughts running rampant in my mind. His eyes zeroed in on the movement, expression deepening, deep pools of green flicking back to mine.

"Now, see," he murmured, voice rough, "you can't be going and doing that."

"Doing what?" I asked, the words trembling as they left my mouth.

"*That*," he said, his tone low, his eyes locked back onto my lips. "Because 'friends' don't do to friends what I'm thinking of doing to that mouth," he said, low and dangerous.

Heat exploded through me, my legs suddenly weak under the weight of his words. I clung tighter to the blanket as if it shielded me from the fire spreading through my veins.

He stepped back, hands running through his hair as if physically restraining himself. "My self-control has its limits." His voice was tight, almost pained.

Something in me wanted to test those limits, to push him. But instead, I awkwardly extended a hand. "Friends?"

The corner of his mouth lifted, and a small laugh escaped him. He took my hand in his, grip warm, the calluses on his palm grazing against my skin. "Friends," he said, though the word felt like an unspoken promise of something more profound.

His hand lingered a moment too long before he released me, stepping back again. He didn't turn away immediately.

Finally, he exhaled and glanced toward the apartment. "Get some rest, Violet," he said softly before heading inside.

I waited, listening to the sound of his footsteps fade. Moments later, his car engine rumbled to life, the sound growing more faint until it disappeared entirely.

'*Friends.*'

The word echoed in my mind, a cruel joke that left me aching for more. My hand drifted to my neck, fingers brushing my shirt collar before trailing downward. My body hummed with restless energy, each nerve screaming for release.

I turned, heading back inside. The apartment was dark and still, save for Cassie and James's quiet breathing.

Slipping into my room, I sank to the edge of my bed. My head in my hands. The scent of Eric's cologne swayed in the air, and I closed my eyes, letting it pull me under.

'*My self-control has its limits.*'

Mine did, too.

Iᴛ ᴡᴀs ᴛoo ǫuɪᴇᴛ.

I'd thought I'd enjoy the silence tonight—just me, my laptop, and the chance to let my mind wander. Cassie pulled another late shift at work, and James was out with Kal. I was initially grateful for the solitude, but now it felt suffocating. The faint hum of my laptop wasn't enough to drown out the gnawing unease creeping up my spine.

I stared at the screen, the search bar blinking impatiently.

Bronson & Bruick Associates.

Just type it. It's nothing.

But my stomach clenched as I hit enter. The law firm's homepage loaded instantly. The scrolling marquee bragged about their high-profile cases and bulletproof defenses. I clicked on the "Our Team" tab.

Scrolling through the endless photos, I nearly convinced myself he wouldn't be there. That I wouldn't find him at all because he wasn't there.

He was *here.*

But that was his face staring back at me, perfectly polished, framed by the corporate backdrop of our downtown law office. That same smirk—the one that promised he'd already won whatever game he thought he was playing. That same photo he had plastered on all his business cards after the firm had welcomed him with a company party.

My hand hovered over the mouse, frozen as memories clawed their way to the surface. I could almost feel the fabric of the dress I'd worn that night, scratchy under Connor's possessive grip as he paraded me through the crowd. He'd insisted on showing me off. And I went, like always, because it was easier than arguing.

But the drive home was anything but easy.

"You were embarrassing," Connor snapped, gripping the Bentley's steering wheel. The sharpness in his tone made my chest tighten.

"What are you talking about?" I asked, my voice barely above a whisper.

"Don't play dumb, Violet. It's not a good look on you. You were flirting with Jeremy all night. Laughing at his jokes, touching his arm—don't you think I saw that? That everyone saw that?"

I clenched my hands in my lap, nails digging into my palms. "I wasn't flirting. I was just being polite—"

"Don't fucking lie to me." His voice rose, echoing in the confined space of the car. "Do you think I'm fucking stupid? You think I don't know what men like him are after? You don't get it. Guys like that will use you the first chance they get. I'm the only one who can protect you."

"I didn't mean—"

"Enough!" The sharpness in his voice silenced me. His grip on the wheel relaxed slightly, though his knuckles still looked tight. "I'm just trying to keep you safe. Why can't you see that? Everything I do, I do for us."

I nodded, murmuring an apology as I fought back the tears that threatened to flow. My eyes fixed on the blur of streetlights outside the window.

The memory burned, leaving my chest knotted and my skin crawling. I squeezed my eyes shut, willing it to fade.

Then I heard it.

A soft sound, like a metallic click.

I looked toward the open bedroom door. The sound came again—quiet, but there—the jiggle of a lock.

My pulse quickened, and my body went cold. I reached for my phone, opening the emergency dial screen, but my fingers froze over the button.

I'm being paranoid. It could be anything.

Or anyone.

My heart thudded against my ribs, each beat louder than the last.

The noise came again, louder this time.

Kitchen.

I moved silently, the chill of the tile floors biting at my bare feet. In the kitchen, my eyes darted to the knife block. My fingers wrapped around the largest blade. My chest heaved as I raised the phone to my ear.

"911, what's your emergency?"

"Someone's trying to break into my house," I whispered, my voice shaking. "Hurry."

"Stay on the line with me, ma'am. Where are you in the house?"

My hands trembled as I pressed my back against the wall near the back door, knife in one hand, phone in the other.

"Ma'am? Officers have been dispatched. Are you there?"

"I'm here," I whispered so low I prayed that she heard me as I slowly bent down and placed the phone on the floor beside me.

Best case, the cops get here before the intruder gets in. Worst case, I have *maybe* a minute once he's in to yell out any descriptions I can manage. He may take me down, but it might get him caught.

Thank you, 'Taken'.

The jiggling grew more insistent as I straightened, followed by the unmistakable click of the lock.

I squeezed the knife's handle tighter. My heart pounded so loudly I thought whoever was on the other side of the door would hear it.

The knob turned. *Slowly.*

The door creaked open, and gloved fingers curled around the edge of the frame.

My body moved before I could think. I shoved my weight against the door, slamming it shut on the intruder's hand. A guttural scream tore through the night, the sound almost feral.

I pulled the door back and slammed it again, the crunch of bone meeting wood reverberating in my ears.

"Fuck!" The voice on the other side howled in pain, and I heard the frantic scuffle of retreating footsteps.

The door slammed shut, and I locked it with trembling fingers. My chest heaved, and adrenaline surged through me as I put every bit of strength I had into shoving my couch into the kitchen and wedging it in front of the back door.

I picked my phone off the floor. "He's gone," I managed to tell the operator, my voice hollow.

I sat on the kitchen counter, phone in hand and knife in the other, as my eyes flitted between the front and back door.

BLUE AND RED LIGHTS FRACTURED THE APARTMENT WALLS, the pulsating patterns jarring and invasive. The static of police radios and clipped voices of officers formed a chaotic backdrop. Each sound grated against my nerves, amplifying the unease crawling under my skin.

"Violet! Oh my *God!*" Cassie's voice cut in like a lifeline, James and Kal trailing in behind her.

She was suddenly in front of me, her hands trembling as they cupped my face. Her sapphire eyes searched me, frantic and full of worry.

"Are you hurt? Are you okay?"

I opened my mouth to speak, to assure her I was fine, but no words came. My throat was dry, and the lump lodged there refused to budge. I managed a nod, but it didn't feel like enough.

The officer's monotone voice dragged me back. He stood a few feet away, notepad in hand, pen moving with the speed of someone handling another mundane call.

"We've checked the doors and windows," he said, not

looking up. "There's no sign of forced entry, and we couldn't find any evidence outside."

Cassie's hands fell away as she whirled on him, her sapphire eyes blazing. "So, what are you saying? That she made it up?"

The officer finally glanced up, his brow furrowing. "No one's saying that, ma'am. I'm just stating what we couldn't find."

Her arms crossed, shoulders squaring like she was gearing up for battle. "You didn't find anything because you weren't looking hard enough. My sister didn't imagine slamming a door on the asshole's hand!"

He was here. I know *he was here.*

James reached out, grasping her wrist. "Cas, it's not—"

"No, James," she snapped, shrugging him off. "This is bullshit. Someone tried to break in, and now you're telling her there's nothing you can do?" She glared at the officer. "Typical."

"Ma'am," the officer sighed. "I'm not saying nothing happened. I'm saying there's no physical evidence to follow up on. Without DNA, video surveillance, or a clear visual identification, there's not much else we can do."

Her frustration mirrored my own, but it wasn't just the officer's words that fed it. It was the helplessness, the suffocating realization that no one could stop him from creeping back into my life whenever he wanted. Shit, I was surprised the cops even showed up in the first place—that Connor didn't have the house marked on some 'do not respond' list.

"Sure, let's just wait for him to come back and finish the job. *Great plan.*" Her sarcasm was wrapped in a scoff-slash-eyeroll.

The officer sighed again, turning to me. "Did you see his

face, ma'am? Hear anything specific—like a name or something distinctive about him?"

I gripped the counter's edge, my knuckles aching from how tightly I held on. My voice wavered as I answered, "No."

Cassie turned back, her expression incredulous. "You know it's him. Just tell them."

"Who's '*him*'?" the officer asked, his pen poised midair.

"Her ex-husband, Connor Allsbrooke. He assaulted her. Now he's stalking her and breaking into her house!"

My pulse spiked at the sound of his name. It was as if saying it gave him power, gave him a presence in the room he didn't deserve.

The officer's gaze returned to me, unreadable and guarded. "Did you report the assault?"

Shame coiled in my throat, squeezing tight. I looked away, nails digging into my palms. "No," I murmured, hardly loud enough for even me to hear.

"Why *would* she?" Cassie interjected, hands gesturing wildly. "When *this* is the kind of help she gets? 'We didn't find anything, so there's nothing we can do.' *Useless*."

My face burned. The weight of the officer's stare made me feel small, as if I had to explain myself when I barely had the strength to hold myself together.

The officer's jaw tightened. "Miss, I understand you're upset, but—"

"No, you don't," she shot back, stepping closer to him. "If you did, you wouldn't be standing here acting like this is just some random break-in. This is a pattern. It's him."

"Do you have any proof it's him?" the officer asked, his calm tone grating against my fraying nerves. "Text messages, threats, anything concrete?"

The flowers. The ring. I had burned the flowers but still had

Connor's wedding band. My stomach churned at the thought of handing over the evidence that would just be dismissed. Still, I forced myself to move to the small table near the front door.

I opened the drawer of the catch-all-table, fingers rubbing the cold metal of the ring. Pulling it out, I turned back to the officer. "This," I said, my voice steadier now, though no less fragile. "He sent this...after he signed the divorce papers."

I placed it on the counter, and the officer studied it with mild interest. "I'll be honest with you. I can take this into evidence, but it doesn't exactly scream stalking or breaking and entering. If anything, it looks like a peace offering."

Cassie's laugh was sharp and humorless. "A peace offering? Are you serious right now?"

The officer straightened, his patience obviously waning. "I'm just saying there's no clear evidence connecting tonight to your ex-husband. And it doesn't really make sense for someone to sign divorce papers and *then* break in."

Cassie scoffed as James added, "Maybe he's just throwing us off his scent."

The officer shrugged. "Could be. But like I said, without something more concrete, it's speculation. You don't live in the safest part of town. It could have been someone looking for a place to crash or a quick score."

Cassie threw up her hands. "Oh, great. Let's blame the neighborhood. Really covering all your bases, huh?"

The officer ignored her and addressed me directly. "My advice? Stay with someone you trust tonight. Install cameras, maybe get an alarm system or a dog. And call us if anything else happens."

"A dog," Cassie muttered, her tone venomous. "That's your big solution? A fucking dog?"

"Cas," James cautioned.

"No! This is ridiculous!" Her voice cracked as she pointed toward the door. "Just get out."

The officer gave me a nod, then glanced back at his partner.

As they stepped out, Cassie yelled after them, "Tremendous help, boys! Really. Stellar work." The door slammed shut, rattling the apartment.

She turned back, her chest heaving. "You're okay," she said, more to herself than me.

I slid back onto the kitchen counter, grabbing the knife I had stashed behind the coffee pot when the cops had arrived. Her eyes softened as she moved toward me and leaned against the counter lip.

I brought my knees to my chest as I stared at the back door. "He'll be back."

Cassie's lips tightened, and she placed a trembling hand on my knee. "We'll be ready for him."

James sat on the kitchen floor, leaning against the cabinet and watching the front door. Kal joined him without a word, resting his head against the cabinet, his hand reaching up to hold the toe of my shoe.

Cassie moved to the coffee maker beside me, her hands vibrating as she set it up. The sound of the machine whirring chased away the silence.

Steam curled through the air, clinging to the mirrors and walls as I stepped out of the shower. The towel I wrapped around myself was too small to fight off the sudden chill seeping into my skin. My fingers left streaks on the fogged mirror as I cleared a patch to look at my reflection. Water dripped from my hair, dark strands sticking to my shoulders and back. I looked like myself, but somehow not. I was glowing —my eyes bright, my skin slightly kissed by the sun, my cheeks rosy and full.

The door creaked behind me.

I stared at the door in the reflection. I turned, clutching the towel tighter. A shadow moved just beyond the threshold, but relief surged when I recognized him.

"Eric," I breathed.

He stepped inside, his movements slow and deliberate, his familiar emeralds locking onto mine. Something in his presence calmed me, warmth spreading up my chest as he closed the space between us.

"I didn't hear you come in," I said, my lips curling into a weak smile.

Eric didn't answer. He just reached for me, his hands steady as they slid around my waist and pulled me close. His chest was solid beneath my palms, his warmth infusing me as I leaned against him.

Everything felt so right, so normal. Like we'd been doing this for centuries. It just felt natural.

"I missed you," I whispered, resting my forehead against his collarbone.

His fingers tilted my chin upward, and my breath caught. His face was so close, his lips just a breath away. I closed my eyes, relaxing into his hold, waiting for his lips to meet mine.

"Till death, babe."

My eyes snapped open at the sound of *that* voice. My heart dropped to the pit of my stomach.

The face staring back at me wasn't Eric's.

"No," I whispered, the name catching in my throat like barbed wire.

Connor's smirk spread, cold and devoid of humanity, as his hand closed around my neck. The pressure was immediate, choking off the scream building in my chest. His grip tightened, shoving me against the bathroom wall. The tiles were cold against my back, the impact jarring.

I clawed at his hand, panic surging as I gasped for air. My legs kicked uselessly, and my vision blurred as tears streamed down my cheeks.

"Stop!" I begged breathless, strangled, and broken.

His face hovered closer, voice dropping to a venomous whisper. "You're mine, Violet. It'll *always* be that way."

Desperation gave me strength, and I shoved him. He staggered back, his grip faltering just enough for me to break free.

I didn't think—I just ran.

The door wasn't there when I reached for it. Instead, I stumbled into a forest, the bathroom gone as if it had never existed. The ground was cold and damp beneath my bare feet, mud squelching between my toes. Shadows twisted through the trees, their gnarled branches clawing at my arms as I ran. The towel clung to my skin, soaked and heavy from the rain pouring, slowing me down. My legs felt like lead, every step harder than the last, as though the earth itself wanted to swallow me.

"Run all you want, *sweet Violet!*"

Connor's voice echoed, a sing-song mockery that sent ice racing up my neck.

I didn't look back. I couldn't. My chest burned with every breath, and my throat ached from the sobs I couldn't release.

The trees blurred past me, but the forest seemed endless. No matter how far I ran, I couldn't escape the sound of his voice.

I turned, just for a second, to see if he was behind me.

He wasn't.

Relief rushed, only to vanish when I turned back and slammed into something—someone.

The impact knocked me back. My towel slipped as I staggered. My eyes darted upward, and I froze.

The man before me was shrouded in darkness, his face hidden beneath a black hood. He didn't speak.

Before I could scream, his hand clamped over my mouth.

I thrashed, my fists pounding against his chest as he dragged me closer. The shadows seemed to cling to him, smothering me.

Connor's laugh cut through the stillness again, closer this time. "Where were you gonna go?"

The hooded man held me tighter, his silence more terrifying than any threat.

Connor appeared from the trees, his smirk stretching wider as his face flickered—human one moment, monstrous the next. His skin darkened, his eyes glowing with a sick, fiery hatred.

I tried to scream, but the hooded man's grip silenced me. I struggled harder, kicking and clawing, but it was useless.

Connor crouched in front of me, his eyes narrowing. "Didn't I tell you?" His hand shot out, gripping my jaw and forcing me to look at him. "No more running."

Terror seized me as he leaned closer, his breath hot against my cheek. His fingers tightened painfully around my jaw.

Then his hand moved to my throat, lifting me off the ground as if I weighed nothing.

"No!" I tried to scream, but the sound wouldn't come.

He threw me to the ground, and the impact knocked the air from my lungs. The earth beneath me shifted, falling away, and I felt myself plummeting—

I woke with a gasp, jerking upright as though I'd been yanked from the nightmare.

"Vi!" A voice pulled me the rest of the way into reality, and my fist shot out, connecting with something solid.

"Shit!" James groaned, stumbling back as his hands flew to his nose. Blood dripped down his arm.

I stared at him, horrified, my chest heaving. "James—Oh my fuck! I didn't mean--God I'm so sorry!"

He waved me off, pinching the bridge of his nose. "I'm fine. Just... remind me not to wake you up."

Cassie stood in the kitchen, holding a mug of coffee. "I'm adding helmets and restraints to our Christmas list," she muttered.

My hands flew to my throat, the phantom grip still there, squeezing the breath from me. My heart wouldn't slow, and I couldn't stop shaking.

"You were screaming," she said quietly, stepping closer.

I wiped my damp face. "I... I'm sorry."

She crouched beside me, her hand reaching to brush my cheek. I flinched and she pulled her hand back with an apologetic smile. "Do you want to talk about it?"

I shook my head, swallowing the lump in my throat. The fear was still there, clawing at me, but something else burned beneath it.

'No running.'

Fine.

I'd show him what *not running* looked like.

THE CLEARING BEHIND THE APARTMENT WAS A WET, miserable pit. Every movement felt heavier, dragged down by the cold rain and thick mud. I didn't know which stung worse—my pride or the icy drizzle soaking through my clothes.

After last night—the helplessness and fear that had gripped me—I needed to do something—anything—to feel like I had control again.

James stood across from me, his stance relaxed. He didn't look like someone about to fight, but I knew better.

"You sure about this?"

"Just show me," I snapped, sharper than I meant to.

He nodded as he stepped closer. "Dicks with weapons aren't going to play fair."

"Got it." I rolled my shoulders back. My frustration bubbled—not at him, but at myself, at how much I still felt like the scared woman Connor had left behind.

He didn't react to my tone. He simply lifted his arm, the dull training knife resting in his grip. He took a slow, measured step forward.

"If someone comes at you like this–" He lunged forward, controlled but deliberate, the blade leading. "—what's your first move?"

I reacted on instinct, grabbing his wrist with both hands.

"Good," he nodded. "Control the weapon hand first. Always."

He shifted his weight before I could adjust my footing, stepping off-center. His free hand shot to my elbow, applying pressure just above the joint. I barely had time to react before my balance was gone, my feet sliding out from under me and my arm pinned behind my back.

My chest hit the wet grass with a thud.

"Dead," he said, his grip firm but not cruel.

The word hit me like a slap. My cheek pressed into the mud. Frustration boiled in my chest as I shoved against him, trying to twist free. He let me go, stepping back and offering his hand.

"You okay?" His voice was softer now.

I ignored his hand, pushing to my feet. My palms stung from the impact, fingers numb with cold. "Fine." I dusted the mud from my sweatpants.

"You hesitated," he said. "That's all it takes."

"I know."

He studied me for a moment. "We'll go slower."

"I'm fine."

He didn't argue, but the concern in his amber eyes made me want to scream. I didn't want pity. I wanted to feel strong, capable. Like I could stand my ground against Connor—against anyone.

"Again." I planted my feet.

James nodded. This time, he came at me a little faster. When his arm shot forward, I stepped off the centerline, turning my body sideways to create a smaller target. My hand latched onto his wrist, twisting it outward as I pivoted my hips.

For a split second, I thought I had him.

Then, his other hand caught my forearm, disrupting my balance. He dropped his weight, using my own momentum against me, and I was on the ground again.

"Dead."

The rain fell harder, soaking through my clothes, stray hairs from my ponytail sticking to my face. I shoved them away angrily, and stood.

"Focus on control," he reminded me. "It's not about strength. He's stronger. You'll lose every time. You need leverage—use his movement against him."

I clenched my fists, nails digging into my palms. "I'm trying."

"I know you are." His voice was quieter now. "You're doing fine, but you're tired. You barely slept. Let's take a brea—"

"No!" The word echoed in the clearing. "I don't need a break. I need to get this right."

He sighed but didn't push. Understanding lit his features. "Alright. Again."

I lunged, stepping off-line too quickly. My grip found his arm, but my footing was off, the mud working against me. James adjusted effortlessly, countering my mistake. A weight shift. A pivot. I was on the ground before I even understood how.

"Dead."

The word echoed in my head, each repetition carving deeper. My chest burned—not just from the exertion but from the anger clawing at me. At James, for being so fucking calm. At the rain, for making this harder. At Connor—at men—for making this necessary in the first place.

I pushed myself up again, breath coming in short bursts.

My muscles ached, and my fingers started to numb, but I didn't care.

"Stay calm," James said in his irritatingly patient way. "Your anger's throwing you off."

I glared at him, wiping the rain from my face. "I know that."

He stepped closer. "We can try again after the rain stops."

"No. I just...." I took a deep breath. "You make this shit look easy."

His brow furrowed. "It's not easy. But you're too in your head—too angry. If he comes back—"

"When," I interrupted bitterly.

His shoulders tensed. For a moment, he just stood there, rain dripping from his hair. "*When* he comes back, you have to stay calm. Your fight, flight, or freeze is going to kick in. Find the middle ground between the anger and the fear. Balance yourself, or you'll be—"

"Dead."

"Yeah."

Something in his voice broke through my frustration. It wasn't pity or condescension.

It was fear. For me.

Balance.

I took a slow, steadying breath, then cracked a soft grin. "Okay, Mr. Miyagi. Again."

'*Between the anger and fear.*'

He nodded, and we went again. The rain poured, the mud pulling at my feet. But this time, when I grabbed his wrist, I didn't just react—I adjusted. I pivoted immediately, guiding his movement instead of fighting against it.

"Better," he said, a small smile breaking through. "Much better."

MY FINGERS TAPPING THE KEYBOARD FILLED THE apartment, blending with the metallic clinking of James's tools by the front door. I slouched deeper into the couch, its worn cushions cradling me as the glow of the laptop hit my face. My eyes darted over Google's latest offering of advice for handling stalkers and unhinged ex-husbands.

My notebook sat open beside me, filled with hastily scrawled and frustratingly obvious notes: Document everything, change your routines, be aware of your surroundings, and —of course—*contact the authorities.*

I huffed through my nose. Sure, the *authorities* would swoop in like knights on white horses. They'd been oh-so-helpful before.

"The locks are in. But cameras won't be here 'til after Thanksgiving," James called out as he moved to the back door. His voice carried over the creak as he tested the handle.

I nodded absently, not looking up. My finger flicked at the trackpad, scrolling further. "Figures," I muttered.

Cassie lounged beside me, her legs sprawled across the

armrest. Fluffy Hello Kitty pajamas and a cropped tank top bared her toned stomach, and sunshine-colored waves framed her face as she glanced at my screen.

"Authorities?" Her lip curled in a wry smirk. "More like numb nuts. Pointless."

I turned to her. "I guess Google doesn't account for megalomaniac stalkers with connections."

She snorted, eyes gleaming with mirth. "Shocking. Might as well tell us to write Connor a strongly worded letter."

Before I could answer, my phone buzzed beside me. Its vibration rattled against the cushion, and I glanced down.

> Eric: What is my brooding little pro-bowler doing?

The heat spread up my neck before I could tamp it down, blooming in my cheeks. My fingers hovered over the screen as I debated a response. Cassie's eyes caught the movement, and her head tilted like a hawk spotting its prey.

"Oh, *Eric*," she crooned, dragging out his name in a syrupy tone. She pressed a hand to her chest, fluttering her lashes as her body gyrated, mouth open and eyes closed.

James paused mid-screw and turned to her with a baffled look. He shook his head, muttered something under his breath, and disappeared down the hall.

"Grow up," I shot at Cassie, though my voice lacked conviction as I typed back a response.

> Me: Thinking I need to get new friends.

She nudged me with her elbow, grin spreading wider. "You've got a cute little crush," she teased, her voice singsong and insufferable.

"I do not," I replied, a little too quickly, the defensiveness in my tone giving me away.

Her grin turned slow and wicked. "That was *so* convincing."

The phone buzzed again.

Eric: Isn't that what we're doing?

The words lingered on the screen, sending a jolt through my chest. I wasn't sure *what* we we're doing. The hang outs, the texts, the lingering touches that sent electricity straight to my vagina—it wasn't something I had the label for. But friends? Hardly.

'Friends don't do what I'm thinking of doing to those plump lips.'

I shifted on the couch, crossing my legs tightly as a flush crept up my skin. Cassie leaned closer, eyes glinting with curiosity as she tried to peek at the screen.

"What are you two talking about?" she asked, sugary sweet.

"Nothing." I pulled the phone closer, shielding it from her prying eyes.

Her laughter bubbled up. "Oh, you're flustered! It's *adorable.*"

"I am *not* flustered, you overgrown noodle," I muttered, typing furiously.

Me: I don't think you're the type of friend I'm talking about.

She smirked. "Ope, another lie. That's two. Want to shoot for a third?"

She lunged suddenly, her limbs flailing as she reached for the phone. I yelped, twisting away and holding it out of her reach.

"Let me see!"

"No!" I laughed despite myself as I wrestled to keep the phone out of her bony fingers.

She sat back on the couch, finally relenting, but her grin was still plastered.

Another buzz.

Eric: And what type of friend am I?

The fuckable kind.
I bit my lip, settling back into the couch.

Me: The dangerous type.

My lips twitched as I hit send. Cassie lunged again, laughing as I fended her off.

"Admit it!" she cried, her hands clawing at my arm.

"It's... he's just... I'm not talking about this with *you!*" I gasped, wrestling her off and collapsing back onto the couch.

She flopped beside me, catching her breath. "Oh, goodie! Something new and different for you. If you ask me—"

"I never do."

She opened her mouth but was silenced by another buzz.

Eric: Who, me? Never.

Yeah, right.
James reappeared, wiping his hands on his jeans. "The control panel for the alarm system is set up by your nightstand and panic buttons in every room. I have to run to my mom's. They finally got back to Jeff about the fire."

"Took them long enough." Cassie rolled her eyes.

"Keep us updated," I said, and he nodded as he walked out the door.

Thankful for James's interruption from Cassie's incessant assault, I briefly returned to my laptop, clicking the tab on the house listing I'd been watching. Selling the house felt like a quiet act of reclaiming something Connor had tried to take. It felt like shedding dead weight, a necessary step forward.

As I switched tabs, a new message popped up.

Eric: Coffee?

I stared at the message, feeling my stomach flip.

Me: Are you asking if I like it or I want it?

Eric: Oh, I know you want it (;

A grin pulled at the edges of my mouth, impossible to fight.

Me: That was very cheeky.

Eric: 15 minutes out of your day. I promise to give you back.

Me: Would that be the 15 minutes women sell their souls for?

Eric: Now, who's being cheeky?

A laugh slipped.

Me: Fine.

"You're smiling like an idiot." Cassie nudged me. "Why?"

"None of your business," I mumbled, already standing and making my way to the bedroom.

She trailed after me, leaning against the doorway as I rummaged through my closet. "Where are you going?"

"Also, none of your business."

"To see Eric?" she asked, all too innocent.

I hesitated, pulling out a sweater, shaking my head and reaching for a jacket, but I tossed that one to the side. Why was finding something to wear so frustrating?

"So, you guys are a thing now?" she pressed.

"No," I yanked another sweater over my head.

"Sure *looks* like a thing." She crossed her arms.

"We're just hanging out," I muttered, rifling through the folded pairs of jeans.

Her eyes narrowed as she watched me. "Yeah, that's what you said at the bowling alley. But that was *clearly* a date. Which would make this your third?" She raised a brow.

I shook my head, searching for my shoes and wanting to pull my hair out.

"You're freaking out. It's definitely a date." Her lips pressed into a thin line. "He's great. Don't get me wrong. But we don't know him, not really."

I dropped to the floor, scanning under my bed.

Finally finding my shoes, I stood and walked into the bathroom. "You all but asked him his blood type. And I've known him for over a year now." I sighed at my reflection, unsatisfied with the outfit, and returned to my closet.

"Yeah, you know him professionally. That doesn't mean you know *him*. Don't go jumping into the first bed, you see."

"Isn't it *my* role to play helicopter mom? You guys said you liked him."

"I'm saying be careful." Worry draped her words. "I just don't want you trading one monster for another."

Her words hit like a slap, but I bit back my retort. She wasn't wrong to be scared, even if I hated the reminder. She was trying to protect me, when it was my job to protect her. *I was supposed to be the big sister, but I kept making her take on that role.*

Cassie broke the heavy silence. "Just... put those expensive psyche classes to use." Her tone lightened as she crossed to my closet, pulling out a low-cut tank top and a sheer mesh long-sleeve. "And don't let your vajeen run the show."

I huffed a laugh, shaking my head as she tossed a pair of ripped skinny jeans with black and gold high heeled booties onto the bed. "Oh, the irony."

Cassie grinned. "Hey! My head and vajeen work in perfect sync."

"I'm sure that's exactly what your 'dates' after the bowling alley said."

She turned, smacking her ass with a grin. "You're goddamn right!" She turned back, pointing to the completed outfit. "If you ruin this with a sweater, I'll drop-kick you so fast."

"So, I'm just supposed to freeze?"

She shrugged. "Being hot requires sacrifice."

33

My car's heater roared, doing its best against the cold that seemed determined to freeze me solid. I rubbed my hands together, the friction barely warming my fingers. My eyes drifted to the back seat, where my black jacket lay crumpled. With a sigh, I twisted awkwardly to grab it, the motion pulling at my muscles, still stiff from the ass-kicking James put me through.

"Screw her," I muttered as I shrugged it on. "Not technically a sweater."

The zipper hissed as I tugged it up, the snug fabric like a makeshift shield. I inhaled deeply as my hand hovered over the door handle. Boots crunched against frosted gravel.

Inside The Coffee House, chatter mingled with the occasional hiss of the espresso machine. I scanned the room for Eric, my heart skipping involuntarily.

No sign of him yet.

Relief mixed with disappointment and unease settled in my chest. I approached the counter, smoothing my expression into something resembling calm.

Cool as a cucumber.

The barista greeted me with a bright smile, her blonde ponytail swaying as she moved. Her youthful energy contrasted sharply with the heaviness I carried, her ease a reminder of a simpler time I couldn't seem to grasp anymore.

"Blonde roast, please," I said, my voice steady even as my chest fluttered with nerves I didn't want to name.

She nodded, the steam from the coffee machine rose in slow curls.

"Violet."

The deep, familiar timbre of his voice slid through me.

I jumped, nearly dropping my wallet as I spun around. Eric stood just behind me, his grin a perfect blend of mischief and charm.

"Why are you so good at that?" I demanded, my heart pounding like a drum behind my ribs.

He chuckled, slipping his hands into the pockets of a black leather jacket that painted his broad shoulders. Beneath it, a navy Henley stretched across his chest, the snug fabric highlighting every defined line. Dark jeans hung low on his hips.

Why was he so easily devastating?

"Trick of the trade," he teased.

"Ninja training included in med school now?" I shot back, willing the heat in my cheeks to subside.

He smirked, leaning in closer as though he were sharing a secret. "Float like a butterfly, sting like a bee."

I swallowed hard, my pulse quickening under his gaze.

The barista fumbled behind the counter, hands trembling as she struggled to take his order. Her cheeks flushed pink, and she couldn't seem to look him in the eye. I couldn't blame her. Eric had that effect on people. I watched her flustered movements with a small, involuntary smile.

We collected our drinks and moved toward the table near the window. *The* table.

Our table.

The thought lingered longer than I wanted, its weight settling somewhere between my heart and stomach. I pushed it aside as I slid into my seat. Eric followed suit.

"Would you prefer I call you Vi?"

I shook my head, peeling off my jacket and draping it over the back of the chair. "Violet is fine."

"Hm," he mused, his gaze trailing over me like a physical touch, making my skin tingle. "Indeed, you are."

My cheeks flushed under his scrutiny, and I shifted in my chair, willing my pulse to slow.

"So many names already," he said, his voice dipping. "I've been dying to know the story behind *Vixen.*"

I forced a laugh. "It's just a nickname." I lied. "Technically, Cassie is a nickname. Her full name is Cassia."

His eyes narrowed slightly, curiosity flashing in his expression before a playful smile curved his full lips. "Were your parents avid gardeners?"

A bitter laugh bubbled out of me unexpectedly.

Dad killed everything he touched.

I hesitated, the weight of old memories pressing down on me. "My mom... she had such a green thumb. She could grow anything. We had this little greenhouse in the backyard. She spent hours in there, reading to all of us. Distracting us...."

The words lodged in my throat as images of my father's rage tore through my mind.

'*WHO TOOK IT?*'

'*No one, honey.*'

'*IT'S GONE!*'

'*Kids, go outside. Now.*'

'*WHERE. IS. IT. ELIZABETH!*'

'David, you're hurting me.'

'TELL ME WHERE IT IS!'

Eric's hand brushed against mine, pulling me back to the present. The simple touch was anchoring. I blinked, meeting those eyes, and the concern there softened the blow of my father's voice.

"Sorry for babbling." I pulled my hand away, curling it into a fist in my lap.

His voice was firm, almost commanding. "I told you, never apologize for that."

I tried to focus on his words, his presence, anything to keep the darkness at bay. But deep down, the familiar ache of guilt crept in.

He didn't belong in this chaos. He deserved a life free of the shadows that followed me—free of Connor, of my baggage. Dragging Eric into my world, into my mess, felt selfish.

But then he smiled, and the weight in my chest lifted momentarily.

His smile softened as he leaned back in his chair, giving me space but still holding my gaze. "So, there are more florally named siblings?"

I snorted. "Yeah, my mom kept it consistent. Ren is the oldest. Then me, then Cassie. And Sage was the baby."

The moment I said Sage's name, surprise and sadness flooded me. It was instinctive, the way my heart ached, and my chest felt hollow all at once. I bit the inside of my cheek to keep the tears at bay, but the grief threatened to claw its way to the surface.

The teasing edge in his expression gave way to something gentler. He didn't press, didn't ask for more than I could give.

"My parents just called me 'shithead,'" he said with that crooked grin I could get lost in. "But in their defense, I deserved it."

His honesty was disarming, and I couldn't help but laugh—an authentic, unguarded sound that felt foreign and strange in its suddenness.

"What was your dad like?" The question slipped out before I could second-guess it.

His grin faltered, his eyes growing distant as he glanced down at his coffee cup. "He was a hard ass, but he was a good man. Even though I spent most of my teenage years denying that fact."

"You guys fought a lot?"

"That's an understatement." He huffed a quiet laugh, fingers idly tracing the rim of his cup. "He was the man with the plan—for everything. Including me and my life. He wanted me to take over the practice, but that wasn't what I had in mind for myself."

I arched a brow, resting my elbows on the table. "What? Modeling?"

Eric's laugh came quickly this time, a rich, warm sound that made my brain short-circuit. "I wanted to get out and see the world. I wanted to experience everything. Different cultures, new languages, exotic food. But he wanted me here, and I hated him for it. So, after high school, I left. I finally got to travel, and I didn't talk to him for almost two years."

"But you obviously came back," I said, watching as his gaze grew shadowed.

"I got into some trouble, and he came and brought me home. After that, I understood why the practice was so important to him, why he was so hard on me."

"How did he...." I trailed off.

Pain flickered across Eric's face, his jaw tightening as he looked out the window. "Brain aneurysm." He paused, his fingers tightening around his coffee cup. "My mom stopped by saying he stood her up for their lunch date. I went into his office, and he was slumped over his desk. I tried to resuscitate him, but he was already gone."

The grief in his voice hit me like a wave, sharp and visceral. The urge to comfort him warring with the knowledge that nothing I said could ever make it better.

"I'm so sorry," I whispered.

He nodded. "He lived a very long, very full life. I'm grateful for the years I had with him. But it changed my mother. Like she lost a piece of her soul that day."

"Is she...." I hesitated, unsure if I was treading too close to something still raw.

"Still calling me a shithead and kicking my ass in chess? Absolutely." The tension in his shoulders eased just a fraction. "She's a force. We have dinner every Friday."

"Hold on, *chess*?"

His grin turned sly, the shadow of grief lifting. "Yes?"

"I'm sorry, it's just surprising that that's one of your skill sets," I teased, leaning forward.

His voice dropped, the playful edge sharpening into something darker, more intimate. "I have lots of surprising skills I can show you."

My breath caught, a shiver running down my spine. Heat pooled low in my stomach, and I struggled to find a response that wouldn't completely give me away.

"Come here," he said softly, his tone shifting so suddenly that I blinked in confusion.

I froze, every muscle in my body tensing. Panic and anticipation battled within me. His eyes held steady, patient, and I found myself leaning forward as though pulled by an invisible thread.

His hand reached across the small table, brushing against my chin with a touch so light it sent goosebumps across my skin. His thumb grazed the corner of my mouth, his face so close that his breath mingled with mine.

"Just a bit of cream on your lip," he murmured, the gravel in his voice melting me.

The heat of his touch burned through me, igniting every nerve. My thoughts scattered, my heartbeat thundering in my ears.

How does he not have coffee breath?

"Favorite color?" I blurted, the words tumbling out in a desperate attempt to break the spell he had over me.

He relaxed back into his chair, a soft chuckle escaping him. *"Violet."*

Oh, he's good—too good.

And I'm in way over my head.

Sunlight streamed through the greenhouse, golden light spilling over the sea of flowers in every direction. Crimson, violet, yellow—each petal seemed impossibly vibrant, impossibly alive, glowing as if lit from within. The cool, soft dirt under my bare feet grounded me as I stepped over the threshold, the scent of earth and blossoms wrapping around me like a comforting embrace.

Birds trilled a gentle melody, the sound threading through the space and blending seamlessly with the lilting cadence of her voice.

My mother.

She sat on a wooden crate in the center of the greenhouse, her golden hair spilling over her shoulders like liquid sunlight. Sage wriggled in her lap, his chubby hands tugging insistently at the loose fabric of her blouse. She laughed, the sound soft.

I inhaled a hard breath, trying to hold on to the scene, to capture every detail. Ren sat cross-legged nearby, his head bent low, dark hair obscuring his face. The scrape of his pocketknife against wood scratched at my hearing. He didn't look up, his focus wholly consumed by the intricate carving taking shape beneath his fingers.

That knife—the twin to mine, carrying it like a talisman of who *he* was and who *we* were.

Mom's voice rose and fell with the words from the worn pages of Frankenstein. Each syllable pulled me closer, soothing me.

I stepped toward her, my chest aching with a yearning so fierce it felt like it might tear me apart.

"Momma," I whispered, my voice thin and trembling.

I knelt before her, tears stinging my eyes as I leaned forward and pressed my forehead to hers. Her sapphire eyes lifted to mine, lips curving into a smile that melted everything around me. Her skin was warm, her breath a hush against my cheek.

"Sugar lump," she hummed, her hand cupping my cheek.

I closed my eyes, trying to etch the moment into my mind. Her touch, her voice, her scent—earthy and floral. If only I could hold on to this....

A cold hand clamped down on my wrist, the grip bruising. I gasped, my eyes snapping open, and the golden light dissolved into shadows.

The greenhouse vanished. The flowers were gone. Mom was gone.

Thrown backward with a force that wrenched a cry from my throat, my back slammed against something hard. The impact rattled through me, knocking the air from my lungs.

"What do you think you're doing?"

The sound of his voice froze my blood.

I looked up, trembling as icy fear rooted me in place. My father loomed over me, his pale blue eyes burning with a hatred that carved through me like a blade.

"N-nothing," I stammered, shaking. "I—I wasn't—"

"Don't lie to me!" he bellowed, his face mere inches from mine.

His hands seized my shoulders, fingers digging in like claws as he shook me violently. My head snapped back, colliding with the wall behind me. Pain exploded through my skull but was muted beneath the rising tide of panic.

"I'm not lying!" I pleaded, tears streaming down my face. "Please, I wasn't—"

"*Stop* crying!" His roar cut through me, raw and poisonous. "You're *always* crying!"

I tried to swallow the sobs clawing up my throat, but they spilled out anyway, choking and ragged.

He slammed me into the wall again. And again. Each jarring impact sent fresh pain radiating through my body, the sickening thud reverberating.

When he let go, I crumpled to the ground, gasping for air, my vision swimming. My hands scrabbled against the cold, unforgiving floor as I tried to crawl away.

A boot struck my stomach, driving the breath from my lungs as I choked on a scream.

"*Hypocrite,*" he spat, dripping with disdain.

I curled into myself, every inch of me aching.

He fisted the back of my shirt, yanking me upward. For a moment, I dangled like a rag doll before he hurled me backward into nothingness.

"Look at what you did!"

I hit the ground hard, the impact stealing the air from my lungs.

When I opened my eyes, my heart stopped.

Mom's body lay sprawled in front of me, her golden locks tangled and matted. Her eyes—once so warm and loving—stared lifelessly into nothing.

"No," I choked, scrambling backward. My hands slipped in

something warm and wet, and I recoiled, bile rising in my throat.

Beside her, Sage lay motionless, his tiny fists curled and still.

"No! No, no, no!" I shook my head violently, my chest heaving as panic and despair raged. "Please, no!"

I turned to see Ren. His face blank, eyes cold and unrecognizable.

"*You* did this."

Cassie appeared beside him, her pigtails swaying as she stared down at me. "You did this," she echoed, her voice void of the warmth I knew.

Their words became a chant, a horrible chorus that threatened to rip me apart.

"I didn't know!" I screamed, clutching my head. "I can fix it! *Please*! Let me fix it!"

I collapsed beside my mother's lifeless body, cradling Sage's limp form in my arms. I brushed a thumb over his cold, pale cheek, my tears falling in hot, endless streams.

"I—I can fix this," I whispered.

A hand gripped my face, the fingers cold and unyielding.

Dad crouched in front of me, his eyes burning into mine. "You can't fix it. You're broken," he hissed.

A sob caught in my throat.

"Who could love a thing like that?"

I couldn't speak. Couldn't breathe.

"Look at what you did to them!" He snapped my face towards the lifeless bodies beneath me before forcing me back to meet his eyes.

Pale blue eyes turned stark white as foam seeped from his mouth. His growl deepened, guttural and monstrous. "Look at what you did to me!"

I squeezed my eyes shut, trying to will the image away.

"Now it's your turn."

I opened my eyes at his words to see the gleam of a syringe, and terror ran rampant through me.

"No, don't. Please. I'm sorry. I'm so, so sorry."

His grip was iron as he plunged the needle into my arm.

The sound of my scream jolted me awake. My chest heaved, and sweat soaked my shirt, clinging to a trembling frame. My hands fumbled for the blankets, shoving them away as I stumbled out of bed.

My legs wobbled beneath me, barely holding me upright as I staggered into the bathroom. I collapsed in front of the toilet just as my stomach convulsed, savagely heaving until there was nothing left.

When it was over, I slumped against the cool porcelain, my forehead pressed to the seat. My entire body shook uncontrollably, his voice still ringing in my ears.

"But you know that none of what happened was your fault, right? You know that you didn't make your mother sick. That your father caused your brother's death and, ultimately, his own. Right?" Dr. Hibani's voice was calm, even gentle, but her words were like salt in an open wound.

The words twisted, sinking deep even as I stared past her. The window offered no solace—just a view of trees lining the street. I latched onto their movement, tracing their dance instead of the words that clung to the room like smoke. My fingers curled into the plush armrest, the pressure a poor substitute for the weight pressing down on my chest.

"Mhm," I muttered, my voice stripped of anything resembling emotion.

Knowing something and feeling it were galaxies apart. Her words scratched at the tightly sealed box in the back of my mind—the one I'd worked so damned hard to keep closed for the past eight years.

Hibani leaned forward slightly. "Do you want to talk about why you might be having these dreams again?"

A sharp, bitter laugh broke from me, unbidden and serrated. "Oh, I don't know. Maybe it's because my ex keeps fucking with me. Maybe it's the paranoia. Or—wait—maybe it's because *you* had the bright idea of *feeling* things, and opening one box gave me more than I bargained for." I paused, letting the words twist into venom. "My life is one long *Dateline* episode waiting for Keith Morrison's voiceover."

Her lips quirked a restrained smile that didn't quite reach her eyes. "Maybe you should write a book."

Maybe you should go fuck yourself.

The thought surfaced, bitter and unfiltered, but I swallowed it back. She wasn't the enemy here. I knew that. Still, the chaos swirling around my life had edges sharp enough to cut, and I was tired of being the one bleeding.

"Dreams can be windows into our psyche."

"And sometimes they're just a bunch of gibberish," I shot back, my arms crossing over my chest.

Her pen tapped once against the edge of her notebook. Her brandy gaze patient. "Irritation and frustration are common and completely expected during stressful times. And you've been under an incredible amount of stress. Your safety has been compromised multiple times. The police couldn't help, triggering you—as it would anyone. Your mind might be trying to connect it to your childhood."

"I doubt anyone cared enough to stalk me back then," I said, my voice clipped, the edge of sarcasm dulled by the rawness creeping in.

I *knew* what she was doing. I *knew* what she was going to say, but I wasn't in the mood to hear it.

"You know I'm talking about the violence you experienced. Watching a parent go through that, let alone experiencing it yourself, is traumatizing."

"Trauma just makes me more interesting." I forced a smirk that felt more like a grimace, my jaw tight.

She ignored the sarcasm. "Your father was supposed to be the protector, but he wasn't. Then there was Ren, and he left. It left *you* to protect your mother, Cassie, and Sage."

"And look how good that turned out." My laugh was brittle, a thin veneer over the splintering cracks inside me.

"You were a child, Violet," she said softly, her tone so steady it felt like it could hold my unraveling pieces together.

"I was old enough to do something, and I didn't!" The words tore from me louder than I intended. A tremor in my voice betrayed me as the tears prickled at the edges of my vision.

Not until it was too late.

"You carry an immense amount of guilt," she continued. "You blame yourself for things that were completely out of your control. It was never your job to do something about any of it. You should have been protected, and you weren't. None of you were. The people who should have kept you safe failed. Not Ren, not Cassie, and not you."

"Debatable," I muttered, swiping angrily at the single tear that slipped free despite my best efforts.

"You hold so much anger—toward yourself, toward your father. This situation with Connor only amplifies it. Your mind and body are reacting as if you were still that little girl trying to protect her family. To protect herself." Her voice softened further, cutting through the tension in the room. "My personal belief is that dreams are always trying to tell us something. Professionally, they're usually connected to deeper fears or unresolved emotions—unresolved trauma."

Her words coiled around my chest, squeezing tighter. My eyes fixed on the cream-colored wall behind her, its blandness a slight reprieve from the storm waging war inside me.

It's resolved. He's gone. It's done. I fixed it.

"Have you ever tried inner child work?" she asked, pulling me from the relentless hum of discomfort under my skin.

I tilted my head, narrowing my eyes at her. "I've got too much going on to worry about my inner child." My tone flat.

Sure, let's just call her up real quick. Hey Violet! Whatcha doin'? Oh, sewing up Mom's face again. Must be a Tuesday!

"It can help us process the present in a healthy manner if we work on the damage of our past," she said, her tone so infuriatingly calm.

My arms tightened around me, fingers digging into my forearms. The pressure was grounding, an anchor against the spiral of my thoughts pushing to the surface. "I think I've processed the stalking pretty healthily."

Her patient smile stayed put in quiet rebuttal. "You've done wonders with finding ways to protect yourself, absolutely. But I mean more how you went from a death sentence to being cancer-free, all while realizing you were in an unstable relationship, being attacked, divorced, and now not feeling safe in your own home. That's a lot to process."

My gaze dropped to the floor, tracing the lines of the rug with my eyes. "Unless someone brings it up, I forget that the cancer thing even happened." I shrugged. "I feel like the bonfire was a good way to let all of it go, and when I did, the pain of it all just... vanished."

"That was a good step toward closure," she nodded. "Do you think it would be helpful to do something similar with your childhood memories?"

My lips tightened, and I shifted, my foot tapping against the floor. "What? Like, burn all of my dad's shit? I didn't keep anything of his."

"I was thinking more along the lines of maybe writing a

letter. No one will see it but you. Write whatever you feel and then burn it."

My nails bit into my arm. A letter? What did it matter what I wanted to say to a dead guy? The words hovered on the edge of my consciousness, but I pushed them back down where they belonged. "I have no idea what I would say to him." The lie soured in my mouth.

"Okay," she said evenly. "We can start small. If he were here right now, what would you say to him? Don't think—just say."

Her gaze held mine, her patience unbearable. Heat rose to my face as my hands clenched tighter, the silence growing louder.

You deserved worse.

My heart thudded painfully, each beat echoing louder than the last. The words clawed at the walls of my mind, desperate to escape, but I hesitated.

I don't regret it.

"You're an asshole, but at least you're a dead asshole?" I shrugged, a smirk pulling my lips.

Hibani didn't fill the silence that followed. her expression soft but unreadable. Her hands rested lightly on her notebook, her posture open, waiting.

The box in my mind creaked under the weight of my thoughts, but I slammed it shut, locking the memories away once more. I let my smirk linger, my defense mechanism as old as the scars he left behind.

She waited, a quiet invitation to say more.

I didn't.

THE FRONT DOOR SLAMMED OPEN AND CRASHED THROUGH the apartment like a thunderclap. I jerked upright on the couch just in time to see Cassie storming in, her phone clutched like a weapon as her thumb jabbed the screen.

"What the fuck is wrong with people?" she snapped, her cheeks flushed, wild eyes blazing as if she were ready to take on the world barehanded. Without breaking stride, she hurled her bag onto the cushion beside me, its force making me flinch.

I arched an eyebrow, leaning back against the couch. "Rough day?"

Her crimped hair swung like The Crimson Banner as she spun to face me. "Some asshole cut me off on the road and almost ran me into a fucking ditch!" she fumed, her voice cracking with the heat of her fury. "I honked at the dick, and he just sped off." She thrusted her phone into the air as if the device itself were to blame. "And then James calls to tell me the cops think the fire was *his* fault!"

My brain buzzed with static. "What?"

"Yeah," she spat, her tone coated in bitter disbelief. "Either that, or some homeless guy trying to light up. James is *drowning* in guilt, but no big deal, right? '*Happens all the time*'. Like, what the fuck, people?"

She dropped onto the couch with a huff, shoved her bag aside, folded her arms, and stared daggers at nothing in particular. Her foot tapped against the floor, each agitated bounce reverberating. Her anger filled the space, crackling like a live wire.

I let the silence stretch, chewing on her words. But the darkness rolling around in my head and the idea of doing nothing—of letting this heaviness consume me—made my skin itch.

I crossed my legs underneath me and braced my elbows on my legs, leaning forward and resting my head in my palms. "Do you meditate?"

Her head whipped toward me, her face screwing up like I'd just suggested she take a vow of silence. "If you're about to suggest I need to meditate, I will shove my foot so far up your ass—"

"Shut up." I sighed, dragging a hand through my hair. The weight of everything—the fire, Hibani, Connor, *Dad*—bricks piling higher with every breath. "The gym's destroyed, you won't run with me, and I can't exactly run alone with a psycho on the loose." The words spilled out like water from a cracked dam. "But my head is full, and I need it to not be."

Her eyebrows rose, the fire in her gaze dimming as she tilted her head. "You want me to help you meditate?"

"Yeah," I admitted, quieter now. Vulnerability wasn't exactly my thing, but desperation was a hell of a motivator. "Unless you've got a better idea for clearing my head." Her eyebrows raised, and a smile crept across her lips. I added, "That *doesn't* include sex or copious amounts of alcohol."

Her smile turned into an exaggerated pout, but she nodded. "Fine. But fair warning—you'll have to listen to me for once."

I snorted, the corner of my mouth twitching into a reluctant smile. "Don't get used to it."

Her laugh broke through the tension in the room, lightening the air just enough to make it breathable again.

"Come on." She stood, motioning for me to follow her. "Let's see if I can teach you to zen the hell out."

And just like that, the storm inside me quieted—if only a little.

"You're not trying hard enough."

The sun dipped low in the sky, casting a golden light, and for once, the weather held—no rain, just the soft thrum of nature. Cassie and I sat cross-legged on the dry grass, the edges of her hair catching the sunlight like a halo.

I leaned back on my hands, scoffing. "Oh, I'm *sorry*, I wasn't aware you're the Dalai Lama now."

Her lips curved, but she didn't open her eyes. "*You're* the one who's supposed to be the therapist, Vi. It's weird you don't know how to meditate."

"I know how to meditate—on paper." I plucked a blade of grass and twirled it between my fingers. "In reality? Not so much."

She cracked an eye open, her baby-blue gaze sparkling with amusement. "Well, maybe if you stopped being such a smartass, you'd figure it out."

I grinned and started humming a ridiculous nonsense tune,

mocking the whole process. Her leg shot out, bare foot colliding with my shin.

"Ow," I muttered, rubbing the spot but unable to wipe the grin from my face.

"You enlisted my help; *I'm helping*." She sat up straighter, her hands resting loosely on her knees. "Now close your eyes and focus on your breathing. Center yourself."

With an exaggerated sigh, I complied, shutting my eyes.

'Center yourself.' Whatever the hell that meant.

The world around me narrowed to the rustle of leaves and the occasional chirp of a bird. My breathing came shallow, stuttering as I tried to match Cassie's calm rhythm. The cool air carried the scent of pine and damp earth, grounding me just enough to ease the tightness in my shoulders.

For a moment, I thought it might work.

But then–

The scent of pine turned sour, like sweat and vinegar.

The air around me felt heavier, pressing against my ribs.

The edges of my mind began to blur, the clearing slipping away like sand between my fingers. The soft sounds of the breeze and Cassie's breathing faded, replaced by an electrical hum that set my teeth on edge.

No.

I tried to open my eyes, to pull myself back, but I was already slipping–

The golden light vanished, swallowed by the dim gray of a poorly lit room.

His room.

'Look!'

The scream shattered the air.

'Look at what you did!'

My fingers trembled around the syringe; it's hard plastic biting into my palm. My grip was too tight—I couldn't let go.

No, no, no.

The stench of failure and fury clung to my skin like oil. Dad's chest barely rose, each ragged breath weaker than the last. Foam bubbled at the corners of his slack mouth, his face pale as ashes.

You're not really here.

The syringe slipped from my fingers, hitting the floor with a muffled clatter that rang too loud in my ears.

Get out. Get out. Get out.

My legs moved on autopilot, propelling me toward the door. The metal handle was cold in my palm as I twisted it and slammed the door shut behind me. The sound reverberated down the hall like a gunshot.

A small voice cut through the chaos.

"VV?" I turned, heart hammering against my ribs.

Cassie.

She was just a kid, her blonde hair falling in a messy braid, her wide eyes filled with confusion as she stared up at me. Her hand reached for the door handle.

I threw myself in front of it. "You can't go in there."

"Why not?" She tugged at my arm.

It needs more time.

"Just grab your stuff and get in my car," I said, forcing a calm I didn't feel. "I'll be out there in a second."

The memory snapped like a taut rubber band.

I gasped, my eyes flying open. The clearing around me swam back into focus, but my chest was still heaving, skin clammy with leftover fear. My nails had bitten into my palms, angry crescent marks blooming red against my skin.

"Vi?" Cassie's voice anchored me further. She was watching me, concern tightening her features.

"It's not working," I muttered, hollow.

"What—"

I was on my feet in an instant, wiping dirt from my jeans as I turned toward the apartment. The clearing felt like it was closing in on me.

I fled inside, barely reaching my bed, before I yanked the blankets over my head, curling in on myself.

I STILL FUCKING HATED THIS.

Each step sent a burning ache through my legs, lungs fighting against the rhythm I forced them to maintain. Eric ran beside me, annoyingly graceful, breathing measured and calm. His long strides carried him forward with ease, making my teeth grind and reminding me *why* I avoided running with others around.

I hated running with him. Well, *hated* was a strong word. I hated that I wasn't as effortless as he was, that next to him, I felt slow, uncoordinated.

And maybe I hated that he looked *this* good while doing it.

But I needed the escape—anything to get out of that house, away from that clearing—from the images. And if I spent another second curled on my bed in the fetal position, I would have drowned myself in the tub. A run with a blisteringly attractive doctor wasn't the worst distraction I could think of.

The incline canted, and I blamed it—not him—for my chest's labored rise and fall.

Definitely not *because of him.*

Eric's shirt clung to his back, damp with sweat, the fabric outlining the definition of his shoulders and the sinuous line of his spine. His legs moved with an almost hypnotic power, the muscles in his calves and thighs flexing under his running shorts. It was impossible not to notice how perfectly built he was. Every movement seemed fluid, his body a precise, well-oiled machine. I tried to look away, but my eyes drifted lower.

Gods, look at that ass.

It was perfect—round, firm, and practically begging to be used as a pillow. It was an ass sculpted by gods to ruin mortal women. My lips twitched, but I shook my head, forcing my focus back on not dying from lack of oxygen.

Ridiculous. This was why I didn't spend time around men who looked like they belonged on marble pedestals.

"I'm surprised you asked me out," he said, voice rippling through me like a warm breeze.

"I didn't ask you out," I replied, my gaze fixed on where my feet landed.

"Hm, that's what you said about bowling."

"I said, '*Show up if you want.*'"

"Yes, and I've learned that that's *Violet language* for asking me on a date."

I threw him a glare as I struggled not to pant. "It wasn't a date! I swear between you and Cassie...."

He grinned, all teasing warmth. "I'm flattered you talk about me with your sister."

"I—we don't talk about you," I shot back, feeling the heat crawl up my neck.

"Mhm." His tone was the verbal equivalent of a wink. "If that wasn't a date, then this is...?"

"Two friends running together?" *Friends.* The word felt like an itchy sweater. It didn't fit, but I shoved it on anyway.

I picked up my pace, leaving him no chance to reply, and

surged ahead. The incline leveled as we reached a clearing, and I slowed to a stop, hands braced on my hips as I fought to catch my breath. He stopped beside me, breath steady because, of *course*, he wasn't even winded.

The valley was a sun-drenched patchwork of trees, and golden light spilled across the horizon. My chest ached, but I wasn't sure if it was from the run or the view.

"Gorgeous," I murmured, more to myself than him

"I agree," Eric said softly, stepping closer. His eyes weren't on the valley.

The weight of his stare prickled along my skin, too heavy, too warm. My stomach clenched with a tangle of nerves and something far more detrimental.

It's just the altitude.

"Is this where you bring all the girls?" I half-joked.

His laugh was deep, easy, and maddeningly attractive. "I've never brought anyone here."

The simplicity of his words knocked the wind from my lungs, but I felt a twinge of comfort. I shifted my footing. "Well, I feel special," I said, reaching for sarcasm.

"You are."

I risked a glance at him, catching the way his green-gold eyes rested on me, their intensity threatening to unravel the threadbare grip I had on myself.

I turned to the horizon, pretending the view was enough to distract me.

"'Friends,'" he said, his tone light but undercut with something significant. "Friends can ask their friends what's bothering them, right?"

I stiffened. "What makes you think something's wrong."

"Call it intuition."

His intuition didn't need to know about the lurking shadows in my life.

You mean being stalked by my ex, having to turn my house into Fort Knox, my best friend nearly getting burned alive, or the random flashbacks of dead daddy dearest?

I continued staring into the view, tapping two fingers to my temple. "There's just a lot going on in here."

"Would it have anything to do with Connor?" His voice softened, but there was no missing the edge beneath it.

My chest tightened. "I just... why do men think that we owe them something? Like we get dressed and live our lives specifically to please them? Like we should be honored to be touched, harassed, assaulted?"

His jaw tensed, his usual easy smile fading into something darker. "He hurt you?" It was a question that sounded more like a statement.

Put a cap on the deep-dark-and-twisties, or you'll run off this God-like man.

I rubbed the back of my neck, searching for a softer version of the chaos my life had turned into that could explain whatever he saw in me that caused him concern without alarm bells going off at my deflection. "There were just these guys at the alley... not when you were there. It was like a week ago. But they were messing with me and Cas."

His expression hardened, the change quick. His jaw ticked before his features settled back into his usual calm.

"People just suck sometimes." I shrugged, forcing a casualness I didn't feel.

Eric's silence dragged. His eyes stayed on me, steady and patient, like he was waiting for me to crack open and spill everything I didn't want to say.

Desperate for a distraction, I let out a dramatic sigh. "It's going to snow soon."

He blinked, cocking his head ever-so-slightly. "Do you like the snow?"

"I love it. Just not the holidays that come along with it."

"Oh, no. Don't tell me you're a scrooge," he teased, and just like that, his smile was back, beautiful and disarming.

I waved a dismissive hand, rolling my eyes. "Christmas is just a way for the corporate elite to capitalize on low-income families."

"Oof, okay. People normally focus on the *joy* of the holidays."

"I'm a cynic," I deadpanned.

"Okay, Grinch. What about Thanksgiving? No gifts, just good food and family."

"My mom couldn't cook worth a damn. Our 'Thanksgiving' was usually cold and out of a can, which there's nothing wrong with. Pork-and-beans is my favorite go-to meal, but Connor's family did the whole 'invite everyone you've ever met over and have it catered.' It always felt more like a business meeting than anything else." I shoved the plethora of vestiges begging to be released as far back as they would go. "But now Cas is trying to get us all together for some kind of 'Friendsgiving' thing, but she took after our mom in the cooking department. It's going to be a complete disaster and will probably end in my apartment burning down." I shook my head, huffing a laugh.

"Good thing I'm handy with a fire extinguisher."

I drew my brows together. "That wasn't an invitation."

"You said *'Friendsgiving.'* Aren't we friends?"

That word again. It rubbed against me the wrong way.

I usually don't want to choke on my friends coc—

"If you go, you can't be all," I waved a hand, gesturing over him and his unholy body.

"All what?" His lips quirked into that sinful, crooked grin that made my heart leap.

"That! You can't look at me like that."

"Like what?" He flashed a knowing grin that equally grated against my nerves and lit a fire low in my belly.

I narrowed my eyes. "With the grin. And the eyes. *I* don't know what it means, but Cassie thinks it means sex."

His grin widened into a devilish smirk.

"Stop it," I tried to hide the smile slowly forcing its way out. "You can't be all flirty and talking like everything you say has a double meaning. If you go, it's just as friends. Because we are *just friends.*"

If I say that word one more time, it will stop sounding like a word.

"Scouts honor," he said, one hand braced behind his back as he raised the other, holding out his pinky.

I stared at him in disbelief. "How juvenile," I muttered before hooking my pinky with his.

With our fingers locked, Eric leaned even closer, his voice dropping to a whisper. "Just friends." His breath was a warm caress against my cheek as he brushed a strand of hair behind my ear.

The skin he touched was too charged, and I stepped back quickly. "We... running. Supposed to be running," I stuttered, my voice embarrassingly high and my mind a sloshing mess that mimicked my panties.

Eric's grin didn't waver as he straightened, stepping beside me again.

FOR BASTET'S SAKE, I JUST WANT SOME FUCKING SLEEP.

I sat up, my damp hair plastered to my forehead. The stale, metallic, and bitter taste of fear rested on my tongue. My throat was tight and dry like I'd swallowed shards of glass. I threw off the covers, my bare feet hitting the cold tile with a muted slap.

The darkness felt alive, pressing against me as I padded down the hall to the kitchen. The refrigerator's thrum the only sound as I poured myself a glass of water. The tap sputtered like it, too, was exhausted. The chill of the glass seeped into my fingers as I stared through the backdoor window.

Snow had finally fallen, each flake catching in the silver glow of moonlight. The clearing lay pristine, untouched, the world outside eerily still. The sight tugged at something deep within me.

Grabbing a blanket from the couch, I wrapped it around my shoulders and stepped outside. The snow crunched beneath my feet, moonlight illuminating the edges of the tree line like something out of a dream. Not mine, clearly, but definitely out of someone else's prettier dreams. One's that someone *normal* would have.

I stopped a few feet in, tilting my face toward the sky. The snowflakes kissed my skin, their delicate touch at odds with the firestorm of emotions within me. The silence here was different —soothing, almost sacred.

Hibani's words echoed in my mind. *"If he was here right now, what would you say to him?"* But it wasn't my father's face I saw when I closed my eyes this time. It was *hers.*

"Momma," I whispered, the word fragile as it left my lips. A single tear slipped free, cutting a warm trail down my cheek.

I swallowed hard, my throat aching as the words bubbled up before I could stop them. "Everything is so *heavy,* all the time... It never stops." My voice cracked, barely audible above the whisper of falling snow.

Her face floated in my mind—soft blonde hair pulled into a loose ponytail draping over her shoulder, wrapped in that ratty pink robe she loved so much. She looked so warm, so alive.

"I thought I was doing something right with Connor. Staying. Making things work. I wanted you to be proud of me. Of my marriage, my work, my career. Like I did something with the life... the life that you should have had." More tears spilled over, hot against the chill of the air. "But all I did was rinse and repeat."

The words tumbled out, raw and unfiltered. "I need you— I've *always* needed you. And I miss you. And I'm so... " My breath hitched, the sob I'd been holding back finally breaking free. "God, I'm *so* fucking sorry. It's not fair that I survived and you... you didn't. Nothing makes sense. You were everything good and all 'sunshine-and-rainbows.' You deserved to be here. Not me. Not with what I've done, who I've become, how *weak* I've been." My knees felt weak, but I stood there, face to the sky, letting the snow and tears mingle. "You were so strong. You just made everything so much better. You were loud and happy and dancing whenever you got the chance—Cassie's a lot like that."

A short huff of a laugh escaped me despite myself. "She just uses way more colorful language. Stubborn and headstrong like Ren, like Dad. She's a lot, but James mellows her out—sometimes. You'd like James. He tries to act tough, but he's just a big softy and a good guy to have on your side. You should...." I took a sharp breath as a few more tears fell. "You should be here to see this... see *them*... see *everything*. I should've done more. I should've... I should've tried harder, been better. Maybe if I had—"

The wind stirred as I tried unsuccessfully to choke back my tears, a soft gust playing against my cheek like a phantom caress. It stopped me mid-breath, the warmth in that touch almost enough to make me believe she'd heard me. The storm inside me eased, even if only a little.

I stood there for what felt like an eternity, breathing in the pine-scented wind as my eyes dried and my mind calmed.

I guess it really does help to get that shit out of your system.

I looked down at my red and near-numb bare feet, wiggling my toes in the snow that had gathered around them. I took one last long and deep breath before turning and making my way back to the door.

A snap echoed as my hand reached for the door handle.

My body locked into place. As I turned, the snow crunched beneath my feet, every nerve screaming at me to get inside. But I saw nothing, just the moonlight slicing through the trees.

What are my chances of it being an animal and not my crazy stalker ex?

A shape emerged—a tall silhouette stepping from the shadowy tree line.

Would've preferred a bear.

Fear crawled up my spine like icy fingers. He stood perfectly still, his arms clasped behind his back, the darkness cloaking his features. But I could feel his gaze—heavy, invasive, slicing through me like a knife.

So what? He hangs out across the country and flies out every so often just to fuck with me? Make that make sense.

But who else would it be if it wasn't Connor? Who else would be this fucking psychotic?

My heart thundered as the memory of his hands on my throat flashed across my mind.

Run.

My body screamed for me to bolt, to get back inside and lock the door, but my legs wouldn't move. It was as if the tree roots had reached out and tangled around my feet, holding me there, making me face him.

He tilted his head to the side, his posture causal—mocking, even.

No. More. Running.

The fear started to crack.

My father's voice—sharp and cruel—surfaced, reminding me of the years he spent tearing us all down. Every insult, every bruise, every piece of us he stole. Every bit of happiness he had taken away.

Cancer. That word *alone* had stolen from me. It had ripped away my strength, my confidence, my peace.

And Connor? He was just a line in a long list of bad decisions and a product of my need for security and love. But that wasn't love. All he ever gave me was a cage. Every sneer, every shove, every decision made without my consent had chipped away at my spirit.

This shadow—this thing—was just another chapter in a

never-ending story of people and circumstances trying to crush me.

And I was sick of it.

The fear ebbed as something hotter, sharper, and far more familiar took its place. Frustration ignited in my chest, burning through the terror. My nails dug into my palms, and my breath came in hard bursts as my thoughts sharpened into a singular realization: I was *done* being the scared and crying little girl.

His head tilted farther, the gesture slow, taunting. Like I was a fucking toy to be played with.

My fists clenched. The words ripped from me before I could stop them. "What is your fucking problem?!"

The sound of my voice startled even me.

He didn't move. Didn't flinch. Just stood there, a living reminder of every nightmare I'd ever faced.

"Seriously, Connor? Enough!" My voice rose, fury giving me strength I didn't know I had. "Can't you just go fuck someone else like a normal person and leave me the hell alone?!"

Still, he didn't move. But his silence wasn't oppressive anymore—it was infuriating.

He took a single step forward, his arms still behind his back. My heart hammered against my ribs, but the anger swelled, overpowering the fear.

"Fine!" I yelled, the rage boiling over. "You want me? Come and fucking get me, pussy!" The clearing fell silent again, the snow absorbing the echo of my voice. For a heartbeat, it felt like time itself had paused.

Then his arms dropped to his sides, and he leaned forward as if preparing to lunge.

The anger wavered for a split second, replaced by raw instinct. I spun on my heel, sprinting into the apartment and slamming the door behind me.

My hands trembled as I locked it, chest heaving with adrenaline.

Yeah, let's tell a psychopath, 'Come and get me'. Real fucking smart, Violet.

I raced to my bedroom, locking that door behind me before turning to my closet and reaching for the gun that James had stashed there. I shut myself in the closet, sliding the hanging shirts and jackets aside as I pressed my back against the wall. I slowly slid down the wall and aimed the gun at the closed door, switching off the safety.

Hours crawled by; each creak of the apartment made me jump. When I heard the front door open, my breathing stopped. Relief flooded through me as Cassie's and James's voices drifted in.

I stashed the gun back on the top shelf after turning the safety on and stepped out, forcing my face into a mask of indifference.

I was too tired to have the hours-long interrogation that I would be subjected to if I told them what had happened, and I hadn't felt like going over how I had grown some balls but lost some—maybe all—of my brain cells.

"We brought you some—" Cassie raised a brow, holding two takeout bags as I met them in the living room. "Why are you sweaty?"

"I'm not sweaty," I lied. "I was outside in the snow. I was just about to change before you guys walked in." I shrugged like I hadn't had a standoff with a psycho in the woods.

James frowned, glaring into my soul, and I knew what he was thinking.

"Alone, outside, in the middle of the night, with everything going on? Are you a fucking moron?"

Why yes, James, it seems that way.

"I was fine. It was only for a second. Give me my food. I'm

going to bed." I snatched one of the bags from Cassie's hands and spun, not waiting for either of them to say anything else.

My legs were still shaking as I reached my bed. But even as the fear set in again, a faint spark of triumph flickered.

Connor is a pussy.

Pots, pans, and half-used ingredients crowded every surface, creating an overwhelming mess that seemed to pulse with Cassie's growing frustration. She stood near her stove, waving a spatula like a weapon of mass destruction. Her hair was pinned back from her face, a few loose strands sticking to her forehead.

James leaned against their fridge, arms crossed, eyes glinting as he watched her psyche unravel.

"It's impossible," she muttered, her jaw tight as she furiously stirred. "This kitchen is too damn small. We'd have so much more room if you hadn't sold the house. We could have used the space."

A wave of nausea threatened to rise. I forced out a laugh that sounded too brittle, begging it would mask how her comment had hit a nerve.

You couldn't pay me to go back there.

His face—furious, towering over me—flashed in my mind like a lightning strike. I felt his grip on my body, hand tracing my cheek, the remnants vivid enough to make my skin crawl. It wasn't a house; it was a prison—one I had barely escaped.

Cassie's eyes darted to me, her expression softening instantly, shifting as guilt crept in. "Kidding," she said, her tone quick and light like she was trying to reel the words back. "Fuck that place. And *fuck* Connor. But not literally, because, well...." Her lips twitched upward in a weak attempt at humor. "That's how we ended up in this whole stalking mess."

The corner of my mouth lifted, the barest shadow of a smile. A dry laugh escaped me before panic reared its ugly head. "When Eric gets here," I blurted, my voice tight, "no more stalker talk. No Connor talk. *None* of it."

Cassie waved her spatula in the air like a flag of surrender, her focus back on the stove. "Yeah, yeah, yeah. No ex-talk to the new beau. *I'm not an idiot.*"

My cheeks flared with heat, and I opened my mouth to protest, to argue against her calling Eric my 'beau,' but James caught my eye. He raised his eyebrows in a silent question, his expression halfway between teasing and genuine curiosity.

"Is she sure about that?"

Cassie spun around just in time to catch the look James gave me. "I saw that!" she exclaimed, lunging at him with the spatula.

James ducked as he sidestepped her. "Careful with that thing!"

"Eat shit!" Cassie shot back, chasing him in circles around the cramped kitchen.

"By the smell in here, I can tell I'm about to," James quipped, his grin widening as he dodged another swat.

The sharp sound of laughter erupted from all of us, shattering the tension and leaving it in pieces on the linoleum floor. I let myself relax briefly, the weight of the past few months lifting just enough to let me breathe.

A KNOCK CAME, PULLING ME FROM THE BATTLEFIELD THAT had become the kitchen. My heart lurched as I opened the door, the sight of Eric standing there. He was immaculate, as always, his dark hair slicked back, and those strong arms wrapped in a black leather jacket.

He held a foil-covered pan, his smile lazy as if he wasn't walking into a disaster.

"Viol—" He started, but his gaze shifted past me, brow furrowing as a thin plume of smoke wafted out into the hallway. The corners of his mouth turned down slightly, a flicker of concern crossing his face. "Is something on *fire?*"

I followed his line of sight and sighed. *Typical.* I ignored his question entirely, my focus zeroing in on the pan he carried. "You cook?" I asked, the words coming out more like an accusation than a question.

"A bit, ye—"

I grabbed his arm, cutting him off and tugging him inside with more force than necessary. My fingers brushed against the bare skin of his wrist, the warmth of it sending an unexpected jolt through me. I dropped his wrist quickly, the sensation lingering longer than it should have.

I gestured toward the kitchen, where Cassie and James were locked in yet another heated exchange over the turkey. "They are at war with the food," I explained, my voice hinting at exasperation. "None of us know what we're doing."

He followed me into the fray, eyes sweeping over the disaster area. Cassie stood at the stove, glaring at James as she brandished her spatula like a weapon. James, arms raised in surrender, looked like he was trying not to laugh.

"Eric brought... well, I don't know what it is," I announced, cutting through their bickering. "But he brought something, which means he can cook."

Both Cassie and James froze, their heads snapping toward Eric in unison. He paused, momentarily caught off guard, confident demeanor faltering as his eyes darted to mine. Uncertainty flickered across his face for a split second. He looked almost... nervous?

Oh, so he is human.

But as quickly as it appeared, it vanished. His smile slid back into place, and he nodded. "I can help."

James visibly relaxed, a grin spreading across his face, but Cassie narrowed her eyes, scanning Eric like she was trying to decide whether to give up the reins. The silence stretched as we all waited for her verdict.

Finally, she threw her hands up in surrender. "Fine," she muttered, stomping out of the kitchen. "I have to change anyway."

Eric stepped forward, his initial hesitance evaporating as his gaze sharpened. "Alright," he said, calm and focused. "What are we working with?"

James immediately launched into an explanation, gesturing at the various dishes. I couldn't fight the eyebrow raise at how easily James seemed to talk with Eric, like they had been friends for years, not mere acquaintances. Eric listened, his attention honing in on each detail with a quiet intensity that seemed to draw the room toward—or, at least, *me.*

His focus shifted toward me, a small smile tugging at the corner of his mouth, and something in my brain melted.

I managed a smile in return, silently mouthing a thank you. Ignoring the flutter in my stomach, I turned and walked down the hall.

I knocked on her bedroom door, pushing it open. "Cas?"

She sat on the floor, back pressed against the foot of her bed frame, knees pulled close to her chest. She sniffled, her head tilted down as she avoided my eyes. I stepped inside the room, closing the door behind me.

"Aw, Cas, come on," I said gently, trying to catch her eye. "It's not that big of a deal."

Her head shook slightly, and her voice cracked as she replied, "It is. I was trying to... it was supposed to be perfect."

I slid down beside her, nudging her shoulder with mine in a small attempt at comfort. "Nothing either of us does ever turns out perfect."

She didn't laugh. Her eyes, glassy with unshed tears, stared straight ahead. "Mom would have made it perfect."

A bittersweet ache bloomed in my chest, and I let out a dry laugh. "Hate to break it to you, but Mom burnt water, too."

That earned me a small, tentative smile. "Remember when she was dog-tired and microwaved a can of ravioli? It *exploded*."

Cassie's laugh was quiet but genuine. "We didn't have power for three days."

"Exactly." I leaned my head back against the bed frame. "So, as long as we don't blow anything up, we'll be alright."

She rested her head on my shoulder as I continued. "Today isn't about the food—I mean, it's kind of about the food. But it's more about being with the people that you give two fucks about."

She tilted her head, her blonde hair tickling my arm as she smirked up at me. "Aw, you give two fucks about me?"

"*Rarely*." I bumped her lightly. "Most of the time, it's just one."

She flicked my nose, her laughter bubbling up again, this time fuller. The mischievous gleam returned to her eyes as she grinned. "So, you give two fucks about Eric then, huh?"

I rolled my eyes, shrugging her head off my shoulder as I stood, extending a hand to help her up. "Uh-huh, sure."

Cassie took my hand, a self-satisfied smirk on her face. "At least you're admitting it now."

Shaking my head, I followed her out of the room. "I was being sarcastic!" I called after her.

I'd like to give him a lot more than two fucks.

"Regrettably *unsalvageable* turkey. But everything else seems alright." Eric placed a platter of deviled eggs on the table.

The aroma of roasted vegetables, buttery mashed potatoes, and paprika from the deviled eggs made my mouth water. Cassie, James, Kal, Kal's *new* boyfriend, Max, and I surrounded the portable table now draped in steaming food prepared by our devastatingly beautiful personal chef.

As Eric turned back toward the kitchen, Cassie's gaze trailed over him, her expression shifting to one of exaggerated appreciation. Her eyes were practically glued to his ass.

Catching my attention, she locked eyes with me and silently mouthed, "*You lucky bitch.*"

I rolled my eyes, a huff of amusement escaping as he returned carrying two glasses of water. He placed one in front of me before sitting down in the chair next to mine.

I glanced at his glass as he lifted it. My mind flashed to the moment last week when he'd casually drunk from my glass, his lips brushing the same spot mine had touched. The idea ignited a spark, making my skin prickle.

When Eric's gaze met mine, a smirk danced as though he knew exactly what I was thinking. My stomach flipped, and I quickly dropped my eyes to my plate.

The evening unfolded easily, the table slowly scattering with empty plates and wine glasses—a testament to the success of Eric's cooking. A rare calm settled over me as I leaned back in my chair, basking in the easy banter filling the room.

Laughter echoed, each note warming me from the inside out, Eric's laugh more than it should have—a deep, rich sound that resonated in places I wasn't going to think about.

Hecate save me, I would pay him to never stop making that sound.

It struck a chord in me, visceral and undeniable, like a song I'd heard in a dream. I glanced at him, his smile radiant, his eyes catching the light and holding it like fireflies in the dark.

"I guess this means you're one of us now," Cassie teased, grinning at Eric.

Kal jumped in, his tone playful. "Yeah, there's no way we're letting you go after the orgasm you just gave my taste buds."

Eric's smile widened, the white of his teeth flashing as he laughed. "James helped," he said, nodding toward him.

James waved a dismissive hand, leaning back in his chair. "Yeah, I cut the carrots."

"And preheated the oven," Eric added, a twinkle of humor in his eye. "Credit where it's due."

Laughter rippled around the table, filling the room with lightness. I joined in, though my focus stuck to Eric—his ease, humor, and how he seemed so engaged with everyone.

Connor would have hated this—loathed the chatter and laughter, made snide comments about my friends, and sulked through the evening—Eric was present, absorbing every word. His attention never wavered as though each shared memory mattered—it was intoxicating.

The corners of my mouth lifted of their own accord, the butterflies in my stomach fluttering with reckless abandon every time his hand brushed mine or he looked my way.

Cassie leaned forward, fixing him with a pointed look. "So, what are your intentions?"

The room fell quiet, the laughter fading like the last note of a song. My stomach knotted as everyone turned their attention to Eric. Even James perked up, his brow arching with interest.

Kal and Max exchanged uneasy glances, their discomfort palpable.

Eric titled his head, smile faltering just slightly. "Eating?" His voice cautious.

Cassie didn't back down. "With my sister."

Heat rushed to my face. "Cas," I warned. "I swear to everything holy and unholy—"

She cut me off with a smug grin. "Thanks, *Eric*," she said, dripping with sarcasm as she waved a hand for him to continue.

His gaze met mine briefly, a flicker of something unreadable passing between us. I wanted to sink to the floor—or, better yet, drag Cassie out by her hair.

Eric remained calm, expression smoothing as he turned back to her. "I enjoy spending time with her. And as I'm sure she's mentioned, we're friends."

The words struck harder than I thought they would, sinking like stones in my chest.

Friends.

I'd drawn that line myself but hearing him say it so easily definitely sent some kind of pang through me.

She leaned back, her lips pursed in thought. "Hm." She let

the silence linger for a beat, then added, "No objections to Vi dating then?"

I held my breath as her question hung. I couldn't stop myself from sneaking a glance at Eric.

"None whatsoever," he said with a shrug. His tone was steady, but the simplicity of his answer twisted something deep inside me, an unwelcome ache.

Part of me was hopeful that Cassie would finally drop the subject for good. Another part of me felt like it crumpled up and died.

I forced my face into a mask of indifference, locking away the sting of disappointment threatening to surface.

Reap what you sow.

Cassie eyed him skeptically, but after a moment, she sighed and shifted the conversation to lighter topics.

But I couldn't shake my irritation. It wasn't just her constant meddling that gnawed at me—it was Eric's nonchalance, his seeming indifference to the idea of me with someone else.

Abruptly, I pushed my chair back and stood. "I'll clear the table."

He rose almost immediately, collecting plates alongside me. We walked into the kitchen, footsteps soft behind.

At the sink, I focused on stacking the dishes. I refused to acknowledge his presence as my emotions swam beneath the concrete wall I was trying so desperately to keep up.

"You okay?" Eric's voice came softly, tinged with something bordering on concern.

I could feel him standing close—closer than he needed to be.

"I'm fine," I replied curtly, bracing both hands against the edge of the sink.

I'm just bitchy because you respected my decision to be friends.

"Agreed." He stepped closer, setting his dishes beside mine. His fingers brushed my wrist.

The spark shot through me, pooling low in my stomach with a maddening intensity.

Damn it. Damn it all to hell.

Fucking ravage me already.

KAL AND MAX BID THEIR GOODBYES, VOICES FADING DOWN the hallway outside Cassie and James's apartment as they headed toward the elevator. I lingered at the doorway, arms crossed loosely. My gaze flickered to Eric as he shrugged into his jacket, the simple movement sparking a nervous flutter in my chest. My heart raced, torn between the comfort of his nearness and the need to keep him as far away as I could.

Eric approached, his steps measured. "Do you want me to walk you to your car?"

I shook my head, tucking a stray strand of hair behind my ear. "I hitched a ride with James. I'm just waiting for him to be ready."

From the kitchen, James's voice carried. "I'll be done in about forty-five."

Eric's eyes shifted toward the kitchen before returning to me, his lips quirking. "I could give you a ride home," he offered.

My hesitation was brief. The idea of being alone with him was equally thrilling and terrifying. "Okay."

His smile deepened into that goddamn gorgeous, crooked grin, a flash of mischief lighting his face. "Lovely."

James, bent over the sink, waved us off with an indifferent nod. "I'll meet you there when I'm done."

The elevator ride was cloaked in silence. Each soft ding announcing the floors felt like a heartbeat echoing through the confined space. I glanced up at Eric, taking in the way he leaned against the wall, hands buried in his pockets, shoulders relaxed. His casualness only heightened the tension weaving its way around me.

I fixed my eyes on the elevator doors, the polished silver reflecting my faint outline. "Thanks for coming tonight," my voice cut through the quiet. "And saving everything."

Eric turned his head, jade eyes glinting under the harsh fluorescent lights. "You never have to thank me for anything."

His words were simple, yet they wrapped around me like an invisible tether, pulling me closer.

Friends.

Fuck that.

I don't want to be friends. I want to be everything *but* friends. Entirely consumed by this unholy mass of muscle and leather.

When we reached his car, Eric opened the passenger door of his classic Camaro with a fluid gesture that seemed as effortless as the man himself. The faint scent of leather and sandalwood greeted me as I slid into the seat.

The low rumble of music filled the space as we pulled onto the street. I recognized the band almost instantly. "I love Arankai," I said, my lips curving into a smile.

Eric's grin tilted mischievously as if he knew something I didn't. "Good taste." His voice smooth as the notes drifted through the speakers.

The drive felt too short, too charged. As he pulled into the concrete driveway of my apartment, I felt an ache of disappointment mingling with relief.

I wasn't ready to leave the delicious scent of cedar and sandalwood that followed Eric everywhere and return to the quiet of my apartment.

The soft glow of the porch light bathed us in a warm haze as we stood by the door. My pulse quickened as I turned to him, unable to stop the words from spilling out. "Did you mean what you said earlier?"

He tilted his head, thick brow arching. "About?"

"The dating thing," I clarified, feeling my cheeks burn as I fidgeted with the cuff of my sweatshirt.

"I rarely say things I don't mean," he replied, his voice low and steady, like a promise etched into the night.

The pit that formed in my stomach was immediate.

Of course, he was just being nice—feeling sorry for the broken, sad little cancer survivor.

Embarrassed, I stumbled over my words, trying to mask the sudden ache I felt. "Yeah, of course. I'm good with that, too. For you. For dating. Going on *alllll* the dates."

Eric chuckled softly, the sound both infuriating and intoxicating. He stepped closer, his eyes locking onto mine with an intensity that made my heart beat painfully against my rib cage. "Let me be *perfectly* clear," his voice dropped to a gravelly murmur that thrummed so low I felt it in my hoo-ha. "I have absolutely no qualms with you dating."

My heart sank, my disappointment flickering before I could mask it. I dropped my eyes, avoiding his piercing gaze. His hand came up, his thumb skimming my chin, tilting my face to look back at him.

"*Me.*" His green eyes burned into mine. "Never anyone else."

His thumb grazed my bottom lip, the touch igniting a shiver that rippled through me. My lips parted without a thought, the unspoken need inside me crackling like static. I bit down absently, and Eric's gaze darkened as he stared at the movement, a low growl rumbling from his chest.

Our faces were inches apart, the tension unbearable, the world narrowing to just the two of us.

Kiss me, goddamn it.

The moment teetered on the edge of—*Fuck.*

Headlights suddenly swept across the porch, breaking the spell.

I turned my head toward the source of the light, my chest heaving as I tried to regain my composure. Eric's hand fell away, and he straightened, expression carefully neutral as James's car pulled up beside mine and Eric's.

James climbed out, smiling at Eric as he joined us on the porch. Eric returned the smile with a single nod before flashing me that maddening crooked grin again and leaving.

I watched him disappear down the street, and I could have *killed* James for showing up when he did.

James's brows rose as he looked at me. I exhaled dramatically, waving a hand to swat away his silent questioning.

"Don't look at me like that," I muttered, my voice sharp despite the lingering heat between my legs.

James smirked, his low chuckle following me as we stepped inside. I felt my shoulders slump as the door clicked shut behind us. I could still feel the ghost of Eric's touch, the fire in his gaze.

What the fuck is wrong with me?

I would have let the man-God take me right there on the porch and not had a second thought about it. And then what?

"Pathetic."

"Nothing but a quick fuck."

"Who could love a thing like that?"

The venomous voices chased me to my room, their chant a

relentless fuel for the self-loathing. I locked the door behind me as I collapsed onto my bed.

I had too many men running rampant in my head to add another. And whether Eric wanted a quick fuck or not, he didn't deserve to deal with my darkness and insecurities and baggage for even a second. I could barely deal with it myself.

This, with him—whatever it was—I had to let it go.

"So, TELL ME AGAIN WHY YOU HAVEN'T TALKED TO SEX-ON-a-stick in four days?" Cassie's voice edged with curiosity as she sprawled on the couch, her feet dangling over the armrest. Her eyes were glued to her phone, thumb scrolling.

I sighed, leaning against the counter as I sipped a lukewarm cup of coffee. The bitter edge scraped against my tongue, but I didn't bother reheating it. "Because I need to get a handle on my shit before I go diving headfirst into... whatever Eric is. I can't go dragging him into all of this."

I'd been making every excuse under the sun to avoid The Coffee House, skipping my usual morning stops and brewing mediocre cups at home instead. The idea of running into him, seeing those green eyes light up when they found me, made my chest ache in a way I couldn't—or wouldn't—explain. I wanted to see him, felt the need, but I couldn't bring myself to.

It was bad enough that Cassie and James were smack dab in the war zone with me, but if Eric got caught in the middle? I wouldn't be able to forgive myself. Cassie and James refused to distance themselves, but at least I could keep Eric as far away from my mess as possible.

Cassie hummed noncommittally, her focus never leaving her screen. "I don't know. He doesn't exactly strike me as someone who's easily dragged. He's more the one... doing the dragging." Her thumb swiped up, her expression shifting between amused and intrigued.

"What are you doing?"

"I can't find any pictures of his ex on here," she replied without a shred of shame.

I pulled my lips into a thin line, staring into my coffee. "If they broke up, he probably deleted them." I set the cup down harder than necessary.

Careful, Vi, your jealousy is showing.

It was none of my business if he had dated someone or a bunch of someone's. It was none of my business if he was dating someone now. I didn't care, and it didn't matter.

Liar.

"Yeah, makes sense. I just wanted to see what his type was besides the obvious." Her gaze swept over me before returning to her phone.

Her words sent an involuntary flicker of warmth through me, reminding me of the almost-kiss on my front porch and how close I was to letting him take whatever he wanted before James—and reality—barged in.

That was as far as it could go. He was... well, *him*. Perfectly put-together, effortlessly charming, and so far out of my league it was almost laughable. But he was happy.

And then there was me. Still working on my shit and getting sucker punched with the unrelenting mayhem at every turn. He didn't need that. He needed someone who could handle themselves and their problems without shutting down, running away, or deflecting. He needed someone who didn't come with so many complications.

And complications seemed to be my middle name.

"Stop lurking," I snapped, crossing my arms as I glared at her.

She glanced up, a sly grin tugging there. "I'm doing the legwork for you."

I rolled my eyes. "With the way you're stalking him, it sounds like *you* want to fuck him."

"Oh, I would," she said without missing a beat, her voice dropping into a playful purr. She sat up, her grin widening like a cat eyeing its next meal. "I'd climb that man like a tree, but, alas, his sights are set on you."

Heat rose to my cheeks, and I turned away, pretending to refill my mug. "You're delusional," I grumbled.

She snorted, clearly enjoying my discomfort. "Says the one ignoring our very own Dr. McSteamy. Can you hurry up and fuck him already? Some of us are trying to live vicariously through you, ya' know."

I shot her a flat look over my shoulder, which only fueled her amusement.

She leaned back against the cushions. "Or just fuck *someone*. It doesn't have to be anything serious. Just get it out of your system. And then we can get back to hunting crazy man-boy."

"*You're not allowed to date just anyone*. You said that."

"I'm not talking about *dating*. I'm talking the beast with two backs, fornication, bumping—"

"Stop."

"*Seeeeexxxxx.*"

I didn't bother with a response, focusing instead on the swirl of coffee in my cup.

Cassie didn't get it. She couldn't. Getting close to anyone—serious or casual—felt like dangling them over an open flame. But that thought made me question if it was really for their sake or my own.

She tapped her phone against her knee, eyeing me. "You really should do something to relieve that tension. You have shit posture."

I straightened instinctively, glaring at her.

She cackled, the sound echoing off the walls. "See? Getting your back blown out will fix that."

"That makes zero sense."

"If you got laid correctly, you'd know exactly what I'm talking about."

A beat of silence stretched between us. I sent up a silent prayer, begging her to let it go though I knew it was all for not. Cassie didn't know what 'let it go' meant. Or she just ignored it all together. Either way, I would be tortured for the rest of my life. The only true escape would be if I ate a bullet. Even then, she would probably get a Ouija board and bug the shit out of me then, too.

Cassie leaned forward, her phone forgotten. "So, what's the plan for catching creepy stalker man-child ex."

"Something incredibly stupid," I admitted, settling against the counter. The cool surface pressed into my spine, keeping the growing anxiety at bay. "And it'll probably get me killed."

Her grin faltered, just for a moment, before it snapped back into place. "Well, at least you'll die interesting. I'll make sure your funeral has an open bar and good music. Not that churchy instrumental bullshit."

I narrowed my eyes at her before shrugging and giving her a single approving nod. "Appreciate it."

Her words lingered, settling heavily in my gut.

This story most likely ended with my death.

And a part of me... felt okay with that.

"THIS IS FUCKING INSANE. YOU'RE FUCKING INSANE." Cassie frowned, her nose wrinkling as I handed her cell phone back to her. She held it up gingerly like it might detonate in her hands at any second.

I shrugged, brushing past her concern with a forced air of calm. "I don't see you throwing out any bright ideas and this is just worst-case scenario," I said, my voice firmer than I felt as I tapped on my phone screen a few times. The words tasted hollow, but I couldn't let myself falter now.

Her lips parted, ready to argue, but James stepped into the doorway before she could speak. "We're all set," he said, though his tone was edged with hesitation. "But I agree this is fucking insane."

"Yeah, yeah. We established that." I waved him off, my patience fraying at the edges. "Now get out."

He crossed his arms and leaned against the door frame, his hazel eyes narrowing as he stared me down. "What? We are not leaving you to fend off a psycho—"

"He didn't show up during Thanksgiving," I interrupted, my voice sharp enough to cut through his objections. My pulse quickened, but I didn't let it show. "My guess? He's watching, he knows you guys are here, and he won't come out of his creepy little hide-a-hole and show his face unless I'm alone."

Cassie lowered the phone slowly, her expression softening into something between frustration and fear. "I'm not okay with this, not in the least."

"No one here is *okay* with it," I admitted, my shoulders tensing as I shifted my weight. "But we don't have a lot of options. And I'm *tired* of being afraid."

The words settled over the room like a shroud. James straightened, tugging at the collar of his shirt as he paced a few steps. His jaw clenched as he looked from me to Cassie.

Cassie crossed her arms over her chest, nails tapping against her lean bicep. "This feels reckless, Vi. What if—"

I held up a hand to stop her. "If it doesn't work, we'll figure something else out." It was a lie. A *necessary* one, but a lie all the same.

If it didn't work, I'd probably be dead. If it did work, I'd still probably be dead. But Cassie needed me to say everything would be okay, even if we all knew that would likely not be the outcome.

The silence between us deepened the weight of their worry making the space thick, and my guilt crept in. My knuckles whitened as I tightened my grip on my phone, and I stared at the glowing screen in my hand.

I let out a shaking breath, forcing my thoughts to settle. *This had to work.* I was done with the endless cycle of fear and helplessness. Done with hiding. Done with feeling like my every move was dictated by a shadow lurking just out of reach.

But even as I resolved to move forward, my mind conjured green eyes and a crooked smile that consistently threatened to undo me at every turn. I clenched my jaw, shoving the image aside. There was no room for distraction—not now.

If he knew what was best for him, he'd get the hell out of dodge and as far from me as he could.

The house was dark and unnervingly still, the kind of silence that pressed in like a weight, wrapping around my chest and squeezing. I sat on the edge of my bed, my back rigid, gripping my phone like a lifeline. The glow of the screen illuminated my face. My fingers moved mechanically, cycling through the camera feeds: front porch, back porch, driveway, living room, kitchen, bedroom.

Nothing.

Every screen showed the same empty stillness, the kind that felt more sinister with each passing second. My muscles burned from the tension coiled in my body, but I didn't dare to relax. My eyes flicked to the windows, only to snap back to the phone. It had to seem like I was sleeping—vulnerable, alone.

> Me: Nothing yet. Just sitting tight.

> Cassie: This is the stupidest idea you've ever had. Can we come back? This is scaring the shit out of me.

> James: I still don't like it.

> Me: 😳

Their messages made my heart twist, but I forced myself to ignore the comfort they offered. Their concern only strengthened my resolve. I wanted this done. *Over.* Whatever the outcome.

Hours bled together, stretching long and thin. My legs ached from sitting too long with them underneath me. I eased myself back, stretching out stiff muscles as I propped myself up with pillows. The feed remained still, every flicker of static on the screen a cruel trick. The house around me felt alive, the oppressive quiet amplifying every creak, every distant groan of old wood.

My eyes burned from staring too long at the screen, but I didn't dare look away—no matter how exhausted I was. If I missed something....

The sharp buzz of my phone shattered the silence, and I jolted upright, heart hammering. The camera alarm blared, the shrill sound clawing at my nerves as the screen flashed:

BACK PORCH MOTION DETECTED.

My hands trembled as I fumbled to open the feed, my breaths coming in shallow gasps. The screen loaded, revealing—

A *raccoon.*

Its striped tail bobbed as it darted across the clearing, its tiny frame disappearing into the night.

Relief hit me like a wave, my body sagging against the bed. "Damn, raccoon," I muttered under my breath, running a hand through my tangled hair. My pulse still thundered in my ears as I pushed myself to my feet, muscles stiff and uncooperative.

The coffee maker gurgled in the kitchen. I leaned heavily against the counter, phone balanced in my hand as I stared at the group chat. My thumb hovered over the keyboard, debating whether to tell them I was calling it a night.

The faint gray light of dawn had begun creeping over the horizon, softening the edges of the darkness. He wasn't going to show.

Just as I started typing, the alarm blared again.

My phone slipped from my hand, clattering against the counter before I caught it. My blood turned to ice, every hair on my body standing on end.

BACK PORCH MOTION DETECTED.

The feed loaded so fucking slowly, the seconds dragging like hours. My breath hitched as the screen lit up, and this time, it wasn't empty or a raccoon.

He was there.

Dressed in black from head to toe, he stood just beyond the door, the hood of his sweatshirt drawn low. A balaclava obscured his face, leaving only his eyes visible—two dark, unblinking voids fixed on the camera.

I couldn't breathe. My chest tightened painfully as he leaned forward, his gloved hand reaching out with deliberate slowness. He waved, his fingers curling in a mocking parody of friendliness like he knew I was there, watching.

My breath came in rapid bursts as I staggered back a step, my phone shaking in my grip. I'd prepared myself for hazel eyes—ones I thought I'd be ready to see—but these were not the eyes staring back at me.

He tilted his head, the gesture almost playful, as if he could see me through the lens. His eyes narrowed, calculating, and then, with agonizing slowness, he lifted a hand to his covered mouth and blew a kiss directly at the camera.

A stifled gasp escaped me, and I pressed my hand to my mouth to silence it. My knees threatened to buckle, the cold tile beneath my feet doing little to ground me.

Reaching into his pocket, he pulled out a small slip of paper. His movements were measured, calm, as though he had all the time in the world. Without hesitation, he tucked it behind the camera, his fingers lingering on the edge of the lens. Then, without a backward glance, he melted away, disappearing as quickly as he had come.

The house felt colder, the walls closing around me as I stood frozen, my body unable to move. My phone vibrated in my hand, the camera feed showing nothing but the empty clearing.

The oppressive silence returned, louder than ever, ringing in my ears. My heart hammered against my ribs as if trying to escape. I didn't move. I couldn't.

The only sound was the faint whirl of the coffee maker, its cheery gurgle at odds with the suffocating dread clawing at my chest.

At least I didn't run.

You can't keep me out

The scratched letters taunted me.

My fingers trembled as I held the note, its weight far heavier than the flimsy paper should have been. The stark black ink seemed to bleed into my skin, a grotesque reminder of the man who stood outside my home, watching, waiting.

Cassie stood nearby, her arms crossed so tightly over her chest it looked like she was trying to stop herself from unraveling. Her jaw was set, blonde hair framing her face flushed with frustration—and something else she was trying to mask. *Fear.* "Okay, so we can go to the police now," she said, her voice decisive, though it cracked just slightly at the end.

James leaned forward, his eyes flicked from the words to the recorded footage on my phone, his mouth pressed into a grim line. "You can't see his face. That's *not* enough. And he was wearing gloves—there's no way he didn't wear them while writing this. They'll set up a patrol, but not much else."

I shifted my gaze to James, studying the hard line of his jaw.

Guilt crept into my bones at the physical manifestation of his stress.

They had both been put through the wringer and here I was, adding to it. They deserved better.

My eyes flicked back to the screen. My voice surprised me with its steadiness, though my insides churned. "But look at the eyes. Tell me those aren't brown. Those *aren't* Connor's."

Cassie snorted, but the sound lacked conviction. Her fingers drummed against her bicep, her restless movements betraying her unease. "I didn't spend hours on end staring into the freak's eyes, so I couldn't tell you if they were brown or blue or blood red. But the lightning could have made them look brown."

James straightened abruptly, his eyes sparking with an idea. "Let's test it," he said, his voice brisk.

James strode to the back door where the camera was mounted.

Cassie cocked an eyebrow, her skepticism barely masking her concern. "J, what the hell are you doing?"

"Seeing if she's right," he said, his voice slightly muffled through the cracked door.

I glanced down at the live feed. Cassie moved closer, her shoulder touching mine as we both stared at the screen. The image of James's face filled the frame, his amber eyes distinct even in the grainy footage.

I gestured at the phone. "See? Not Connor. Whoever was here—not him."

James pushed the door shut behind him as he stepped back into the kitchen. His brows drawn together as though he was trying to solve a puzzle that refused to fit. "I still maintain he could've hired someone."

Cassie let out a quick laugh, though it lacked her usual bite, like it might shatter under its own weight. "So, what? Now we start suspecting everyone?" She threw her hands up.

James and I exchanged a look, the unspoken agreement between us clear. Our voices overlapped. "Yep."

Cassie rolled her eyes. "Paranoia it is."

The three of us stood in the kitchen, the note still lying on the counter, a threat etched in ink. It felt like even the house itself was holding its breath.

Lights buzzed overhead, beating down and worming their way into my skull as I stared at the endless rows of cereal boxes. My shopping list sat crumpled in my pocket. I couldn't focus long enough to remember if I even needed cereal, but I grabbed a box anyway, the plastic bag inside crinkling as it landed in the cart with a thud.

I pushed the cart forward, the uneven squeak of the wheels grating on my nerves like nails on a chalkboard.

Just a regular grocery store trip.

Just another chore.

Everything around me felt infuriatingly normal, but my skin prickled, every nerve alight as though I were being watched.

A man stood at the end of the aisle. Hood pulled up, shadowing his face. He shuffled closer to the edge, hesitating long enough to draw my attention. My stomach tightened.

Stop. You're being stupid. It's broad daylight.

I tore my eyes away, the rational part of me trying to regain control and turned down the next aisle. My focus flitted from shelf to shelf, but the bright packaging blurred together, meaningless. I reached for a can of soup before my eyes caught a flash of the hoodie again.

People get abducted in broad daylight all the time.

This time, they didn't even pause. They just walked past the aisle. It felt intentional as if they were looking for something.

Or someone.

My chest felt tight, and I forced myself to breathe, but the air seemed too thin. Clammy and trembling, my fingers wrapped around the cart handle.

It's nothing. It's nothing.

I moved faster, the wheels squeaking louder with each hurried step, but the unease coiled tighter around my ribs, squeezing every time I told myself to stop overreacting. When I reached checkout, the cheerful beeping of the scanner drilled into my brain—too sharp, too loud. Each sound made me flinch, my patience fraying.

Once the groceries were loaded in the trunk, I slid into the driver's seat, locking the doors. The car engine purred to life, but the parking lot was quiet. My heart thundered in my chest, and despite the empty spaces around me, I couldn't shake the feeling of eyes on me.

The drive home should have settled me, but halfway there, a car appeared in my rearview mirror. It was an ordinary SUV that blended into traffic without a second thought, but it had been behind me for too long.

Plenty of people go this way. Stop being ridiculous.

Even as I repeated the words in my head, my body rebelled, tension seeping into my muscles. My knuckles whitened around the steering wheel. When I turned left, the sedan turned, too. Another right, another left—it mirrored me at every turn.

My palms slicked with sweat, and my breaths became

faster, shallower. Each random street I chose only seemed to lead them closer, and the panic clawed through me and up my throat.

I wanted to scream.

Where could I go? The police station. That would at least get them to back off.

Their blinker flicked on. They slowed, turning into a driveway without hesitation.

The realization hit so fast it made my head spin. I wasn't being followed. They weren't watching me. They were just going home.

I stared at the sedan parked neatly in the driveway as it faded in my rearview mirror, heat rising in a wave of embarrassment and frustration. I gripped the steering wheel, the tremble in my hands now fueled by anger instead of fear.

How the hell was I supposed to handle this when it really happened? I'd already unraveled over a fucking minivan.

Hot tears threatened to sting my eyes. I was supposed to stay calm, to be prepared. Instead, I was breaking apart at the seams.

I turned back toward my street. The rational part of me knew I'd overreacted, but the rest of me—the part that hadn't slept properly in weeks—clung to the unease, refusing to let go.

Much to my delight, the restaurant smelled of sizzling burgers and freshly brewed coffee. Avoiding my regular coffee shop routine had its consequences, and I was dying for a non-home-brewed cup. Cassie threw the door open with dramatic flair as if we were about to step onto a stage instead of scuffing across a linoleum floor. Her hair bounced with each step, drawing attention like she always seemed to do without trying.

I trailed behind her, regretting every moment of letting her talk me into this outing. My mood had been too raw to face the world, but Cassie insisted I needed a break from the *How to Catch a Stalker* TV show that had quickly become my life. The hostess smiled at us, menus in hand, but before we could follow her to a table, Cassie froze mid-step.

Her nails dug into my arm. "Oh my god," she whispered, her voice brimming with excitement.

"What?" I muttered, following her wide-eyed gaze.

At a corner booth, hunched over his phone, sat the blonde vigilante from the bowling alley. He glanced up, recognition dawning in his eyes as Cassie waved like a woman flagging down a lifeboat.

"Hey!"

I groaned, wishing I could shrink into my sweater. "*Really,* Cas?"

But she was already tugging me toward him, her smile wide and her enthusiasm impossible to contain. He looked up fully now, his grin splitting across his face like we were old friends instead of complete strangers.

"Bowling alley!" he greeted, standing as we approached.

"Blonde vigilante," I said, keeping my tone polite but flat.

"Logan, but that works too."

Cassie elbowed me before flashing Logan her signature bright smile. "What are you doing here all alone? Come eat with us!" she chirped.

"Cas—" I started, but she shot me a quick glare, daring me to argue.

Logan hesitated before nodding. "Sure, why not? Better than eating alone."

He grabbed his drink and slid out of the booth, following us to a new table. She practically skipped into her seat beside me, leaving Logan to sit across from us.

"Kismet," she declared as she opened her menu, her eyes twinkling.

I forced a tight smile and glanced at Logan, who was now looking at me with a self-assured grin. I fought back an eye roll.

Just what I need.

Chatter and the clinking of silverware droned, but all I could hear was his booming voice. He dove into a story about his latest hiking trip, hands gesturing wildly as he described some impossible peak.

Cassie ate it up. Her head propped on her hands, face alight with fascination as she chimed in with her usual brand of over-the-top enthusiasm. "That's insane! You climbed all of that in one day?"

He leaned back. "Yup. Wasn't easy, but I'm not one to back down from a challenge."

I sipped my coffee, masking my disinterest with polite nods. My jaw ached from holding a fixed smile.

The conversation became a showcase for his accomplishments, each story louder and more exaggerated than the last. Cassie egged him on, chiming in wide-eyed and amazed at all the right moments, nudging me when my smile faltered.

My mind wandered to Eric—his deep, teasing voice. The way those eyes seemed to hold a secret just for me.

Stop comparing. Let it go.

Logan launched into another story about his gym routine, gesturing animatedly with his hands. I nodded when appropriate, added a "wow" here and there, and mentally counted the minutes until I could escape.

His voice droned on, a deep rumble that lacked the warmth or charm I realized I craved. Eric's voice had that smooth edge, that teasing lilt that sent shivers down my spine. Logan's voice was just noise.

"...So, what about you?" Logan's question yanked me back into the present. His brown eyes locked onto mine.

I blinked, my grip tightening on my coffee mug. "Sorry, what?"

He chuckled, mistaking my disinterest for coyness. "What do *you* like to do? For fun?"

Avoid situations like this, for starters.

And green-eyed Man-Gods that could ruin me with a glance.

I cleared my throat. "Bowling. Movies. Normal stuff, I guess."

"We should go together sometime," he said, flashing another grin. "I'm pretty good with a ball."

I could not give a shit less.

I didn't bother to fake enthusiasm. "Maybe." I busied myself with a napkin, folding and unfolding it as my foot bounced under the table.

I glanced at the clock on my phone. Two hours. Two whole goddamn hours of this

Cassie, noticing my disinterest, leaned into me with a conspiratorial whisper, "Even stressed, stalked bitches need to get laid." She nudged me playfully.

I shot her a glare, but she only giggled, her mischievousness unrelenting.

By the time the check came, my patience had frayed to a thin thread. Logan showed no signs of slowing down, and Cassie wasn't helping. She winked at me as he went on, her expression practically screaming, *"You need this."*

Yeah, like I need a lobotomy.

Cassie excused herself to the bathroom. "I'll be right back." She shot me a look that clearly meant, *'Don't fuck this up.'*

Logan insisted on paying, and I didn't bother arguing. As he and I stepped outside into the crisp night air that hit like a blessing, I made a beeline for my car. Determined to wait for Cassie behind the locked door of the vehicle that would—if there was a god—give Logan the hint to shut the fuck up.

"So, tonight was fun," he said, catching up to me.

"Sure," I replied, reaching into my bag for my keys.

Before I could process his movement, he leaned in. His lips pressed against mine—soft but utterly devoid of any spark. My body stiffened as his mouth moved awkwardly over mine, my eyes wide open, staring at the parking lot lights above us.

What. The. Fuck.

The moment stretched unbearably long before he finally pulled back, grinning like he'd just won a prize.

"That was nice, huh?"

I gaped at him, fumbling for words.

"There you two are!" Cassie called, her steps quick as she approached, hands rubbing her biceps to keep warm. "What'd I miss?"

Relief flooded me, and I stepped away from Logan. "Nothing. Just saying goodbye."

Cassie's eyes darted between us, her lips twitching with barely concealed amusement. "Goodbye, huh? Looked a little more exciting than that."

I shot her a sharp look, my cheeks burning. "Let's go."

She looped her arm through mine, casting Logan a wink. "Nice seeing you again! Don't be a stranger!"

I felt his gaze on my back as we walked to the car. She waited until we were safely inside before bursting into laughter.

"Well, that was something," she teased, clutching her stomach.

I groaned, gripping the steering wheel tighter than necessary and resting my forehead against it. "Never again."

Her laughter only grew, but I couldn't bring myself to join in. The thought of Logan's kiss faded quickly, replaced by a lingering, frustrating ache for something—or someone—else entirely.

THE APARTMENT DOOR HAD BARELY CLICKED SHUT BEHIND

me before James's voice drifted down the hallway, laced with confusion and weariness. "Why are you guys yelling?"

I kicked off my shoes with more force than necessary, the sharp thunk echoing down the hallway. My glare snapped to Cassie like a whip. "Because *someone* doesn't know how to keep her nose out of my business and stop meddling in my love life!"

She threw her hands up in dramatic surrender, her bracelets clinking as her eyes rolled. "*I'm sorry,* I was trying to give you a little fun amidst the fucking *TMZ special* that has become our lives. I thought a distraction would be nice!"

"He thought it was a date! A *date,* Cassie!" I spun to James, who was now leaning against the kitchen doorway, eyebrows raised in what looked like equal parts amusement and dread. My arms flailed as I struggled to contain my rising frustration. "She made me spend hours listening to some guy drone on and on about himself, basically doing a mating dance in the restaurant!"

James raised a hand like he was about to play referee. "Cas—"

"What?" She cut him off, her tone sharp and defensive. "I was trying to help! She's busy concocting plans that are going to get her killed, and you're putting up cameras! I'm just trying to keep some semblance of normalcy in her life!"

I let out a humorless laugh and jabbed a finger in her direction. "Why don't you worry about your own vagina instead of constantly trying to fill mine?"

She snorted—then burst into full-blown laughter, doubling over as if I'd just delivered the punchline of the century. "One, that's incest. Two, my *vajeen* is very well taken care of, thank *you.*"

Something flickered between her and James—a glance that lasted just a second too long. My eyes narrowed, suspicion prickling at the back of my mind as they both looked away almost in unison, their movements too quick, too rehearsed.

Cassie was the first to recover, her smirk resurfacing as if she hadn't just been caught. "Which is why I'm *not* a massive ball of stress. Unlike our favorite little emotionally constipated gremlin."

"I am handling everything just fine!" I snapped. My fists clenched at my sides as I stomped toward my bedroom. "Leave me *and* my vagina alone!" I hurled over my shoulder before slamming the door shut hard enough to rattle the hinges.

I collapsed on my bed. Arms crossed over my chest as if I could physically contain the annoyance. The muffled sounds of the apartment hummed outside my door, but I blocked them out, stewing in the mix of frustration and exhaustion curling in my gut.

Minutes later, a soft knock broke through the quiet. I didn't bother answering before the door creaked open, revealing Cassie's sheepish face. She held up two cups of steaming hot cocoa like peace offerings, her smile cautious but endearing. "Olive branch?"

I sighed, pushing up on my elbows. "I hate you."

She took that as an invitation, slipping inside and nudging the door closed with her hip. "Yeah, but you're stuck with me."

"How unfortunate."

She handed me a cup and plopped down on the bed beside me, careful not to spill. The rich aroma of chocolate and cinnamon filled the room, melting some of my lingering irritation.

We sat in silence for a moment, sipping the warm drinks. The heat seeped into my hands. Finally, I reached for my laptop on the nightstand. "Want to watch something?"

She grinned. "Always."

I pulled up The X-Files. The opening credits barely began

to roll when she nudged me with her elbow. "So...he kissed you."

I groaned, setting my mug aside. "Yeah. I was there."

"And you...."

"Hated it," I admitted, my eyes glued to the screen as though it could shield me from her probing sapphires.

She tilted her head, expression too knowing for my liking. "Would you have hated it if it was Eric?"

My jaw tightened. "What does that matter?" I shot back, my voice more defensive than I intended. "Why are we even talking about this? Can't we just have a single moment where we don't talk about stalkers, guys, or the state of my vagina? I *just* want to watch this movie."

She rolled her eyes, her smirk softening. "You've seen this movie a hundred times."

"Because I like it," I said, waving a hand at the screen.

Cassie wasn't deterred. "Answer the question."

I snapped the laptop shut with a groan. "Why? So, you can rub it in my face that I like someone? Fine. No, I wouldn't have been mad if it was Eric. Happy?"

Her grin widened, her expression positively gleeful. "Immensely."

I tugged the drawstrings of my hoodie, pulling the fabric over my face as I flopped back against the pillows. "You're the worst."

She leaned back beside me. "Why is it such a bad thing to like him?"

Her question hung in the air, heavy and unavoidable. I grumbled from beneath the hood, "Because."

"Because...?"

"Because look at him and then look at me! It doesn't make sense."

She nudged me again. "Shut up."

I waved her off, my hand limp. "What sane person would want to be with me? With everything I have going on? He's probably just trying to feed some morbid curiosity of fucking one of his patients."

Her smile faltered, replaced by a quiet intensity. "Those sound a lot like Connor's words."

"And what if he was right?"

Cassie set her mug down, turning to face me fully. "Dipshit has never been right in the history of anything he's ever said or done. He's a piece of shit who said whatever he could to make you small and keep you under his thumb."

I didn't respond, chewing on her words in the uncomfortable silence.

"What happened to not running? Not letting him win? This—" She gestured to me. "—is you letting him win. So what if you've got a lot of shit going on? Who doesn't? You may have left Connor, but he's still controlling you—controlling who you let yourself see, how you see yourself."

She took a breath, her smirk returning as she added, "And I highly doubt Eric is hanging around just to get his dick wet. I mean, that's probably part of it, but he seems... invested."

I glared at her from under my hood.

"So, Vi," she said, her tone laced with affection, "with love —if you *don't* get your head out of your ass and stop ignoring tall-dark-and-fuckable, I *am* going to beat the ever-loving shit out of you."

A reluctant laugh shot out, and I shook my head. "You're ridiculous."

"Well, you're a stick in the motherfuckin' mud."

A LIGHT DUSTING OF SNOW CRUNCHED BENEATH MY BOOTS, the sound mingling with the frosty puff of each breath. Even with my hands jammed deep into my pockets, my fingers felt like icicles.

"It's too cold for this," I muttered, my voice muffled by the scarf wrapped tightly around my neck. The petulance in my tone didn't escape me, but I was too miserable to care.

The cold weather aesthetic? Great. Snow? Magical. My toes on the verge of falling off—*not stellar.*

Eric glanced back, his honey-colored cheeks tinged pink from the crisp air. His maddeningly serene expression, glinting green eyes, and that damn dimple etched deeper as he grinned. "You're the one who said you wanted to get out of the house."

I glared at him, though I doubted it had much effect. "I meant coffee, not hiking this frozen hellscape."

"This way, I get you all to myself," he countered, grin widening into a wink that sent a traitorous flutter through my stomach. He slowed, motioning to the trees ahead. "Come on. I want to show you something."

The crunch of snow softened as we veered off the main trail, weaving through the dense forest. Towering trunks shielded us from the worst of the wind, and the bitter edge of my irritation dulled, replaced by reluctant curiosity. Eric strode ahead with effortless grace, his broad shoulders cutting through the broken sunlight spilling through the branches.

I, on the other hand, stumbled over every hidden root and fallen branch my feet could find. Each misstep burned my cheeks, especially when Eric reached back to steady me. His hands always lingered for just a moment too long, his touch igniting a frustrating, delicious warmth that the cold couldn't compete with.

The trees opened, and we stepped into the clearing. The cliff's edge overlooked a sprawling valley, every tree below blanketed in a pristine layer of snow. The setting sun painted the horizon in fiery gold, amber, and crimson hues, each shade bleeding seamlessly into the next. Its light scattered across the snowy landscape like molten glass.

It was breathtaking. Beauty that silenced everything else.

The same way Eric did.

An ache I couldn't quite name filled me. "Holy shit...."

Eric turned to me, the golden light catching the sharp angles of his face, softening his features into something even more devastatingly perfect. His eyes held mine. "Worth the cold?"

I nodded, unable to speak. Seeing him against the painted horizon burned itself into my memory.

We stood there in a silence too delicate to disturb. The moment stretched, heavy with unspoken words, until the thoughts pounding on my brain demanded to be free.

"I've been avoiding you," I admitted, my voice barely audible over the soft rustle of the wind through the trees.

He gave a soft smile. "I know."

"I'm sorry," I murmured, guilt threading through each word.

He shook his head, gaze softening, piercing through the walls I always tried—and failed—to keep up around him. "You don't have to apologize, Violet. You've got a lot going on." His tone was calm, reassuring—too understanding.

You have no idea.

"You're allowed to take time for yourself," he continued, voice dipping. He hesitated, his eyes briefly dropping to the snow before returning to mine. "But I'll admit... I was worried I pushed you too far after dinner."

I swallowed hard, the weight of my guilt doubling. "It wasn't that—or you. I just...." My words faltered, and I looked away, unable to meet his gaze. "I'm worried about dragging you into all of my bullshit."

He stepped closer. The warmth of his presence enveloped me. His fingers ghosted over mine—hesitant, testing—before lifting to tuck a loose strand of hair behind my ear. His fingers feather-light, my breath hitching at the electric jolt his touch sent racing down my spine.

"I'd let you drag me to hell if you asked," he said, his voice low and rough and so full of conviction it stole my breath. Heat spiraled through my chest, settling low in my stomach and curling my toes.

A laugh burst out—too loud, too awkward—fracturing the fragile tension. "I actually might...." I trailed off. "Cassie wants us all to go to this Christmas pub crawl thing tonight. I can come up with an excuse...."

His grin returned. "Why would I miss that? I'd love to go."

I blinked. "You would?"

"Absolutely." His hand dropped to his side, leaving my skin tingling in its absence. "Drunk holiday chaos? Sounds like my kind of night."

"You might be insane," I muttered, shaking my head to hide the involuntary smile that made its way out.

He shrugged, the gold in his eyes catching the last light of the setting sun. "For you? Always."

I turned back toward the valley, pretending to study the view. But the heat crawling up my neck was impossible to ignore. Eric fell silent, his eyes lingering on me as twilight crept across the horizon.

And a selfish part of me begged to let him in.

THE WIND TORE THROUGH MY SWEATER LIKE IT HAD A personal vendetta. I rubbed my hands together, desperate for any kind of heat, but the friction was laughably inadequate. My fingers felt stiff, useless. The line to the bar was endless, each second feeling like a deliberate punishment.

Cassie stood a few steps ahead, somehow grinning through the misery.

"You know," I shuffled from one numb foot to the other, "we could just make drinks at home. Where it's warm. And *civilized.*"

She didn't even glance back. "It's for the experience!" she called over her shoulder, like freezing to death was a badge of honor.

"Losing my extremities isn't exactly on my bucket list," I shot back, my teeth chattering.

From near the front of the line, Kal turned to shout over the wind, his laughter booming. "Come on, Vi. You've gotta suffer for the memories. It's the rule."

I rolled my eyes and resumed my futile attempt to regain

feeling in my toes, bouncing in place. A low, velvety chuckle drifted from behind me. My head turned almost instinctively.

Eric leaned casually against the exterior wall of the bar with his hands tucked into his jacket pockets, looking like the cold didn't dare touch him. His dark hair was tousled just enough to make my mouth water, the flashing neon sign from the bar reflecting in the deep green of his eyes. Those eyes met mine, filled with a teasing warmth more potent than any heater could manage.

I shoved my hands deeper into my sweater pockets, masking the idea of how those eyes would look from between my legs. A gentle touch at my elbow startled me, gliding down my arm before depositing something soft into my pocket. My fingers closed around it—a small, heated hand warmer.

I looked back at him. His lips curled into that infuriatingly perfect half-smile.

"Thanks," I murmured, quiet enough that no one else would hear.

He dipped his head, his gaze holding mine just long enough to make my stomach do a somersault before looking away.

The line finally began moving, and stepping into the bar was like falling into a furnace. Heat rushed over me, thick with the tang of cigarettes and sweat mixed with the thrum of too-loud music. Cassie bolted ahead, weaving through the crowd with single-minded determination to claim a table.

I peeled off my coat and sank into the seat she had secured. The table was barely big enough for all of us, the glasses clinking as the first round of ridiculous Christmas-themed cocktails arrived. I sipped mine, hiding my amusement as James grimaced at his drink, a concoction the color of radioactive tinsel.

The night blurred into laughter, clinking glasses, and sporadic bursts of cheesy holiday songs. Eric stayed close, always within reach, always nudging food and water my way. Every brush of his hand against mine, every accidental graze of his knee beneath the table, the contact searing despite the layers of denim.

I told myself it was nothing, a series of coincidences. But every glance he sent my way, those burning eyes—made that lie harder to believe.

Cassie was right. It did look like he wanted to eat me.

By the time we reached Tumbleweeds, our usual haunt, it felt like coming home—if home had sticky floors and smelt like sex.

"...and he was so obsessed with Vi." Cassie's voice cut through the noise, her tone dripping with mischief. "It was *actually* kind of cute, the way he was shamelessly flirting with her. Poor guy."

Her words hit me like a bucket of ice water. I'd been mid-glance at Eric—again—and now I couldn't decide whether to glare at her or crawl under the table. Eric's attention snapped to Cassie, his easygoing posture stiffening, and the heat of my cheeks rivaled the fire of her grin.

"Who?" His voice was calm, but a sharp edge was beneath the surface.

"Oh, just some guy we met a while ago," Cassie replied breezily, waving a hand like it was a passing thought, though her sly grin betrayed her. "We grabbed some food, and he talked to Vi for hours."

"He talked *at* me for hours," I corrected, cringing at the memory of Logan's one-man Broadway show.

"And then I witnessed the most awkward lip-lock in the history of ever," she added, her grin as wicked as her delight.

I caught the faintest tick of Eric's jaw from the corner of my eye. His lips turned into a polite smile. It was subtle, controlled, but something dark flickered in his expression. Jealousy?

Anger? Whatever it was, he buried it almost immediately, leaning back into his chair like the conversation hadn't affected him.

My core almost sang at the idea of Eric being jealous, though he had no reason to be. No one held a candle to him, least of all Logan.

Connor would have reacted differently. He would have plastered on a tight-lipped smile, made some flimsy excuse, and dragged me out of the bar. The fight would have been inevitable, his fury simmering beneath a mask of control. And I would spend *months* apologizing for something I didn't ask for or even want.

But Eric wasn't Connor. He wasn't shooting silent daggers at me or painfully squeezing my leg under the table. He was smiling and laughing and teasing James and Max for babysitting their drinks.

Eric's fingers brushed mine under the table—a barely-there touch, but it felt almost... reassuring, *grounding*, like he knew exactly where my thoughts had gone.

I relaxed my shoulders, unaware of how tight they had wound, and felt the invisible weight lift from my body.

Cassie, seemingly satisfied with whatever she saw cross Eric's face, leapt to her feet, dragging Kal, Max, and James with her. "This is my song!" She glanced at me expectantly.

I shook my head. "I'm good here."

She frowned, narrowing her eyes. "Stick-in-the-mud." She tapped her index finger to my forehead with each syllable.

I swatted her hand away, shooing her off. She stuck out her tongue, turning and leading the others to the dance floor.

Eric stood, extending a hand. "Come on. One dance and then back to brooding."

I hesitated before slipping my hand into his. His palm was warm, his fingers curling around mine in a way that felt too intimate. Everything about this man felt too intimate, but something about me craved it.

The music was loud, lively. The kind that you couldn't help but smile to. Cassie twirled me into her orbit, her laugh radiant. For a moment, I felt like my old self, the version of me that wasn't so tightly wound. I felt light, free, as my feet danced along the floor. Laughter left my lips as we all huddled together, jumping and throwing our hands in the air as we shouted the words to every song.

A bead of sweat dripped down my temple as the tempo changed. A sensual beat thrummed through the air. Max and Kal roamed their hands over each other as their bodies moved to the music. Cassie's grin widened as she spun me again, straight into Eric.

I stumbled, and my hands landed, splaying against his chest. Solid muscle met my fingertips as his arm caught me, his hand pressing low against my back.

The room seemed to melt away. Pulsing lights danced across the darkened bar, the crowd reduced to a distant hum. His hand traced my shoulder to where mine braced against him, fingers curling around mine. Gently, he lifted my arm, guiding me into a slow spin.

When I faced him again, he didn't let go, drawing our joined hands behind my back as he dipped me. His free hand cupped the nape of my neck, thumb brushing along my jawline.

My pulse thundered. His face was so close, his breath warm against my lips. The room was too hot, too small, too crowded.

"I'll be right back," I blurted, straightening abruptly. The tension in my chest was too much, the pull toward him overwhelming. I needed air.

The cold hit me as I stepped outside, sharp and biting but

welcome after the stifling heat. My breath clouded the air as I wandered down the sidewalk, away from the noise and the smokers. My pulse slowed, my body temperature returning to a semi-normal level, when an arm snaked around my waist and jerked me into the shadows.

I GASPED, A SCREAM CATCHING IN MY THROAT AS A HAND clamped over my mouth, silencing me. My eyes flew open, wild with panic, and I twisted instinctively at the sudden restraint. A hand braced the back of my head as I was pinned against the wooden exterior of the bar. My gaze darted upward, locking with searing green eyes flecked with molten gold.

Eric.

His face was so close that the heat of his breath brushed my skin. His pupils dilated, holding me in place more effectively than his hands.

"What the fuc—" My muffled words were barely audible against the press of his palm.

Eric moved slowly. His free hand released the back of my head, and he brought a single finger to his lips, silencing me with a smirk. Then, as if to tease every nerve in my body, he tugged his bottom lip between his thumb and forefinger, the movement slow, sensual, devastating. My pulse raced at the sight, and I could've easily come undone right then.

His other hand left my mouth, biting the tip of his thumb as his eyes roved over me, devouring every inch of exposed skin like a predator savoring its prey. The hunger in his gaze was raw and wild. It was the same look he'd given me that night in the clearing—the night we'd agreed to be friends.

Friends.

Oh, Shiva.

If I were truly his friend, I'd tell him to run. To cut his losses and escape the wreckage of my life. To find someone that wasn't so fucked up. He had no idea what kind of chaos he was inviting in. And the selfish part of me just kept letting him.

Eric's hand lifted to cup my jaw, his thumb moving over my cheek with tenderness. His touch burned, branding me—and Artemis bless me, I wanted it *everywhere.*

"Eric...." My voice trembled, weak and betraying the storm raging inside. A heady mix of guilt and liquid desire churning, battling for dominance.

The sound of his name leaving my lips seemed to unhinge him. His eyes darkened, his jaw tightening before his tongue darted out to wet his bottom lip. "Say it again," he demanded, his voice low and rough, curling around me like smoke.

My lips parted, but no words came. Instead, I felt the pad of his thumb trace the column of my neck, trailing fire as it slid along my collarbone. My head tipped back against the wall, exposing more of my throat to his touch.

"Stop thinking, Violet," he murmured, his lips brushing the shell of my ear. The gravel in his voice made my knees weak, and I clung to the wood at my back for support. His fingers danced lower, skimming the exposed valley between my breasts with agonizing precision. Each swipe of his fingers unraveled me, my body betraying me in ways I was so tired of denying.

"*Stop thinking.*"

And for once, I did.

I reached up and grabbed his face, pulling him down to me as I crashed my lips against his in a feverish kiss. His groan vibrated against my mouth, deep and raw, as his hands gripped my waist, yanking me flush against him. My fingers tangled in his dark, silken waves, tugging hard enough to draw a growl from deep in his throat.

His erection pressed against my stomach, hard and insistent, igniting a frenzy of need. I moaned against his lips, rolling my hips, desperate for friction. He tasted like sweet spearmint with the sinful burn of rum—and I drank him in, letting myself drown. His mouth devoured mine like he had been waiting for this, too—*starving* for it.

Eric tore his mouth from mine, his eyes blazing as they followed the path of his hand. He plucked the waistband of my jeans, his grin devilish. His gaze met mine again, barely controlled as he waited.

I pulled my bottom lip between my teeth, and that was all the confirmation he needed. His hand slid beneath my thigh, lifting my leg to hook around his hip. His other hand dipped past the hem of my jeans, his fingers brushing against the thin fabric.

"Dripping for me already?"

If I'd been in my right mind, I might've snapped back with something smart, but all I could do was cling to him, trembling as his fingers slipped beneath my panties.

The first brush of his fingers against my clit sent a surge through me, and I gasped, my head falling back. He rubbed small circles against my center, his touch awakening a hungry beast inside me that demanded to be sated.

My body tightened around his touch as he slid a finger inside. Eric's lips parted, lust pooling in the depths of his eyes as he watched me.

His lips crashed into mine again, muffling my moan. I

ground against his hand, crying soft desperate sounds into the kiss.

"Hold on to me," he commanded, the words possessive as they sent shock waves to where his fingers danced on my body.

My hands found his biceps, clinging to the solid muscle as he worked me with slow, torturous pumps. His lips latched onto my neck, the scrape of teeth against skin drawing a broken moan from my lips as he added another finger.

My world narrowed to the sensation of him—his fingers curling inside me, thumb circling my clit, the way my body arched into his, grounding me even as he unraveled me.

Eric's face twisted in a painful groan as I clenched around him, my legs trembling as I writhed against him, aching for more—for *everything* this Adonis would give me.

"So *eager.*" His words sent a pang of embarrassment through me, but they were clipped as if he were struggling to stay composed.

"Apparently... I'm... I'm not the only one," I panted.

His fingers continued their ministrations, and a low chuckle vibrated under my ear. His free hand cupped my breast, and I reached between us to palm his cock through his jeans. Eric hissed, pressing himself further into my hand.

If rational Violet were present, she would worry about someone—or *many someone's*—seeing us. But she was nowhere to be found, so instead, I gripped the button of his pants between my fingers, desperately trying to unbutton them. Eric grasped my hand, stopping the movement and I nearly screamed with frustration.

I needed more, *so much more.*

"I will have *every* single part of you. I've never needed anything so much. But not here. If anyone saw you, even partially exposed... Well, I *couldn't* have that, could I?"

Something about his words sent a raging fire through me.

He raised my arms above my head, pressing them back into the brick and holding them in a single hand. Twisting the wrist nestled between my thighs and curling his fingers inside of me, he slid firmly along that sensitive spot deep within me. My head lolled back as I grabbed his wrist, grinding myself against him again.

His pumps quickened, reaching deeper, and my body became rigid.

"Look at me," his voice hoarse. "I want to see how pretty you are when you come on my fingers."

His words sent me over the edge. My gaze locked with his, and I shattered, my body trembling as my release crashed over me. His name left my tongue on a scream, and Eric caught it with his lips, muffling the sound as he held me upright, his fingers coaxing every last wave of pleasure from me.

When he pulled away, I was boneless, leaning against him as he steadied me. His shaky breath matched my own as he gently removed his fingers and cupped the sensitive skin. His hand slid from between my thighs, and I watched, breathless, as he brought his fingers to his lips. I watched in pure avidity as he placed one by one into his mouth, sucking them clean.

He released each finger with a pop and licked across his kiss-swollen lips. "Divine." His grin was unapologetic and smug. I'd be damned if it weren't the most beautiful thing I'd ever seen. "Who knew you'd taste so sweet under all that sass?"

I swatted his arm with the back of my hand, earning a rich laugh. He straightened, grabbing his arm, his mouth gaping as if I had hurt him.

My eyes narrowed before dropping back to his lips. Heat crept back in. I wanted to kiss him again, to taste him, to feel that sinful mouth where his fingers had been.

Those eyes glinted. "Your sister will send an army out if I don't return you. I won't be able to if you keep looking at me like that." His hand rested on my back as he guided me toward the dark alley's entrance.

He just fingered me in an alley.

I just let him finger me in an alley.

Reality loomed, threatening to come crashing back with embarrassment not far behind. But my body didn't care—still buzzing from his touch, still yearning.

I pressed my lips into a hard line, battling the emotions warring in my chest.

Cassie would know. And she'd mock me for an eternity.

Or she might finally stop hassling me and find someone else to hyper-fixate on.

Yeah, right.

As we emerged, Eric's hand at my waist sent prickles of awareness rippling over my skin. The bar's doors burst open, spilling raucous laughter.

Cassie, James, Kal, and Max strolled toward us.

"Found you!" She winked at me, her grin stretching wide, bordering on obnoxious.

Heat surged to my cheeks, spreading like wildfire. I was sure it was written all over me—or, more accurately, all over the damp cotton between my legs. My lips still tingled from Eric's kiss.

Kal slung an arm around Max's shoulders, his grin infectious as he bounced on his heels. "Greasy food run. Let's go!"

I opened my mouth, scrambling for a response—anything to hide that greasy food wasn't what I was starving for. My eyes moved to Eric, who remained composed. But the faint curve of his lips told a different story—one of quiet, male satisfaction that sent my pulse into overdrive once again.

"I'm tired." I let out the fakest yawn ever concocted by man. "Eric's dropping me at home."

Kal groaned, clasping his hands in a plea. "Oh, come on, Vi! It's my one night off—"

Cassie cut in. "Oh, please. I doubt *any* sleep is happening tonight."

Her eyebrow wagging dripped innuendo, and my stomach plummeted. Fire crawled up my skin, reaching a blistering peak. I mustered a tight, sarcastic laugh paired with a glare, my mortification too overwhelming for a clever retort.

Eric said nothing, his amusement radiating as I turned toward his car, desperate to escape.

"Have fun fucking!" She called, voice carrying down the street as the group strolled away, their laughter fading into the darkness beyond the shuttered buildings.

Subtle as ever, Cas.

Eric's hand on my lower back guided me forward. The simple touch reignited another surge of electricity, melting my embarrassment into something far more dangerous and primal.

Too fast. Too soon.

The thought screamed louder with every step I took. But underneath it, a quieter, more feral voice rose in defiance—the one that had been aching to touch him, to feel his skin against mine again.

Just one taste and this man had turned me into an addict. I needed *more.* I needed *all* of him. Damn the consequences.

The drive to my apartment passed in heavy silence, broken only by the engine's rumble and the erratic pounding of my heart. I couldn't help but steal glances at Eric's profile—the tight clench of his muscles showcasing his own internal war.

We pulled into my driveway, the car settling into stillness. The cool night air kissed my flushed skin as I stepped out of the Camaro. My keys felt heavier than they should have as I led Eric toward the concrete porch.

At the top of the steps, I paused, fumbling with my keys. Eric hesitated below, bathed in the soft glow of the porch light.

"Violet."

I turned halfway, my brows knitting with apprehension. His hand reached out, catching mine. The warmth of his touch rippled through me, silencing my fumbling.

"I need to tell you...." he began, his expression raw, almost vulnerable, as though he were peeling back layers he rarely shared.

I turned to face him head-on, the keys dangling forgotten between my fingers as I searched his face.

This is it. This is the moment he tells me I'm a mistake. He doesn't actually *want me, and now I look like a desperate idiot.*

From where I stood, he was nearly eye level with me, which felt strange and oddly intimate. The gold in his eyes shimmered under the light, catching like embers.

"I don't want you to feel obligated," he said, his voice dipping to a softer register. "To do anything tonight. I'm content just being near you. It doesn't have to go any further than that. If I crossed a line earlier—"

Relief crashed over me like a wave, sweeping away the tension I hadn't realized I was holding.

"Eric," I interrupted my voice firm.

His brow lifted, his hand holding, anchoring us both in the moment. "Yes?"

"Shut the fuck up."

His surprise was fleeting as I stepped down a concrete stair, closing the space between us. My hands found his face, pulling him into a kiss that dissolved the world around us.

His lips softened under mine, the taste of him reigniting that primal need within me. The pressure of his hold was electric, and I melted into him, surrendering.

With a fluid motion, he lifted me, my legs wrapping instinctively around his waist. A soft gasp escaped me, and I smiled against his mouth as he carried me back up the steps.

The door swung open, and we stumbled inside. I lost track of where one kiss ended, and the next began—and I loved every second of it. His lips trailed from my mouth to my jaw, down the column of my neck, leaving a searing path in their wake.

My fingers tangled in his hair, and his grip on me tightened, anchoring us as he moved toward my bedroom like he had done this a thousand times before—and I'd let him do it a thousand times more. Every thought I had been fighting—the doubts, the fears—dissolved under his touch, replaced with the simple, undeniable truth.

I wanted him. *Needed* him. And nothing else mattered.

We reached the bed, the door clicking shut behind us. Eric laid me down with a tenderness that belied the fire in his gaze. The mattress groaned under our weight as his hands traced the curve of my thighs, his lips leaving a trail across my jaw and neck.

His fingers tightened around my legs, holding me firm, his growing length pressed between the apex of my thighs. I rolled my hips instinctively, grinding against him.

A low, gravelly groan escaped him, vibrating against my skin. His hands moved with purpose, unbuttoning my pants, fingers deft yet impatient. I scrambled to help, desperate to rid myself of the barrier.

He chuckled, eyes dark but amused. "Still so eager, are we?"

"Oh, like you're so unbothered," I shot back, breathless.

His lips curved into a wicked smirk. "Let me show you just how *unbothered* I am." He leaned closer, pressing his cock against me again, harder this time.

I didn't care about the logistics of how I would fit that massive thing inside me at some point tonight. I hardly even noticed as my pants were tossed aside. I arched beneath him.

My hands found his waistband, fumbling to feel more of him, but he caught my wrists, his grip firm yet gentle.

"Not yet," he murmured, his voice rough and commanding.

Disappointment flickered before vanishing the moment his lips returned to my skin, each kiss deliberate and maddeningly slow. He lifted my leg, pressing a kiss to the curve of my ankle, his tongue dragging up the length of my calf with torturous precision. His teeth grazed the sensitive skin of my inner thigh, and I gasped, my head tipping back as pleasure coiled.

His breath ghosted over the thin barrier of my underwear. He hooked a finger into the waistband playfully before nipping at the material.

A sudden vibration shattered the spell. My pants tossed haphazardly across the room, buzzed where they had landed.

Eric ignored it, his focus unwavering as his finger traced a feather-light line over the soaked fabric of my panties.

"Mmm," he hummed, his voice thick with satisfaction. "You respond so *beautifully* to me."

The phone buzzed again, and frustration bubbled inside me, compounded by his torturous pace. My breath hitched as I pleaded, "Eric."

His mouth pressed to my clit through the fabric, the vibration of his chuckle traveling straight through me and leaving me trembling.

Another buzz.

With a sigh, Eric pulled back and retrieved the phone, handing it to me with a soft smile. "Could be important."

I shot him a disbelieving look but reached for the phone. Before I could answer, Eric sank back between my thighs, his finger snapping the elastic against my clit with a sharp flick.

I yelped, glaring at him as he smirked. "Answer it."

Biting my lip, I swiped the screen. I didn't get a word out before his tongue darted out, licking over the cotton.

My voice came out breathy. "I'm a little busy, Cas."

Cassie's voice broke through, trembling and soaked with tears. "Vi."

The single syllable shattered the moment, dousing the flames building in my groin. I shot upright, the sudden movement startling Eric. His expression mirrored the alarm blaring in my head.

He didn't hesitate. In an instant, he was gathering my pants and shoes, placing them into my hands as if sensing the urgency.

Cassie's sobs filled my ear. "Something happened."

"WHAT THE FUCK HAPPENED?" I DEMANDED, BURSTING into the hospital room. Eric trailed close behind, his presence steady but silent. My chest tightened with every shallow breath, each inhale pulling me closer to the suffocating spiral I was dancing on the edge of.

Cassie sat slumped by James's bedside, her fingers clinging to his like it was the only thing tethering her to the earth. James lay motionless, wrapped in a cruel mosaic of bandages, cuts, and bruises. The sight of him sent a wave of helpless fury crashing over me.

Her head jerked up at my voice. Her eyes red-rimmed, clouded with tears she'd clearly been shedding for hours. Dried blood streaked her arms, and a sling cradled her shoulder, the physical injuries jarring against the raw grief written across her face.

"Jay...." My voice cracked as I crossed to James's side. I took his hand, brushing my thumb over his battered knuckles. The small gesture was all I could manage as my other hand ghosted over his forehead. The coolness of his skin under my trembling fingers sent a chill through me as I struggled to force the rising panic back down where it belonged.

"He pushed me out of the way," Cassie said, her voice splintering as she forced the words out. Her gaze dropped to James's hand in hers. "We'd just said goodbye to Max and Kal. The Uber was taking forever... I wanted a donut." Her words tripped over each other as though rushing to outrun themselves. "There were no cars, Vi. I swear we looked. He shoved me, and I hit the ground. When I looked back... he was...."

Her words crumbled into broken sobs, body shaking as though her grief might tear her apart. Guilt and anguish poured from her in waves, each tear carving deeper lines of pain into her already bruised face.

"It's my fault," she choked, her grip on James's hand tightening so much that her fingers turned bone white.

"Cas," I murmured, stepping away from James to wrap my arms around her. Her sobs wracked her body as I pulled her close, her pain like a live current sparking against my own. I ran my hand along her back in slow, soothing strokes, though I felt anything but calm. "Look at me."

She didn't.

"Cassie, look at me."

Her swollen eyes finally met mine.

"This isn't your fault," I said, enunciating each word. "Do you hear me? None of this is on you."

It's on me.

Her lip trembled as she whispered, "I can't lose him, V. I can't."

My chest ached, but I forced my voice to steady. "I know. You won't. *We* won't."

I glanced down at her scratched and bruised arms, the sight turning my stomach with guilt and anger all at once. "They checked you out? You're okay?"

She nodded weakly, her face crumpling as another sob broke free.

"Okay, did you call anyone else? Dianna? Jeff?"

She shook her head. "Just you."

"Alright. I'll be right back." I squeezed her shoulder.

Her hand jutted out, grabbing my arm and stopping me from turning toward the door. "Vi," she whispered, her voice like sandpaper, "I think.... It sounded like they hit the gas."

"After they hit James?"

"...Before."

You know those cartoon characters, when they get scared and their color drains completely, until all that's left is a black and white outline?

Yeah.

I blinked, my jaw clenching, as I nodded and stepped out into the hallway. The hospital lights were harsh and unrelenting against my already pounding head.

Eric followed me, but I ignored him. His hand settled on my shoulder. I ignored that, too.

My hands shook as I scrolled through my contacts, every name blurring.

"Violet," he said softly, his voice a lifeline I refused to grab.

I clenched the phone tighter, the edges digging into my palm as if the pain could help me focus.

I wasn't ready to let the dam break, and I could tell by how Eric looked at me, he expected it--was waiting for it. And another part of me whispered that he was ready to catch me as I fell apart. But I couldn't. Cassie, James... they needed me to keep it together. And for them, I would.

"Violet," he said again, still gentle, but his tone held a hint of sternness. "Let me—"

"You can go," I snapped, my tone harsh—sharp enough to draw blood. But he needed to leave. He needed to run.

Please, just go. Before you get hurt, too.

He didn't move, his determination unwavering. "I'm not going anywhere."

I opened my mouth to argue, but the phone in my hand connected to Dianna, and I was forced to explain. The words came out brittle and mechanical as I recited what little information I had—minus the fact that the accident might have, and most likely was, intentional—and completely and utterly my fault. Dianna's panic swelled with each passing second, her questions bleeding into one another until I couldn't process them anymore.

After hanging up, I repeated the process with Kal. Each call stripped me bare, scraping away the thin armor I had left. I felt brittle, fragile, like a single misstep could shatter me.

Less than twenty minutes later, Dianna, Jeff, and Kal's faces were drawn with exhaustion and dread. Dianna still wore her pajamas, her chocolate hair a wild tangle. Kal's breath carried faint traces of the holiday cocktails from earlier, and Jeff looked like he'd aged ten years in mere hours.

Hours faded into each other as we waited for news. When the doctor finally appeared, we hung on to every calm, clinical word she spoke. Each phrase—internal bleeding, broken ribs, punctured lung—driving the air from my own lungs.

"He's stable now, but the next 24 hours are critical," the doctor finished.

Every word etched itself into my chest, fueling the inferno of rage and helplessness burning inside me. I clenched my fists until my nails bit into my palms.

A bitter mantra looped in my mind.

"You did this. You did this. You did this."

Twenty-six hours.

Twenty-six hours of watching James's chest rise and fall, the only reassurance that he was still here. Twenty-six hours of staring at that stupid, beeping monitor, its steady rhythm a cruel taunt.

Wake up, goddamn it.

Twenty-six hours of hearing Cassie's muffled sobs, the scrape of tissues against her nose, her occasional snoring when exhaustion overtook her.

And twenty-six goddamn hours of Eric's presence, a constant heat at my side, his nearness both grounding *and* suffocating.

Why the fuck is he still here?

"You should get some rest." Dianna's voice broke through the weighted silence as she entered the room, arms cradling a pot of bright yellow roses. She set them down on the side table with a soft thud.

"I'm fine," I replied automatically.

Dianna shot me a knowing look. Her lips pressed into a thin line. "Honey, I haven't seen you leave that chair. Or eat."

I opened my mouth to argue—to tell her about the muffin Eric practically shoved down my throat that morning—but she cut me off with a raised hand.

"James would throw a fit if he knew everyone was making such a big fuss over him. Go stretch your legs, shower. I promise to call if there's any change."

"Cassie hasn't left his side either," I countered, gesturing to where my sister sat, her hand glued to James's. "Why aren't you telling her to go?"

Dianna sighed as she glanced at Cassie. "I don't think an army could pry her away. But she at least lets me feed her."

"Alright, fine," I murmured.

Eric moved without hesitation, holding out my coat before I could even stand. I glanced at him, lips twitching in annoyance, but I grabbed the coat anyway.

Stop trying to take care of me.

He was giving me the room to break, to be weak, with the silent promise that he would pick up the pieces when I was done. But I wasn't going to be weak, not now, never again, and his hovering only made that harder for me to stick to.

I slipped on my coat and realized how stale my clothes felt, how foreign my own body seemed.

The walk to his car was quiet, the silence heavy but not unbearable. He didn't push me to talk, and for that, I was grateful.

But I could still feel my anger and frustration prickling at the edges of my skin. It didn't matter that it was directed at someone else entirely and had nothing to do with him. I didn't want Eric seeing me like this... but he *just wouldn't leave.*

When we reached the apartment, he followed me up the porch steps. The questions clawed out of me before I could stop them.

"Why are you here?"

He blinked, startled by my sudden venom. "Because I—"

"You saw a broken and sad girl and thought, 'Hey! sounds like a good time'?" I interrupted, my voice rising, each word laced with bitterness. "You want to fix me? Or are you just that desperate to fuck your patients?"

His expression shifted, disbelief darkening his features before he steadied himself. His jaw tightened, but his voice remained calm. "I care about you. That's why I'm here. No ulterior motives."

I shook my head, turning away, anger in my chest bubbling over and melting everything in its path. "Just leave."

I stepped inside, ready to shut the door behind me, but Eric followed, his presence like a second shadow. I spun to tell him off, but the sight of my living room stopped me cold.

The space was a battlefield.

The couch had been gutted, its stuffing strewn like shredded clouds. Shattered dishes glinted like jagged stars beneath dim light, and on the wall, scrawled in thick, jagged letters of dark red paint, one word screamed back at me:

WHORE

Smoke billowed from the hallway, acrid and sharp, triggering the shrill wail of the fire alarm.

Eric bolted toward the bedroom without hesitation, and moments later, he returned, coughing and clutching a charred bundle—my comforter, reduced to blackened tatters.

I couldn't move, couldn't breathe. My eyes were locked on the word defacing the wall, the letters a grotesque accusation that burned into my skin.

Of course he saw us, of course he knew.

Stupid, stupid, stupid.

"Violet."

I ignored Eric, marching into the kitchen and grabbing a sponge. My hands attacked the wall, the paint smearing and staining my skin a sickening red.

"Violet," he said again, closer now.

I couldn't stop, couldn't think. My mind spun, each thought lashing like a whip.

Mom. Dad. Sage. Cassie. James.

Every name carved a fresh wound, every memory an

agonizing reminder of the destruction that followed me like a curse.

"You *care* about me?" I snapped, spinning to face Eric, the sponge slipping from my hand. I gestured wildly to the wreckage around us. "This is what caring about me gets you! Attacked, hurt, *dead!*" My voice cracked, the words dragging me like an undertow.

I felt the tears coming, but I fought them back, my body shaking with the effort. "People drop like flies around me unless they are smart enough to stay the hell away. *Please*, Eric. I am begging you. Be one of the smart ones."

Eric didn't flinch. His hands cradled my face, his touch an anchor. I tried to pull away, but his grip held steady, grounding me in a way that made my knees weak.

"You can't get rid of me," he said, his voice low and resolute. He pressed his forehead gently against mine, his breath warm against the bridge of my nose. "Whatever *this* is, it doesn't scare me. So, stop shutting me out and let me help you."

I shook my head, the tears spilling over. "Helping me is going to get you killed."

"Nothing could keep me from you," he murmured a quiet vow that cut through my despair. "Not you, not this, not even death."

His words shattered something inside me and seemed to mend other parts right along with it.

THE CAR RUMBLED TO A STOP ON THE GRAVEL DRIVE, ITS tires grinding against the loose stones. I stepped out and stood between the open car door and the frame, staring at the sprawling structure in front of me.

How much money does this guy make?

The house was a lumberjack millionaire's fever dream. Towering redwood beams supported a wraparound deck of the cabin-turned-mansion. Floor-to-ceiling windows faced west, catching the dying sunlight and throwing back hues of molten gold. The polished redwood exterior blended so seamlessly with the surrounding ancient forest that it looked like the house had grown there, cradled by nature. Shadows stretched long and protective, the towering trees like sentinels around the property.

"It's... I mean... oh, my god," I inched closer to the car's hood as if moving might help me process what I saw.

Behind me, Eric's deep chuckle rumbled like distant thunder. "It used to be just a plot of land with a hunting bunker before my dad got ahold of it and put up a cabin. We spent a lot of time out here when I was younger."

I turned to find him leaning against the car. A faint, wistful smile tugged at his lips as his gaze lingered on the house, the look in his eyes heavy with unspoken memories.

"He gave it to me after bringing me back home," he continued, voice lower now, almost reverent. "He said I needed something to focus on—to keep my head above water. So, I turned it into this."

My mouth fell open before I could stop it. "You *built* this?"

"Crazy what you can learn online." His grin widened, playful and infuriatingly perfect.

I rolled my eyes, crossing my arms. "Oh, now you're just showing off."

He laughed the sound light and gestured toward the house. "Come on, I'll give you the tour."

I followed him to the front steps, crunching gravel replaced by the hollow thud of wood as we climbed. The scent of aged timber mingled with the earthy smell of the forest, rooting me even as my thoughts threatened to spiral.

Here I was, trailing behind this tree of a man, smiling while James lay unconscious in a hospital bed—because of me. Because I couldn't figure out how to stop a random psycho from trying to burn my friends alive or hit them with cars.

Eric opened the heavy wooden door, releasing a sweet, familiar scent—vanilla, like the perfume I bought in Costco-sized quantities.

I hesitated in the doorway, my eyes sweeping across the expansive living room. The space felt like a warm embrace. Rich redwood beams arched high above, framing an open area. Plush leather couches faced a massive stone fireplace. Polished wood floors gleamed, accentuated by the thick woven rugs that looked so soft I had to resist the urge to slip off my shoes and feel them under my toes.

"Well," I said dryly, blinking back the awe threatening to creep into my voice, "it's absolutely atrocious. Ugliest thing I've ever seen."

Eric huffed, shaking his head as he shut the door behind us. "I'll take that under advisement."

He led me through the house, pointing out rooms with an understated pride that made me smile. His quiet confidence was disarming, even endearing. I bit back a gasp as we reached a library tucked at the back of the house.

The room was a sanctuary of books; its walls filled with shelves that stretched from floor to ceiling. A ladder on wheels slid smoothly along one shelf, and the window on the far wall offered a view of the forest that was almost as stunning as the books themselves.

"I take it back," I said, spinning slowly to take it all in. "*This* is the ugliest thing I've ever seen."

Eric exhaled through his nose from the doorway, his broad shoulders leaning against the frame. "Duly noted."

We moved on, the tour revealing more of the cabin-mansion-that-cost-more-than-I-could-make-in-seventy-life-times. My amazement only deepened as we passed a spiral stone staircase leading to six upper-level bedrooms and an office that looked fit for a CEO.

The kitchen was a masterpiece of natural light and polished finishes. Sunlight streamed through high windows, dancing across the countertops. It felt lived-in, filled with small touches that made it worlds apart from the sterile perfection I was used to with Connor.

"And you live here all by yourself?" I asked.

"Just me and Gemma."

"Gemma?"

"Yeah, my dog."

"You have a dog?"

His smirk was smug like he enjoyed keeping me on my toes. "She's usually out running around, but she'll be back soon. You'll love her."

Almost on cue, a mass of black and tan fur bounded through a doggy door, her glossy coat glistening. She shook herself off, sending water droplets across the floor.

Eric crouched low, and his entire soul lit up. I'd never seen such a broad smile in my life. "Hey, Gem," he murmured as the sheltie pranced toward him, her tail wagging furiously.

Gemma nuzzled his hand, giving it a few affectionate licks before her almond eyes turned to me. I didn't move, worried I might piss off the beautiful beast, and well aware of how territorial females could be of their owners.

Eric glanced up at me, his grin encouraging as he waved to join him on the ground.

Swallowing my hesitation, I bent down, extending the back of my hand to Gemma, whose heterochromia eyes watched my every movement.

You and your dad have a lot in common, then.

Gemma sniffed, her nose cool against my skin, before her tail wagged in a blur. She tapped her front feet, body vibrating with excitement as she pressed against my hand and rolled over to expose her pink-and-white belly.

A reluctant laugh bubbled out of me, and the smile that broke across my face hurt my cheeks. I crossed my legs and settled on the floor, rubbing her belly. "Such a good baby," I hummed as her tail thumped wildly.

I could feel the weight of Eric's eyes on me and the smile that plastered his face as he watched Gemma stand and curl into my lap, licking my face, arms, and any exposed skin she could get ahold of.

"We weren't allowed to have pets." The words left my lips in a whisper as I felt my heart clench with a memory that I had shoved down almost as deep as I'd shoved down Sage's. "My brother found a kitten behind his work. The mom had been dead for a while, but it still stayed with her. Cassie and I buried her and took the kitten home to our mom. She was so good with animals. We hid it in the greenhouse, like we did with everything we didn't want our dad seeing." The words tumbled out in a rush, like an extreme case of word vomit. I couldn't stop them or the ache they caused. "I don't even remember what he was so mad about...." A short and bitter laugh escaped me. "He destroyed the greenhouse, and when he found the cat... he made me scrub the blood from his boot." I paused, my hand stilling on Gemma. "And we never tried something that stupid again."

His jaw ticked, fierce, quiet anger flaring. "It wasn't stupid," he said firmly, rough with conviction.

My lips pulled into a thin line, petting Gemma absently as the memory lingered. Eric rose, his movements precise, almost tense, as he crossed to the fridge. He pulled out a cut of raw beef, plated it with calm efficiency, and set it down for Gemma. She padded over, wagging her tail, oblivious to the turmoil.

Dusting dog hair from my jeans, I stood just as Eric turned back to me. His expression was a storm of emotion—rage, sadness, and something I couldn't name. The space between us vanished, his lips crashing into mine with an urgency that threw me. The kiss was raw and angry, his grip on my waist rough. As if he wanted to erase the hurt with the pressure of his mouth and fingers. It stole my breath as I leaned into him, the intensity overwhelming but strangely comforting.

When he finally pulled back, his green eyes glimmered with a sadness that made my heart lurch. Without a word, he cupped my hand and led me toward a sleek black door that looked out of place in his house's rustic charm.

He hovered his hand over a small panel beside the door. The light blinked from red to green as it scanned his fingerprint, followed by the soft click of the lock.

I arched a brow as the door eased open. "That's not weird at all."

He chuckled, his grin genuine, the kind that made his eyes crinkle just enough to soften his features. He gestured for me to follow as he stepped through the threshold.

The staircase beyond was polished stone, its winding descent casting shadows.

Yeah, let's hop, skip, and jump into the creepy dark pit. Definitely not *about to get murdered or anything.*

Alarm bells should have been ringing in my head. My gut, however, remained oddly calm. So, instead of doing the logical thing, I followed the man who set my skin on fire down into the abyss.

The air grew cooler with each step, brushing against my skin like a whispered warning. My fingers skimmed the iron railing.

"Any second now, you're going to whip out a knife and slice me open," I said lightly as the stairs ended.

Eric glanced back, amusement flickering in his eyes. "Kiss you, then kill you? How little you think of me." He pressed a hand dramatically to his chest. "You said you needed somewhere safe to work out. I can offer that."

He stepped aside, revealing a massive space lined with mirrored walls, reflecting pristine equipment: a treadmill, rowing machine, free weights. A boxing ring anchored the corner. The floor was an immaculate white, shining like freshly fallen snow.

I paused on the last step. "So, not a dungeon."

"Violet, if you wanted to be chained up, all you had to do was ask." He flashed that stupid grin, and my throat went dry as he sauntered further into the room.

Oh, you cheeky, cheeky bastard.

Biting back a retort, I found myself watching how his shoulders flexed beneath his shirt as he picked up a dumbbell and returned it to its rack. My body screamed with need.

Stop staring.

I cleared my throat, determined to calm that annoying little voice that resonated low in my belly. My fingers grazed the leather of a weight bench.

It made sense now, seeing this place. His lean athletic frame wasn't just the result of good genes—it was dedication, focus. I could picture him here, shirt damp with sweat, his skin flushed and gleaming as he pushed through another set of reps. My mind wandered further, unbidden, to the sounds he might make as his body worked and if they matched the rough groans he'd let slip in the alley—in my room. I wondered if he would let me run my tongue between his sweat-slick pectorals as he lifted weights.

Focus, Violet.

I bit the inside of my cheek, dragging my attention to a punching bag. "Pretty impressive," I admitted, giving the bag a slight push, watching it sway back and forth, before my eyes locked on another metal door at the far end of the room. "That's where you keep the bodies, huh?"

Eric followed my line of sight, his body stilling. His expression didn't falter, but the way his shoulders squared felt deliberate. "Something like that."

For once, his smile didn't touch his eyes, and something cold twisted in my gut as he walked to the door, his fingerprint unlocking it. When it swung open, I stepped closer.

Oh shit. He might actually kill me.

Behind the door, walls bordered with shelves held guns of every size and type. Drawers were mounted beneath, their handles gleaming from the linear lights attached to the shelves.

I exhaled slowly. "I was kidding about the dead bodies, but now I'm a bit concerned."

Eric leaned against the doorframe, watching me, almost assessing. "It was my dad's hobby," he said quietly. "I just add to the collection here and there."

His tone carried something—hesitation, maybe even vulnerability. Like he was waiting for me to say something, anything.

I raised a brow, glancing around the dustless room. "Are you a neat freak? James is, and it drives me fucking wild. Not a speck of dust in here."

Shock crossed his face before he smiled, the tension in his face easing. "I have a maid."

"Of course you do," I muttered, rolling my eyes.

"You could stay here."

"I beg your *finest* pardon?"

"You could stay with me. Your apartment isn't safe. I doubt that Cassie and James's would be any different."

"I'm not moving in with you."

"I'm not asking you to move in. I'm saying stay here until I— until *we*—figure out how to handle whatever's going on."

I crossed my arms, glaring up at him. "I can handle it. I am handling it. I don't need some white knight swooping in to save me and my friends. You don't know me well enough to go running into my mess trying to fix everything. What're you gonna do? Blow something up? Shoot it? And what about James and Cas? I hide here while they deal with everything on their own? I can't leave them."

He smirked, his sarcasm cutting as he slapped a palm to his forehead. "If only I had a place full of empty rooms."

I opened my mouth to argue—because fuck him for thinking I needed to be rescued—but his hand reached out and traced from my shoulder down to my fingertips, effectively shutting my ass up.

"There's one more thing I want to show you." Large fingers wrapped around mine. My annoyance evacuated.

"What? A tank?"

His laugh echoed as he led me back upstairs.

We reached the living room again, where twilight spilled through the tall windows. Without hesitation, Eric crossed the room and opened the glass double doors leading to the wooden deck.

He turned back to me, extending a hand. I hesitated for a heartbeat before slipping my hand in his. His grip was firm but gentle as he pulled me outside.

Above us stretched an unbroken canopy of stars, their brilliance untainted by city lights. Galaxies spiraled, their ethereal glow like strokes of a celestial artist. The air was still, wrapping around us with an infinite quiet.

I drifted to the railing, my fingers brushing the cold iron to anchor myself to something tangible. A few shooting stars streaked across the sky, and for a moment, I couldn't look away. The quiet was so profound—not empty, but full— like nothing else existed, just this, us.

Eric moved to stand beside me, his shoulder brushing mine. The brief contact grounded me in ways I hadn't realized I needed. He didn't speak right away, letting the quiet settle. When he finally broke it, his voice was low, a rough edge to his words.

"You're *not* some itch I'm trying to scratch," he said.

The unexpected confession pulled my gaze to him. The moonlight caught the sharp lines of his profile, softening them just enough to make him look untouchable and achingly human at the same time.

"Eric, when I said that...." I started, the words catching in my throat. "I didn't mean—"

He silenced me with the gentle press of the pad of his thumb against my lips. His touch was careful, securing and unraveling all at once.

"I don't want to fix you," he said, his tone final. His eyes, those striking green and gold depths, held mine. "You're not broken. I don't understand why you see yourself as such."

I turned away, my chest tightening as shame bubbled. My eyes settled on the moonlight dancing across the surface of the nearby lake, its ripples glittering like a thousand tiny secrets. Secrets I *know*--that he never would.

Before I could retreat too far into myself, his hand caught my chin, gently guiding my face back to his.

"You are not less," he said. "No matter what *lies* you've been told."

Tears came, stinging my eyes as his words settled deep inside me. Words I didn't know I needed to hear so badly, filling an ache that I had been carrying for so damn long. My throat tightened, and my fingers curled against his on my cheek, clinging to them.

"Anything you throw at me, I can take it. Just promise to keep throwing it," he continued, his words weaving through the cracks in my defenses. "Scream, cry, laugh. I want every inch of you—every ounce of sarcasm, every eye roll.' His lips teased into that goddamn crooked grin. "I want it all."

A bittersweet sigh slipped from me, barely more than a whisper, as his words wrapped around my heart and held it. "You couldn't possibly understand what you're getting yourself into," I said, an armor of defiance barely concealing my vulnerability.

He stepped closer, the warmth of his body chasing away the chill. His free hand cupped my jaw, the calloused pad of his thumb brushing against my cheek. Slowly, he leaned down and pressed his lips to my forehead. The tenderness of the gesture undid me, and my eyes fluttered shut as I leaned into him.

"Then show me," he murmured, a soft rumble against my skin.

For the first time in so very long, I felt the slightest flicker of something I barely recognized.

Home.

And it terrified me.

THE WHIR OF MONITORS WAS LIKE A CONSTANT, unwelcome reminder of how out of control everything was. James lay too still, his amber skin faded to a pale shadow of itself. He looked *wrong*, like a stranger was wearing his face.

Cassie sat slumped in the chair beside him, her usual bouncy blonde hair hanging limp and dull. Her broken arm rested in a sling, but her other hand clung to his limp fingers, her thumb brushing over his knuckles like she could will him to respond. The red stain that typically coated her lips was gone, leaving them bare and colorless. Her spark that always annoyed me had vanished—and God, did I miss it. In its place was a tight, hollow smile that didn't reach her eyes.

"So let me get this straight," she said, her voice dry but edged with disbelief. "Eric has an arsenal, a mansion-slash-fortress, wants to help, and you didn't sleep with him? He is clearly head over heels for you. And you're completely obsessed with him. Just let him love you already—and maybe mess up your guts a little."

I leaned against the door frame, arms crossed, and raised an eyebrow. "Pot, kettle."

Cassie stopped mid-shift, her brow creasing. "What?"

My eyes drifted to James and then back to her, letting the weight of my silence do the talking.

Her jaw tightened, and the corners of her lips pressed into a thin, strained line. Her grip on James's hand shifted, tightening momentarily before easing. Her tough facade cracked, her gaze softening as she looked at him with a tenderness she rarely let show.

"He deserves more than what I can give him," she said finally, the words quiet, stripped of the flare she wielded like a shield.

"I get it."

You have no idea how much I do.

She shifted in her chair, hand dragging across her face like she could scrub away her discomfort. "Okay," she said after a pause, voice steadier now. "So, Eric's in on it? You told him everything?"

I glanced at my hands, realizing too late that I was twisting them together like I could wring the tension out of my skin. "I gave him the basics. Not sure what he thinks he's going to do, but he's...*determined* to be a part of whatever we're doing."

Her golden brow arched, a flicker of her usual sharpness flickering back into place. "And what exactly are we doing?"

A breath of bitter laughter slipped out. "Illegal things."

Cassie's lips twitched, the faintest hint of her usual grin ghosting over her face before it vanished again. Her gaze returned to James, and she let out a soft sigh, her thumb absently brushing over his knuckles again. Her eyes fixed on him, a silent plea.

The silence that followed was heavy with unspoken fear

and fractured hope. I stayed where I was, pretending that the ache in my chest wasn't tearing me apart piece by torturous fucking piece.

I'm going to fix this, bud. I promise.

THE ALLEY SWALLOWED ME IN SHADOWS, BROKEN ONLY BY the weak glow of a distant streetlamp. My breath fogged the icy air as I crouched by the back door of the donut shop, the lock pick fluttering in my gloved hand. The silence pressed against my ears, amplifying every scrape of metal and rustle of fabric.

With a click, the lock gave, and I fought the urge to happy dance. I straightened, hand closing around the door handle.

"Such lengths for a donut."

I spun around, my pulse spiking as Eric stepped out of the shadows. He leaned against the wall with infuriating ease, arms crossed, a smug grin illuminating his perfect face.

I swallowed the scream that rose in my throat, my heart pounding against my ribs as I struggled to regain composure. "What the hell are you doing here?" I hissed, clutching the doorframe.

He shrugged, the motion almost lazy. "Taking in the scenery," he drawled, gesturing toward the trash-strewn alley. "What are *you* doing here?"

I exhaled, slumping against the door. "They wouldn't let me

see the footage from the night James was hit," I admitted, the frustration in my voice as raw as my nerves. "I had to get creative."

His eyebrows shot up, and for a moment, he just stared. Then, with a shrug, he pushed the door open and stepped inside like he owned the place.

"Wait—" I whispered harshly, but he was already disappearing inside. Grinding my teeth, I followed, shutting the door behind me.

The red glow of the "Closed" sign buzzed, sending long shadows across the counters.

Eric turned to me. "Where'd you learn to pick locks?"

"I grew up poor," I said, pulling out my phone to use as a flashlight. "Let your imagination run wild with that."

His smile widened, the kind that could melt ice and set nerves on fire.

Not the time, Vi.

"Well," he said, his voice dipping lower, "I do love you in all black. Like my very own little night stalker."

"Yeah," I muttered, scanning the shelves beneath the counter. "Except I'm not into murder as a hobby."

"No," Eric murmured, his lips curving into a sly grin. "But you look gorgeous committing a felony."

A flicker of heat crept up my neck, and I clenched my jaw, refusing to indulge him. "I'm not comm—they won't even know I was here! I just need to see the video. Then we're gone."

He raised his hands, palms out. "Whatever you say, Bonnie."

"Don't touch anything!" I snapped as his fingers inched toward a stack of fliers. He froze, eyebrows arching. I held up my gloved hand for emphasis. "Fingerprints."

He glanced at his bare hands, sighing, and clasped them behind his back as he wandered around.

"You're not concerned about cameras?" He continued glancing around the opposite side of the counter as I crouched, sifting through papers under the register.

Where is it?

"What are you looking for?" Eric leaned over the counter, watching me.

"There's only one camera, and it's facing the street," I bit out, rifling through folders. "There's an office door with a pin pad back here." I threw my thumb over my shoulder. "It's probably where they keep the—*Ha!* Found it."

I tugged a slip of paper from beneath the register, standing up to examine it. The pin code was scrawled in faded ink. I moved to the office door, punching it in as Eric appeared at my side.

He watched me with an amused smile as the pin pad beeped, and the door unlocked. "Impressive." He followed me inside.

The cramped office was filled with filing cabinets and a tiny desk barely big enough to hold the computer. I slid into the chair and jiggled the mouse, the screen blinking to life with a password prompt. I groaned under my breath, frustration mounting as I rifled through sticky notes scattered across the desk.

"Looking for the password?" Eric asked, voice dripping with feigned innocence.

"No," I snapped, not looking up. "The Krabby Patty Formula." He chuckled a low sound that sent an unwelcome shiver down my spine. "Okay, Mr. White Knight. You want to help so badly? Start looking around!"

"Don't need to." I could almost hear the shrug and pursed lips in his voice.

I stopped, slowly turning to him with narrowed eyes. "And why not?"

With a toothy shit-eating grin, he pulled a flash drive from behind his back, dangling it like a prize. "Because Reggie already downloaded everything for me. I was on my way to pick it up. Then I saw you."

Heat flared in my chest—half embarrassment, half fury—as I stood to face him. "Reggie? You know the owner? And you didn't say anything?"

He shrugged. "Watching how your brain works is... entertaining. It does something to me."

Oh, I'm about to do something to you, asshole.

His eyes drifted over me again, this time slower. He licked his lips like he was savoring the moment. Heat bloomed on my cheeks, though whether from anger or something else, I wasn't willing to decipher.

"And you look so cute when you're pissed off," he added, eyes glinting.

I snatched the flash drive from his hand, ignoring the ache pooling in my stomach as I stalked toward the door. "You're a real pain in my ass."

Eric followed, his laughter a soft rumble. "And what a magnificent ass it is."

"A NORMAL PERSON WOULD TELL ME TO GO TO THE COPS and *not* make coffee while we watch my friend get hit with a car." My voice was sharp, a brittle edge to it, as I leaned against the cold wooden top of the island. The laptop sat in front of me, its screen dim. My fingers fumbled to plug in the flash drive.

The sound of Eric's coffee machine—which looked like it cost more than my car—filled the silence. The sound blended with the soft clink of mugs as he moved through the kitchen. I barely glanced at him as he placed a steaming cup beside me, the rich aroma curling upward.

He took a slow sip, his stance loose and casual as he leaned against the island across from me. His eyes sparkled with that infuriating mix of amusement and curiosity like I was a puzzle he was piecing together just for fun.

"The police would've taken a copy of the footage after hearing Cassie's statement," he said, setting his cup down. "So, it's moot. I figured if you were going to *this* much trouble, you had your reasons for not trusting their abilities." His tone was calm like this was all just logic and not me spiraling into fear-induced crime.

I studied his face, searching for any crack in his composure, any hint of the weight this might carry for him. *Nothing*. He was unreadable. Smug, even. "And you're just *okay* with that?"

His lips twitched into that half-smile, the kind that always made me want to smack him or tear off his clothes, depending on how powerful my vagina was that day.

"I liked our little breaking-and-entering date."

My eyes rolled so hard I could have sworn I saw my brain. Allah, the man was vexing. If he wanted to call it a date, *fine*. At least it was wildly better—even fun, if I was being honest— than any dates I had been on in... *ever*.

Despite the circumstances.

Not to mention, he'd also been knuckle-deep inside me that night, but I still wasn't sure how to categorize that. We had been spending more time together, but I hadn't paused long enough to analyze what that meant.

The spinning wheel on the screen mocked me with its endless rotations. I ground my teeth, irritation buzzing in my veins.

"What's the plan?"

"Wait for this slow-ass thing to load." My words clipped as my focus glued to the screen. "Hopefully, see a face, a license plate. Or at least the make and model."

He didn't look away, his lips pulling tight. 'I mean when we figure out who it is. What are we doing with that information?"

See how he *likes being hit by a car?*

My fingers stilled, resting on the counter's edge as Eric's question hung. The logical thing would be to turn him in. I knew that. And yet....

"I hadn't really thought that far," I half-lied. "I just want it over."

The atmosphere in the room shifted, the teasing glint in his eyes replaced by something sharper, darker. He leaned forward slightly, his mug cradled in one hand, his expression unnervingly focused. "Do you want him dead?"

I turned to him, my breath catching. His face was still so damn unreadable, but there was something in his voice—a subtle challenge, a faint trace of curiosity, maybe both. But not a single hint of judgment. My brows knitted as my thoughts tangled around themselves.

"I—"

The laptop chimed. My eyes darted back to the screen, relief and dread warring as the video finally loaded.

The footage was grainy, streetlights casting weak halos over the sidewalk as Cassie and James came into view. My heart kicked against my ribs as I watched Cassie grab James's hand, tugging him forward into the street with a laugh I couldn't hear.

The headlights cut through the darkness without warning, and my stomach lurched. The car barreled toward. James turned at the last second, shoving Cassie out of the way as the vehicle hit him. My body jerked like *I* was the one that had been hit as the car smacked James with a sickening force, his body folding like paper before he rolled off the hood and out of the frame.

A raw sound tore from my throat, pain rippling through me. Tears burned at the edges of my vision, but I blinked them away, refusing to let them fall. My hands moved of their own accord, rewinding the video and replaying it over and over and over again.

"I can do this," Eric said softly, his hand resting on mine as my fingers hovered over the mouse pad. "You don't have to—"

My head snapped so fast I thought my neck might break as I shot him a glare that could've cut glass. The heat of my anger kept my tears at bay as I yanked my hand away from his.

I slowed the footage, forcing myself to study every second, every frame. The driver's face was impossible to see—just shadows and reflections on the windshield. The license plate was a blur, the camera too cheap to catch it. Even the car's color was indistinct, a dark shade that could've been black, blue, or green.

"It's an Accord," Eric said, confident.

I didn't respond. My eyes glued to the screen as I rewound the footage again, watching James go down. Watching that car disappear.

My hands gripped the counter as the weight of it all pressed in. I kept my eyes on the screen, kept watching until the images blurred together, mixing with the painted *"Whore"* on my apartment wall, brown eyes staring through my doorbell camera, the gloved hand breaking into my house.

"Yeah." A whisper edged with steel. "I want him dead."

EACH OF MY STEPS CRUNCHED OVER BRITTLE LEAVES ON the cracked sidewalk. The wind snuck beneath my scarf. I gripped my phone tighter, pressing it to my ear as Cassie's voice crackled over the line, full of energy.

"You shouldn't go to the apartment alone." Her words came out fast.

"I planned on asking Eric to come," I tugged my coat tighter. "I'm just going to try and clean what I can, but I'm pretty sure my deposit is fucked."

She snorted, and I could almost see her smirking on the other end. "Good thing you've got a hot, rich boyfriend with an impenetrable fortress to shack up with."

I rolled my eyes, my breath misting in the cold air. "He's not my—"

"Don't forget the extra whip and Kal's scone!" She cut in before I could finish. The line went dead, leaving me standing there, phone in hand, staring at the *call-ended* screen.

I slipped the phone back into my pocket.

At least she's doing better.

It was undoubtedly thanks to James. He was awake, stubbornly pushing himself to walk even though the doctors told him to take it slow.

Typical male.

I hadn't gone to see him yet. Thinking about it made my chest heavy, guilt pressing down like a stone. I should have been there. But I wasn't. Because I had nothing to give him—no answers, no justice, nothing except the sickening realization that I was no closer to finding the piece of human garbage who had done this to him.

The silence on that front was maddening.

What was I missing?

I had watched that damn tape over and over. Scanned the stolen cars list, checked every Honda Accord in town and the surrounding areas, even cross-referenced arrest records. Nothing. The only thing I hadn't done was go around town, physically checking every Accord for a James-sized dent. Which, honestly, I hadn't completely taken off the table.

I was lost in thought when a parked car across the street caught my eye.

My feet slowed. My stomach turned to ice.

No. Fucking. Way.

The sleek dark paint. The shape of the grille.

No way that just landed in my lap.

My pulse thundered in my ears. I tilted my head, narrowing my eyes as a tall man in a hoodie walked across the street, moving toward the car. His posture relaxed, his movements casual. But my instincts screamed.

I ducked into the nearest store, the bell jingling as I slipped inside.

The shop smelled like incense, the shelves crammed with

tie-dye ceramic mugs and overpriced crystal jewelry. I crouched behind a display, heart hammering, peering through the floor-to-ceiling window facing the street.

Turn around. Come on, just turn around.

The man leaned against the car, phone in hand, his back to me.

Show me your face, asshole.

"Can I help you?"

I jolted so hard I nearly knocked over the shelf. A cheerful sales clerk flashed a polite smile, her perfect ebony skin and deep brown eyes oblivious to the fact that my soul had just left my body.

Heat rushed to my cheeks as I scrambled, grabbing the nearest mug and twirling it absently. "Oh, uh... no. I'm just looking for...." I trailed off, eyes snapping back to the window.

He ended his call and opened the car door.

Shit.

I dropped the mug onto the shelf with a clatter, muttered a distracted, "*Sorry!*", to the clerk, and bolted out the door.

My Vans hit the pavement hard, pace quickening as the car rumbled to life. My hands curled into fists, each step fueled by adrenaline and not much else.

I was only a few feet away when I slammed into something solid.

"What are you doing?"

Eric's hands gripped my shoulders to steady me. I barely registered the touch; my focus locked on the car.

"Eric, I don't have time for this," I snapped, trying to side-step him.

The engine roared, and my breath caught. The car peeled away from the curb, disappearing down the street, taking the man—and my chance for answers—with it.

My anger boiled over.

I shoved Eric's chest, frustration exploding out of me. "What the fuck? I almost—Why'd you stop me?"

His face was stone, that usual smirk nowhere to be found. "You were about to do something incredibly stupid and incredibly dangerous," he said, the heat behind his words barely hidden. "Worst case scenario, it's him, and you walk right into his hands. Best case, you look like a lunatic screaming at an innocent guy."

I ran my hands through my hair, tugging at the roots, desperate to ground myself, desperate to keep the frustration from swallowing me whole. "So what?! *God!*" I spun on my heel, then back to face him, my voice rising. "What are you even doing here? Are you following me now, too? Take the fucking hint! Just because I let you do your little finger tap dance doesn't mean you get some primal claim over me! *Stop* showing up. *Stop* getting involved. *Stop* trying to save me. Just *stop*. Go home and fucking *stay* there. I don't need you!"

A few people on the street had stopped, their eyes pressing in like a cage. But I didn't care.

Let them watch. Let them see the girl who was getting really sick and tired of people trying to control her and tell her what to do.

Eric's jaw ticked. His nostrils flared. His pools of green darkened with something unnamed. Anger, maybe. Or something deeper.

I turned away from him, my feet moving before my mind could catch up. The Coffee Shop was only a few doors down. I could make it there without looking back.

Eric's footsteps followed.

I whipped around, my chest heaving. "Do. *Not.* Follow me."

For a long moment, he didn't move—his gaze right where it always was, as if debating whether to ignore my demand.

Then, finally, he stepped back.

I turned away, pushing through the doors of The Coffee Shop, forcing myself to keep walking.

And use every fragile, fraying piece of willpower *not* to look back.

I balanced the coffee tray against my hip as I nudged open the hospital room door with my shoulder, my other hand clutching a paper bag with Kal's obnoxiously specific scone order.

Cassie stood near James's bed, her posture casual, but eyes locked on him as if she was scanning for signs of distress. Pale but smirking, James leaned back against a mountain of pillows, the massive bandage wrapping his torso impossible to miss.

"About time," he rasped.

"Patience," I shot back, my first words to him since he had woken up. Setting the tray on the small rolling table beside his bed, I handed Cassie her chai with *extra whip* and passed Kal his scone. "You're Highness," I teased.

"Finally," Kal said, snatching the scone. "Can't you see I'm wasting away?"

I rolled my eyes, turning back to James, nodding toward the evidence of his punctured lung and subsequent surgery. "You definitely have to quit smoking now." My tone was light, even though the sight of him lying there made my stomach twist.

Kal, who had been perched on the windowsill tearing into his scone, chimed in without missing a beat. "But what will he do to keep up the mysterious bad-boy facade?" Kal's stuffed cheeks muffled his words.

James raised a brow, his lips quirking. "They'd have to pry my cigs out of my cold, dead fingers."

A laugh escaped me, lifting whatever weight was sitting on my shoulders as James and Kal joined in.

Cassie didn't. She shifted her weight from one foot to the other, a tight smile pulling at her mouth before she mumbled something and bolted for the door.

James's smile faded as his gaze trailed after her. He attempted to sit up as if he would follow her. "Cas—"

I moved to follow, but Kal stopped me with a hand on my arm. "I've got it."

The door clicked shut behind him, and the silence that followed was damn near suffocating, the earlier weight on my shoulders returning. I leaned against the wall, cradling my coffee as if it were my last line of defense against the guilt trying to seep into my bones and take over.

Maybe trying to go after the stalker alone was reckless. Maybe I hadn't thought things through. But damn, Eric sure knew how to get in the way. I could've—well, I didn't know what I could've done, but *anything* was better than nothing. So what if it wasn't the guy? I'd rather be called crazy and be wrong than be right, and the guy got away. Why couldn't Eric understand that?

Maybe it was stupid, but I didn't care.

And James. I wanted some kind of good news for him. Some lead to show him I wasn't just sitting on my hands—or, more correctly, Eric's hands.

"You look like you haven't slept in decades. You should try a medically induced coma. Ten-ten, best sleep of my life."

I huffed a laugh through my nose, my arms dropping to my sides. "Yeah, like I could afford this lavish lifestyle." I gestured vaguely to him.

He tsked. "Shoulda been born a Native." He grinned. "Got those Tribal Benefits for life."

This time, the laughter came easier. But as the quiet settled again, I stared at the floor.

"Car accidents aren't contagious, you know," he said after a minute, his voice softer. "You can come sit." He gestured to the chair next to his bed.

I shook my head. "Debatable if you keep hanging out with me."

He didn't respond immediately, but when I looked up, his expression was serious. His eyes flicked from me to the chair, a silent demand.

"Fine," I rolled my eyes as I sank into the seat. "Happy?"

"Ecstatic," he deadpanned, but a smile pulled at the corner of his lips.

I picked at my nails, avoiding his gaze.

"Vi—"

"I'm sorry," I choked out. The sting in my eyes threatened to spill over, but I looked to the ceiling, refusing to let them fall.

The last thing James needed to do was comfort me when he was the one hurting.

His confusion softened into something quieter. He shifted, wincing as he scooted over in the bed. My brows furrowed as he patted the now-empty space beside him.

I hesitated, but his expectant look made it clear he wouldn't let it go. With a sigh, I climbed into the bed next to him, careful not to jostle his injuries. We lay there side by side, staring at the ceiling as if it held answers we couldn't find anywhere else.

"Not as cool as laying on the roof watching the stars, but...." James shrugged a single shoulder, pursing his lips.

I didn't respond, and neither of us looked away from the ceiling.

"I'm okay." His words were almost a whisper but still firm.

"Still debatable." I chewed on the inside of my cheek.

He waited, giving me the space to speak, but the words wouldn't come. Finally, he broke the silence. "Do you think it's my mom's fault for what my dad did to us?"

I turned my head to look at him, stunned. "No? The *fuck?*"

"And if the roles were reversed," he continued, no emotion crossing his face as he continued to stared up, "if you were in this bed instead of me, would you blame me for you being here?"

I rolled my eyes. "It's not the same."

"It *is* the same," he said firmly. "You just have a nasty habit of blaming yourself for everything. None of this is your fault. You didn't ask for this. The only difference between you getting stalked and me not getting stalked is luck—or bad luck, I guess. *You* didn't hit me with a car, Vi. We're dealing with shitty people doing shitty things. That's on them, *not* you."

I snorted, bitterness thick in my voice. "No, I just have a bright flashing sign on my head that screams, '*I have trauma, psychos welcome.*'"

James laughed, the sound rough but genuine. "Cas has the same trauma, and no one's ever hit me with a car over her."

"There was that one fight outside tumbleweeds with the guy who had the massive gap in his two front teeth." I pointed out, smirking.

James grinned. "'*Thee led me on!*'" he mocked the man's heavy lisp. We both chuckled.

"Speaking of Cas...." I trailed off, watching his face carefully as I tried to find the words. "She was here... the whole time. Never left. I'm not even sure she showered." A soft, awkward laugh left me.

He sighed heavily, running a hand over his face and wincing at the movement. "I knew from the moment we met, her screaming at me in that stupid little hole-in-the-wall pie shop for grabbing the last chocolate slice, that I wanted to spend the rest of my life getting yelled at by her," he admitted, his voice thick. "But she's not ready, and maybe she never will be. I'm okay with that. I'll be whatever she needs, no matter what that means."

His words hit hard, not expecting a damn near love confession from him. I had known they both harbored feelings for each other, but they both slept with other people and often. I had just assumed whatever they had fizzled out like small-time crushes did. But after seeing Cassie not just in the hospital with James but even after the gym burnt down... What they had was a lot more than just a crush.

"She cares, I know that. But I also know that there's some shit inside her that makes her feel like she can't love, or be loved, without someone getting hurt in the process," he finished.

He eyed me as if silently accusing me of something.

I furrowed my brows. "What? That's not what I'm doing," I lied, knowing it was pointless because he always saw right through everyone.

"You guys are literally carbon copies of each other. It's like you both were made from the same star or whatever she says. Split right down the middle. You both hide when things get too emotional. She's quick to anger and dramatics, while you shut down and use sarcasm for defense."

"So now you're giving me the boy talk, too? Maybe *you* and Cas are carbon copies." I tried to deflect, but he wasn't having it.

"I don't give a shit if you get with Eric or not. I only want you to stop beating yourself up for shit *none* of us can control."

The door swung open, and Cassie walked in, her hand on her hip and her annoying confidence back in full force. "Well, *I* give a shit! For the love of Gaia, please just fuck the man."

I couldn't help but smile, the memory of how close I had gotten to doing just that flashing through my mind.

I'm supposed to be mad at him.

She flopped onto the foot of the bed, her head lading on my legs as her calves dangled over the railing at the end. Kal appeared moments later, arms full of baked goods.

"*Ope*, didn't know I was crashing the long-awaited threesome," he quipped.

Without missing a beat, all three of us lifted a middle finger to Kal in unison.

My Camry's interior was dark, except for the dim glow of the dashboard and the distant hospital parking lot lights. Derik Feiin's voice poured through the speakers, gravelly yet smooth, the melody of *The Sun* wrapping around me. My fingers curled around the steering wheel, squeezing tight enough to turn my knuckles white.

I should have gone home days ago. Instead, I'd dreaded it, circling the idea of stepping inside the apartment as if it were a crime scene—because, well, it *was*. My space had been defiled, my walls marked with a deranged message I still wasn't ready to process. I knew what the cops would say, what everyone *kept* saying. That I should be scared. That I should let them help. That it wasn't my job to be brave, that I didn't have to.

But I wasn't being brave—didn't *feel* brave.

I felt pissed.

Let them help? That was the problem, wasn't it? The proprietors of testosterone and overcompensation always thought they had to handle things *for* you. Whether it was Connor forcing me to live the life he wanted, moving me across the board like some chess piece, my father who etched himself so deep into mine and Cassie's bones that it still shaped our outlook on love, or the faceless coward who had crept into my home, carving his obsession into my walls. Always men deciding, acting, *taking*.

I gritted my teeth and hit the gas, driving through empty streets. The song played on, but my mind was somewhere else. Anger gnawed at my ribs, clawed at the inside of my throat, begging to be let out. I wasn't some weak, fragile thing waiting to be taken care of who needed a man to complete her. I didn't *need* protecting. I needed men to stop thinking they could dictate me, own me.

James was the only exception. He never tried to fix us. Never smothered us in the name of protection or wanted to mold us into something easier to handle. He just existed beside Cassie and me, letting us be as fucked up and reckless as we needed to be. Cassie deserved someone like that. Someone who saw her—really saw her—and didn't try to dull her edges. James could be that person—was that person. I just hoped she would let herself have it.

I pulled in front of my apartment, the engine idling as I stared at the dark windows. The last time I was here, Eric had whisked me away to show me his mansion-fortress, trying to help in his own way by offering me one of his many guest rooms. But I had refused and opted to stay the nights at the hospital while James slept, and Cassie watched over him. Now, heat curled in my chest, twisting into something volatile.

I climbed out of the car and stalked up the steps, already bracing myself for what I would find.

But when I opened the door, my stomach dropped.

The place was spotless.

Not a single sign of the destruction that had been here before. No broken glass. No spray paint scarring the walls. The air smelled clean, like someone had erased every trace of what had happened—lemon, bleach, and... *vanilla.*

I didn't need to ask who had done it.

"MEN!" I shouted, throwing my arms up before storming back outside.

Eric. *Of course,* it was Eric. Of course, he thought he was helping. Of course, he believed he could take this off my hands, fix it like I was some helpless little thing who couldn't face the damage on my own.

I wasn't grateful.

I was furious.

I stomped toward my car, ready to drive straight to his place and tell him exactly where he could shove his good intentions.

A figure stood at the driveway's edge, and I stopped cold.

I forgot how to breathe.

He didn't move.

Didn't speak.

Just *watched.*

The night air suddenly too sharp, too thin, my pulse slammed against my ribs, each beat a warning, a frantic plea for me to run. But I couldn't.

The world around me shrank, the edges of my vision narrowing until all I could see was *him.*

THE FIGURE STOOD JUST BEYOND THE STREETLIGHTS' reach, wrapped in black. His hoodie sat low over his brow, hands loose at his sides, head slightly tilted. The only visible part of him—the glint of his eyes beneath the balaclava—watched me.

A slow, deliberate breath rattled out of me.

Then, he moved.

One exaggerated, taunting step. His leg swung out almost mockingly before planting on the pavement with a hollow thud.

I fixated on the movement, my brain unraveling every possible scenario. If he got to me, I couldn't fight him off. He was taller, broader—his presence alone devoured the air between us. But I wouldn't go down without a fight.

I had one chance. One shot to outmaneuver him.

And I needed him closer.

I swallowed hard and shifted my weight, taking a single, measured step back. The moment my foot moved, he mirrored, stepping forward as if we were locked in some grotesque, demented dance.

The front door was too far—and locked. He'd be on me before I even got the key in. My neighbors were out, the two other apartments vacant. James was in the hospital, Cassie by his side, and Eric... I had pushed Eric away for trying to prevent this *exact* situation.

The weight of it crashed over me.

He had been watching me. Watching them. Watching every tiny detail of my life, waiting for the perfect moment. And I had basically served myself on a platter.

I could scream, but how long before someone got to me? Before he shoved a knife in my gut? Or take me?

"Never let them take you to a second location. No one will find you, and that's where they'll kill you."

James's words rang in my head.

So, this was it. I'd fight here. I'd die here.

Poetic.

My phone was already in my hand from when I had texted Cassie that I had gotten here safely.

Safe. What a fucking joke.

I curled my fingers around it behind my back, trying to unlock it by feeling alone.

Stupid fucking touchscreen.

My thumb trembled over the screen.

Come on. Come on.

Psycho dickhead tilted his head again as if he were trying to see past me. My heart slammed against my ribs. There was no way he could see what I was doing from that distance.

Then, slowly, he straightened and shook his head.

A silent command.

I must have been transported to Pluto, because there was no fucking oxygen in my goddamn lungs.

The night pressed in—thick and suffocating. The silence wasn't *empty*. It was alive, coiling like an unseen force waiting to snap.

He took another step.

I took one back. My heel hit the first porch step.

I will not let him take me.

My stomach clenched. My mind raced. I had to make this count.

Another step back.

Another step forward.

I inhaled slowly and deeply, the breath filling my lungs as if it might be my last. My pulse roared in my ears, drowning out the quiet.

Love you, Cas.

I turned and bolted for the door.

He lunged.

A hand slammed over my mouth before I could scream. A thick arm locked around both of mine, pinning them to my ribs. My back crashed against his chest, the heat of him burning through my clothes.

I thrashed. Kicked. Twisted. My heel stomped hard onto his foot, but he drove me forward before I could do it again, slamming me against the front door. My cheek struck the door, the impact rattling my teeth.

"Shhh," he murmured, the sound almost tender—a sick parody of comfort. His breath fanned over my skin. Fingers combed through my hair in slow, strokes, grotesquely gentle.

A violent shudder crawled down my spine, the hair on the back of my neck standing on edge.

He sighed, deep and contented, his mask shifting. A breath later, his nose pressed into the back of my hair. He inhaled as if he were *savoring* it.

"God, that smell," he groaned. "It's fucking addictive."

My stomach twisted. I twisted with it, but his grip was unyielding.

"What a pretty little thing you are when you're scared," he purred.

The voice scratched at something distant in my memory. Familiar, but just out of reach.

Not Connor.

But I *knew* this voice.

His fingers fisted in my hair, yanking my head back from the door. Pain splintered across my scalp as he knocked my skull against the wood—not hard enough to knock me out, but enough to hurt something fierce.

"Unlock the door," he ordered.

I didn't move.

His grip tightened. A sharp sting tore through my scalp.

My fingers fumbled into my pocket, trembling as I fished out the keys. The door blurred, my vision spinning.

Think. Think. Think.

I dropped the keys.

The slight clatter echoed like a gunshot in the quiet. My pulse pounded as I waited, prayed, for him to bend down and move just enough to expose himself to the doorbell camera above the handle.

He didn't.

A slow, knowing exhale left him.

"Hm."

His body pressed harder against mine. His fingers slid over the back of my head before twisting cruelly in my hair again, forcing my head back. I strained to see past the edge of my vision, to catch any part of his now unmasked face.

"You think I won't fuck you right here?" His voice dipped, dark amusement laced with cruelty. "Think I won't *smile* into that little camera when I'm done?"

The hard press of his arousal ground against my ass. Bile burned up my throat.

I swallowed it down. I refused to let him see the fear clawing its way up.

Instead, I forced my voice into something sharp and cruel.

"I've had bigger."

His body went rigid, and a low growl rumbled from his throat.

"I'm going to *cut out* every inch of you that they've touched."

Through the terror, something reckless flared inside me.

"Better get a move on, then," I whispered. "It'll take you a while."

His grip *wrenched* at my scalp.

"You ruin the pretty parts every time you open that *goddamn* mouth."

A humorless laugh scraped up my throat. "Just get it over with."

I needed time. Just a little more time.

He exhaled. "Unfortunately, I have other plans for us right now." His mask slipped back into place, and I had to fight the frustrated cry that tried to leave my lips.

He shoved me down. I hit the porch hard, the keys just inches from my nose. I snatched them up with shaking fingers, shoving the right one in the lock.

The moment the door creaked open, he kicked it wide. I was flung inside. Pain jolted through my knees and my arm as I caught myself against the floor.

He waltzed in, swinging the door shut with a dramatic flourish.

I rolled to my ass, scrambling backward and dragging myself across the floor to get away.

His steps were unhurried as he stalked toward me.

"Oh, no point in any of that, now," he drawled.

He reached for my arm, but I kicked at him.

He laughed—short, amused. Then, he grabbed my foot mid-kick and yanked, pulling me closer.

He drove his boot into my stomach.

Once, twice.

Air ripped from my lungs. My body curled in on itself.

Fingers wrapped around my throat.

I barely had time to react before he hauled me up, my toes barely brushing the ground. His grip crushed my windpipe, pressure mounting as I clawed at his arm, but his reach was too long.

My legs kicked out, desperate. My knee slammed into his gut. The force of it knocked me from his grip. I dropped, collapsing onto the floor. My body screamed in protest.

I had *seconds*.

I pushed up, bolting toward my bedroom.

The gun. If I could get to my closet—

A brutal arm locked around my waist just as I reached the hallway threshold, wrenching me back.

He lifted me in the air as I kicked and swung my elbows back violently.

He threw me onto the couch, his weight caging me down.

"Stop being such a fucking bitch." His face hovered inches from mine, breath sour with rage. "You let everyone else inside you. It's *my* fucking turn."

I thrashed—desperate to move, to breathe, to fight. But he was stronger.

They were always stronger.

He dipped his face closer.

I lunged, my teeth sinking into his cheek through the fabric of his mask.

His scream ripped through the apartment.

A fist cracked against the side of my face.

The world tilted. A wave of static buzzed in my skull. I watched, motionless, as he reached behind his back, pulling out a gun.

"Thank you." He lifted the Glock, waving it haphazardly between us.

The barrel found my chin, nudging it up. "Now, act right."

One slight movement, and he'd shoot me.

At least it would be over.

I inhaled, closing my eyes and readying myself to move—

Headlights slashed through the window. He stiffened, his grip on the gun tightening as his head snapped toward the interruption.

"You've got to be *kidding* me." His voice dripped with irritation.

The gun never wavered. Even as he turned his head toward the window, his arm remained locked, the cold barrel still pressing against my chin. I swallowed hard, forcing my body to remain motionless, though my pulse thundered in my ears.

Don't be Cassie. Don't be Cassie.

I could deal with this. But I couldn't deal with anything happening to her.

He huffed, head tilted slightly as if piecing something together. Then, his gaze flicked back to me, a cruel smirk curling beneath the mask.

"Your little boyfriend is here to ruin all the fun."

Eric.

Relief and dread crashed into me all at once, a brutal tide pulling me under.

Psycho douche bag stood, finally peeling his weight off me, but the gun remained trained on my chest. My body sagged into the couch, but I still couldn't move. My limbs were locked, frozen in the shape he'd left me in.

"Don't move. Don't make a sound," he ordered.

As if I could. As if my body wouldn't have listened to him if I *tried*.

Outside, the car engine cut off. The sound sent another rush of panic through me.

He moved toward the back of the kitchen, his steps slow. My breath came in shallow pants, the world narrowing to the lethal weight of the weapon pointed at me.

At the back door, he hesitated. His head tilted once more, listening. Then, his gaze slid back to me, something almost... playful in his eyes.

"Another time then, sunshine."

Then he was gone.

The door was left slightly ajar.

I stayed where I was. I couldn't move. My lungs burned from the shallow, ragged breaths I forced out. I couldn't even make a sound.

A knock at the front door.

"Violet," Eric's voice came through, tight with concern. "Please, let me in."

I tried to speak. My lips parted, but only a weak, broken squeak escaped. I swallowed, forcing air into my lungs, and tried again.

"Eric." It was barely more than a whisper, but somehow, he heard it.

The door burst open, the sharp crack of wood and metal splitting as the door slammed against the wall. Eric was kneeling in front of me in an instant. His hands were on my face the moment I finally was able to sit up, his touch impossibly gentle as he brushed over my already bruising skin.

His eyes—wild, frantic— scanned me as if he were searching for something irreparably broken. His fingers hovered near my cheekbone, his jaw clenching so hard I thought his teeth might crack.

His gaze met mine, demanding answers. Then his head turned, scanning the room like a predator seeking its target. His body remained in front of me, hands still gingerly on my skin, but his eyes locked onto the back door.

I saw the wheels turning in his head immediately.

The shift in his stance, the tightening of his muscles, the way his breathing slowed as raw fury set it.

No.

Panic jolted through me as he moved. My hand shot out, gripping his wrist before he could take another step.

He whirled back to me so fast it made my head spin. His face darkened, confusion flickering before giving way to something far more dangerous.

"He has a gun," I whispered.

Eric's nostrils flared. His lips parted, his breath uneven. "I could not possibly give *any* less of a shit."

I yanked harder on his wrist, forcing his attention back to me. "Just... grab me my phone."

His brow furrowed, hesitation creeping into his expression. But there was something else, too—understanding. A realization that sent something awful flickering behind his eyes.

I didn't have to guess what he was thinking.

His gaze dropped to my body. Not in the way it usually did, not with heat or teasing, but with a quiet, devastating kind of horror.

My throat tightened. My grip on his wrist did, too. "It didn't get that far. I'm *fine*. Eric. My phone."

His jaw flexed, the muscle ticking violently, but he nodded. He strode across the room, snatching up my phone from where it had landed in the struggle. His hands were steady when he handed it to me, but his eyes were a storm of barely contained rage.

He watched as I unlocked it, his eyes never leaving my

movements. Pain, confusion, fury—they all fought for dominance within him, but he said nothing.

I opened an app and turned the screen toward him, a slow, satisfied smile tugging at my lips despite the fear still rolling through me.

His eyes flicked down, scanning the screen. His brows pulled together, then snapped back to me. "You...." The word barely left his lips, more breath than voice.

I finished for him "Planted a locator on him. Yeah."

His head snapped up, stunned silence stretching.

"So you planned for him to—" He cut himself off, his throat working around the words he couldn't bring himself to say.

I nodded. "This was going to happen eventually."

He didn't move. His hands flexed at his sides, body coiled tight, rage boiling over.

"I needed some kind of insurance that he'd be caught even if I was... dead."

He exhaled sharply as if I'd punched the air from his lungs. He dragged a hand down his face, shaking his head.

"I've never been so equally turned on by your brains as I am pissed off in my life."

A snort escaped me, and pain lanced through my bruised cheek, making me wince. "Okay, well, get over it. Pretty sure I have a concussion, so I can't drive. And we need to go stalk a stalker."

"We should talk about what happened." Eric's words were slow, testing.

The tires of his Camaro hummed against the road, a steady vibration beneath me, but my focus never wavered from the glowing red dot crawling across my screen. My fingers ached from how tightly I gripped my phone. My breath stayed controlled, measured—because if I let it slip, if I let myself truly *feel*, I'd come undone.

I knew this was reckless. I knew chasing the fuckwad without a solid plan was stupid, that I should wait, call the cops, do *anything* but barrel headfirst into danger. But I couldn't. Not after everything he'd done. Not after what he took from me—what he had almost taken.

There was no time to run to Eric's arsenal of weaponry, though he tried to convince me we should. There was this nagging feeling in my gut screaming that if we didn't follow this asshole now—if we gave him a chance to find the device and disappear—he'd hurt someone I loved again, or *worse*.

We had to do this now.

"Turn here." My voice came out harsher than I intended.

He sighed but obeyed, the wheel shifting smoothly under his hand. His knuckles were tight, gaze flickering toward my lap—toward the gun resting there.

"At least tell me you're okay enough to handle that."

"I'm fine," I snapped. "Turn here."

His fingers flexed against the leather, but he didn't argue. The weight of the gun had become an extension of me. A constant reminder of what I was willing to do—about to do.

"You know how to use it?" He asked, his voice too calm.

I rolled my eyes. "Yes—"

"It's different when you're pointing it at someone."

My head snapped toward him at the obvious statement. "And you would know that better than me?"

His jaw tightened. A muscle ticked near his temple. He started to answer, but my phone screen blinked—the red dot had stopped moving. My stomach clenched.

"He's in there," I said, my pulse hammering.

I pointed to the looming structure ahead—a factory. It was old and abandoned, its windows gaping black voids, cardboard covering the broken glass, and layers of graffiti bleeding into the rusting metal.

A short, bitter laugh slipped from my throat. "How cliche."

Eric pulled to the curb, killing the engine, but I was already moving. My fingers tightened around the Glock as I shoved the door open.

"Wait." His voice cut through the night as he climbed out of the car.

I spun. Anger and exhaustion crashed over me in waves. Or maybe it was the lingering concussion. "I thought I was going to die," I said, the words thick in my throat. "He nearly killed James, tried to kill Cassie. You can come, or you can stay out here. But it ends now."

Eric grunted, crossing his arms over his chest. "I'm saying we don't know what we're walking into. Running in there guns blazing isn't the best idea."

I let out a sharp breath. "Fine. What would you suggest, Mr. Secret Agent?"

He dragged a hand through his hair. "I'd love if you'd let me handle this myself...."

I glared at him.

He sighed. "But I know you'd kill me, and then run in there anyway."

I lifted a shoulder in silent confirmation.

He turned toward the building, his gaze sweeping over it with unnerving precision. He wasn't just looking—he was assessing.

This isn't new territory for you, is it, Mr. Bond?

"This isn't where he lives."

I frowned. "And you think that because?"

"If he was smart, he wouldn't go home in case he was followed," Eric murmured. "He'd go somewhere with cover. Somewhere with lots of places to hide."

My fingers tightened around my phone. "Why do you know that?"

He didn't answer right away. His gaze was still fixed on the factory, his shoulders coiled with tension. "It's what I'd do."

That shouldn't have sent a thrill through me, but it did.

"He doesn't know we're here," he muttered, "but I doubt he picked a random building to hide. This could be his... home away from home."

"You were going to say lair."

"Forgive me for not being well versed in labeling your attackers hideout." A pause before he says, "we need to be quiet, careful."

I rolled my eyes. "No shit."

He turned to me. "I don't doubt you can handle yourself, but emotions make people unsteady. You can't hesitate. Aim for the chest—it's the biggest surface area. Always make sure they're dead, but don't get close in case they aren't. And never turn your back."

I narrowed my eyes. "I'm choosing to ignore the massive red flag that's screaming at me about how you know all of this, and pretending it's because you *really* like action movies."

He just looked at me, and something in my stomach coiled even tighter.

I exhaled shifting my weight. "You know this makes you guilty by association, right? You walk in there with me, you're just as guilty as I am. No tattling."

A slow, crooked grin tugged at his lips. "I'll follow you anywhere, gorgeous."

Even now—right before we stepped into hell—he still managed to make my heart stutter.

I'll analyze that later.

I didn't think. I just moved, pushing up onto my toes and pressing my lips to his. It was quick, familiar, as if we'd done it a thousand times over a thousand lifetimes before. A kiss that felt like a habit—natural, normal.

But we weren't normal. We weren't coming home from work, greeting each other after a long day.

We were on the cusp of damning ourselves together.

Eric's fingers brushed my wrist when I pulled away, his eyes searching mine. "Once we do this, there's no going back."

I turned toward the factory, gripping the gun tighter.

"I don't want to go back."

We stepped into the dark together.

55

THE AIR INSIDE THE FACTORY WAS FILLED WITH DUST, rust, and the stench of something rotting. My boots barely made a sound against the concrete as I moved forward, the gun cold in my grip. The factory spread in every direction, a maze of corroded machinery and towering metal beams.

Eric moved just ahead of me, his steps controlled. His gaze moved across the shadows as if he could see straight through them. His body was tense, but eerily composed.

This definitely isn't your first rodeo, buckeroo.

A metallic creak echoed from somewhere in the dark.

I stilled, my heart slamming into my ribs.

He motioned for me to stay close before crouching behind a rusted crate. I followed, swallowing the tightness in my throat. The locator on my phone showed the red dot unmoving, pulsing on the screen like a beacon.

I frowned, my grip tightening on the gun as I moved toward the signal. It led us deeper, past collapsed scaffolding and empty oil drums.

Something's not right.

Unless he was hanging out on the roof above us, he should have been right—

My eyes latched onto a small familiar sticker stuck to the side of an empty oil drum.

Trapped. Trapped. Trapped.

A gunshot cracked through the air.

Eric moved faster than I could process. One second he was behind me, the next he was shoving me aside, his body twisting as the bullet struck.

He grunted, stumbling back, his hand snapping to his thigh.

My breath locked in my chest.

Stupid, *stupid* man.

A shadow moved in the rafters—then another shot rang out. I ducked, my back slamming against the nearest beam as Eric shoved me back again. Then footsteps faded like an echo of my own racing heart.

Go after him.

But I didn't.

I was too focused on the fact that this man—this godlike man who looked like the devil but smelt like heaven—literally took a bullet for me.

The sound of a car engine turning over broke me from my thoughts, and I bolted toward it. I reached the spot where we had squeezed into the building, Eric in tow, only to see the dark Honda peel away.

MOTHERFUCKER.

I turned to Eric. He was standing, weight shifted to one side, barely wincing as blood stained his ripped pant leg.

I stared at him, breathless. "Are you even human?"

He glanced down at his leg as if he was only now remembering he'd been shot. His gaze lifted to mine. "Are you okay?"

I let out a sharp, disbelieving laugh. "*Me?* Am *I* okay? You just got shot!"

He examined the torn fabric, blood soaking through. He exhaled through his nose, unimpressed. "Just a scratch."

I wanted to throttle him—or let him throttle me.

Adrenaline really did mess with your brain, or maybe it was still the concussion.

I dragged a hand down my face, forcing myself to breathe and shut down the thoughts my vagina had sprung on me.

The bastard got away.

Again.

IT WAS SILENT NOW, EXCEPT FOR THE DRIPPING OF WATER from some unseen leak and the slow, steady rhythm of Eric's breathing beside me. My pulse still pounded from the moment we walked into this place, from the sickening panic that surged through me when I saw Eric hit the ground.

"You need a doctor."

"I *am* a doctor."

I rolled my eyes.

Stubborn, stupid, stupid *man.*

I swept my flashlight over the dark expanse of the factory floor. It was a one-in-a-million chance that the psycho would have left anything behind, but I held out hope that this might be his regular haunt when he wasn't at home or stalking unsuspecting, fed-up women.

Frustration burned beneath my skin. "You were shot."

"Was I?" His sarcasm was going to be his death. I swore it.

I gritted my teeth, trying to focus on the task at hand.

A door loomed ahead, slightly ajar, its chipped paint

curling away from the wood—a forgotten office tucked into the far end of the factory.

He noticed it the exact moment I did.

"Ten bucks says we're about to walk into some creepy shit," I muttered, more to myself than him.

He chuckled. We moved carefully, the floor groaning beneath us. When I pushed the door further open, the hinges let out a low, eerie whine.

Definitely creepy.

My flashlight cut through the darkness, illuminating the space inside—

A sharp breath rushed from my lungs, and I fought back the bile rising in my throat.

Eric tensed beside me as his eyes scanned the room.

"What. The. Fuck."

ERIC'S CAR BARELY ROLLED TO A STOP BEFORE HE THREW the door open and rounded the vehicle, moving toward me before I could unbuckle my seat belt.

I wrenched the handle and stepped out before he could get any closer. "Don't," I warned, my clenched fists aching from the pressure.

This man. This stupid, stupid man with his bullet wound and his need to make sure I was okay when *he* was the one who needed a fucking doctor. This man and his refusing to let me drive when his leg had nearly been blown off.

I hate him. I hate him. I... might be in love with the stupid, stupid man.

"Violet—"

"I mean it," I bit out, moving toward his house.

He barely limped as he followed, as if taking a bullet was just a mild inconvenience. As if it still wasn't bleeding beneath his jeans.

As if he hadn't nearly *died*.

Another fucking person I care about hurt.

Inside, he sat on the closed toilet lid, leaning back like he hadn't saved me... like he hadn't made everything worse. The wound wasn't terribly deep, but the sight of his blood still sent something dark spiraling through me.

This was why I needed to do this alone. At least that way, everyone would stop trying to be a hero and risking themselves.

"This is exactly why," I muttered, yanking the first aid kit from under his sink. My hands shook as I set it down. "*This* is why I didn't want you to help."

He exhaled, dragging a hand through his hair. "This is exactly why you *can't* do this alone. If he had... I'd skin him alive and sew him back together just to do it again. He will already die a slow, painful death for what he's done to you, but I'd love to let my creativity soar."

I cringed at the imagery, but my thighs clenched at the thought of what he might do to someone for touching me—hurting me.

He's still stupid.

"That isn't helping. Throwing yourself in front of a goddamn bullet isn't helping."

His expression remained infuriatingly steady. "My bad. Next time, I'll just let you take the brunt of it all," he deadpanned.

The words lodged in my throat, tangled with rage and something dangerously close to desperation. I grabbed a gauze pad and pressed it against the wound harder than necessary. "I can take care of myself."

He barely flinched, the bastard.

"Sure, and I'd believe you if I hadn't watched you repeatedly prove that you have a death wish." He smirked, teasing but laced with something more serious. "Plus, I'll take any excuse to get your hands on me."

I nearly dropped the gauze.

I shot him a glare, but he just watched me, his eyes dark. "Eric."

He hummed in acknowledgment, utterly unrepentant.

I pressed harder against the wound, and this time, he sucked in a breath. "Sadist," he murmured.

"Funny, I was just thinking the same thing about you."

Among other things.

His voice lowered. "Glad to hear thinking about me has become a habit. What an honor it is to grace this beautiful mind." He reached up and brushed a strand of hair behind my ear as I leaned over his leg.

I ignored the heat curling in my stomach, ignored the way his flirting sent something unwanted—something stupid—fluttering in my chest. I focused on the blood staining my fingers, on the memories clawing their way to the surface.

My hands were shaking.

"I used to do this for my mom," I heard myself say. The words came from somewhere distant, pulled from a place I didn't want to go. "After my dad would go off on one of his drug-fueled come-downs."

Eric's gaze didn't waver, steady, patient, waiting.

"I perfected my running stitch on her face." A bitter laugh escaped. "Patching her up like it meant anything... like it would stop it from happening again." I focused intensely on the wound and what my hands were doing. "It never did."

His hand reached down, brushing my arm in comfort.

"You're an idiot," I muttered.

His lips quirked. "And so I've been told."

I shook my head, sealing the bandage with medical tape, fighting the unwanted warmth in my chest that battled with my anger.

Angry butterflies. Stupid, infuriating, lovesick butterflies.

He stood, moving into his bedroom, and I followed.

"You told me I was stupid. Yet, you didn't hesitate to do an arguably more fucking dumb thing. Don't do that again." I felt my anger rising back up.

Something flashed in his eyes as he faced me. "That's not how this works. You can command me to do whatever you wish. But when it comes to you and your safety, I will always—"

"Stop doing that! " The words ripped from my throat, raw with frustration. The helplessness, the guilt, the suffocating weight of everything crashed over me, and I shoved at his chest. He barely moved, his body solid, unyielding.

That only made it worse.

I pushed again, harder this time, forcing him further into the room. My breaths came fast, my pulse hammering. "I'm not some damsel in distress! You're not a hero. You're a dumbass! The dumbest ass that *ever* assed!"

His mouth parted, likely ready to say something salacious, but I didn't give him the chance. My fingers went to the buttons of his shirt, tearing them open with sharp, frantic movements.

He stilled.

His eyes burned into mine.

I pushed him again, backing him up until his knees hit the edge of the bed. My fingers worked another button free. "I don't need to be saved." Another. "I don't need to be shielded." My hands slid beneath the fabric, tracing the hard planes of his chest, the warmth of his skin branding my fingertips. "I'm not a fragile thing."

He sucked in a breath, a muscle jumping in his jaw, but he didn't stop me.

I dipped lower, unfastening his jeans, slipping my fingers just beneath the waistband, teasing, tempting. His eyes traced every movement my hands made as I released his hardened length that looked like it could rip me in two.

I dragged my lips down his abdomen before running my tongue up the expanse of his shaft. I paused, removing my tongue and watching Eric, feeling like someone completely other than myself—like some kind of sexual deviant had taken over—and I was obsessed with the feeling. "Are you *listening?*"

His head fell back for half a second, his restraint hanging by a thread.

"Violet," he growled, warning and plea tangled into one.

I smiled—a slow, wicked thing—and moved my lips close enough to the soft tip of his cock, but didn't touch it. "Say it."

His hand shot out, gripping my wrist and pulling me to my feet before tossing me back onto the bed. My leggings were gone in a flash of black fabric flying across the room, and he kneeled at the end of the bed, placing his torso between my bare thighs and spreading them wide for him. His gaze trailed over me, landing on the blood red fabric of my panties, and he licked his lips.

"This may be my new favorite color." His finger traced the front of the fabric, sending shock waves and anticipation through me. His touch slipped beneath the band and ripped them off with such ease I nearly gasped.

His head dipped closer to my exposed flesh and ran a single finger down my slit. "I *lied.* This is my favorite color." I barely had a moment to see the smirk that played on his plump lips before he attached them to my core. A moan left my lips as he feverishly licked, nipped, and sucked at the sensitive skin. I clenched my thighs around his head, reaching a hand down to grip his inky black waves.

A growl left his chest, vibrating through my core as he lifted his head, and I whimpered from the loss of contact. "You could never be fragile or weak. But that *does not* mean I would let someone hurt you and still allow them to breathe." He ran his tongue up my center, before removing his touch all together and staring into the soul that was fast becoming his.

A smirk played on those taunting lips. "Are *you* listening, Violet?"

Oh, you cheeky bastard.

He stood in my silence, his body lowering over me, pressing me into the mattress. His jeans and boxers long gone and forgotten, lips brushing my ear, voice dark and deep and utterly consuming. "I will die for what is mine." His teeth grazed my earlobe, then the sensitive skin below it. He traveled lower, and a yelp left me as his teeth sank into my breast through the material of my shirt. "*Say it*." he ordered.

Knowing what he wanted, and dying to comply—but that sneaky little devil inside me resurfaced.

I hooked one leg around his waist, and in one swift movement, pushed with the other off the bed and flipped him. I straddled him, our naked lower halves millimeters apart. "Make. Me." I narrowed my eyes, dragging the words out in a slow challenge.

His arms shot out to grab ahold of me, but I caught them, pinning them on either side of him. He kept his hands there as I straightened and removed my shirt, exposing myself to him completely and earning another lick of his lips as he took me in.

I ran my slick center along his length and he groaned, the muscles in his arms straining. His hands darted out again, but I pinned them back down as I placed my lips a breath away from his.

His head lifted, trying to connect our lips, but I pulled back just enough to stay out of his reach. "I can take care of myself...." I nipped at his bottom lip. "*Eric*," I purred his name.

A growl left his throat again as he flipped us once more, pinning my arms above my head with one large hand. "But it's so much more fun when I do it." His head dipped down and bit at my exposed nipple, a gasp leaving my lips. I lifted my hips, grinding against his cock, desperately aching for him to be closer—deeper.

"Mmm." Eric closed his eyes at the sensation before grabbing my hip with his free hand, pulling me closer as the tip of his cock brushed my entrance.

I had less than a second to prepare myself before he pushed a few inches inside me. "I will always," he said, his fingers digging into my hip, holding me exactly where he wanted. "Do whatever." —deeper— "It takes." His mouth skimmed my throat, and he went deeper still. "To protect you." He buried himself to the hilt inside me in a brutal thrust, and the noise that escaped me was *animalistic*, so far from human.

I arched into him, dragging my nails down his back, meeting his gaze with fire in my own.

I didn't want to be saved.

But I *did* want to breathe in his scent and taste his soul.

Among other things.

My hands clutched at his shoulders, fingernails digging into his skin as I stretched around his cock with each brutal thrust. His teeth grazed the curve of my neck, a sharp nip that made me gasp, and I retaliated, sinking my teeth into his shoulder. He groaned, the sound deep and primal, and it only spurred him on.

"Fuck, you're divine," he growled, his hands sliding down my thighs, gripping them tight, pulling them higher. He pulled himself fully out of me before sliding his cock back inside in one deep, hard thrust that made me cry out, my back arching off the bed.

"God, you feel so fucking good," he groaned, voice thick with pleasure and something else, something darker, more possessive. His hands were everywhere, exploring, claiming, touching me like he couldn't get enough. One hand slid up my side, his thumb brushing over my nipple, sending a jolt of pleasure straight to my core.

I bit down on my lip, trying to stifle the moans that threatened to escape, but it was useless. He was too much, too deep, too *everything*. My body was on fire, every nerve alight, every touch, every thrust sending waves of pleasure crashing through me. I could feel the tension building, coiling tighter and tighter inside me, and I knew I wouldn't last long.

"Look at me," he demanded roughly. I opened my eyes, meeting his gaze. Those green eyes I loved so much were dark, the gold almost glowing, and the way he looked at me–like I was his, like he would never let me go–sent a thrill through me.

The pad of his thumb rubbed circles on my clit, his hips never stopping, his thrusts hard and unrelenting. He raised his thumb to his lips, sucking lightly. "You taste like *mine*."

"I am." The words left me on a whimper and against my wishes. I wanted so desperately to hold onto that last shred of defiance, but it was clear that I was well and truly his.

A low sound rumbled through his chest, a sound of pure satisfaction, and his hips slammed into me even harder, his cock hitting that spot inside me that made me see stars. His fingers found my clit again, and I cried out. My thighs around his waist, ankles locked behind his back, squeezing and pulling him deeper.

His free hand gripped my hair, pulling my head back as his eyes met mine. "So needy." That crooked smile quirked and I damn near combusted at the sight.

His tongue ran along the exposed flesh of my neck, trailing along my jawline before he pulled my bottom lip between his teeth.

"You're so fucking beautiful," he groaned, his voice thick with need. The thrusts became sloppy, and it drove me wild.

"So fucking perfect. I've wanted you—needed you for so long. To feel you, taste you, to fuck that smart mouth."

"Then do it." The sexual deviant was back and ready to take everything he could give. I needed him everywhere I could get him.

He let out a soft chuckle against my lips before removing his cock, making me whimper at the emptiness. I immediately slid out from underneath him and off the bed, my knees hitting the floor before him.

Eric's hand slid through my hair, fingers tangling in the dark waves as he tilted my head back. The pad of his thumb grazed my chin, coaxing my mouth open with a slow, deliberate pressure. His other hand gripped his cock, gliding it towards my lips. I could feel the heat radiating from him, the thick, hard length of his brushing against my mouth. I parted my lips wider, inviting him in.

He pushed himself slowly into my mouth, the head of his cock pressing against my tongue. The taste of his was heavy, salty, and addictive. I could feel the weight of him, the way he filled my mouth, and it sent a rush of heat straight to my pussy. But I wasn't satisfied with his slow, teasing movements. I wanted more.

Needed more.

I wrapped my lips tighter around him and began to move, sucking him deeper, faster. My tongue swirled around the shaft, teasing the sensitive underside as I took him as far as I could. The sound of his sharp intake of breath only fueled me, and I increased the pace, my hands gripping his thighs for balance as I worked him.

"*Violet*," he hissed through clenched teeth. "If you keep that up, I'll come. And I'm nowhere near done with you."

I didn't listen. I couldn't. The taste of him, the way he felt in my mouth—it was intoxicating. I wanted him to lose control, to give in to the same desperate need that was pulsing through me. I moved faster, my mouth sliding up and down his length, my tongue pressing against him in tight, demanding strokes.

His hand tightened in my hair, yanking my head back with a force that made me gasp. My eyes met his—dark, almost predatory, as he stared down at me.

"You never fucking listen," he said, his voice a mixture of frustration and arousal.

He thrust into my mouth, deeper and harsher than before. I gagged slightly, but he didn't slow. Still gripped my hair, he held me in place as he fucked my mouth with relentless punishing strokes. Tears pricked at the corner of my eyes, but I loved it. The feeling of him taking what he wanted, of him claiming my mouth like it was his—it was overwhelming. A few tears spilled down my cheeks, and Eric caught one with his thumb, brushing it away with a tenderness that contrasted with the roughness of his movements.

"Such a gorgeous sight," he murmured, his voice rough. "You crying over my cock. But now, I want you screaming my name."

In one swift motion, he flipped me onto my hands and knees, my back arched and my ass in the air. The sudden change in position left me breathless, but before I could adjust, I felt the sharp sting of his hand against my ass. The sound of the smack echoed in the room, and I yelped, the pain blending with the pleasure in a way that made my head spin.

"That was for not listening," he said, full of promise.

His hand rubbed the spot he had just slapped, soothing the sting before he bent over me, chest pressed against my back. His breath was hot against my ear when he whispered, "And this... this is for putting yourself in danger."

His hands gripped my ass, spreading me open before he leaned down and bit one cheek. The sharp sting of his teeth made me gasp, but he didn't stop there. He licked over the spot he had bitten, his tongue soft and soothing against my skin. Then he bit the other cheek, his teeth sinking into my flesh before he licked that spot too.

"And that," he said, his voice a low growl, but I could hear the smirk behind it, "denying me such a beautiful ass for so long."

His tongue moved lower, tracing a path down the center of my ass before reaching my core. He wasted no time, burying his face between my thighs and fucking me with his tongue. The sensation was electric. His tongue thrust into me, deep and unrelenting, while his arms hooked themselves under my thighs, holding me in place. I was completely at his mercy, and I loved it.

In one swift motion, he pressed himself against me, the head of his cock brushing against my entrance. He didn't wait, didn't tease—he thrust into me in one smooth, deep stroke. I gasped, my body stretching to accommodate him, the fullness of him inside me sending waves of pleasure through me.

"You take me so well," he groaned, his voice thick with need.

He began to move, each thrust driving me closer to the edge. Hands gripped my hips, holding me steady as he fucked me with an intensity that left me breathless. Then he reached forward, tangling his fingers in my hair and wrenching my head back. I had to rise onto my knees, my back arching as he forced me to look at him. Our eyes locked, and pools of molten green washed over me.

He needed this as much as I did.

He leaned down, capturing my lips in a searing kiss. His tongue explored my mouth, mimicking the rhythm of his thrusts, and I moaned into him, my arms reaching behind me and locking around his neck for balance. The feeling of him inside me, his lips on mine, his hands on my body—it was way too much. The coil was going to break.

"That's it," he moaned against my lips. "Let me feel how much I ruin you."

His words were enough to push me over the edge. My body convulsed, the orgasm tearing through me with a force that left me trembling. I cried out, my nails digging into his neck as I came, my body clenching around him.

But Eric didn't stop. He kept thrusting, his movements becoming even more intense, more desperate. I could feel him getting closer, his rhythm faltering as his own release approached.

"Mine," he growled, his voice full of possession. "Fucking *mine.*"

His movements became erratic, and with one final, deep thrust, he came, body shuddering as he spilled inside me. The warmth of him, the way he filled me completely, it sent a shiver a pleasure through me.

But even as we both came down from the high, the tension was still there. Eric pulled out of me, his breath heavy as he placed a gentle kiss to the top of my hair. I tried to stand, but he hugged me tighter to him, his grip unyielding.

"I told you I was nowhere near done with you."

I opened my mouth to respond, but before I could say anything, he was on me again.

My body was still trembling, my legs weak beneath me, but his arms were there, steadying me, holding me up as if I were the most precious thing in the world. His hands moved over my skin, tracing the curves of my body with a gentleness that surprised me, given the depravity of what just happened.

"Absolutely divine," he murmured against my lips. "Every. Single. Inch." His fingers brushed against my sensitive skin, eliciting a gasp from me.

There was something in his gaze, something raw and unguarded, that made my heart skip a beat. He scooped me up into his arms, holding me bridal style as if I weighed nothing.

"Eric," I protested weakly, but he just smirked down at me.

"Hush," he said, voice teasing, but with an undercurrent that made my stomach flutter. "Let me take care of you for once."

He carried me back through the threshold of the bathroom, I could feel his heartbeat, steady and strong against his chest, and it grounded me.

If I hadn't already fallen for him, the things he did to my body would have done me in.

He set me down gently on the edge of the massive bathtub, his hands lingering on my hips for a moment before he moved to turn on the water.

The sound of the water filling the tub was soothing, and the scent of vanilla, cedar, and sandalwood filled the air as Eric poured in a generous amount of soap. I watched him, my eyes tracing the lines of his back, the way his muscles moved beneath his skin. There was something almost hypnotic about him, something that drew even the strongest of us in and made it impossible to look away.

When the tub was full, he turned to me, gaze soft but still holding that edge of possessiveness. "In you go."

I hesitated for a moment, but his eyes held no room for argument. I slid into the warm water, sighing as it enveloped me, soothing my sore muscles. He knelt beside the tub, eyes never leaving mine as he reached for the sponge and began to wash me, his touch so gentle it almost made me want to cry.

I had never been taken care of like this. A part of me felt weak for letting him, but another part wanted to lean into the feeling.

So I did.

His hands moved over my body, washing away the sweat and the remnants of our passion. He took his time, fingers brushing against my skin with a reverence that made my chest ache. When he reached my arms, he pressed a kiss to my shoulder, lips lingering for a moment before he moved on.

"So beautiful," he murmured.

I couldn't help but laugh, the sound soft and a little breathless. "You're such a bad liar."

Eric's lips curved into a smirk, but his eyes were serious as they met mine. "I don't lie," he said, his voice firm. "Not to you, not about this."

His words sent a shiver through me, and I was suddenly acutely aware of how vulnerable I was, how completely he had me in his grasp. But instead of fear, all I felt was a strange sense of safety, as if I *knew,* deep down, that he would never let anything hurt me.

When he was done, he grabbed a towel and gently helped me out of the tub, drying me off with the same care he had shown before.

"Stay here." He disappeared into the bedroom, leaving me standing there wrapped in a plush towel that cost more than my life savings, and feeling more exposed than I ever had before.

When he returned, he was holding one of his plain black t-shirts, and he held it out to me with a shit-eating grin. I raised an eyebrow at him, my lips curving into a teasing smile.

"Really?" I said, my voice dripping with sarcasm. "Trying to *thoroughly* claim, are you?"

Eric's smile only widened, and he stepped closer, his eyes dark and filled with promise. "I'll spend the rest of my life *thoroughly* claiming you."

I fought the urge to melt right there. He slipped the shirt over my head, fingers brushing against my skin as he helped me into it. The fabric was soft against my skin, and it smelled like him.

He stepped back, eyes scanning me. "Mm, there's something about seeing you in my clothes." His voice was filled with pure male satisfaction.

I rolled my eyes, but there was no real annoyance behind the gesture. Instead, I felt something warm and soft curling in my chest.

"Come on." He offered his hand. "I'm dying to hold you."

I placed my hand in his, letting him lead me back into the bedroom. A soft glow of the moonlight filtering through the floor-to-ceiling windows. He pulled back the covers and helped me into the massive bed, his touch gentle.

He climbed in beside me, pulling me into his arms. His body was warm against mine and I closed my eyes, drifting off to the steady rhythm of our heartbeats synchronizing.

THE SHEETS TANGLED AROUND US, THE ROOM STEEPED IN steady breathing and fading heat. Eric lay on his back, one arm folded behind his head, his skin still warm beneath my touch. I traced a lazy finger along his chest, dragging my fingers over the hard planes, following the steady rise and fall of his breath.

His skin was smooth, except for the faint ridges of old scars, each one a story I hadn't asked him to tell yet.

But I would, as soon as the need to jump his bones every second subsided.

A slow smile pulled at my lips. "Are we still *just* friends?"

His chest vibrated as he let out a low chuckle. His other hand reached for mine, stilling my movements against his skin. His fingers curled around mine, anchoring me, keeping me there with him.

"We are whatever you want us to be," he murmured, his voice thick with sleep. He lifted our joined hands, pressing my palm flat against his lips and kissing it before placing it right over his heart. His gaze caught mine, dark and unguarded. "As long as this...." His thumb brushed the back of my hand, sending a slow ache through me. "Never stops."

Something in my chest clenched—something raw, something terrified.

This wasn't just about the heat, the desperation, the way we had crashed together as if we were the only thing left in the world that made sense. It was about *this*. The quiet. The aftermath. The way he was still here, still looking at me as if I was something worth holding onto.

And I didn't know what to do with that.

I swallowed, letting my fingers move again, tracing over his heartbeat like I could memorize the rhythm. "Is this covered under the doctor-patient confidentiality clause?"

His lips quirked. "Technically, I'm not your doctor anymore."

I hummed, tilting my head. "Fine. Is this covered under the 'hot guy with an arsenal of weapons and questionable motives' confidentiality clause?"

His smirk deepened, but there was a flicker of something else in his eyes. "Hot, huh?"

"Don't get a big head. It's basically the *only* thing I know about you," I said, pressing my palm a little more firmly against his chest.

His gaze flickered, and for a moment, I thought he might deflect, might bury himself in another teasing remark. Instead, he said, "I disagree. But ask me anything."

I hesitated, biting my lip before finally settling on one of the ten million questions I had running through my mind. "How'd you get that scar?" I traced a faint line at the corner of his eyebrow.

His fingers covered mine, his thumb brushing absently over my knuckles as he answered. "Got in a fight when I was sixteen. He was bigger, stronger. But I was faster. I still won." His lips twitched. "Well... mostly."

"Mostly?"

"He got one good punch in before I put him on the ground."

I huffed a quiet laugh. "Sounds about right."

A comfortable silence stretched, but the question gnawed at me, the one I wasn't sure I wanted the answer to. I stared at the play of sunlight over his skin before finally saying, "Why were you so okay with me going after him? With what I'd planned to do if we got to him?"

Eric didn't pretend not to know who I meant. His hand tightened around mine for a fraction of a second before he spoke. "Sometimes, the ends justify the means."

I exhaled sharply, dragging a free hand down my face in frustration. "You and your vague answers."

He chuckled at my irritation, and despite myself, I fought back a smile.

Another silence. This one heavier.

I let out a slow breath and murmured, "I don't know if I could actually do it."

His expression shifted. "*It?*"

"*Kill* him."

The words felt foreign on my tongue, even after all the rage, all the certainty I'd built up in my head. I clenched the sheet in my fist. "I'm just so angry. So tired of feeling out of control. Of feeling... helpless."

Eric sat up on one elbow, turning fully toward me, eyes locking onto mine. "You are not helpless, nor have you ever been."

He kissed me then, softly—no urgency, no desperation, just warmth. Just quiet understanding.

When we broke apart, I searched his face, my heart hammering against my ribs. "Why are you here?"

The bastard chuckled. "I live here."

I smacked his arm, rolling my eyes. "You know what I mean. *Here*. With me."

His smile lingered, but then he sighed, leaning back against his pillow, staring at the ceiling. "I've asked myself that question a thousand times."

I scoffed. "Oh, thanks."

He turned his head. "Could be the sarcasm."

"Eric, I'm being serious."

His gaze held mine, and something in his expression shifted, the teasing fading. "Do you want the truth? Or do you want me to make it sound pretty?"

I swallowed. "The truth."

His voice was quiet, but steady. "I don't know."

My breath caught, but before I could process the sting of his words, he continued.

"I admire your strength... but I would love you without it."

My heart stopped.

"Love?" I whispered, the word barely making it past my lips.

His eyes never left mine, steady as the tide. "Your fire, your beauty, the sharp wit that keeps me on my toes—I love it all. But even stripped of those things, I would still be helplessly, *irreversibly* in love with you."

He paused, searching for the right words, as if even language was inadequate to contain what he felt. Then, softer, "You've carved yourself into me, embedded beneath my skin, wrapped around my soul like a warmth I never knew I was missing. Before you, there was only the cold, an endless stretch of days that felt more like existence than living. And then you —" He exhaled, shaking his head slightly, almost in disbelief. "You stormed into my life, mean and sarcastic, and suddenly, I wasn't just existing—I was alive."

A faint chuckle escaped him. "Of course, our little possible-prison-time escapades keeps things interesting. But none of that is why I can't close my eyes without seeing you. Why my world tilts when you're around."

His fingers traced lazy patterns along my bare skin. "It's the way your laugh gets stuck in my head like a song I never want to forget. The way your smile feels like the first hint of sunrise after so long in the dark. It's the way you make that little noise when I do this–" He ran his tongue along my collarbone, and a soft moan slipped from my lips, making my cheeks burn.

"There's nothing I wouldn't do for you." His voice was like a vow, whispered against my skin. "No length I wouldn't go, no line I wouldn't cross. And let me be *entirely* clear when I say–I do not love you in halves, in hesitation, in conditions."

His hand found my cheek, tilting my face toward his, eyes dark with a devotion that burned through him like an unquenchable fire. "I want you and everything that comes along with having you. You are not too much for me. You could never be. If anything, I'd say you're too infinite, too consuming, too everything. And still, I will never have enough of you."

His eyes darkened, voice drooping to something nearly

sinful. "From the moment you walked into my office, I knew I would die to spend the rest of my life between your thighs, beneath your fingertips, and drowning in your divinity."

My breath faltered, my pulse hammering like the wings of a caged bird. He wasn't just offering words—he was offering ruin, devotion, worship. A love that would consume, devour, and never let go.

And Gaia help me, I *wanted* to be consumed.

I had no words to give him, nothing that could compete with such poetry. Instead, I threw my leg over him and straddled his lap, leaning down to plant a kiss on his bare chest. "That was a lot more than *pretty*."

His hands gripped my hips, pulling his bottom lip between his teeth. "Must have been a poet in a past life."

I rolled my eyes, smirking. My fingers tangled in his hair, pulling just enough to make him groan. "You love me?"

His tone firm. "No pretty words could ever explain how much."

My heart jumped, flipped, somersaulted. I leaned down, brushing my lips against his ear. "Tell me you're mine."

He groaned, his teeth grazing my neck. "You already know I am."

I didn't let up, my voice low, teasing—but I needed it more than I would ever admit. "*Say* it."

He gripped my jaw, pulling my eyes to meet his. "I'm yours, Violet. Every fucking part of me."

Something inside me clicked in place and I kissed him hard, my nails digging into his back as I rolled my hips against him. His hands moved, touching, teasing, pulling me apart piece by piece.

I moaned, feeling dizzy, and he laughed, his lips trailing down my neck, hands gripped my thighs as he whispered against my skin. "I need you. All of you."

I pulled back, hands tugging at the inky black waves, forcing him to look at me. "Prove it."

His grin was wicked, his hands moving to my hips as he rolled his own, grinding against me, his hardened cock sliding against my already soaking core.

"That it's, love," he groaned, guiding me. "Fuck, you feel too good. But I need to taste it."

Smoother than I could comprehend, his arms hooked under my thighs and lifted me until I was straddling his face. I yelped as his tongue swiped against the sensitive flesh between my thighs. The sound that escaped me was somewhere between a gasp and a moan, my thighs trembling as his mouth latched onto me with a hunger that left me breathless. His tongue was relentless, swirling and prodding, teasing every inch of me until I was writhing above him, my hands clutching the headboard for stability.

"Eric—oh my god, Eric—" I choked out, voice breaking as his lips sealed around my clit, sucking in a way that sent shock-waves of pleasure through my body. His hands dug into my ass, holding me in place as he devoured me like a man starved. His tongue dipped lower, thrusting into me, and I cried out, my body arching off the bed.

Fuck.

I was already on the edge, teetering, my legs shaking uncontrollably.

"Let me taste your undoing." His words vibrated against my core and sent me spiraling. I shattered, my body convulsing as waves of pleasure crashed over me. He didn't let up, his tongue working me through it, drawing out every last shuddering moan until I was limp, my chest heaving, my vision blurry.

Before I could even catch my breath, his hands were on me again, lifting me away from his face and pulling me back down onto his lap. His cock pressed against my entrance, the tip barely teasing me, and I whimpered, my body still sensitive from his mouth. I sank down slowly, taking only the tip, relishing in the way his breath caught, the way his hands gripped my hips like he was struggling to hold himself back.

"So fucking cruel," he growled, his voice strained. I grinned wickedly, rolling my hips *just* enough to elicit those sweet sounds he made. With a low growl, his hands tightened on my hips, and he thrust up, burying himself deep inside me. I screamed, the sudden stretch overwhelming, my nails digging into his shoulders as he filled me completely.

His hands moved to my waist as he sat up, face buried in my breasts. His tongue lapped at my skin, licking and nipping every inch he could reach, leaving marks that made me shiver. "Make me come, Violet." His words came out in heavy pants as he thrust into me, movements deep and unrelenting.

My head leaned back, my hands braced against his thighs, riding him with a rhythm that had us both gasping. The sound of our bodies crashing together filled the room, mingling with ragged breathing and desperate moans. I could feel him every-where—inside me, around me, his hands on my skin, his lips on my neck, his claim on my soul.

"Eric," I whispered, voice shaking as I moved. His thrusts became more erratic, his grip tightening as he urged me on. I could feel the tension building, coiling low in my stomach, my body tightening around him.

"Fuck, Violet. I love you. I love you. I love you," he chanted, voice breaking as he slammed into me one final time, spilling inside of me. I came undone. My body shook with pleasure as I screamed his name, my mind blank, my body limp as I collapsed against him, bodies slick with sweat.

For a moment, we just clung to each other, our hearts racing but somehow in sync, our bodies intertwined. His hands moved over me, gentle now. His lips brushed against my shoulder, soft and tender.

I buried my face in his neck, breathing him in, my body still trembling with the aftermath of the vaginal destruction it just endured. I didn't want to let go—didn't think I could.

I would never get enough of this—of him.

Eric wrapped his arms around me, delivering sweet, soft kisses to the valley of my breasts. "Ruin me. *Please.*"

But I was the one who had been *thoroughly* ruined.

The thought sent another wave of heat crashing through me and I moved down between his legs, running my tongue along his glistening shaft, tasting both of our arousals and humming.

Eric watched every swipe of my tongue with that damn crooked grin. "Absolutely insatiable."

James sat propped against his pillows, looking better than before—still pale, still bruised, but less like he might keel over if he so much as moved. His leg remained in a cast, body still healing from the punctured lung, but when the doctor walked in, clipboard in hand, there was something almost triumphant in the way James lifted his chin as if he was daring them to give him bad news.

"Looks like you're good to go home tomorrow," the doctor announced, flipping through James' chart. "You'll still need to take it easy—"

James let out a heavy sigh, already exasperated.

"—but as long as you don't push yourself, you should be fine." The doctor lowered the clipboard. "That means *no* lifting, no strenuous activity."

James gave him a tight-lipped smile that said *I will absolutely not be following that advice.*

Cassie, sitting cross-legged in the chair beside his bed, pointed a finger at him. "That means *no* more playing hero, dumbass."

His lip twitched, but he didn't argue. Max chuckled beside Cassie, shaking his head. Kal, sprawled out in the other chair.

"Okay, enough about *Wonder Boy*," Kal sighed, standing up, "I'm starving. What do you guys want?"

Cassie and Max immediately launched into their orders. Max wildly gestured as he described some sandwich that probably didn't exist in a hospital cafeteria. Eric just asked for a coffee.

Kal, nodding absently, turned to me last. "And you?"

I shook my head. "I'd rather eat my hair than hospital food."

Kal clicked his tongue, rolling his eyes. "Ugh, you're so hard to please." Before he dipped out of the room.

Eric muttered under his breath, "*Debatable.*"

Heat flickered up my spine, a small smile threatening to curl at the edges of my lips as the memory of last night—and this morning—rushed back. My stomach dipped, recalling the way his hands had gripped my waist, the way his mouth had—

James moved.

Subtle, just a small shift in the bed, but when I looked up, his amber eyes were locked onto Eric, then flicked to me with a raised brow, sharp with unspoken meaning.

'You guys fucked?'

I sucked my lips in, resting them between my teeth, and kicked a spot on the floor with the toe of my shoe. A tiny shrug, casual, indifferent. His gaze darted back to Eric—who was now fully engaged in conversation with Cassie and Max, completely oblivious—before cutting back to me.

Another flick of his eyes. This time toward Cassie and back.

'Does she know?'

I pursed my lips.

James' expression shifted—eyes going wide, eyebrows almost meeting his hairline, as he puffed out his cheeks before quickly dropping his gaze to his phone, pretending to be deeply engrossed in whatever was on the screen.

A laugh bubbled up in my chest before I could stop it. Soft, barely audible, but enough.

Cassie turned sharply, her hair swaying. "What's so funny?"

I straightened, schooling my features. "Nothing."

Cassie narrowed her eyes at me, and then James. James, for his part, didn't look up from his phone, but I caught the way his shoulders shook with muted laughter.

She huffed and went back to her conversation, and I leaned back in my chair, biting back another smile.

James stretched his arms over his head, wincing slightly before he settled back against the pillows. "Any more signs of our friendly neighbor stalker-slash-almost-murderer?"

Everyone's attention turned to me.

I hesitated, feeling Eric's gaze flick toward me, quick and assessing.

"Nothing new." The lie felt thin in my mouth, stretched over the truth like worn fabric.

I wasn't just keeping the sex-a-thon with Eric a secret, and I hated myself for it. The factory, the chase, the way my blood had turned to ice when we found the douche bag with a god complex and a pension for making women cower—and how easily it went south. I was hiding the risk I took, and the way Eric had nearly paid for it.

James was healing, Cassie was stressed, and the last thing either of them needed was to findout I was still playing this dangerous game with a psychopath.

Cassie tilted her head, those sapphires narrowing again, and I was sure she saw right through me. "Weird."

I forced a shrug. "Guess he gave up."

She pursed her lips. "That makes zero sense."

Eric chimed in, Allah bless him. "He tried to kill you two and failed. He's probably terrified that one of you saw him and could identify him to the police. Most likely skipped town."

"I mean, obviously, we're still being cautious."

She looked between Eric and me. "Hm. So what were you doing last night, then?" *Fuck.* "You're the one that put the location of that device thing on my phone, stupid." She crossed her arms.

"I was showing her a property I'm thinking of grabbing in town," Eric replied, smooth as ever.

Why is he so good at that?

"What would you want with an abandoned factory?" James questioned, and I shot him a look. He shrugged. "What? You thought I wasn't going to google that shit? I sent the police there when you didn't text us back." His attention turned back to Eric, waiting for an answer.

"It's got good bones."

"Okay...." Cassie's words trailed off. "Well, you can't be going radio silent like that. And the quick '*all good*' text from Eric isn't good enough."

"Okay, okay. I'm sorry. I was honestly just exhausted and a little... distracted." My eyes flicked to Eric, then to my hands as I picked my nails, avoiding Cassie's glare like the plague.

"Yeah, good dick'll do that to ya'," She deadpanned.

Max choked, coughing into his fist. James snorted.

Eric just smirked, leaning back against the wall, smug as all hell.

I glared at Cassie. "I hate you."

She grinned, all teeth. "You love me."

"Wish I didn't."

58

ERIC'S KITCHEN HAD ALWAYS FELT SO INVITING, comforting even, much like the man himself. A place where comfort carried in the scent of his intoxicating aftershave that clung to my soul. But, right *now*, it felt more like a war room than a sanctuary.

The island was littered with photographs, each one a silent, *invasive* witness to the past few months of my life. My breath felt tight in my chest as I stared down at them, my stomach twisting with something ugly.

We had walked into that dark office in the abandoned factory, and my heart and stomach dropped to the depths of hell. The walls were covered in these pictures of *me*, of my friends with their faces burned. I didn't spend much time looking at them before I had to leave the room and empty my stomach in a violent fit of anxiety and nerves. Eric had collected them all while I had gathered myself.

The images weren't just stolen moments—they were proof. Proof that someone had been watching me, shadowing my steps, slipping into my world unnoticed until he'd decided to grace me with his appearance.

I picked up a photo with trembling fingers. It was me at The Coffee House, my eyes distant as I sipped my drink, oblivious to the unseen lens that had captured me. Another showed my silhouette through my apartment window, framed in the warm glow of my living room lamp.

But the worst ones—The ones that turned my blood to ice—were the ones of me asleep.

On Connor's couch.

My fingers clenched around the photograph's edges, the glossy paper crinkling under the pressure. A slow-creeping nausea curled through my gut. He had been inside that house. Inside my apartment. Watching me. Standing over me, while I slept completely unaware of the danger hovering just beyond my consciousness.

I swallowed hard, trying to breathe around the pressure against my ribs.

"He's been watching for much longer than I thought," I murmured.

So why hadn't he acted then? He was right there, had the perfect opportunity, and yet... he *waited?*

Beside me, Eric stood with his arms crossed, his jaw locked so tightly I could see the muscle flex beneath the golden warmth of his skin. His usual air of casual confidence was gone, replaced by something sharper, something lethal. He had been combing through the photos with me, his mind dissecting every detail, searching for anything that could give us a face, a reflection, a clue.

But there was nothing.

Psycho dickhead had been careful. *Calculated.*

I exhaled, dragging a hand through my hair. Frustration burned behind my eyes, a wildfire spreading beneath my skin.

"I *know* his voice. It's right there," I gestured vaguely as if the motion might shake something loose in my brain. "I know it. I just... *don't* know it."

I sounded like a lunatic, but it made sense to me.

Eric hummed in response, a sound of understanding rather than a dismissal. "I get what you mean." His voice was softer now, edged with something close to concern. "Let's take a break and come back to it with fresh eyes. I haven't seen you sleep in three days."

I looked up at him. "We've been a bit *busy*."

His lips quirked, the brief flicker of amusement cutting through the darkness. "Ah, what a lovely *busy* it's been," he said, voice teasing before the seriousness settled back into his features. "You still need sleep."

I scoffed, crossing my arms. "I couldn't sleep even if I tried."

"Looking at this over and over again isn't going to help that." He shifted slightly, his fingers pressing against the counter like he was grounding himself. "Go see James. Take a break with your friends. We can come back to this later."

I clenched my jaw. I knew he was right. But the idea of leaving—of stepping away from this, from him—made something uneasy stir inside me. I had gotten used to Eric's presence, the steady, unwavering certainty of him, and the thought of being away from him, even for a moment, made me feel... *unmoored*.

Desperate.

Pathetic.

My brain was a frayed wire, buzzing with exhaustion and paranoia, and I couldn't help but wonder if he was trying to get rid of me. If he was tired of me hovering over his shoulder, tired of me bringing all of this baggage into his space. Maybe he was shoving me off on my friends because he wanted a break.

The thought stung more than I wanted to admit.

I let out a slow breath, pushing the feeling down where it couldn't sink its claws into me. "Okay." The word came out hesitant, unsure. I covered it quickly with a shrug. "But only because I think my eyes might fall out of my head if I keep looking at these."

Eric huffed a quiet laugh, the warmth in it easing some of the tension in my chest. His lips curved into that dangerously charming smirk that always sent a slow, unwelcome heat curling through my stomach. "It'd be a shame to lose such devastating eyes."

I rolled my *devastating* eyes, ignoring the way my pulse kicked up at his words, and grabbed my jacket.

ERIC'S FINGERS THRUMMED AGAINST THE STEERING wheel; an aimless, rhythmic tapping. His expression remained unreadable—*always* so fucking unreadable. The glow from the dashboard cast sharp shadows across his face, accentuating the tension in his jaw, the slight furrow between his brows. But he didn't look at me. Not once.

A hollow ache settled in my chest, twisting, pressing.

"Nothing but a quick fuck."

Was that all it had been? He got his fill of fucking and almost murdering *together*, and now he was done? Decided I wasn't worth the aftermath?

I wanted to push, to know what the hell had happened to the, *"I'd follow you into hell if you asked"*, Eric. I wanted to demand answers, to claw my way through whatever wall he had just put up between us. But I was drained. Physically. Emotionally. My limbs felt heavy, my mind sluggish, every nerve in my body frayed to the point of breaking. I wasn't sure I could survive his rejection and still hold my head high. Not from someone I had fallen so hard and fast for.

The hospital's fluorescent lights bled into the darkness as we pulled into the parking lot. He shifted gears, the soft click of the car going into park unnervingly final. But he didn't cut the engine.

This was it.

The first time we'd be apart in three days.

I shouldn't have cared so much. But the thought of stepping out of his car, of not having his constant cedar and sandalwood-scented warmth wrapping around me, made my throat close up.

Now, you sound like a psycho-obsessed stalker.

Silence, brittle and unbearable.

What happened to the *"I don't need a man"* Violet? Where was she when I needed her?

I hesitated, my fingers tightening around the door handle.

"Text me if you need me."

His voice was low and careful—too careful—like he was holding something back, pressing it down beneath that mask.

Maybe he was just tired.

Tired of you.

A lump formed in my throat. "Okay," I murmured. My hand lingered on the handle a second longer, like some pathetic part of me was waiting for him to stop me, to say something—that same something he'd already confessed—that I was dying to reciprocate, but couldn't find the words.

He didn't.

I swallowed hard. Forced myself to move.

One foot out the door. Then the other.

I didn't look back.

"See you later," I said, even though it didn't feel like I would.

I STEPPED INTO THE ELEVATOR, PRESSING THE BUTTON FOR James's floor. My reflection stared back at me in the polished metal doors. The yellowing bruise on my cheek was barely visible under the layers of makeup, but I still felt it—an aching reminder of how close he had gotten. How close he could still get.

You need to be smarter.

The only reason I was still here, still breathing, was because of Eric.

Whether I would admit it out loud or not, I really *was* a damsel in distress, and he really *was* a white knight.

My stupid, reckless, white knight.

I *hated* that. *Hated* knowing I needed saving.

And the cold shoulder he gave me when dropping me off seemed to scream how much he hated it, too.

The elevator dinged. I stepped into the hallway, quiet except for the distant murmur of nurses and the occasional beep of machines from the patient rooms. My steps were slow, my body still aching from the factory—and Eric.

I let out a slow breath, packing the heartache into a box labeled *'Deal with later.'*

Cold fingers clamped around my wrist.

An abrupt yank pulled me sideways, my shoulder colliding with something solid as I stumbled into the stairwell.

Panic detonated inside me.

I twisted, trying to wrench free, a scream building behind

my lips. A hand pressed over my mouth and nose, cutting off my air.

A sickly-sweet scent flooded my senses.

No. No. No.

I thrashed, my nails clawing at the iron grip on my face, my lungs burning as my scream died in my throat. My vision blurred, the world spinning in nauseating waves.

Shadows bled into the edges of my sight.

The stairwell blurred, tilting, shrinking.

My knees buckled.

The last thing I saw was the faint glow of the hospital corridor beyond the stairwell door—so close, yet entirely out of reach.

Then—utter darkness.

A SLOW, HAZY AWARENESS BLED INTO THE DARKNESS, hauling me from the depths of unconsciousness like a body pulled from deep water. My head throbbed, a dull, pulsing ache at the base of my skull, my limbs impossibly heavy, immobilized. The effects of whatever he had used to knock me out still clung to my muscles, making each sluggish attempt to move feel like trying to swim through tar.

My eyelids fluttered, the world beyond them swirling in a nauseating blur of weak light and shifting shadows. I struggled to focus, my breath shallow, uneven.

It took a moment to realize I was moving—not on my own, but the car beneath me was in motion, the engine's rumble vibrating through the seat pressed against my cheek.

I was lying across a backseat.

Panic surged, but my body barely responded. My fingers twitched uselessly, my wrists constricted behind me, bound so tightly the rough material bit into my skin. I tried to shift my legs—rope, tight around my ankles. A muted sound of frustration slipped from my lips, barely more than a breath, my throat too dry to make anything louder.

The car rocked gently, the passing streetlights casting fleeting glimpses of my captor in the driver's seat. His face was turned away, but he wasn't wearing a mask. That fact alone sent a new kind of terror creeping in, cold and insidious.

Why wear a mask when he isn't letting you go?

I forced myself to focus, to memorize what little I could through the lingering haze. The dashboard light outlined his profile in eerie half-light—a broad shoulder, a clean-shaven jaw, and fingers that curled loosely around the wheel relaxed. Too relaxed. Like he was enjoying this.

Because *of course* he was. This was the *whole* point. The whole fucked up plan of finally catching his prey, like the disgusting predator he was.

I swallowed hard, willing my voice to work. If I could get him to turn around.... Maybe I'd die tonight, but at least I'd see his face. But my tongue felt thick. My body screamed for me to fight, to kick, to claw—but I was useless, a puppet with its strings cut.

He must have noticed me stirring. His voice wading through the fog in my mind.

"Don't worry," he murmured, amused. "We're almost there."

The words slithered through me, cold and wrong. My lips parted with the monumental need to speak. My voice came out weak, slurred.

"Where?"

A pause.

"Where we started."

My pulse pounded against my skull, a frenzied, worthless thing. My vision tunneled again. I fought against the weight dragging me under, against the fog threatening to pull me back into oblivion. But it was no use. The world tilted, darkened at the edges again, the creeping horror sinking its claws into my chest.

Everything slipped away.

THE SUDDEN, JARRING STOP OF THE CAR RIPPED ME FROM the suffocating dark, yanking me back into the nightmare that had become my reality. My head lolled to the side, the sickly fog of chloroform still clinging to my limbs, weighing them down.

The back door opened. The bitter cold burned against my clammy skin, shocking my lungs into a rattling inhale.

A pair of rough hands seized me, fingers digging into my arms as I was dragged forward. My legs buckled the moment my feet touched the pavement. The hands didn't falter, tightening like a vice, keeping me from crumbling.

Dark shapes of buildings and late-night traffic, it all bled together, twisting, unfamiliar—yet familiar.

My mind fought to place it through fogged memories. The buildings were indistinct, identical in this part of town—*my town*.

We were still here. Not miles away in some unknown place.

I couldn't have been out that long, then.

I turned my head, straining to glimpse the man dragging me forward. But his grip was ironclad, holding me flush against him, his breath warm—too warm, too close—ghosting against my ear as he fumbled with a set of keys.

A scent hit me then—thick and cloying, a mix of sweat,

something sharp and chemical, scorched sugar? And beneath it... *coffee beans.*

Then the door opened, and the scent hit harder.

The realization crashed into me with the force of a freight train.

The Coffee Shop.

My stomach twisted violently, bile rising.

As the thought clicked into place, so did something else— something more profound, more horrifying.

A voice.

His voice.

A rasped whisper inside my head, screaming his name before my lips could form it.

"Oliver."

The man pulled me inside, slamming the door shut with a sharp kick of his foot. At the sound of his name, he let out a breath, almost... amused.

"Duh."

He turned to me, and I saw him fully in the glow spilling from the shop. His grin stretched unnaturally wide, his teeth catching the light in a way that made my skin crawl. His pupils swallowed the brown in his irises, his eyes feverish, burning.

"*What?* Who did you think? Your husband?" His voice dripped with mockery, lips curled higher, near predatory. Then, he shrugged. "Makes sense. Luckily, he's not a problem anymore."

A cold blade of dread carved through my chest.

"What did you do to him?"

I didn't care. Not really. If he had killed Connor, I wouldn't shed a single tear. But I needed to know if he had done it—if he was truly capable of killing. If he had been... *successful* before. If he would do it again. If I was next.

His face twisted. His amusement flickered like a dying

flame, darkening into instability. "Stop talking about *him*," he snapped, taut with venom, possession. His grip around me flexed, nails pressing into flesh. "Or you'll ruin this."

A cold sweat broke out along my neck.

He released me just enough, eyes trailing over me as if assessing my state. My feet were planted firmly on the ground, still tied at the ankle, but more sturdy than before. He gripped my shoulder with a large hand, swaying me from side to side, testing my ability to stand independently.

He *humphed* in some kind of acceptance before dropping to my ankles and removing the rope around them.

My pulse hammered, my gaze flicking a glance toward the exit. The door was right there. So close. Oliver had moved further into The shop, putting space between us. If I ran—

"You could try," he mused, singsong and teasing. He didn't even turn to look at me, as if he already knew my thoughts. "But again, *you'd ruin this.*"

Candles flickered around me, their warm hue stretching long, distorted shadows across the shop. They weren't just on the counter. They were *everywhere*. The tables. The shelves. The floor. A demented version of romance.

My stomach coiled tight.

"What is *this*, exactly?" My voice barely sounded like my own, raw and thin.

Oliver gestured with a flourish, manic energy vibrating beneath his skin. "You don't remember?"

I didn't answer. My throat had closed.

His grin faltered, eyes scanning my face as if searching for recognition. When he didn't find it, something ugly slithered. "How could you not remember?"

Tension snapped through the air, electric, volatile.

I braced for his anger, for the inevitable eruption. But then —just as quickly as the storm gathered—it passed. He inhaled slowly, shaking his head. "No, *no*, it's okay," he soothed himself. His fingers twitched. "It's probably hard to keep them straight with how many we've had."

He beamed suddenly, giddy, his eyes bright. "Here, I'll show you!"

Before I could recoil, he grabbed me, fingers latching onto my wrist like a shackle, dragging me from behind the counter and around it.

Think. Think. Think.

He stopped abruptly, spinning me around like a marionette. "You were... here."

He adjusted me like a doll until I stood precisely where he wanted. Then, with a burst of energy, he darted back behind the counter, stopping in front of the register. His eyes gleamed. "And I was right *here!*"

My breath came in shallow gasps, my mind racing.

Play along.

I fought to still the tremors wracking my body.

"It was such a busy day," he continued, his voice slipping into a reverent hum. "You walked up and ordered...." He trailed off, waiting.

I hesitated. "Coffee."

His brows furrowed. "A large blonde roast," he corrected, voice sharp. "You smelled of vanilla and sunshine when you walked in." He closed his eyes, inhaling deeply. "The scent *burned* into my brain."

My skin crawled.

"You asked me...." Again, he left the sentence hanging.

I swallowed hard, grasping for anything. "How much?"

The sharp crack of his fist slamming against the counter made me flinch. "NO! YOU ASKED—"

He stopped himself, taking a shuddering breath. His fingers twitched against the wood as he forced a smile, though his body vibrated with barely restrained fury. "You asked me how I was doing."

I stared at him, dread pooling in my stomach.

His voice softened again. "You were the first person to ask me that all day. The first person... probably *ever*, actually." He tilted his head, watching me with something disturbingly close to affection. "I said, 'Peachy if peaches were constantly on fire.' And you laughed. Really laughed. At *my* dumb joke."

My lips pressed together.

"And I saw it then." He stepped forward, eyes burning into me as he braced himself against the counter lip. "You *understood* me. We share a sadness no one else knows. But you got it. You knew my loneliness because you were lonely, too."

My stomach twisted, my mind racing for a way out.

"And then that fucking guy yelled at us for taking too long." His voice grew venomous again. "And you told him...."

The memory surfaced.

"Deep breaths," I murmured, the words monotone. "Big emotions are hard."

Oliver's face lit with delight. He laughed, throwing his head back, the sound bursting from him like a joyous, unhinged melody. "That wasn't even the best part!" He gasped. "Your voice made it *perfect*. You sounded so condescending, and his face went bright red!"

He kept laughing, shaking his head like a man recalling the best day of his life.

I didn't move.

Slowly, his laughter faded. "You went to bat for me. Like I was someone important to you." He glanced down at the register, his fingers tracing the worn wood. "You are a fighter. Just like me. We're the same." His eyes flicked back to me, filled with unhinged darkness. "I realized then that I would do anything for that feeling, for that connection, for *you*."

A cold chill slid down my spine.

Then, his lips curled into a smirk. "Obviously, I couldn't let that pussy continue breathing, mumbling under his breath that you were a bitch after you walked away."

Need I remind him that he also called me a bitch? Pot, Kettle.

"Did you kill him?"

His grin widened. "Burned him alive, more specifically, but *yes.*"

A slow, terrible realization settled over me as he gazed at me, eyes alight with twisted devotion.

"His *end*," Oliver continued, tilting his head, "marked *our* beginning."

He darted around the counter with manic energy. His movements were erratic, fueled by something unnatural, something feverish. I instinctively flinched as he reached for me, but his fingers dug into my arm as he tugged me forward.

"Come here, *look*," he urged, dragging me across the shop floor.

I stumbled, my heart hammering against my ribs. But when he stopped, I froze—not out of fear of running but because of what lay before me.

The table was a grotesque shrine. Pictures of me—some familiar, most taken without my knowledge—were arranged like relics. Lingerie and underwear I had thought disappeared into the abyss of my washer was neatly folded alongside stolen clothes, a toothbrush, and a vial of yellow liquid that made my stomach turn. My favorite oversized band tee, the one I had slept in for years before it mysteriously vanished, draped over the table. A hairbrush, used-up lip balm, socks, a near-empty bottle of my perfume—every object was so deeply personal, so *mine*, and yet *he* had them.

I swallowed back bile.

Oliver's grin stretched wide, his head tilting as he gestured at the collection. "You stole some of my pictures, or I would've put out more. But I grabbed a few from my stash at home. I did this for *you*."

My skin crawled. My throat was dry as I forced myself to respond. "I really... appreciate it."

His expression briefly melted into something almost... lovesick. "*See?* I knew you'd come around. I knew you'd get it, even if it took a bit. Love can be scary. I get that. I was scared, too."

He tugged me down onto a nest of blankets and pillows on the floor, his excitement palpable as he positioned me just so. I barely had time to register the candlelit nightmare surrounding us before he thrust a steaming cup to me.

I hesitated.

Probably—most definitely—drugged.

His onyx eyes darkened instantly. His nostrils flared, fingers twitching. "What?"

I forced myself to stay calm, leaning and shrugging a shoulder to showcase my bound hands as an excuse. His eyes flicked down, realization dawning. "Oh. *Duh.*" He scrambled behind me, fingers working quickly to untie the restraints. As soon as they were free, I rubbed my aching wrists, resisting the urge to recoil as he settled back in front of me, eagerly sipping from his own cup.

I lifted the cup to my lips, pretending to drink.

Oliver sighed, pleased. "Now it's like every time you came to see me. I was *always* right here, waiting."

I had to keep him talking, to understand what made him into this... and *maybe* that would give me a way out. "Thank you for being so patient with me," I said carefully.

He ran a hand through his hair like a nervous boy on his

first date. "You really mean that?" His voice was breathless, awed.

I nodded, trying to keep the tremor from my hands. "Why didn't you just tell me… why hurt my friends?"

The mood shifted like a snapped wire. His face twisted with fury as he lunged forward, his hand latching onto my jaw with bruising force.

"Don't bring them up ever again!" His voice was low, seething. He shoved me back with a sharp jerk of his wrist and reclined again, fingers flexing, stretching, as though shaking off his anger.

"They don't matter," he muttered, more to himself than me. "*They* never did. *They* were just in the way, poisoning you against me. Trying to take what's *mine*." His gaze snapped back to mine. "Drink!"

I lifted the cup to my lips again, pretending once more.

He exhaled slowly, rolling his shoulders, fingers tapping the side of his cup. "Funny how the universe works. Shows you something so *delicate*, so *intoxicating*, and just when you think it's *yours*—" His fingers tightened. "—it always finds a way to rip it from you."

There is it. Something had been taken from him before.

I chose my words carefully. "The universe has taken a lot from me, too. My brother. My mom. My da—"

"Don't say *dad*. You'd be *lying*." His eyes snapped to mine.

I blinked. "I'm sorry?"

He smiled, slow and knowing, before rolling his eyes. "*Come on*. You and I are the *same*, remember? You *get* me."

No.

"To everyone else, it looked like an overdose. The coroner ruled it that way. An addict who'd been using for *thirty years* suddenly dies with a morphine and 6-MAM level of 240?

That's like, 15 grams." He scoffed. "You'd think he would've known how to *not* overdose after all that time."

My pulse roared in my ears.

No.

"But no one cares about addicts," he continued, thoughtful. "Or better yet... no one pays attention to their daughters. Daughters who skipped town the same day he died and *only* returned once he'd been long buried."

No.

He grinned. "At first, I thought maybe the blonde witch did it—since she was the only one living in the house at the time. But then I read her therapy notes." He chuckled, shaking his head. "*Wildly* different from yours."

I felt sick.

His voice softened, almost affectionate. "She still holds love for him, you know, which I'll never understand. But *you*? You mentioned him *once*. 'I have no idea what I'd say to him,' But I bet that's also a lie." He leaned in, eyes gleaming. "*Because you saw him for what he was. And you* protected *her from it.*"

My breaths came short and shallow.

"So, your brother dies—wrongfully ruled, by the way. We *all* know your dad did it. Then your poor mother gets sick by a *terrible* twist of fate. Your older brother disappears. And *you*? You *left*. Abandoning the only sibling you had left."

I clenched my fists.

Oliver's grin stretched wider. "*Then* the hospital reports. The ones about a sixteen-year-old blondie showing up battered and bruised. And the *next day*—your dad? *Dead.*"

His voice dropped to a whisper.

"Weird how that works... isn't it?"

60

*H*E KNOWS.

The realization echoed in my mind, drowning out Oliver's voice as he prattled on like we were on a first date and just casually getting to know each other. I sat frozen on the makeshift pallet, my body numb.

Oliver knows.

I forced a breath through my nose, steady, measured—desperate to keep my face impassive despite the slow, twisting dread in my stomach.

'We're the same.'

That's what he had said. And for one terrifying second, a part of me *almost* believed it.

I *had* killed. My actions ended someone's life. And I felt no regret—only that I hadn't done it sooner. That I wasn't able to protect Sage, to protect my mom.

But I was able to protect Cassie.

'You get me.'

No—my actions had been about protection, about justice

for what our dad had taken from me, what he had taken from Cassie—what he had *done* to her in my absence.

Oliver did what he did because he felt *entitled* and thought he *owned* me. He slaughtered people who so much as *looked* at me the wrong way. He hurt the people I cared about. Hurt me when I didn't conform to whatever delusional fantasy he had built in his head.

I'm nothing *like him.*

And yet, here I was, sitting across from a man who had studied my every move, who had stripped away the darkest moment of my past and laid it bare between us like a shared secret.

I have to get out.

"Your coffee is getting cold."

My mind raced. I needed a distraction. Something that might give me an edge. I plastered a smile on my face, stretching it just enough to look natural—like I was enjoying this.

"My bladder might burst if I drink any more without peeing first."

Oliver stilled, his brown eyes narrowing with suspicion as he surveyed my body. His fingers twisted at his sides, hands flexing like he was debating whether to let me move.

Seconds stretched unbearably.

Then, with unsettling ease, he pushed himself up and stepped toward me.

I didn't flinch as he reached down, grabbing my arm to help me stand. The heat of his fingers seared against my skin, but I willed my muscles to stay loose, relaxed. The moment I was upright, I forced another breathy, casual *"Thanks,"* hoping he wouldn't hear the tremor beneath it.

A sharp sting pricked the side of my neck.

My breath hitched, and I turned to see Oliver withdrawing

a syringe, his expression alight with amusement and satisfaction.

"Apologies," he mused, as if he had simply bumped into me rather than injected some unknown substance into my system. "But the coffee wasn't working fast enough, and I'm getting impatient."

Panic surged through my chest.

No, no, no.

A creeping numbness began devouring my limbs. My knees buckled, and before I could brace myself, I collapsed onto the blankets with a painful thud, knocking over the coffee cups. Liquid seeped into the fabric.

He crouched over me, watching with fascination as my body refused to obey me.

Trapped. Trapped. Trapped.

A breathless chuckle. "Woah. That worked fast." He grinned, rocking back on his heels like a child marveling at his experiment. "Sorry—I'm still learning my dosages."

A single tear slipped free, trailing hot against my skin.

His pupils dilated.

His gaze darkened as he leaned in—too close—his tongue flicked against my cheek, tasting my tear like something sacred.

I wanted to scream.

"You're scared," he murmured, breath ghosting against my skin. "Of course you are! But you can trust me." His fingers brushed against my hair, the touch disturbingly gentle. "You have no idea what lengths I've gone to—what lengths I'll *go*— for you. But I'll show you. I'll show what *real* love is, not that artificial shit Connor gave you. He was too distracted, his priorities too unfocused. He left you. He *gave up* on you. But I—" His fingers curled against my scalp. "I'll never do that."

His tone was affectionate. "I just had to get everything out of the way first. You'll understand."

I wanted to shove him away, spit in his face, but my body remained motionless.

Helpless.

Again.

His lips barely moved as he whispered, "James had to die."

My stomach plummeted.

Oliver tilted his head, observing me, gauging my reaction. "I thought the car was enough," he said conversationally as if we were discussing the weather. "But damn, he's strong. And the fire? I didn't think about the windows." He sighed, shaking his head. "I did use a bit too much on him, but hey! It's all part of the learning process." A pause. A slow, satisfied smirk. "But lucky for you, now I know *exactly* how much kills someone."

That's why he'd been at the hospital.

He went back for James.

Where is Cassie?

The world blurred as an endless stream of silent tears slipped from my eyes.

Oliver's expression twisted with rage at the sight of my tears. He shot to his feet, pacing, his fingers raking over his close-cropped brown hair. He whipped back toward me, eyes burning.

"See?" His voice was frantic. "*This* is why they have to die! You're so attached to *them* that you never see me! *You don't need them!* What you're feeling right now?" He jabbed a finger toward my chest. "That should be reserved for *me! Not them!* They don't care about you! *Not like I do!* They use you! They—"

A breath. A shudder.

Then—calm.

Like someone had flipped a switch inside him.

He knelt back down, fingers cradling my face as if I were a precious thing.

His voice dropped into a whisper, brushing against my lips like a lover's secret. "We'll deal with them soon enough."

His mouth claimed mine, lingering, possessive—owning me in a way that made me want to die.

His eyes brown burned with fevered devotion as he pulled back. "Running the witch off the road was a half-baked idea anyway, so I didn't have high hopes to begin with. But I have ideas for that." He sneered. "The doctors a pain in my ass, but I need him... for now," he mused, pouting. "But Cassie? Kal? Even that new one—what's his name? Max?" His lips curled. "'*Free, creative reign.*'" He lifted his fingers into air quotes, and his voice changed like a mimick.

I barely had time to register the thought before my vision blurred. My eyelids drooped, the edges of the world going dark.

Stay awake.

Please stay awake.

Oliver cursed. "Wait! That's right! You don't even know the best part!" He let out a breathless laugh, shaking his head. "I can't believe I forgot! We have a surprise for you!"

We?

I barely heard him. The world spun violently. I tried to fight it, tried to stay awake, but my body betrayed me.

He moved out of my line of vision, scrambling excitedly to an unseen part of The Coffee House.

My vision was nearly gone as my ears strained, grasping for any detail. Oliver's frantic footsteps, then suddenly, a slower, *heavier* set joined his.

Something—*someone* moving closer.

Then—warm breath against my cheek.

I blinked, trying to see, but the darkness pulled.

A sharp, piercing pain.

Green-gold eyes.

And then—*nothing.*

ACKNOWLEDGMENTS

To my son, who isn't even old enough to read, but is the reason I am here today, *and* the reason I keep breathing. I hope to instill in you to never take anyone's shit, know your worth, and never apologize for existing in a world full of people who would make you feel small. May you always rise above, and when you can't, I'll help you burn it all to the ground.

To my family, for listening to my incessant, "I'm writing a book!", and supporting it the entire way. For being a safe space for me to be creative. For helping me through treatment, doubt, and near death. For loving my son just as much as I do. For healing the very broken little girl who craved love and affection.

To my chosen family, I sincerely have never met a greater group of people in my life. I am grateful that I have you all on my team. I couldn't have asked for a better gaggle of friends to stand beside me. **Kyra**, for keeping me sane, for fighting for me when I couldn't fight for myself. For accepting my decisions in life and being a second mother to my son. **Sarah**, whose soul mirrors my own, because she was carved from the same stone and ruined in the same blood. **Erin**, who laughed and cried with me and saved my life on multiple occasions, like the healer she is, for the cards that made me cry, for the dino tattoos that ended up melted into my couch, for the reminders that not once will I ever be alone again. **Amaris**, for pushing me to aggressively love myself the way we aggressively love others. **PATRICIA PINEAPPLE PERSIMMON PIZZA PURPLE PEOPLE PETER** (iykyk), for making the gosh darndest best BB Special cover I have ever seen, and for reminding me that I am doing a good job—also for making me fall in love with rom coms, you bastard. **Milli**, for dancing with me at the buttcrack of dawn and giving me an escape. **Amanda**, for your positive words and encouragement that kept me going, even when it was too dark for me to see the end. You kept me alive more often than you realize. You all did and still do. I would be nothing without you.

To The Indie Author Revolution, for giving me a space to be creative, a community to feel a part of, and a chosen family I didn't know I was missing.

And lastly, to the cancer that tried to end my writing and my life. You're gonna have to try harder than that, bucko.

ABOUT THE AUTHOR

Black Dahlia is a writer, mom—and cancer survivor—who was really just looking for an excuse to avoid the week-old pile of laundry waiting for her. Her debut novel, This Quiet Violence, is a spicy, psychologically twisted tale of feminine rage, with so much more planned for the series. Known for emotionally wrecking her readers with alarming consistency, Dahlia writes dark romance, horror, and tragedy, all laced with sharp wit and a very dark sense of humor.

As President of The Indie Author Revolution NonProfit, she's also notorious for her all-caps pep talks and unapologetic passion for indie voices.

This Quiet Violence is the first book in the Violent Violets Series. Black Dahlia is already hard at work on the second book, This Quiet Revenge. She has many more books planned, and intends to stay true to her brand of female rage and dark romance, even branching out into dark romantasy.